BEYOND T
BOOK 1
THE GIRL WITH SILVER EYES

FABIO FURLANETTO

For more information visit www.beyondtheimpossible.org

Special thanks to Michele Miglionico and Valerio Pastore

THE GIRL WITH SILVER EYES

THE GIRL WITH SILVER EYES

Art by KodamaCreative

1- Before the beginning

What if the universe didn't care about you?

If nothing about you mattered. If your life, your family, your world were just irrelevant in the grand scheme of things. If you could as well be nothing and the universe wouldn't notice.

If your world were Drylon, it would drive you insane.

When time was young, the Drylon were obsessed with proving they owned the universe.

Their empire grew to conquer dozens of galaxies. Their weakest weapon could vaporize an entire solar system. Their technology laughed in the face of the impossible.

Five billion years ago, the Drylon disappeared. The legend goes that the Drylon waged war against the universe and lost. They lost so bad that hardly anybody remembers them.

Today, the universe is filled with gods and monsters and scary things born out of the burned ashes of the Drylon.

There is a planet called Earth where people believe their lives matter. The universe disagrees.

What if you could go beyond the impossible and prove the universe wrong?

2- The vanguard

My name is Noriko Null and I've never met my mother before.

There was never a picture of her in the house. Dad never mentioned her unless I asked first, and he always seemed very careful to say as little as possible. All he ever said was that my mother had to go back to Japan when I was very young.

I always asked him why, and the answer was always the same: she was a very busy woman and he'd explain when I was older. I'm eighteen and I still don't have the answer.

While it's not really that rare to be biracial, especially when you live in New York, it's impossible to avoid questions when people hear my full name or see me with my father: he's white and I look distinctly Japanese. Which would be fine if I knew how to answer, but the mystery's always been there for me.

Until this week, when I received a letter from Tokyo...an actual paper letter inside an envelope, with a hundred-dollar bill.

"Meet me at the Empire State Building, 87th floor, next Friday at eight PM. Don't tell anyone. Leiko Tanaka, your mother".

Every fantasy I've ever had about my mother flared up when I received that letter. I still have it in my pocket, together with the hundred dollar bill.

Sneaking out of the house, catching a cab to the other side of the city, taking the longest elevator ride of my life, my heart feels like it's going to explode.

What will she look like? Why hasn't she said a word all these years? Why did she leave me?

An Asian man in a business suit is waiting for me, quickly showing me his card.

-Miss Null, I presume. I represent Miss Tanaka; follow me, please.

I mumble something and follow him. Before you know it we're in some kind of brand new conference room. I couldn't miss the Scion Corporation logo if I wanted to.

There's a woman in front of the window overlooking the city. She's wearing a stark white office suit, in contrast with the very dark hair reaching her shoulders.

She turns and walks towards the table. I don't know why I'm surprised by the resemblance: I knew I'd look more like my mother.

She's beautiful, more than I'll ever be. But beneath the makeup and the confidence that clearly sets us apart, you can see that she's my mother. It's the first time in my life I experience family resemblance and I can't help staring at her. Probably looking like an idiot.

-Sit down. Don't just stand there looking at me like an idiot – she says.

-Miss Null, as you may know, as daughter of a Japanese citizen born in the United States, you currently have both citizenships. However Japanese law does not recognize dual citizenship: before you reach age 22 you are required to choose one of the two nationalities.

-What? I'm sorry, but…this is the first time I see my mother…what's this got to do with anything?

-Miss Tanaka wishes you to renounce Japanese citizenship, never visit Japan, never acknowledge your mother's identity and sign a nondisclosure agreement. In exchange, miss Tanaka agrees to pay you one hundred thousand American dollars.

I feel the weight of my fantasies crashing down. My mother stares at me like she's studying a clinical case. I've never seen so much coldness in someone's eyes.

-Wait wait wait. You're showing up after all this time to give me hush money!?

-Miss Tanaka is a very important person, miss Null. News of a secret teenage pregnancy could damage her image – the lawyer explains very calmly.

-That's what you care about? Your image? Is it more important than me? – I shout at her.

-Yes.

The black hair slips in front of her left eye, but she doesn't even blink as she looks at me and explains:

-Life is full of disappointments. You are one of them, just like your father. Your name suits you well: you are nothing and will always be nothing. If it had been up to me, you wouldn't even exist. Take the money, it's probably the best thing that will ever happen to you.

-Miss Tanaka, please, is this really the best way to handle the situation? – asks the lawyer, his voice a mix of embarrassment and fear.

She answers something in Japanese. I don't understand a word. All I understand is that I've never felt this insulted and betrayed in my life.

I reach for the letter in my pocket and throw it at her. It's still got the hundred dollar bill inside.

-Don't worry. You don't have a daughter.

I manage to hold the tears until I've stormed out of that horrible place. There's no way to explain what's going on inside my head right now, but as soon as I reach the elevator I hear a voice:

-Your mother's quite something, isn't she?

She startles me: I have no idea how I missed her. Admittedly it's easier to see other people as giants when you're only five feet tall, but she must be at least seven feet. Long blond hair and a yellow office suite that doesn't come even close to hiding the figure of a swimsuit model. Pretty hard to miss.

-You have no idea – I tell her.

-Maybe I do. I've never met my mother, actually, she was eaten by my father before I was born.

-...

-It's not as bad as it sounds, he turned her into a fly first. He doesn't like eating people. Family issue.

-O-okay. Nice meeting you.

This isn't the best day to deal with crazy people, so I decide to ignore her. The elevator door opens, but on the other side there's no elevator: just a grass field. I turn around and all of a sudden I'm no longer in the building.

-Central Park, in case you're wondering – the woman clarifies.

For some reason I'm not freaking out. Part of me wants to run away, sure, but a much bigger part wants to understand what the heck is going on. She nods approvingly.

-You didn't scream. I'm not easily surprised, but I didn't expect that.

-Why am I here?

-I like the place and I didn't want to blow up the building. Listen, this is awkward enough...

I'd laugh if the situation wasn't so absurd. I'm arguing with someone who just teleported me!

-Awkward!? What happened in that office was awkward, this... this is crazy!

-I'll get to the point: I am Athena, goddess of wisdom and war.

-A goddess – I repeat.

-I assume you are familiar with the concept. I want to offer you a job.

-What… what kind of job?

-The universe is far stranger than you know. Things you thought fictional like gods, aliens and monsters are real. Humanity is ridiculously unprepared and I can't shield you forever.

-I don't understand.

-You will – she answers, reaching inside her jacket. She shows me something fitting in the palm of her hand: a swirling path of energy, shaped like the symbol for infinity.

It looks like electricity, but at the same time it feels like nothing else.

-This is human knowledge. All of it, throughout the ages of mankind. It will make you the most intelligent being native to this planet. The vanguard of Earth's defense against the impossible.

-And you're giving this to *me*?

-You have determination, you don't scare easily, and I have a thing for heroes with family issues. Heroes have been chosen on far shakier grounds.

She leaves the energy glow floating, right in front of me. I stare into her silver eyes, my mother's voice still echoing in my mind. "You will always be nothing", she said.

-What does this have to do with my mother?

-Let's just say that your family makes mine look normal, and my uncle is the Lord of the Dead.

-Where's the catch?

-The catch is you'll have to live with the darkest part of humanity crawling inside your head. If you can live with that and with the responsibility of my gift, just touch the energy.

I hesitate. This is too crazy to be true. But it would be crazier to throw away something like this.

My hand gets closer to the infinity symbol. It's not warm like I thought it would be.

-Will it hurt?

-Immensely. But it's worth it.

-This is probably a bad idea – I say, touching the energy.

The energy flows from my hand to the rest of my body. All my pain receptors go into overdrive; I can't move a finger. This is the easy part.

11

Then the process reaches my head; I feel like somebody's peeling off my brain with a rake and pouring acid into it. Making new space. Every man, woman and child feels something at the exact same moment, like they've heard a distant sound they don't recognize. They don't know their mind is being linked to mine.

As this happens, the sky over New York is lit by a lighting storm the likes of which has never been seen, mostly because there's almost no cloud. It's literally a storm of knowledge, as the information is reaching it from all over the world.

As I look up to watch it, the download starts. No wonder Athena didn't want to do this indoors: a massive bolt of lightning strikes me. It takes seventeen seconds. Seventeen seconds to download EVERYTHING.

You think it's not much? Try squeezing ten thousand years of civilization into it, in a continuous stream of data. Think of every book and magazine ever written, every song and speech ever recorded, every theory and fantasy and nightmare and hope ever passed to future generation.

I fall on my knees. The grass has been burned to ashes but there's not even a scratch on my clothes. My brain is still stitching together neural pathways to process the new information. I will probably need to rewrite neuroscience from scratch to understand what's going on inside my head. Suddenly I realize two things: I can do it, and it will be *easy*.

I stand up. I can see Athena as the ancient Greeks saw her, with her golden helmet and majestic shield. I also see my reflection in the shield. My eyes are now bright silver.

-How do you feel? – Athena asks.

"You are nothing and will always be nothing" – says my mother's voice.

I feel like I can do anything. I feel like showing my mother what I have become.

But I am not the sweet innocent Noriko anymore. I am something more, something born out of every battle that's ever been fought, every mystery that's ever been solved, every threshold that's ever been shattered.

I am a single mind backed by seven billion souls, and there's only one thing that I can answer, the one thought that keeps the other seven billions in check.

-I am Null. I feel like I could take over the world.

Athena looks at me approvingly, with half a smile on her face. I see her differently now... not just because I can see her armor. I can see everything now.

Suddenly I know how she's been represented over the centuries. I know how every single statue of her looks like, I know the name of each sculptor. I read the entire Odyssey in the time I need to blink, which leads to all the translations, to the biography of every translator.

It's too much in such a short time; I have to close my eyes. I feel them burning.

-Relax, my child. It will take time to adjust to your new mind – Athena tells me; her motherly voice makes things easier, but just barely.

When I open my eyes, they shine so brightly that I can see the reflection on her armor.

-Bioluminescence. You didn't just download information into my brain, you have also physically altered my body. Why?

-You tell me.

I feel a surge in my head, reverberating through my eyes. I know they are shining again.

-The human brain isn't supposed to handle this much work. I'm constantly overclocking. Did you give me new eyes to discharge the energy in excess?

-I see you are adjusting just fine. I'm sure the next time we see each other you'll have grown to your full potential – she tells me, taking a step back.

-What, you're leaving? Already?

-I am a busy goddess, Noriko. I have other matters that require my presence.

-But... but what am I supposed to do now?

Athena smiles. Not the way you do when you're happy or you're having fun, but the way you smile when you've won the game before everyone realized you were playing. Somehow, I have a feeling that's the only way Athena smiles.

-Anything you want, Noriko. This world is yours now.

She disappears in a cloud of golden light, leaving me alone. Now that the adrenaline rush is going away, I begin to realize the magnitude of what just happened.

The Greek gods are real! And they've chosen me as their... their what, really? She said I was supposed to be "the vanguard". What's that supposed to mean?

Vanguard, the leading part of an advancing military formation that seeks out the enemy and secures ground in advance of the main force.

The answer comes to me before I ask it. It will take time to get used to this.

I look around, feeling slightly disoriented. How am supposed to get home from here? It should be easy: apparently I know New York's map into its finest details now. I can see all the ways I can get home on foot, and I know the number of every taxi I can call.

I decide to take a walk, to clear out my head. Easier said than done with all the stuff that's been put there: I feel like my mind has indigestion.

I know I'm in Central Park. I've been here before, of course: you can't live in New York all your life and miss it. But everything is different now. Or really, I am different now.

I get some stares from a couple of tourists; I must look drunk by the way I'm watching everything with amazement. Wait, how do I know they're tourists?

Faces. Driver's license. Job application. Internet profile. I don't want to know the details of what they've posted online for the last twenty years, but it comes automatically.

It's just a couple people several feet away and I have to look away. Find something to focus on.

I get to Cleopatra's Needle, the park's obelisk. I already know it has nothing to do with Cleopatra, but I don't want to know its full history. It comes anyway.

It's overwhelming, I don't know where to look now. I stare at the hieroglyphs on the obelisk, will that help? "The crowned Horus, Bull of Victory, Arisen in Thebes", yes, I can read that.

I reach the nearest bench and sit down. I'm reading thousands of pages of Egyptian history, how do I get this to stop!?

Take a deep breath. Don't panic. No I don't want to know about the respiratory system, you stupid brain, can't you slow down just a minute!?

Calm down, Noriko. You can do this. You can focus. You are Null. Take a deep breath. Open your eyes, you can handle this. I'm looking down, all I can see are my boots on the grass.

Biker boots. Paid 39.99 dollars. A list of where they're sold. Financial records of all the manufacturers. Grass. Poa pratensis, commonly known as Kentucky bluegrass. There are more than 12,000 grass species, about 800 genera that are classified into 12 subfamilies.

No no no. Stop it. Focus focus focus. I have to stop this.

This is just noise, useless junk information. It's all the same to me. I take another deep breath. My eyes shine, discharging excess thought process. It gives me a solution.

It's called the von Restorff effect: when multiple homogeneous stimuli are presented, the stimulus that differs from the rest is more likely to be remembered. In other words, if I isolate the one thing that I can't mistake for anything else an focus on that, I should be able to filter the rest.

-I am Null – I say out loud.

It's just a name. It means "zero" in German. "You are nothing and will always be nothing", isn't that what my mother said? Focus. Focus everything through my sense of identity. Filter the rest.

Seven billion minds back off. The collective brainpower and experience of an entire planet is at my fingertips now. I wonder if they feel who's the boss now.

I seem to have gained more interest than Cleopatra's Needle, because there's half a dozen people around me. This is still a short distance from the absolutely massive lightning strike that everybody in the state must've seen, but I can understand that from their perspective I'm acting strange.

They probably think I'm high as a kite.

Maybe it's best to avoid attracting too much attention at this point: I'm still new at this. I take my leave and start thinking again, but this time my head feels a little clearer.

I think about Athena. So many implications in the fact that gods are real, I have no clear basis on how to deal with that. She mentioned

Zeus, so I have to assume that other gods are real as well; at the very least, the Greek ones are.

Are there any others on Earth? Athena looks human, but not exactly the kind that goes unnoticed. A quick glance at all the photographic records in existence doesn't show a match; I do that by reflex before I realize I can do it. This might prove to be a useful skill. Let's try it out.

I turn around. And sure enough, I face I see is accompanied by an instantaneous background check.

Except one. There's a woman with long black hair and a green office suit staring at me, immobile. She's not even blinking, and I have no idea about who she is.

Something's not right. I walk away, speeding up my pace until I'm out of the park, before I turn again. And there she is again, still staring. Still unknown.

I try not to be paranoid. But she's the only face I can't recognize, and she's following me. Even after I've left the park, sure enough, she's still at the same distance from me. Still staring.

Think. Is she working with Athena? Or against her? The term "vanguard" that she used suggests the existence of an enemy. Should I confront her? I'm not ready for this.

My subconscious provides a suggestion, again. Or at least I think it's subconscious; can I hold two simultaneous trains of thought, now? I'm confused. It's still hard to avoid thinking too much.

So I run away. I need to shake off the adrenaline rush, and I won't do that if I keep overthinking every little thing. I run by familiar buildings that now feel like they belong to a different life.

I stop when I come by a shop window, looking at myself in the reflection.

I see an eighteen year old Asian American girl with a green leather jacket. I see the faint glow coming from my new silver eyes, and my new abilities come bite me in the ass to hammer down how truly unremarkable I am.

A teenage girl like a million others. With the brainpower of a planet. And I smile the same way Athena did when I see my stalker's reflection in the distance.

Lady, if I'm right... and I know I am... you won't like where I'm going now.

3- A goddess walks into a bar

Vesta is a very strange waitress: she never wears shoes. She's also immortal.

You'd think people would complain, but you've never seen Vesta. If your waitress had a girl-next-door smile, a body an Amazon would kill for, and never served your order more than a second late, would you complain about the shoes?

You'd also think more people would notice she's immortal, but she's very careful. She never works in the same place for more than five years, never talks about her previous jobs, and moves to another city every ten or fifteen years.

It used to be far easier. Back in the day, she could stay in the same town for a century before someone would notice the stunning beauty with bright red hair looked exactly like the young lady that grandpa was always talking about.

But then again, back in the day people died more often.

-Does anything weird ever happen here?

The customer's question distracts her from her memories. She glances the man asking: mid-twenties, African-American, wearing a grey hoodie and reading a comic book.

-Normal weird or New York weird?

-You know that thing in comics and movies where the hero asks the bartender if there's anything weird or suspicious? I don't think actual bartenders answer that kind of question.

-I wouldn't know, I'm just a waitress.

-Isn't it weird how it's just ten PM and there's only us here?

-A little.

-So, you doin' anything after this? I'm Max, by the way.

Just then, an Asian girl slams the door open. She looks like she's been to hell and back.

-Your new lord and master demands coffee!

-All right, *that* is weird – Vesta admits.

Both Vesta and Max watch the girl drink three full cups, one after the other. No sugar.

They figure she must be sixteen or seventeen; she's wearing a black T-shirt underneath a green leather jacket that seems almost oversized for her tiny frame.

17

The situation is too strange to miss the opportunity to strike an interesting conversation.

-So. Shouldn't it be "your new *lady* and master"? – Max asks.

-Shouldn't we take her to the hospital? She doesn't look well – Vesta notices.

-Lady. From Old English *hlæfdige*, literally "bread-kneader"; I am Null. It's getting difficult to think straight; bring me more coffee.

-Yep, definitely not well.

-I think you've had enough. Why don't you go home and get some sleep? – Vesta asks.

-After drinking that much, I don't think she can.

-*Both* of you – she clarifies.

-Vesta. Your name is Vesta Dicrono – the girl suddenly realizes.

-Do I know you? – the waitress asks; after all the tag on her shirt doesn't show her surname.

-I am Null; I know everything.

-Really? What's my name? – interrupts the customer.

-Maximilian Black. Age 27, unemployed.

-Nice trick. When is Stan Lee's birthday?

-December 28th.

-Air date of the first Star Trek episode?

-September 15th,1966.

-She *does* know everything! Even I don't know this stuff on the fly.

-I have all the information in the world in my head.

Maybe it's the coffee, maybe it's her new brain stitching together all the evidence, but Noriko seems to come to her senses and stands up.

-You. You've been using the name "Vesta Dicrono" for two hundred years. Possibly more, but evidence in earlier centuries is sketchy at best.

-I don't like where this is going.

-You are the Roman goddess of the hearth; don't insult my intelligence pretending otherwise.

-Don't insult mine with tricks like that – she tries to defend herself, and Noriko understands why Athena smiled like that. The feeling of being so much ahead in the game is almost intoxicating.

-Should I list all the tiny mistakes you've made updating your documents? Such a sloppy work, really. Or would you prefer a detailed list of the body language clues that tell me you're about to lie? You returned the library a Sherlock Holmes book a month late in

1917, so maybe you would appreciate it, but I'd prefer going straight to the point.

The girl and the goddess look at each other in the eye. Silver eyes flash, and the goddess backs off.

-I'm not the Roman goddess. You would consider me Greek – she corrects.

-Wait, isn't *Venus* the goddess of the heart? – Max asks.

Vesta replies by showing him the palm of her hand, where a live flame appears out of thin air.

-*Hearth*, the household fire. I was born Hestia, firstborn of Kronos. I've been using the name Vesta since leaving Olympus twenty-seven centuries ago. You have my attention, "Null"; what do you *really* want from me?

-I don't know. I'm working on it.

-You two are working on some kind of act, right? I know, you've got a lighter up your sleeve!

-Go home, mr. Black. Gods are speaking here – Null declares.

-You're not a goddess, you know – Vesta replies, making the fire disappear.

Null smirks, looking down at the now empty cup of coffee.

-A black-haired woman in a green suit will come through that door. She wants to kill me.

-Let me guess, you can see the future? – Max asks.

-I can think. I saw her after I left the park. I couldn't recognize her, so her face is not on any database on the planet. I could've lost her easily, but I let her come close enough to make sure she was following me. I suspected Athena may have set me up, so my subconscious found the only other goddess in New York. I also really like coffee.

-What a load of bull...oh crap – Max says when the door opens: there's a black-haired woman in a green suit, standing right there.

-Lucky guess – he mumbles.

Vesta reacts as she would with any customer: with a warm and sincere smile.

-Welcome. Can I get you anything?

-The Heart of the Universe – the woman answers with a cold voice.

Right after that, two other women walk through the door: twins of the first one, wearing the same green office suit.

-I'm sorry, we don't serve that...I think.

The three women walk towards Null's table, standing behind her. Yet another two women, again looking exactly like the first one, walk in and start closing the blinds to cover the windows. They even change the "we're open" sign with the "we're closed" one, even though Vesta tries to stop them.

-I'm sorry, we're still open. Wait, that sounds wrong.

-Vesta. You are known to us – says one of the twins.

-Do not interfere – continues another.

-You. You are the Nexus. You will take us to the Heart of the Universe – concludes the third, placing her hand on Noriko's shoulder.

Noriko react so fast that Max and Vesta aren't really sure how the woman who touched her ends up with her head smashed on the table.

-Explain yourselves or I will not be so gentle with you – Null says, her silver eyes shining briefly.

-I told you that was way too much coffee! – warns Max.

The other women dressed in green don't do anything. The one that attacked Noriko pulls herself together; her nose has been squished into her head, but she doesn't seem to feel the slightest pain.

-Perfect sphere. Rocky exterior. Size of a human hand. High density.

-Like the object my father keeps besides his bed – Null answers, without even noticing the woman she's talking to probably shouldn't be alive with a wound like that.

-Thank you. You may die now.

Four out of the five women in green exploded with the force of a small bomb, seemingly without warning or reason.

The force of the explosion shatters everything in the room, yet nothing is burned. Max Black opens his eyes: he looks like he's been through the dirtiest chimney in history, and the Asian teen with the silver eyes doesn't look much better.

-How the heck did we survive that!? – he wonders.

-Hello? Goddess of the fire here? – says Vesta, who doesn't have a single speck of dust on her clothes or on her red hair.

-That doesn't even begin to…nevermind. Someone just tried to kill us!

-But did not succeed. I have an idea – Noriko says, wiping the dirt from her face as best as she can while trying not to trip on the debris.

-Where are you going? – he asks.
-I think I know what is happening here. I must follow that woman.
-Which one?
-The one that didn't explode into my face.
-But she tried to kill you!
-I don't see your point – she cuts him, storming to what's left of the door.

The cliché goes that people in New York will shrug off anything, but blowing up a building will get their attention. Just outside the bar, Noriko finds people gathered to understand what's going on.
The explosion should've been far worse: the sidewalk is full of shattered glass, but that's it.
"Could Vesta have contained the blast somehow?" she wonders.
-Are you all right? – a random guy asks. Just with one glance Noriko knows his name, his job, how many kids he has, and so many details that she has to make an effort to stop thinking about them.
As soon as she turns her silver eyes to the next person, a woman asks:
-Is anybody still inside? What happened?
Noriko doesn't know what to answer, as her eyes shift from person to person. Every information the world knows about the twelve people in front of her is flowing through her head: birthdays, phone numbers, medical histories, job résumés, social security numbers, everything.
Only now Vesta and Max come out of the bar. They see Noriko in the middle of the crowd, seemingly lost and confused. They've known her for less than fifteen minutes, granted, but this is her first human reaction to anything.
-Enough! – Noriko finally shouts. Her silver eyes flash for a second when she says it.
-Where did the woman dressed in green go? – she asks angrily.
-That way – mumbles one of the witnesses, pointing at the street. There's no need to clarify: if you see a woman walking out of a place before it explodes, you tend to remember it.
Noriko just pushes aside the people in front of her, looking at the street: it would take too long to wait for the streetlight to turn green before crossing. She just makes a step forward.

A motorbike comes to a screeching halt just a second before hitting Noriko. It was a calculated risk, since her brain decided the driver had enough reaction time to avoid her. The driver doesn't seem to think the same, shouting at the top of his lungs:

-Are you insane!?

-I am Null – she answers, just grabbing the driver by the shoulder and pushing him out of his seat.

It's hard to say what's more impressive, that she just shoved aside a man twice her weight or that she's stealing a bike in front of a dozen witnesses.

-Vesta, Black, deal with the authorities: I have to save my father – Noriko says before hitting on the accelerator and running out. Driving in the wrong direction.

Rarely has a crowd been made more speechless than now. Only Max has something to say:

-That was freakin' awesome!!!

-She's gonna to get herself killed! Come on!

A bright flame suddenly appears in front of Vesta, causing enough distraction to sweep Max off his feet and fly away, following Null's bike.

To recap. Noriko is driving in the wrong direction on a stolen bike, followed by a goddess who his flying ten feet off the ground, carrying a grown man in her arms. And all of them survived an explosion five minutes earlier. In other words, this is Max's greatest day ever.

-You can *fly*!? – he asks.

-Oh so *now* you believe I'm a goddess?

-You didn't tell me you could fly!

-It's not something you tell to strangers.

-Why not? I wouldn't shut up about it!

-It's a long story. Let's save it for when I don't have to avoid trucks.

A building several blocks away

Bob Null is late again. It's not his fault, really: he tried to leave the party earlier, but the girl just wouldn't let him go. In fact, she's still clinging to his arm, and they are both right in front of the building where he lives.

-Listen...Tina, right?

-Deena.

-Sure. Listen, it's been a great night but I really have to go home now, okay?

-Can I come up for a drink?

-No, because A) you're already drunk and B) I promised my daughter I would let in only girls ten years older than she is, remember?

-Riiight, the kid you've never let me talk to. You sure she's not adopted or somethin'? You don't look old enough to have a kid that age.

-I'll send you some pictures of how awesome I was at fifteen. You sure you can make it to your house alone?

-I'm not drunk! Y'know what I think? I think you don't really have a daughter and you're making things up 'cause you're seeing other girls.

-Now, come on, Tina…

-Deena!

-Whatever; I'm not seeing anyone else, okay?

Just then, something smashes right through the walls of the building, five stories up. The wall smashes on the ground along with something else; Bob's first reaction is to push Deena out of harm's way. He makes sure she's okay, despite throwing up on the street, before looking back.

There's a puddle of green goo in the middle of the wall debris. The puddle grows very quickly, taking a rough human form, before splitting in two equal parts.

In less than five seconds, the puddle has turned into two identical women with long black hair, dressed in green. One of them holds in her hand an object which Bob recognizes immediately: a perfectly round sphere of solid rock.

-Hey, that's mine!

-And who the heck is she? – Deena asks.

-We are the Many. The Heart is ours now. All witnesses must be eliminated.

The second woman makes a step forward. While Bob is still struggling to understand what's going on, he hears the sound of a very fast motorbike approaching.

The bike then hits he woman, turning her back into goo and smashing against the building.

Someone jumped off the bike at the very last second. She stands up, bruised but completely unfazed. Her silver eyes glow in the night.
-Father. What did I tell you about taking home girls?

4- Once in a blue moon

For all his family's complicated history, Bob's world used to make sense. He was a single father in his middle thirties with an eighteen year old daughter; remembering his date's name and making sure her daughter's life was going to be better than his own was really the extent of his whishes.

That was five minutes ago.

Now some kind of green blob who can take the form of a beautiful woman and calls itself "the Many" has broken into his house, has stolen the most valuable thing Bob has ever owned, and her twin was smashed into a wall by a bike driven by Bob's daughter. Who apparently now has silver glowing eyes and has learned to drive. And for some reason Bob's most valuable possession looks like a perfectly spherical rock. To sum: things just got really weird, really fast. And Bob still can't remember his date's name.

The rock has rolled towards the Many, who doesn't seem to mind the destruction of its twin.

-Step away from the sphere. NOW.

Noriko's voice is firm and convincing. The Many hesitates.

-We wish to avoid conflict if possible. We have what we came for; we will not harm you.

-You exploded in my face!!!

-All witnesses must be eliminated.

The Many quickly picks up the sphere, slowly looking around. It's hard to crash a bike a few blocks away from a very recent explosion without attracting a lot of attention, especially in New York.

Sirens are approaching quickly. People are looking out the window to find out what all this noise is about. The traffic jam is picking up the pace.

And there's a flying goddess in a waitress dress with no shoes landing at Noriko's side, with an African-American man in her arms. This is what finally ticks off the Many.

-We are not prepared to face an Olympian. The Heart will take care of this.

The rocks glows blue.

A blue energy bubble surrounds this very, very strange group of people. When it disappears just a blink afterwards, there's only a huge hole in the ground.

Mare Crisium

You have seen this place before. It's a small dark spot on the edge of the Moon's face. When you looked it didn't have a New York sidewalk with half a wall and six people, but it does now.

-No. Freakin'. Way – is Bob's reaction when he looks up, seeing only stars surrounded by grey mountains. He doesn't have much chance to marvel at the beauty of the universe, since Deena has thrown herself into his arms screaming in terror:

-WHAT THE HELL IS GOING ON!?

-We did not anticipate this. The Heart is malfunctioning.

-Shouldn't you be suffocating? – Vesta asks, just as confused as anyone else.

-Don't you mean "we" should be suffocating? – Max replies.

-Oh, I don't really need to breathe. Hey, why aren't *you* freakin' out at this?

-Why should I? This is awesome! I'm on the Moon!!!

-We have less than two minutes before the air that's been teleported with us fades away and lets us here to die alone – Noriko clarifies.

-You just *had* to spoil the moment, didn't you?

-Listen, Many or whatever your name is. If you didn't want any witness, it's too late. This diversion might kill us, but Vesta will survive. And I can assure you, she will not rest until she has taken the Heart from you.

-I didn't say an…oh yeah, I get it. Sure, I'll never rest until I catch you, Many. Totally. To get away with this, you'll have to go through me – Vesta plays along.

-We agree with your suggestion – the Many answers, shooting a blue ray through the rock.

Max immediately jumps in front of the ray, pushing Vesta and taking the full blast.

The blue energy rips his body apart, hollowing his body from the inside out. He barely has time to scream, since his lungs are one of the first things to disappear. All it takes are two, maybe three seconds, before all that's left of Max Black is blue mist on the surface of the Moon.

-No! – Vesta shouts, grabbing the mist with both hands and…well *compressing* it, for lack of a better word, back into human shape.

Noriko is watching speechless; she has all of mankind's experience at her disposal and yet she can't believe what she's seeing. Max's body is re-forming while he screams in reverse: Vesta is basically putting his atoms back together.

-Is he going to be all right?

-I don't know! I have no idea what I'm doing! – Vesta admits: most of Max's body is intact, but there's still a lot of blue mist around him…which as far as she knows could be a good sign.

-Nori, behind you! – Bob shouts.

Noriko avoids another blast from the Many by moving to her left a couple of inches; just enough to grab the Many's arm and twist it.

Any human would try to resist or scream in pain, but the Many simply stares as her arm twists unnaturally. She still has the sphere in her hand and is not letting go.

-If you are the best this world has to offer, we are not impressed.

-Neither am I – Noriko answers, using all of her strength to smash the sphere right into the Many's face…literally, since the woman's face seems to have the consistency of jelly.

Amazingly she's still alive, and only takes a step back. It will probably take her a moment to recover from the injury, but Noriko's not going to give her one.

-Nobody steals from Null and lives – she threatens before touching the sphere.

Then everything goes blue.

Earth, New York City
Empire State Building, 87th floor

Leiko is standing in front of the window, hands behind her back, overlooking the city. Her daughter's reaction wasn't entirely unexpected: she was raised by her useless father, after all. A part of her can't help but admire the girl's will to stand up for herself, though.

She walks to her desk, where a small wooden box is waiting for her. She opens the lock and a metallic sphere, not much larger than her fist, starts rising in the air.

-*You are late* – it says, using a voice far deeper than humanly possible.
-I decide when to let you out of the box, Core. Never forget who is in charge.
-*Leadership is meaningless to me. I have no interest in being in charge of amoebas like you.*
-Really. Then maybe I should bury you again where my grandfather found you.
-*I will concede that our alliance has been useful. Your father had a much smaller vision for this planet than yours.*
-I had my own reasons for killing him.
-*Of course. But unlike him, you are willing to use my knowledge to its fullest potential. It may take some time, as inferior beings like you measure these things, but there is no doubt: the future is ours.*
Someone knocks at the door. The Core floats back to the box, which Leiko closes before her secretary enters the room.
-Miss Tanaka, I'm sorry to disturb you, but you asked to be notified immediately.
-Did you find her?
-No, ma'am. We haven't been able to locate miss Null after she left the building. However, the surveillance cameras in her apartment show that the sphere has been stolen.
-Was it a dark haired woman dressed in green?
-Y-Yes, ma'am. How did you…
Leiko smiles. She rarely does, but this time it's worth it.
-Then it worked. My daughter may still be worthless, but we finally caught the gods' attention.

Mare Crisium
The moon dust settles slowly, thanks to the lower gravity. Noriko Null stands on the green ashes that used to be a woman a few seconds earlier.
-You…you vaporized her – Max says.
-You have a real talent for stating the obvious, mr. Black. Is everyone alright? – Noriko asks.
This is the last straw for Deena. She's been clinging to Bob, her date and Noriko's father, since they've all been teleported here.
-WE'RE ON THE MOON! WHY ISN'T ANYONE FREAKIN OUT!? – she shrieks.

28

Noriko is not amused; she stares at her father, stating with supreme annoyance:

-Father, either slap some sense into that woman or I will do it myself.

-"Father"? What happened to "dad"? – Bob answers, visibly puzzled.

Noriko sighs, massaging her temples: this is a very long night.

-This isn't the right moment, Father. Our priority should be to go back to Earth before we asphyxiate or freeze to death. Vesta, am I to understand you're the reason we're not dead?

The immortal waitress without shoes just shrugs.

-I'd be a pretty bad goddess of the hearth if I didn't keep my guests warm and breathing, now, wouldn't I?

-That almost makes sense – Max notes – Hey, why don't you use that gizmo to beam us back?

-I'm working on it – Null answers, concentrating on the sphere in her hands, which looks like a rock. For as long as she can remember, it's always been on her father's nightstand and it's never looked interesting…she never even asked where it came from.

She was able to control it briefly before, using its power to disintegrate the Many; it can't be that hard to do it again.

There's a blue flash of light. When it disappears, the Earth is filling the entire sky. And it's becoming visibly larger each second.

-Honey, maybe you should keep working – Bob suggests to his daughter.

The Earth is getting bigger because Noriko teleported a chunk of moon rock just above the atmosphere. A football-stadium-sized chunk.

The air surrounding the newly formed asteroid starts burning thanks to the friction with the Earth's atmosphere. The fire moves towards Vesta's hands, who shouts:

-I can't keep us alive much longer! DO SOMETHING!

-I said I'm working on it! – Noriko answers, looking intensely at the rock in her hands. So intensely that her silver eyes are shining: she's actually concentrating a small fraction of humanity's thinking power on the problem at hand.

-Done – she says before another bright flash of blue light.

Everyone hits the sand, falling from a couple of feet off the ground. Everyone except Vesta, who is floating in the exact place where she was teleported.

-Where are we now? – she asks.

-Coney Island – Noriko answers, wiping the sand off her face.

Bob Null tries to get on his feet again, stumbling and falling again right on top of Deena. She passed out two teleportations ago.

-Nice work, Nori…whatever you did… - he mumbles.

-I'm afraid we didn't do enough – Vesta says, pointing at the sky.

The football-stadium-sized chunk of Moon rock is about to fall on top of New York City.

Max Black was pretty much raised by comic books and television; his father was a cop and his mother never had less than two jobs at a time.

Contrary to the cliché, he wasn't the black nerdy kid with glasses that always gets bullied; he was the high school quarterback who could kick your ass if you said anything funny about Superman's costume. Since knowing the full Avengers roster by heart didn't get him a job in Chicago, he moved to New York as soon as he could…most of his heroes lived there. Well, a fictional and highly idealized version of New York, at the very least.

He was almost surprised that the city wasn't always about to be destroyed by a supervillain or an alien invasion. Even more surprisingly, the fact that an asteroid is about to wipe the city out of the map doesn't make New York look more real in his eyes.

-Now what? – he asks to the silver eyed eighteen year old Asian girl that's turned his life upside down in less than an hour.

She's holding to the spherical rock called the Heart of the Universe as if her life depends on it, mostly because it actually does.

-This thing isn't working. I think it's resisting me somehow.

-So…we're going to die, right? – Max asks.

-Sorry, I'm really not good at that – Vesta answers, leaving the ground and flying towards the asteroid; there's a huge boom when she reaches the speed of sound a hundred feet above.

But that's nothing compared to the deafening explosion of the meteorite; it's loud enough to shatter windows several miles away.

Max isn't watching the explosion; he's covering his eyes from the sand lifted by the first sonic boom. Vesta caused quite a little sandstorm when she kicked off.

-Next time give us a warning shot or something! – Max complains, trying to move the sand.

But the sand isn't moving. It's still in the air.

-What the heck is going on? Why is everything so quiet? – he asks, even though he can't hear his own voice.

Just outside the sandstorm, the picture is clear. And it's very much like walking through a picture: everything's perfectly still. Noriko is concentrating on the sphere.

Max waves his hand in front of her eyes: she's not blinking. She's not even breathing. A drop of sweat on her forehead is absolutely immobile.

That's not the weirdest thing: Max's hand is now made of bright yellow light, like the rest of his body. His mind struggles with the change for the briefest of times, before he comes to the sudden realization that will change his life forever:

-I have super-powers! Whoo-hoo!

As he shouts with all the joy of the world, he looks up. Frozen in time, the asteroid's explosion is filling the entire sky.

-Crap. The end of the world stuff. Forgot about that.

Later, Max is lying on the beach with his hands behind his head. It's impossible to know how much later: it feels like an eternity, but nothing is changing.

"Okay, let's see what we've got here. I probably didn't stop time; I don't have problems breathing. Actually, now that I think about it, I'm not actually breathing. That rules out super-speed I guess. And how did I get superpowers anyway?"

Max steps up, walking towards Noriko. Actually *walking* is misleading: he just wills himself in another place and appears there. The drop of sweat on her forehead hasn't moved.

"Too bad I can't ask *you*, little miss genius. Maybe that gizmo can unfreeze time" – he guesses, trying to touch the Heart of the Universe. His hand phases right through it.

"Figures. Maybe it's for the best, I don't want that thing to disintegrate me tw…wait a second".

31

He pictures a familiar scene again: him pushing Vesta out of harm's way, the Heart's death ray disintegrating him, and Vest pulling him back together.

"That's it! She did something wrong putting me back together, like mixing that thing's energy with my body or something. That means…"

He looks up. The explosion hasn't moved.

"That means absolutely nothing. I'm still stuck here. What kind of lame superpower is this?"

Max then wills himself right inside the explosion. Vesta is still there, still frozen in time after punching the asteroid. And her waitress dress doesn't even have a scratch.

"So you turned into what…energy?" – he wonders. Then something in his mind just connects all the right dots; he snaps is intangible fingers, making no sound.

He tries to grab a fragment of the meteorite; his hand passes through it at first, but when he puts his mind into it the space rock explodes.

-Max? What are you doing up here? – Vesta asks.

-I can turn my body into energy!– he shouts with all the joy in the world, before flying away literally at the speed of light. Turning his body into a laser.

Imagine you live in New York. You hear a loud noise and you look up: the sky's on fire.

Then you hear a much louder noise, loud enough to drown all the voices in the world, even the noise of the millions of windows shattered.

If you're not too terrified to keep looking at the sky, you see the most fantastic light show imaginable as a streak of light ricochets between rocks the size of cars to incinerate them, one by one. Finally, if you haven't completely lost your mind yet, every impossible thing you've just seen… the fire, the meteorite, even the fine dust falling to the ground after the laser hit the rocks… everything just disappears in a blue streak of light.

It was quick. Everything happened in less than a minute, when even a lifetime wouldn't be enough to really understand.

Because what just happened was simply impossible. And this is the night when the world begins to understand that the impossible is now real.

32

Max flies back to the beach, turning his body into human flesh again. After an eternity, the wind is finally letting the sand fall to the ground.

Noriko Null is standing on the sand, with the Heart of the Universe in her hand and half a smile on her face.

-Told you I was working on it.

5- Breakfast with the goddess

Bob Null wakes up with the smell of bacon. It's not a bad way to wake up, the only problem is that there shouldn't be anyone cooking it.

His daughter couldn't cook even if her life depended on it. Did he bring anyone home last night? No, he's pretty sure he didn't, he slept alone this time. He gets out of bed and grabs the baseball bat he keeps under it, then drops it.

"Yeah, great idea Bob, somebody must have broken in to steal cash and got hungry. Did I lend the keys to anyone? Nori's gonna kill me" he thinks.

Walking slowly to the kitchen he's speechless for how clean everything is. There's not even a single shard of glass on the floor; after the windows shattered the night before, it was everywhere.

There's a woman with red hair in the kitchen. She's wearing orange pants and tube top, no shoes, she's floating a couple of inches from the floor, and she's humming.

-Vesta!?

-Good morning! Pancakes or bacon? – she asks cheerfully.

-How did you get in?

-I flew. There's no glass on the windows.

-So you decided to fly in and make breakfast?

-I made quite a mess when I blew up the asteroid and you all looked exhausted. I tried to tidy up a bit; is everything fine?

-I...guess it is – Bob answers, flabbergasted; the apartment was a disaster area, but now it looks perfect. That's not the only thing he's looking at. Vesta is floating towards the table, humming a cheerful tune, looking absolutely perfect.

-Null is your daughter, right? – she asks.

-You mean Noriko, yeah. How did you meet her?

-She walked into the bar where I worked before it exploded. She never told me her name. You look...I'm sorry, I never know how to talk about these things...you have different...eyes? And skin color? – she says nervously.

-It's okay, I get that a lot. Her mother's Japanese. Wait, your bar *exploded*?

-Well, no, somebody inside it did. Is Noriko alright after what happened tonight?

34

-I don't know...with all the police and firemen and all that mess tonight I haven't really had the chance to talk to her. I figured I'd let her have a good night's sleep.

-I tried to clean her room but she yelled at me.

-Let *me* try it.

It doesn't take much to get to Noriko's room: with his salary, he can't afford a decent place.

Bob is used to find a mess in her daughter's room; it's what you expect from a teenager. But what he finds is excessive even for her.

She's sitting on the floor, in her underwear and the same T-shirt of the night before, tinkering with some electronic parts. She has dismantled a TV, a cell phone and her alarm clock; the remains are scattered everywhere together with dozens of sheets of paper, filled from top to bottom with formulas and diagrams.

She's even torn the posters of her favorite bands from the wall, drawing some kind of spherical machine. Bob doesn't recognize the design, but the amount of details she came up with is insane.

-What the hell happened here?

-It's a matter of processing power – Noriko answers, not looking up from the device she's building.

-What?

-The Heart of the Universe – she answers, pointing vaguely towards the drawing on the wall; now that he thinks about it, Bob can see that the drawing is the cutaway of the spherical rock on the floor.

-It needs a very high number of inputs in order to work, and they need to be very precise. That's why the Many and I had so much trouble working it; even my brain can't generate easily that many instructions.

-Did you even sleep, Nori?

-Little less than an hour. I kept having nightmares about concentration camps and wars so I decided to keep myself busy.

-Well, we're gonna be late. You've got time for a shower; we'll talk about this...mess after school.

-Father, understanding this alien technology could be humanity's greatest technological achievement!

-It can wait after breakfast.

Marbella, Spain

35

Hours ahead of the cold New York morning, the sun is shining on a magnificent beach.

Tourists in bathing suits are watching an African-American throw rocks in the air, then seemingly shooting at them with lasers coming out of the palm of his hand.

For Max Black, this is the best day of his life. People are cheering, thinking this is some sort of performance, but he's doing much more: he's learning how to use his newfound power.

As far as he can tell, he can turn his body into energy. It didn't take long to understand how to turn a very small part of himself, much less than a drop of blood, into pure light.

Too bad he doesn't speak more than three words of Spanish, because he would love to shout at the top of his lungs that he's the world's first superhero now.

His cell phone starts ringing, singing the theme song of a cartoon show. He almost forgot about it, but it's in his pocket. He excuses himself from the applauding crowd to answer:

-Hello?

-*Max, thank God you're alright! I tried to call you all night!* - says his sister Kayla.

-Uhm, yeah, I've been kinda busy. What's up?

-*What's up? A meteor almost landed on New York, you dumbass, that's what!*

-Oh, right, that. Don't worry, everything's fine, I was...I was out of town, yes. Would you hang on a second?

Max puts the call on hold, grabs the shirt from the sand, and turns his body into light again.

Chicago, Illinois

Kayla is tapping her foot. It's just like her brother to scare her half to death and then disappear.

Somebody knocks at the door. She lowers the volume on the TV, where they're showing the walking disaster area that is New York City, and looks through the peephole.

-Oh you've got to be kidding me! – she shouts opening the door.

Max is just outside, shaking the sand out of his shirt before putting it on again.

-Mind if I drop by?

-Don't tell me: you were fired.

36

-What? Oh, the job interview, right, I never got the job in the first place. But something came up and I wanted to talk to you about it.

-You can't stay – she says bluntly, walking in. Just from the way she walks, it's clear she's upset.

-Oh come on!

-I helped you move to New York but that's it; you think it's easy with a security guard's salary?

-Hey I never asked you for money!

Kayla's death stare is more than enough to convince Max to reconsider his statement.

-Okay, two or three times. But I paid it back. Mostly. It's just for a few days anyway, my place is a mess! You should see what happened last night.

-I thought you were out of town.

-Uhm, yeah, it's like…Oh, the heck with it, I suck at this. Kayla, I've got superpowers now.

-Max, I don't care about your latest game, I have a job remember? Unless they fired me 'cause I was on the phone all morning trying to reach my…idiot…brother….

Kayla's jaw drops watching her brother's body turn into light, floating on air, with a gleeful smile.

-See? I'm a superhero! How cool is that!?

-I'll call in sick.

6- Homecoming

Noriko never really cared about high school. She always thought it was a colossal waste of time and couldn't wait to finish it. She knew her father was looking forward to her graduation: he had to drop out of his school when she was born. There was no way she would be able to go to college: her father didn't have remotely that much money, and her grades were nothing to be proud of.

That was yesterday, before she became the smartest being on the planet.

Now she's just standing in the hallway, her mind overwhelmed by the stream of information. Every face is connected to thousands of emails, forum discussions, tweets. The noise is too chaotic to understand any of it. Unable to disconnect from it, Noriko's mind is in overdrive.

-You okay there? – Jane asks her, snapping her fingers in front of her eyes.

Noriko comes back to Earth looking at Jane and the noise disappears. She already knows everything there is to know about Jane Blake, after all: they've been best friends for most of their lives. She's always been one of the few constants in her life and a stable reminder of what it means to come from a normal family. And as always, she has no problem figuring out when Noriko is trying to hide something.

-You kinda zoned out for a moment – she notes.

-I was…distracted. What was the question again?

-I said, where were you last night?

-Why do you ask?

-Gee, could it be 'cause something crashed every window in the city? They say it was a meteor. I can't believe they're making us go to school today – Jane answers, opening her locker.

Noriko's seen her do this almost every day since she was ten years old. But now something's off. Something about her feels alien.

-Come on, you can tell me. You weren't home 'cause you went out with Jeff, didn't you? I thought you two broke up last month, but…Nori? Hello?

Noriko has frozen in place again, staring at her locker. She takes a book, looking at its cover with a mixture of fear and disgust.

-This is all so…small. So very small. Everything I used to know wouldn't even fill half of this.

-Is this your way to tell me that you didn't study for today's test?

-This is all wrong!!! – Noriko shouts, drawing the hallway's attention.

She's not used to being the center of attention. She's not exactly a wallflower; most of the students would recognize her as "the five feet tall Asian tomboy that always wear an ugly green jacket and hangs out with that white girl", at the very least.

-We split the atom, we went to other planets, we discovered the origin of the universe! We rule this world! Why are we wasting time like this!?

Noriko slams the locker shut and Jane takes a step back. There was enough rage and volume in Noriko's voice to silence the lively chatter of a high school hallway.

She turns towards them, and her silver eyes glow for an instant.

-What are you looking at?

The bell rings. This is the first time Jane's ever been truly scared of her best friend.

-Let's just get this over with – Noriko says, walking towards the classroom.

Noriko's never been good at math. Her grades have never been something to brag about in any subject, but math's been her sworn enemy since grade school.

Mr. Bennett has been her teacher for the last three years and knows this very well. When he notices she's started to write furiously as soon as he's handled her the test, the first thing he thinks is that she's joking or cheating. He stands right besides her, waiting until she finishes in record time.

Noriko draws a circle on the first page and slashes it, like the symbol Ø for the null set, and handles it to Mr. Bennett.

-Is that your signature or did you just grade yourself? – he asks, causing the classroom to laugh.

-I am the only one qualified to – she answers, deadly serious.

-Very funny, miss Null – he says, ready to reprimand her, when his eyes pause on the test for a little while. Everything is right. He checks it twice; even he couldn't finish the test in such record time.

39

-How did you do this? – he asks. She couldn't have cheated, he was looking at her the whole time.

-I know all the answers.

-Really – he says sarcastically, looking at the test again. He just can't believe his eyes; Noriko's best grade ever was a C minus. This is easily an A plus.

-Would you mind to come to the blackboard? The rest of you, keep working – he says to the rest of the class, which has lost what little interest it had on the test.

-Let's do another test. Can you solve this? – mr. Bennett asks, writing something on the wall. Last time Noriko tried to do this in her last test, she got an F.

-Too easy – she answers, wiping out the expression with her sleeve. Not even bothering with an answer.

-Very well, Noriko. Show me what you know.

Bob Null walks towards the classroom, ignoring the smiles and giggles of the girls. It's not easy being the janitor in your daughter's school, but it can be worse if all of her friends have had a crush on you. He only recognizes Jane, walking towards him; she looks distressed.

-Mr Null, what are you doing here?

-Bennett called me while I definitely wasn't in the storage room with mrs. DeMartino.

-What? Nevermind. Did something happen to Noriko? She's kind of crazy today. I'm really worried about her.

-It's probably just a phase – he answers, walking past her and into the classroom.

Mr Bennett is sitting on his desk and looks devastated. His tie is loose, the hair is a mess, and he looks like he's smoked a thousand cigarettes.

Noriko is writing something on the blackboard. Bob doesn't recognize it and can't keep up with it: as soon as she's finished filling the blackboard, she wipes it clean and just goes on.

-I've been teaching math for thirty years, Bob, but now I feel like I've failed kindergarten. Your kid... she went from calculus to chaos theory in ten minutes. She said something about string theory and quantum chromodynamics twenty minutes ago and I just lost her.

-What is she writing?

-I have no idea. I can't follow her anymore. Bob...has your daughter ever taken an IQ test?

-Years ago – Bob nods, looking at her daughter writing like she's in some sort of trance - She scored 101. Just...average, they said.

Noriko is drinking her soda, sitting on the sidewalk in front of the school. Between her feet there are six empty cans and a dozen sheets of paper, all full of writings from top to bottom.

-Two hundred and sixty-five – Jane says, approaching her friend.

-It's not accurate. It needs to be adjusted for age and other variables – Noriko clarifies.

-So what's your real IQ, genius?

-Unlikely to be measured in a meaningful way.

-Come on, Nori, talk to me. The least you can do is tell me what's happening.

-Stop calling me that.

-What?

-I'm not Nori anymore. I am Null – Noriko answers, standing up and showing her friend a sheet of paper with the same symbol she used to sign the test. A slashed zero.

-Noriko is a drop in the ocean and I feel like I'm drowning. There's so much stuff in my head now I feel like it can explode if I relax for a second. I am Null; I *must* be Null.

-Nori, you're scaring me now. Nothing you say makes any sense, you know that?

Noriko smiles and shakes Jane's hand.

-Of course. Null knows everything. Goodbye, Jane Blake, you were a good friend.

Just like that, Noriko leaves. Jane still can't believe they're having this conversation. Noriko has always had her quirks, but she sounds crazy now. Would a crazy person become that smart that quickly?

-Where are you going? – she asks.

-I'm leaving high school – Noriko answers without even looking back.

-What!? Why?

-I don't want anyone else to be caught in the explosion.

-What does that even mean!? – Jane insists.

-Excuse me – a female voice interrupts. Jane turns towards it, looking at the impossibly beautiful woman with long red hair and no shoes.

-Vesta. My father asked to come here, I suppose.

-Well, yes. He's very worried about you... are you okay?

-Better than okay. Way better. Follow me – Noriko orders, walking away from the school without giving Jane any more attention. Vesta seems conflicted, hesitating before following Noriko, but after mouthing a polite "I'm sorry" to Jane she complies with the request.

-That was very rude, Null. What about your friend?

-She'll get over it. I'm sorry if that makes me sound cold, but there are larger issues at hand.

-Such as?

Noriko looks at her; the silver eyes shine in a way that make her understand she means business.

-You're a goddess.

-Don't say it out loud – Vesta whispers, looking around to make sure nobody heard her.

-Why not?

-It's not something I'd like to go public. I try to keep a low profile.

-You didn't seem to have much trouble telling me.

-Well yeah but... you already knew. And you can be quite intimidating with that eye thing, despite being... well...

-If you're looking for a politically correct way to say "mortal", don't bother. And you shouldn't be ashamed of what you are: without you, the Many would've gained the Heart Of The Universe. Speaking of which, are you familiar with them?

-I've seen creatures like them a few times, but nothing so advanced.

-Interesting. The work of another god?

-Perhaps. Listen, Null, I didn't come here just because your father asked me...

-How *did* he ask you, anyway?

-I gave him my number.

-You literally met him *yesterday* and he's already... who am I kidding, you're an attractive woman, *of course* he got your number without even trying – she rolls her eyes.

-He just reminds me of one of my brothers, that's all – Vesta replies defensively, although Noriko notices she's still blushing. Again, something she should've seen coming.

-Anyway, I wanted to thank you for stopping the Many, and to tell you that I'm leaving the city.

-What? Why?

-People saw me flying, remember? It's too risky to stay here. I have to move somewhere else for a decade or two, just to be sure.

-That's the dumbest idea I've ever heard. You will stay here, and you will help me.

-Help you with what?

-Vesta, you're easily the most powerful being on the planet, and you work as a waitress. Why don't you use your powers in a more productive way?

-I tried. Believe me, I did. But the world just isn't ready.

Noriko smiles at her, while her eyes shine brightly. It's the smile of a person who has just figured out how to accomplish the impossible.

-Then let's fix the world together, shall we?

7- The hero of another story

Chicago

Kayla still isn't really sure she isn't dreaming. Her brother Max, who is supposed to be in New York, has been telling the story of what happened to him the night before.

When he first showed her his powers, she almost fainted. Not her proudest moment as security guard! But how do you react logically to the news that your slacking younger brother can turn into a laser now?

He's been going on for hours now. First he wanted to show her how many tricks he's already mastered. Then how awesome the situation is. Then he bragged that he went to the Moon and how awesome it was. Then what he's going to do with this awesome powers, that he's going to be a superhero and fight evil. Then he said how everything is awesome now, to the point that the word "awesome" is starting to make her sick.

-Okay, let me get this straight – she interrupts him – You went to a bar where the waitress was a goddess. Then an alien blob that looked like a woman teleported you on the Moon with a rock, then used the rock to disintegrate you, the goddess put you back together and now you've got powers?

-Pretty much. Isn't it…

-If the next word that comes out of your mouth is "awesome" I swear to God I'm gonna shoot you.

-…cool? We also saved New York from a meteor!

-Nice job at that; did you see the news? It looks like a warzone!

-I sort of did see it. I turned into radio waves and bounced between a few stations, but it gave me a headache so I stopped.

-You made billions of damages…wait, you can turn into radio waves too?

-I think I can turn into any kind of energy.

-You *think*.

-Have you ever turned into energy before, sis? It's not like you see a giant neon sign telling you what you've turned into.

-Or you could ask the goddess – Kayla answers.

Max opens his mouth to answer, then stops realizing he really doesn't have anything to say except:

-You know, that's actually a good idea.

-Max, you mean it never came to your mind to ask some questions to the person that gave you superpowers!?
-Hey! You came up with that idea! Wait, that's actually worse, isn't it?

Kayla sighs. Her brother has never been the sharpest mind in the world, but now he's trapped in a permanent sugar high. Just then, her phone starts ringing.

-Just pray this isn't my boss calling – she warns him, answering the phone.
-Hello?
-*I am Null* – answers a female voice on the other side.
-Do I know you?
-*I must speak to your brother. Now.*

Kayla looks at her brother, then puts the call on speaker and hands the phone to Max.

-Hello? Is this Null?
-*Drop the speaker, mister Black. I have no need to talk to miss Black.*
-Definitely Null. What's up?
-*This is supposed to be a private conversation, mister Black.*
-Call me Max. So, do you want me to join your team?
-*My what?*
-Your superhero team!
-*What are you talking about?*
-I can turn into energy, Vesta can fly and shoot fire, and you've got that glowing eyes thing.
-...
-Hello?
-*Can I speak to your sister?*
-I've got a better idea! – Max answers, disappearing so quickly to let the phone fall to the ground.

New York
Noriko also drops the phone when Max appears right in front of her in the blink of an eye, on the other side of the phone booth. This being New York, very few people notice.

-These things still work? I thought everyone had a cell these days – he wonders.

45

-I did own a cell phone. I dismantled it before breakfast to build a spectrometer – she answers, stepping out of the booth.

She takes a long look; she really didn't have the time the night before. He's still wearing the same T-shirt and grey hoodie.

-So. How did you know I was at my sister's?

-I know everything. I am...

-Yes, yes, you're Null, I know that. You don't need to tell me every five minutes. What does it mean, exactly? Is that, like, your codename? 'Cause it sucks.

-Excuse me? – she asks, raising an eyebrow.

-Well I don't get "supersmart Asian chick with freaky silver eyes" from "Null".

-It's my last name.

-But it doesn't mean anything! Now if your surname was Danger or Doom, I'd understand you hammering on the point. Hey, you know what? You should call yourself Doctor Null!

-That doesn't make any sense, I'm not a doctor. Is there any chance you may listen to me?

-I've been thinking about my name too. All the good ones are taken. I was thinking something that starts with The, but I can't think of anything that's not been done before or which doesn't sound dumb. I'll probably have to go with something very generic, but do you have any idea how many superhero names sound corny when you say them out loud?

Noriko sighs. This is probably a bad idea.

-Max, you're giving me seven billion headaches right now. I was going to ask you if I could study your powers, so that I could get an insight on how the Heart of the Universe works.

-Sure. Which way's the base, Doctor Null?

-Just Null. Noriko, if you absolutely must.

Inside the building, Noriko is opening the door to the apartment. Max is still talking.

-Maybe The Laser. Too bad The Flash is taken. Hey Nori, if you know everything, does that mean that if someone tries to rob a bank you know it immediately?

-No, I don't have access to this level of detail. I only know something if enough people already know; I can tell you how many banks were robbed yesterday. None in this city, by the way.

-Then how do we stop bank robbers?
-Why do you want to do that?
-'Cause it's what superheroes do. What if I fly around at the speed of light looking for crime?
-Because then you'd need to...Max?
Noriko turns around, discovering that he's disappeared. She sighs again, looking for the keys in her pocket. Before she can open the door, he's behind her again.
-I didn't find anything.
-Of course you didn't; in your light form you're too fast to experience more than very quick snapshots. You'd need to fly everywhere twenty four-seven. Can you even see things when you're made of light?
-Sort of. What if I stop time like I did yesterday?
-What are you talking about?
-I dunno. I thought I was light, but it felt very different from what I've been able to do so far.
-I don't think that was light; possibly neutrinos or some unknown particle. Amazing. The first time I have a free afternoon I'll rewrite quantum physics just to explain you.
-Hey, what about Quantum? That sounds cool, right?
-If I agree, will you shut up?
-"Quantum, the man of energy". Or something like that.
-It sounds totally cool – Noriko says with the most bored and deadpan voice ever heard.
Then she opens the door. Vesta greets her with a warm smile; her hands are holding something.
-Welcome home! I removed all the surveillance cameras. I hope you don't mind.
-I didn't build those. How...nevermind. We've got work to do. This is Max Black.
-Call me Quantum - Max adds.
-We've met. You guys hungry? I made cookies!

Noriko just pushes Vesta aside, walking nervously inside and grabbing a cookie.
-Whoever was monitoring us knows what happened tonight. The world is likely to know the truth sooner than expected...that the

47

impossible is very real. I must take action to protect the Heart of the Universe from inferior minds.

-Which means… - says Max.

-I need a million dollars.

-To do what? – the goddess asks.

-Miracles – answers the teenager with a mind the size of a planet, while eating a cookie.

8- Pandora never learns

The Scion Corporation has made quite an impression on Japan in the last few months. Its creation has been the result of the biggest merger of the year, spearheaded by none other than Leiko Tanaka.

Daughter of the late Daichi Tanaka, pioneer of consumer electronics rumored to be heavily involved in organized crime, Leiko has turned hostile takeovers into a brutal art form.

When she enters the main R&D lab, a dozen of the most highly paid scientists on the planet bow respectfully. They wonder about the wooden box she's carrying around, but don't dare say a word to her. They know what happens to those who disrespect any member of the Tanaka family, after all.

She barely acknowledges their presence. Her eyes are only for the centerpiece of the laboratory, protected by thick bulletproof glass and surrounded by very expensive sensors.

It's a vase. Specifically, a Greek amphora.

-Report – she orders. One of the scientists answers:

-We have not been able to determine its age, ma'am. The circuitry inside the vase extends to microscopic scale; it would take a lifetime to understand what it is, but it is definitely far older than ancient Greece.

-Is it working?

-It causes radio interference at short distance, but we're not sure why. It's not emitting radio waves.

-That would be all. Now leave, all of you.

The scientists are perplexed for a moment, but exit the room one by one. Leiko watches their reflections on the glass.

Only after everyone has left, she opens the box. A metallic sphere rises into the air, speaking with a deep voice.

-*Such primitive technology. You might as well throw rocks at it* – the Core says.

-You helped me find it. I assume this is Drylon technology?

-*Hardly. A cheap Olympian copy, but still superior to your pitiful instruments.*

-Then you certainly know how to activate it.

-*Of course. The device is causing interference because it is waiting for a signal. I have already deciphered what it wants to hear.*

-Wait. The vase depicts the story of Pandora. If the Olympians made this, it must have been some sort of warning from them.

-*Impressive. You almost come close to redeeming the intellectual abilities of your species. Have you suddenly developed their affinity with childish fears as well?*

-Don't patronize me, Core. There are two pieces of Drylon technology on Earth. The Many know one is in New York City; it won't be long before they find you too.

-*Wisely said. Then, shall I say the word to activate the device?*

-Yes. It's time to open the box.

-*Very well.* **Καταπορεύομαι.**

The Core's voice is not only sound: it also transmitted a very specific radio signal. The vase glows brightly before shattering into millions of pieces.

Every computer screen in the building goes blank, then shows a wall of text. A single word repeated over and over again: *Καταπορεύομαι.*
It's only the beginning. In less than a second, every single screen in Tokyo shows the same wall of text. The wall of text spreads everywhere: every computer and TV screen fills with endless repetitions of *Καταπορεύομαι.* A second later, the same thing is happening in all of Japan.

Every single cellphone sends and receives thousands of messages with only one word: *Καταπορεύομαι.* Every single email account does the same.

Then the phenomenon reaches South Korea. China. Russia. India. Half of the planet's communications have been taken over by a single word in less than five seconds, and it doesn't seem to slow down.

Chicago, Illinois

Kayla Black is watching the news in her apartment. The reporter is talking over images of a man walking outside of a building, with his hands raised.

-I'm speaking with Mayor Corgain who, along with six people from his staff, was held hostage by a man identified as John Rhoades for over an hour. Our cameras caught Rhoades surrendering himself to the police. Mayor Corgain, what happened before this unexpected surrender?

-I still can't believe what I saw. A man appeared out of thin air in my office. Rhoades tried to shoot him, but his gun just...just melted.
-What do you mean with "melted"?
-It glowed red for a second and Rhoades let it fall to the ground. Now it's just a puddle of metal...like someone microwaved it.
-Did you recognize this man?
-He was wearing some sort of mask. Rhoades bailed out screaming, and this man...the masked man asked us if anyone was injured, then he just vanished. Just like that, in the blink of an eye. Most unbelievable thing I've ever seen.
Kayla is feeling a migraine coming up. This is the third time in a week: as soon as some crime or crisis is shown on TV, a masked man appears out of nowhere and fixes everything.
The same man has appeared behind the couch, asking:
-Did they get to the final answer yet?
-AAH! Don't...DO that thing, Max! Ever heard of knocking!?
-Too slow. What are you doing watching the news? This is Nori's big night!
Max waves at the TV screen, changing the channel without the need of a remote.
-Good, they're still on commercials.
-Max, that stunt you pulled in the Mayor's office was reckless. What if that Rhoades guy shot you before you could...could...what did you did to him, anyway?
-I turned my hand into microwaves and disarmed him. Nobody got hurt and nobody recognized me; what's wrong with that? You're a security guard, you do dangerous stuff all the time.
-Yeah, but I carry a gun!
-And I can shoot lasers if I want to, what's your point? Look, it's back on!
Max sits on his sister's couch, without a care in the world.
-I'm just killing time, waiting for Nori to do her next big thing.

On the screen, the host is sitting in front of a computer screen. On the other side of the table there's a half-Japanese girl, wearing brown contact lenses to disguise her silver eyes.
-Welcome back to the show! For those joining us now, our contestant today is Noriko Null from New York. At eighteen, she's one of our youngest contestants, and she has answered correctly all

51

of our questions so far. Are you ready to answer our One Million Dollar Question, Noriko?

-Of course. I am Null.

-What are you going to do with all this money?

-First I need to repay a motorbike I recently crashed. I will use the rest to take over the world.

The host and the audience laugh, but Noriko doesn't even smile.

-Good luck with that, Noriko, I thing the price tag's gonna be a little higher. But before you start conquering us all, you must answer the following question.

Kayla looks at her brother, with a curious look.

-"Take over the world"?

-She's kidding. I hope – he answers.

The TV is showing Noriko's face as the graphics write the question, read aloud by the host.

-"Flowers for Algernon" is a famous 1959 short story by Daniel Keyes about a man whose intelligence is artificially increased. Which science fiction magazine first published the story?

-Oh come on, that's a lame question! Anyone can look it up! – Max protests.

Then the screen goes blank, showing a wall of text. A single word repeated continuously: *Καταπορεύομαι.*

-This show is getting weird – Max adds.

In the studio, the screen showing the question does the same thing. The host looks around, to understand what is happening.

-There…there seem to be some problem with our screen. This is not one of the answers.

-It's Ancient Greek – Noriko explains.

-What? Are you sure?

-I am Null.

-What does it mean?

-"Come back".

The wall of text disappears. The host is still perplexed, but Noriko doesn't waste any time:

-The correct answer is "The Magazine of Fantasy and Science Fiction". Now give me my million dollars; I have work to do.

Tokyo, Scion Corporation R&D labs

Leiko is holding in her hand the ashes that remain from the ancient vase.

-Did it work? – she asks.

-*The message was repeated seven hundred trillion times before breaking your primitive communication networks.*

-Will it be heard beyond Earth?

-*Are you seriously asking me if a tachyon relay is somehow limited to a single planet? This is such an ignorant question that, were I not far above these things, it could very well be considered offensive.*

-I can afford to be merciful to you, Core. You have just delivered me the galaxy, after all. But never forget who is the master. Now, the dust left behind by the device…

-*Nanoscopic entanglement generators.*

-Teach me how to reverse-engineer them.

9- They do come back after all

Vesta is sitting on the edge of the roof on Two East River Place, the skyscraper that is her home now. She always liked watching the city from the sky, and she's glad that mortals in the last century have been able to do the same.

Noriko is approaching her, with a cup of coffee in her hands.

-Penny for your thoughts – she says.

-I didn't know you could read minds – Vesta answers.

-In a way. I have all of mankind's knowledge, remember? It includes noticing when someone is feeling blue. Here, this will help – she says, handling the cup to the goddess.

Noriko sits down next to her, and the two couldn't look more different if they tried. Noriko is a black-haired eighteen-year-old with short black hair, wearing jeans, sneakers and a leather jacket with a horrible shade of green. Vesta is a redhead of ageless beauty, wearing orange cut-offs and a pink T-shirt, going barefoot.

-Aren't you cold dressed like that? We're close to zero degrees up here.

-It's not *that* cold – the goddess answers. Her hands catch fire for a couple of seconds, heating the cup.

-You're right. I've started thinking in Celsius instead of Fahrenheit, probably because most of the world does the same. Now, would you mind telling me why you're feeling down?

-It's nothing, really – Vesta answers, standing up in front of the roof. Her feet don't touch the ground, in fact she simply walks on air as she talks.

-I guess you want to know why I'm paying your rent now – Noriko says.

-I've been wondering about that. You just rented…what, the top ten floors?

-Just the top five. You'd be amazed how little a million dollars can buy. Vesta, I've seen what you can do, and I'm not talking just about the fire and the flying and the strength. On the Moon, the Many ripped Max to shreds and you pulled him back together.

-It's not a big deal. I'm not even sure how I did it.

-Max was basically turned into ashes and you took him back, Vesta. When I met you, you were working as a waitress. To say that I think you can do more would be the understatement of the millennium. And since you're thousands of years old, you know that's true.

-You're very sweet, Nori. My niece Athena must have chosen wisely before making you...whatever you are now. Yes, my niece is always about wise choices – she says bitterly.

-Including disappearing right after turning me into the smartest person in the world, apparently. I take it there's quite some history between you two.

-Nori, it's been twenty-five hundred years since I last saw my family. Athena was here, in the same city where I live, and she didn't even say a word. How long will it be before I meet her again?

-Probably not as long as you think. Take a look at this – Noriko says, unfolding a large sheet of paper. It's a blueprint, highly technical and highly detailed, but it's drawn in pencil.

-You did this?

-Last night. I had trouble sleeping. Some nightmare about war.

-This is wonderful! What...what is it?

-The world's first quantum computer. The only thing powerful enough to crack the operating code of the Heart of the Universe.

-Cool! Can I see it? – Max shouts excitedly.

Noriko almost falls down the roof thanks to the surprise of someone appearing out of nowhere shouting right behind you.

-What did I tell about doing stuff like this, Max!?

-Yeah, yeah, whatever. I get it, you plan on selling them?

-Once completed it will be the most advanced technological device on the planet, Max; I estimate the prototype will cost about 200.000 dollars to assemble.

-That's nice, but is this really the sort of thing Athena had in mind? – Vesta asks, confused.

-Once I understand how the Heart works, we'll be able to ask her. Don't you see? I'm the smartest person ever and I've got my hands on an alien device that can do anything, a man who somehow can turn into energy at will, and a goddess. If I've got enough time to concentrate, I can do *anything*. Everything is going exactly as planned.

Just then, something flies by the skyscraper, with the sound of a roaring motor and the speed of a fighter jet, leaving behind a red streak of light.

-So what part of the plan is this, little miss evil genius?

55

The first thing on everybody's mind is "not meteors again", but the falling object is clearly slowing down. It falls into the water, right in front of Liberty Island, making it boil thanks to the residual head of the atmospheric re-entry.

People on the island, here to visit the Statue of Liberty, have already stormed the waterfront and start taking pictures. A robot emerges from the water.

It looks like a man in a futuristic white and black armor, and from the sound of its boots it must weigh several tons.

Its head is similar in shape to a Corinthian helmet, but instead of eyes it has a single red visor burning with a fierce atomic flame.

-**Ωηιcη γοδ οωνσ τηισ ωορλδ?** – it asks, with a metallic voice.

The crowd is loving this: there isn't a single person looking at it who isn't taking a picture or shooting a video.

-**Ι δεμανδ αν ανσωερ. Ωηιcη γοδ οωνσ τηισ ωορλδ?** – it repeats, this time with an angrier tone and stepping towards the crowd.

Nobody seems to take a hint, thinking this is some kind of incredible publicity stunt. Only when the robot grabs one of the smartphones shooting a video that the protests start. The phone's owner tries to take it back, but the robot is holding it too tightly.

-Hey, give it back! That's mine!

-**Βε qθιετ. Ι αμ σcαννινγ** – the robot replies, showing the man the palm of its hand.

An energy blast blows away the poor man's head, and with good reason the crowd goes into panic immediately. There are screams, male and female, but the robot is only hearing its own voice.

-**Σcαννινγ. Native language decoded. I will repeat the original question: which god owns this world?**

It's too late: everybody has run away from the scary killer robot. It almost looks confused from the reaction, then it looks around.

There is a very prominent statue of a woman in front of him, holding a torch in her hand. To the robot, this can only mean one thing.

-**This is Hestia's world. Beginning takeover.**

10- Ready for prime time

Bob hates moving. He should be used to it by now: he's never lived in the same place for more than a couple of years, but he's never appreciated it in any way. Maybe that's because this is the first time this happened without anyone kicking him out of the previous house. Deena doesn't seem to think so: she's admiring the view of the city, and she's been smiling for hours now.

-This place is so cool! I can't believe you live here now!

-I can't believe this couch is so heavy – Bob complains, struggling to move the furniture.

-Really? That's your biggest concern now?

-What is this thing made of anyway, lead? No wonder they left it in front of the door – he keeps complaining, throwing all of his weight to move the couch.

-Y'know, you've got a lot of space in here. How many floors did your daughter rent?

-Top five. I mean what kind of people move a couch up sixty stores and leave it *outside* the room?

-Would you forget about the couch!?

-It's the most comfortable couch in the world. And the heaviest – he points out.

-Bob…your daughter isn't going to live on this floor, right? – Deena asks, walking towards Bob who is still struggling with the couch.

-No, I think she likes the top floor better.

-Well, I don't want you to feel lonely, all alone up here. You've got a lot of free space. And since you're not going to be a janitor anymore, I think you'll also find a lot of spare time. I can help with that, too – she says, moving her hands through his hair.

-You wanna move to my place because I'm the sexiest man alive or because my daughter's a genius millionaire?

-Uhm…both. Is that a problem, Bob?

-Not if you help me move the couch.

-FATHER! – Noriko shouts, slamming the door open.

Despite being ten years older than her, Deena feels like she's just been scolded by her mother. She steps back, raising her hands to surrender:

-We weren't doing anything!

-Where is the Heart of the Universe? – Noriko asks.

-The what?

-The spherical rock that teleported us to the Moon!

-Oh that thing. I put it in the fridge.

-You put the most valuable device in the world *in the fridge* – Noriko repeats skeptically.

-Yeah.

-I'm afraid to ask why.

-Nobody would search there. Unless it was an hungry thief or something.

-I knew I had reason to be afraid.

Max and Vesta enter the room now, both visibly worried.

-You guys may want to watch the news – Max says, pointing at the TV and turning it on.

Deena wants to ask how he did it without a remote, but there's something far more interesting on the screen.

It's footage of a black and white robot walking through the city, ignoring the dozen shots from the police officers that are shouting empty threats. The journalist describing the scene is trying to be professional, but this is something straight from a movie.

-This is live from State Street, where a…a man in some kind of battle suit is attacking the city. Several people are reported injured after the man walked right into traffic fired an unknown kind of weapon.

The footage changes from an earlier scene: the robot blasting a car with an energy beam coming from its hands, splitting it in half.

Bob, Deena and Max are watching speechless. Noriko has a determined look on her face. Vesta looks like she's going to faint at any moment.

-It's a Talos. Good Gaea, he sent a freakin' Talos.

-You recognize it? – Noriko asks.

-One of my nephew's automatons. A virtually unstoppable war machine.

-"Nephew"? You mean that thing was built by Hephaestus?

-They used to be made of bronze but the design is unmistakable. Why do you have to ask? I thought you knew everything.

-Only if it's part of human knowledge. Which apparently doesn't cover as much as I thought – Noriko answers.

-So what are we waiting for? Let's go kick some robot butt! – Max shouts, disappearing in a flash of light. Half a second later, he's on the screen wearing a black mask.

-*Not so fast, robot! This city is under the protection of Quantum, the man of energy!*

-Hey Nori, that masked guy on TV looks just like your friend! – Bob says.

-Father, stay here and guard the Heart of the Universe; Vesta and I will deal with the robot.

Noriko walks away from the screen, but stops when she notices that Vesta isn't moving.

-I can't go – the goddess protests.

-Why not? You know this being better than anyone. For the moment, even better than me.

-I can't go out there and fight a Talos in broad daylight! People will see me!

-Didn't picture you as the shy type, Vesta.

-I kept a low profile for thousands of years, Nori. Every time someone sees me fly or make fire, bad things happen. Very bad things.

-You used your powers to rescue me from the Many when we first met. This is the same thing.

-This is different! The entire world will be watching!

The girl and the goddess stare at each other. Noriko has seen her smash to pieces a meteor the size of a stadium, but now she looks scared to death.

-Very well. Let's try a different approach – Noriko says, her silver eyes flashing briefly.

-What…what do you have in mind?

-Nothing special – Noriko answers, picking up a chair and walking towards the window.

-Your eyes flashed for a second. Your eyes always flash when you're thinking.

-Very observant – Noriko says, throwing the chair and smashing the window.

-What are you doing!?

-You kept a low profile for so long, now you don't think you're ready for prime time. I think we're late for the opening act - Noriko says before jumping out the window.

Noriko falls to her death for more than twenty stories; she can even hear Deena's screech.
-You know you're just about impossible, right? – Vesta asks, rescuing her from certain death and slowing her descent. When they're about ten stories above ground, she just stops mid-air.
-Speaking of impossible, we have an unstoppable war machine to stop – Noriko answers.

Deena is looking down from the crashed window, where she can see the goddess flying away carrying her boyfriend's daughter in her arms.
-I'll take the alien doomsday device from the fridge. You want a soda? – Bob asks.
A moment of silence.
-Well I'm not moving the couch now – Deena says.

11- Don't quote anything

It's amazing how fast people can run after they see an alien robot.

The Talos looks like some sort of futuristic knight, with a black and white armor and a shining red visor over its eyes. Not very scary, until it starts shooting death rays from its hands.

The people running have seen it a million times in movies: cars exploding left and right, bullets ricocheting on the bad guy, alarms and screams from every direction.

Now they're watching it live from their homes, courtesy of the lone cameraman recording the action and trying not to wet himself.

The Talos isn't doing this for the sake of it, of course. If you're new in town and want to speak to the person in charge, the fastest way is to make such a huge mess.

The primitives throwing bullets at it don't seem to think so. They have assembled a makeshift barricade in its tracks, placing police cars right in front of it in an attempt to slow it down.

The Talos could easily walk through it, or vaporize it. But the situation is clearly requiring an escalation of noise. It lifts one of the cars above its head, ready to use it to mash the cops to a fine pulp.

-**Ask your god to hurry** – it says with a deep metallic voice.

A ray of light cuts the car in half. When what's left of it touches the ground, there is a masked African American in front of the robot. He appeared out of nowhere, shouting:

-Not so fast, robot! This city is under the protection of Quantum, the man of energy!

"God I hope we're still live" the cameraman thinks, taking his best shot of the hero.

-**I am Talos, harbinger of Hephaestus. Are you a god?**

Quantum answers with a smile that practically screams "I've got this":

-When someone asks me if I'm a god, I always say "yes".

-**Then DIE!!!** – the robot replies, opening its chest uncovering a nuclear reactor.

A six feet wide plasma beam hits Quantum, vaporizing him and anything even remotely on its path.

This includes two cars, two hotdog stands, four parking meters, seven desks, nine walls and one ego. Everything took place almost at the speed of light.

That "almost" is why Quantum's body reforms at the fifth floor of an office building, several blocks away from the Talos.

-Note to self: next time don't quote movies to crazy alien robots.

The Talos walks over one of the police cars, which struggles to hold the weight of the robot. It stands tall, like this is some sort of solemn pulpit, raising the volume of its voice.

-I claim this world in the name of Hephaestus, son of Zeus. If any god objects to his claim, speak now or forever be silent.

A huge fireball hits the Talos, seemingly coming from nowhere. It doesn't hurt it: the robot just stands there, waiting for the flame to vanish to see who issued the challenge.

It's a teenage girl with silver eyes and an horrible green leather jacket.

-I object. This world is mine – she boasts.

The robot is confused. On the left side of the girl there is a being made of energy that identified himself as a god only minutes earlier. On her right side floats a redhead goddess.

According to the robot's database the goddess is Hestia, daughter of Kronos and sister of Zeus.

The artificial mind behind the red visor studies the silver eyes, and has only one question for Noriko:

-Are you a goddess?

-Don't quote anything – Quantum suggests.

-I am Null. Now get out of my planet.

-Scanning. You are mortal. Why do you challenge a herald of the gods?

-It was not a request, robot: I gave you an order. Vesta, do you mind?

The goddess flies forward faster than the eye can see, punching the Talos so hard that the robot is launched into the sky.

-Now *that*'s an homerun! - Quantum says, while the robot and the goddess disappear into the distance.

-Follow them and... – Noriko says, immediately interrupted by Quantum:

-Make sure that civilians don't get hurt, yeah, I know.

-...

-What?

-I was gonna say "and help her", but your idea is…I can't believe it, but your idea is actually *better*.

-Nobody knows superhero battles better than me, Nori. Relax, I've got this.

Quantum disappears in a flash of light, leaving Noriko alone.

Well, relatively speaking. She's still in the middle of the barricade of police cars, where some extremely confused cops are looking at her.

-What are you looking at? – she asks, her eyes flashing briefly.

-Should…should we arrest her or something? – one of the cops asks.

-Who the hell were these people!? –asks another.

-A waitress and a slacker. They're probably the most powerful people on the planet.

Noriko turns her attention to the cameraman, who's filmed the most breathtaking action of his career.

-I'm gonna need that – she says, turning off the camera with one swift motion.

That's the last thing people can see on their TV.

12- Let's get dangerous

Grand Central Terminal, New York

Two thousand pounds of alien metal crash through the ceiling, and the Talos falls to the ground with the sound of a bomb.

Most of the windows are already in pieces, thanks to the recent near miss of a meteor, otherwise they would've exploded by now. Still, people are understandably freaking out and fleeing the scene.

Vesta flies in, passing through the hole left by the robot, saying nervously:

-I'm sorry! I didn't mean to send it here…I was aiming for Central Park!

-Hestia, daughter of Kronos. Do you claim this planet as your dominion?

-My name's Vesta now. Look, this world doesn't belong to anyone, okay? Tell Hephaestus to choose another one or…

Vesta hesitates, as the Talos walks towards her. The black and white robot is significantly heavier and taller than her.

-Or what?

-Or…or we'll…we'll stop you – she answers timidly, visibly intimidated.

-Challenge accepted. Activating battle mode.

The robot punches Vesta in the stomach, with enough force to be louder than an explosion. Vesta had braced for the impact, which is the only reason why she isn't flying over to the next state.

Instead she kneels in pain, unable to do anything except attempting to breathe. It's quite hard to do, even for a goddess, when your internal organs have been subject to a shockwave the size of a tsunami.

-You have been away for a long time, Hestia. Technology has caught up with the power of the gods: you cannot hope to defeat me.

The Talos grabs Vesta by the hair, holding her steady for a second punch. This time even the ground shakes for the sheer force of the impact.

-What you are feeling is pain. You may not be familiar with it, dwelling in this primitive wasteland. You must have thought yourself invincible. You were mistaken. Let me show what invincibility really is.

Another punch, this time right on the nose. And another one. And another one. When the robot stops, it leaves Vesta lying on the floor, curled up in pain.

-**You can surrender now.**

-**Go to Hades** – Vesta answers, her body suddenly wreathed in flames.

The Talos takes a step back.

Vesta stands up, slowly and painfully, grinning her teeth. She's hurt, but she doesn't have a scratch.

-**You think you can scare me? I am the Firstborn of Kronos the God-Eater, I am the older sister of the Lord of the Dead Hades and of the Supreme Ruler of the Universe Zeus. Tell Hephaestus what I've already told them: NOBODY touches Earth!!!**

Once again, Vesta shoots fire at the robot, but this is no ordinary fire. It burns so hot that the air turns into white hot plasma just by touching it. The floor melts, and it's a good thing that civilians have already fled the scene, since anybody standing within ten feet of her would be burned alive.

Luckily for him, Quantum appears in holographic form.

-Sorry I'm late.

-**You move at the speed of light, how can you be late!?**

-Had to stop a dozen car accidents and a couple of robberies. People will take any excuse to steal stuff, won't they? Blackouts, crazy robots...Hey, what's up with the giant barbecue? – he asks, pointing at the sphere of flame right in front of him

-**Oh, that. Turns out** I'm too hot to handle.

-Is that why you're on fire?

-Sorry. It happens when I'm upset – she answers, making the flames surrounding her body disappear.

Quantum turns back to flesh and blood, giving her a puzzled look.

-What?

-How come you still have clothes? Shouldn't they burn when you do that?

Vesta is even more puzzled than him, looking at herself. Her orange tube top and jeans are still perfectly in shape.

-I have no idea. How can you turn yourself *and* your clothes into energy?

-How am I supposed to know? You're the one who gave me super-powers. Hey, do you mind turning down the heat just a little bit here?

The sphere of fire is still burning. Vesta simply wills it to vanish, and the fire disappears leaving only a trail of black smoke rising to the roof.

And a Talos.

-Oh cραπ – she exclaims. Suddenly, her stomach starts to hurt again.

-This body is composed of neutral matter, capable to withstand the heat and pressure of star cores. You cannot harm me.

-That…that was my best shot – Vesta admits.

Quantum smiles, cracking his knuckles.

-I've got this.

He turns his body into a laser, shooting right at the Talos' visor. It's a sound strategy, since it's the only spot not protected by its indestructible shell, but Vesta whishes she had the time to discourage him.

Max Black alias Quantum doesn't really have much experience with his energy transformations; in fact, he's only been able to do it for a few days.

His senses take a completely different form once he's no longer composed of matter. He just *feels* other things, some sort of instinct; he's already learned to associate certain feels to certain types of energy, but the robot's power core is completely alien to him.

There's something inside its core that defies his senses. It's placed in his chest, where a human heart would be, and it's constantly generating new power.

Max tries to overload it, merging with the energy which is already there. He finds himself absorbed by the veins of power that run through the robot's body, then sucked back into his visor, until he's finally released.

All of this takes a microscopic fraction of a second. From Vesta's perspective, the Talos simply looks up and releases a massive energy blast towards the roof.

"That's a cheapshot!!!" Max protests, without a voice to shout. Right now he's just a stream of photons, a living laser running straight towards the vacuum of space.

"Well this sucks. I can't slow down, at all. Why can't I slow down? Maybe that's because I'm in space...I think. I can't see anything when I'm made of light. I don't even know how I'm able to think! Okay Max, calm down. You just need to change into something else".

He tries to turn himself into a different wavelength, with no success. Then he tries electricity, then radio waves, but without success: he's stuck in light form.

"Don't panic. Once I reach the Moon or some planet I'll be able to bounce back. Unless there's nothing in my path, in which case I can go on forever. Right. This may be the best time to panic after all, now, wouldn't it? No! I have to keep thinking! Why can't I change? What's different from before? I'm in space, *and* most of this energy isn't mine. It's from the robot! As long as I'm in the middle of this light stream, I can't turn into anything but light! Which means..."

Time passes. Not much, but even in a second light can shoot past the Moon.

"Which means I'm screwed. I can't move, I can't turn into energy, what can I do?"

Then he understands. In the blink of an eye Max Black is in space, flesh and blood.

The light that came from the robot continues its flight into infinity. Max doesn't stay in human form for long, for obvious reasons, but he's now free to come back to Earth.

Ten seconds later, he lands on the collapsed roof of Grand Central Terminal, where Vesta is rising the ruins shaking pieces of bricks from her hair and giving him a dirty look.

-I *don't* got this – he admits.

While all this is going on, Noriko Null is busy dismantling the radio inside one of the police cars wrecked by the Talos. Not an easy task, since she didn't bother to take any instruments with her.

A man in his early forties is looking at her expertly fidgeting with wires.

-Kid, we've managed to clear the street; we can get you home now.

-This will only take another couple of minutes, officer O'Malley – she answers, without caring enough to look at him as she keeps working.

-You are unusually cooperative – she adds.

-What?

-I am dismantling your car. I was expecting the need to explain why, but you don't seem to mind.

-You look like you're the only person around here who understands what's going on.

-Of course; I am Null. I know everything.

O'Malley puts an hand on her shoulder, causing her to look him in the eye for the first time.

-That robot is dangerous, kid. If you know anything about it…

-It decoded human language in a matter of seconds; I plan to use that against it. If you let me finish, I may be able to do it before more people die.

-Okay, I'll buy it. What the heck are you talking about?

Noriko sighs.

-It was on the Internet one minute after it happened. When the Talos landed, it didn't speak English. It just grabbed a phone, connected to the web, and learned the language. This means its artificial intelligence is able to process vast amounts of data in a fraction of a second; I can use this to shut it down.

-How?

-Exposing it to an highly complex mathematical formula…an arithmetic description of a paradoxical geometric design. Its mind will try to decode it, diverting more and more processing power into spawning an infinite number of anomalous solutions until its mind is overloaded.

-And you're planning to do it…with this?

-No. This is to get its attention – Noriko answers, turning the radio on.

When she talks, her voice is amplified a thousand times by every single radio in the city, talking at the same time as loud as possible.

-ROBOT. I CHALLENGE YOU FOR THIS WORLD.

His ears still ringing, O'Malley looks at Noriko. Her silver eyes are shining, meaning she's devoting a significant part of humanity's knowledge to fixing the problem.

-That'll get its attention. Do you have a pencil and a sheet of paper? I need to write down the formula before the Talos kills me.

13- Deep Thought

Even though they don't know it, all the people on Earth are thinking at the same thing: how to write a formula that can kill an alien robot.

Not consciously, of course. Many of them are asleep. Many don't know how to count. They don't focus their attention to the task; in fact, they don't even know how they're doing it.

Noriko's brain is doing most of the work, actually. Every other mind is handling a microscopic part of it…seven billions are starting to add up.

When Noriko's silver eyes disconnect from the human mental network, they stop shining: the formula is complete, ready to be written down.

A pity she can't do it, because two thousand pounds of alien robot have just landed in front of her.

The Talos grabs her by the leather jacket, unfazed by its horrible shade of green, lifting her as if she didn't weight anything at all.

-**You again. Do you speak for this planet?** – it asks.

-More than you know.

-**You are mortal. You are only allowed to be ruled or to be killed. You cannot challenge me.**

-Not physically, maybe. Can someone from this planet be smarter than you?

The robot hesitates to answer. It's subtle, lasting maybe a second, but Noriko notices it.

-**According to my analysis, no.**

-What if I could prove otherwise? – Noriko asks, smirking.

-**I would kill you** – the Talos answers, throwing Noriko away like a boring toy.

Even when it isn't accessing the collective knowledge of humanity, Noriko's brain works faster than it should. She calculates that the force of the impact with the nearest wall will be enough to kill her, and that she doesn't have enough time to do anything about it.

Luckily for her, Vesta can fly fast enough to catch her. It's not a pleasant experience either, but it's more like getting the wind knocked out of you than being killed.

-Why did you challenge it? It could've killed you! –Vesta shouts.

-Just…just one minute… - Noriko mumbles, still out of breath but refusing to lose consciousness.

The Talos notices that its target is still alive, but is distracted by the lightning strike.

The electricity flows through the body of the robot, before turning back into human form.

-Somebody shoot this thing or something!!! – Quantum yells, transforming its body into pure concussive force and throwing all he's got at the robot.

Concrete and asphalt get blown away like sand in the wind, but he Talos doesn't slow down. It keeps walking towards Noriko.

-Buy me twenty seconds – she orders, writing down symbols as fast as possible.

-You got it.

Vesta flies right in the middle of Quantum's energy form, pushing the Talos in a desperate attempt to slow it down. Noriko doesn't look up: she has no time to worry about them.

She knows she will only get one shot. She has to double check an impossible mathematical expression and estimate the inner workings of an alien artificial intelligence, based on second hand data. And she has to do it all in ten seconds now.

-Analysis completed: planetary defenses are insufficient. Proceeding with hostile takeover.

-Analyze this – Noriko answers defiantly, showing the Talos a single sheet of paper crammed with information.

At first glance, the formula is impossible. But why would a mortal show you this information at such a crucial moment? It warrants more scrutiny. And when the solution doesn't make any sense, there is only one course of action in your programming: think harder.

Imagine for a second you were designed to be an unstoppable force. You are not allowed to consider anything as a threat: everything that isn't a god is to be steamrolled in your path.

If presented with an intellectual challenge, you would treat it as any other opponent: with overwhelming, unadulterated brute force. Even when brute force is meaningless.

-Divide by zero. Total system fa-

And that's when the unstoppable force stops.

The moment of silence following a battle is a weird thing. Your body is still high on adrenaline, still expecting danger to come from any direction. Then the rush disappears, and you feel more tired than you ever thought possible.

The utterly devastated road. The car carcasses. The smell of molten asphalt. The distant sound of sirens and alarms.

The Talos is at last immobile, a black and white statue frozen in place. Vesta knocks lightly on its head, but the robot is dead.

-Did…did we win? – she asks timidly.

-That was AWESOME! – Quantum shouts.

-We won – Noriko admits tiredly, leaning on one of the police cars and looking miserable.

-Is everything alright? – Quantum asks.

-Just catching my breath. Connecting to the collective consciousness takes a lot out of me.

Vesta seems more interested in the robot, looking it straight in the visor.

-We took down a Talos. Good Gaea, we took town *a Talos*. I can't believe this.

-Technically, *I* took it down. But I appreciate your attempts at helping me.

Quantum and Vesta look at each other.

"You were expecting her to say something like that too, didn't you?" – they both think.

Noriko closes her eyes for a second, whishing she could turn off her brain for just a few minutes.

Of course she can't do that, because a cop is shouting on a microphone.

-HANDS UP AND STEP AWAY FROM THE ROBOT.

-Aw man, now what? – Quantum whines.

-Just go, I'll handle this – Noriko orders, standing up and dusting herself off.

Quantum disappears in a flash of light. Vesta simply flies upwards, faster than the eye can see.

Noriko adjusts her leather jacket of a horrible shade of green, walking defiantly towards the group of shell-shocked officers.

-Let's make this quick. I need coffee.

Two East River Place, Later that evening

The crowd of journalists is so thick that Noriko almost can't see the lobby. She understands the interest, even if she finds it annoying. Today the city was attacked by an unstoppable robot and only three people showed up to stop it: a red haired flying woman that nobody has been able to recognize, an African American man with a mask that has literally disappeared into thin air, and an half-Asian teenager that made the news only days earlier as "the smartest girl on the planet".

-Miss Null, why were you detained after the attack? – is the first question.

-Who were the two people at your side? – is another.

-What was the creature? Where is it now? How was it defeated? - are some of the others.

The rest are unintelligible. Noriko doesn't acknowledge them or the dozens of cameras waiting for her word. Instead she takes her phone from one of the pockets of the jacket.

She's been fiddling with it all day, to the point that it's no more recognizable as a phone.

It's hard to pass the time with people asking questions you can't answer without causing widespread panic, so she built the first handheld sonic neutralizer.

When she activates it, everything goes silent. For a few seconds, it's physically impossible to make any sort of sound. Noriko walks calmly towards the lobby, and people step back in awe and terror.

What did Athena say, when she gave her a new mind? "Humanity is ridiculously unprepared". She was right, as a goddess of wisdom should be: if it hadn't been for Noriko and her allies, the Talos would probably have taken over the city by now.

She looks at the crowd, visibly shaken by today's events. She understand that they deserve an answer to the questions that now are in the minds of millions of people:"Who are you? What happened today?"

She allows sound to exist again and answers the first question.

-I am Null. I am the vanguard of Earth's defense against the impossible; I saved your lives today. You're welcome.

Closing the door behind her, Noriko starts working on an answer to the last question:

"What will happen if something like that shows up again?"

Noriko Null by KodamaCreative

Leiko Tanaka by KodamaCreative

Vesta by KodamaCreative

Max Black by KodamaCreative

14- World, meet Null

At first glance, the scene is nothing strange: a teenage girl sitting on a chair, waiting impatiently for the makeup artist to finish the job.

It becomes interesting when you think that the girl is Noriko Null, also known as the world's smartest person, and the artist is Deena Zylberman, current flame of Noriko's father.

-Would you *please* stay still? I swear, you act like you never had makeup before.

-I'm perfectly capable of applying cosmetics, Deena. I simply find the effort unnecessary.

-Look, you can walk in front of a camera with millions of people watching that hideous green leather jacket of yours, but I *refuse* to let you do it without proper foundation and eye shadow.

-I like that jacket – Noriko pouts.

Deena smiles. It's one of those rare moments where Noriko lets down her guard and acts like the eighteen year old girl that she is.

-Y'know, this may be the first time we've had a chance to talk since I met your father.

-I will try to control my excitement – Noriko answers with deadpan voice.

-You don't really like me, now, do you?

-No.

-But you pay my rent.

-You make my father happy, for reasons I force myself not to dwell upon. As long as that doesn't change, the rest is inconsequential to me. Are we done now?

-Sure. Well, tell me, what do you think?

-Inertial electrostatic confinement is the most promising path towards successful nuclear fusion.

-About the makeup.

-Oh. I could've done a better job if I wanted to, but I appreciate the effort.

Noriko steps up, putting on the green leather jacket. She looks at herself in the mirror, specifically at the white symbol on her black T-shirt. The symbol for a null set: Ø. Now *her* symbol.

Her silver eyes glow suddenly. She's feeling the moment.

-I'd tone down the glowy-eyes thing if I were you. It messes with the eye shadow.

77

"And it gives me the creeps every time you do that" – Deena adds without saying it out loud.

The press room is lit by tens of flashes when Noriko walks into the room. The five feet tall teenager steps on the blue podium with the large Ø symbol and turns on the microphone.
-I am Null. Get used to hear this often.
Backstage, Deena chuckles thinking that, for Noriko's standards, it was kinda funny.
-The press has called me "the smartest girl in the world", which is of course correct if a bit reductive. As of today, I am also the sole owner of Null Technologies. Since you have never heard of it, you are probably wondering what Null Technologies does. Luckily for you, I am a firm believer in the "show, don't tell" philosophy.-
Noriko places a cylindrical object on the podium, something that looks like fancy camera lens.
When she turns it on, the air is filled with a spectacular tri-dimensional projection of the schematics of this device. She needs to raise her voice above the sudden chatter in the audience.
-The Null Holographic Projector is just the first of many scientific breakthroughs you can expect from Null Technologies. Investors can find all the information they need to know on our website; you can see the address in the projection. Now, onto more trivial matters…
Noriko presses a few buttons on the dedicated remote, and the hologram changes form. Now it shows an outside view of the skyscraper where Noriko is keeping the presentation, but with one major difference: the big Ø symbol added on top.
-Two East River Place will be renamed Null Tower; it will serve as headquarters of Null Technologies and my personal residence. Résumés can also be submitted to our website; don't worry, I have assembled a dedicated server to back up the increase in traffic.-
She pauses. Right now, you could probably hear all the jaws hitting the floor.
-Any questions?
Every single hand in the room goes up.

White House Situation Room
Washington, D.C.

A live feed of the press conference is playing on one of the many flat screens. Others show stills from the Talos attack; others yet focus on Vesta and Quantum. A man breaks the silence:

-So this is the girl you guys are all so worried about.

-Mister President, if I may – another man answers, standing up and replacing the live video with a still picture. It shows a big hole in the ground.

-This picture was taken the morning after the New York Air Impact. The building houses the former residence of Noriko Null. You can see the signs of an impact in the left corner, which from our analysis was caused by a motorcycle crashing into the wall. According to police reports, people first heard an explosion and saw a very bright blue light. When they looked at the street, it had simply vanished. The description matches the blue light that accompanied the sudden appearance and later the sudden disappearance of the meteor that caused the air impact.

-The same meteor that NASA says wasn't a meteor at all – the President remembers.

-We have recovered parts of the motorcycle and identified it as belonging to a Marco Sanchez, who reported it was stolen by, quote, "an Asian girl with glowing eyes". Mister Sanchez received several thousand dollars in his mailbox the day after miss Null won one million dollars on a TV show.

-I remember the show. She said she needed to repay a motorcycle she had crashed.

-The theft of mister Sanchez's vehicle was witnessed by several people, who also reported the unexplained explosion of a bar called Moonbucks. A girl whose description matches miss Null was present right after the explosion, together with an unidentified African American male in his mid-twenties and a Caucasian woman with long red hair who was later identified as one of the waitresses of said bar. According the bar's hiring records, the woman was identified as Vesta Dicrono.

-You are suggesting that the waitress is the flying woman who fought the robot and the African American male is Quantum. And that what caused the street to disappear was the same thing that made a meteor first appear and then disappear over New York – the President summarizes.

-That's correct, mister President. Our telescopes also picked up an unexpected blue flash on the surface of the Moon. Further investigation proves that that part of the Moon is now missing.

-A piece of the Moon is missing? – the President repeats, incredulous.

-Yes Mister President. As you can see, all these…impossible things point to miss Null.

The President leans back, sighing. This is going to be one of the days when he whishes somebody else had this job.

-What do we know about her? – he asks.

-As far as we can tell, sir, until the night before the impact she was an ordinary teenager. We have studied her student records and tracked her activity on the Internet: she didn't show any sign of high intellect. We did find, however, that her family has a very unusual history.

-How so?

-Her mother disappeared right after she was born. Her father Robert worked as a school janitor until recently; he is the grandson of professor Heinrich Null.

The screen now shows a very old black and white picture, showing a smiling man shaking hands with a Nazi officer.

-Heinrich was an highly respected professor of geology in Germany in the 1930s.

-Excuse me, how did we jump from teen supergenius to Nazis?

-Look at what professor Null is holding in his right hand. He found it in an excavation in Greenland, enclosed in a zircon shell that he believed was older than the Earth.

-It looks like a rock. Shaped like a baseball – the President notes, squinting.

-Yes, Mister President. Professor Null claimed it showed him images of an alien civilization who used it to, quote, throw away stars when they didn't need them anymore. He called it the Heart of the Universe. The Nazis took some interest in his discovery at first, but when he failed to show any kind of proof he was isolated from the scientific community. His son Conrad, Noriko's grandfather, emigrated to the United States in the early 1950s. We believe he took the Heart of the Universe with him.

-So, to recap – the President interrupts, rubbing his eyes – A Nazi recovered an alien artifact that somehow turned his great-

80

granddaughter into a genius, gave super-powers to a waitress and some guy who thinks he's a super-hero, and was used to teleport a piece of the Moon over New York.

-Yes, Mister President.

-How does this lead to an alien robot who thinks he's working for a Greek god?

-We…we're still working on that, sir – the man answers nervously.

Tokyo, Scion Corporation R&D labs
The day after

Leiko Tanaka hasn't said a word the whole meeting. The scientists across the table have dreaded her voice for some time now: they know she can destroy their lives with a sentence.

They know what happened to the people who questioned her orders, or who dared to leak any sort of information to outsiders. They know that, at Scion Corporation, Leiko's voice is law.

-According to the Null website, the holographic project works by controlling the position of photons composing the image, causing them to freeze in mid-air in the desired configuration. Which, as far as we know, is completely physically impossible.

-Could she have reversed engineered this technology from the robot? – Leiko asks.

-Unlikely. The Talos is still under custody of the United States military and she hasn't had the time to study it. We only managed to do it with the same technology recovered from the Greek vase that allowed us to control it.

-Are we certain it hasn't communicated with anyone after we sent it to New York? – she asks.

-Absolutely, ma'am.

-How about our surveillance? Do we know what she's doing?

-The surveillance cameras in her older residence have been destroyed. We have tried to infiltrate listening devices or hack into their database, but Null Tower is impregnable.

Leiko inhales sharply. The scientists wait for her lead.

"The robot didn't mention the Heart of the Universe. That means that Hephaestus wasn't the one that enhanced my daughter's intelligence. How needlessly sentimental of me to keep her alive".

-Buy Null Technologies. I don't care about the cost.

-Mistress – a female voice interrupts.

A dark haired woman dressed in green, the only Caucasian in the room, stands up.

The woman's body quickly splits in two, and a second body of the Many walks towards Leiko.

-We think we have another way.

15-Under construction

Null Tower has been a permanent construction site for weeks now. Every day there's something new to replace or update, to the point that it doesn't resemble the original building anymore.

Today there's quite a crowd to watch the helicopters delivering the pieces that will become the massive Ø symbol that will identify the tower from any point in the city.

Vesta is watching from afar, sitting barefoot on a crane two blocks away.

Quantum appears in the blink of an eye, sitting next to her. She's starting to be used to his sudden appearances.

-Hey. I thought you'd be working today – he greets her.

-I am. If a construction worker falls down, I can save him before he hits the ground.

-Sounds like wasting your powers. Weren't you supposed to assemble the big zero yourself?

-It's not "a big zero", it's the symbol of a null set.

-Which is…

-I have no idea, but Noriko keeps saying that. Hiring people to work on it was her idea: "we should avoid looking like overbearing gods, if possible". Her exact words.

-Yeah, that sounds like her.

-By the way, what are *you* doing here, Max?

-Sshh! I'm Quantum, when I wear the mask! – he answers with a whispering voice.

-Max, we're four hundred feet in the air. I think your secret identity is safe.

-Right. To answer your question, I'm eating. Cheeseburger? – he offers, recovering his lunch from a fast food bag.

-No thanks. I don't really need to eat and that looks…what's the opposite of tasty?

-It's awful, yeah – he answers, taking a big bite and then talking with his mouth full – But it's the best I can afford now.

-Doesn't Noriko pay you enough to buy a decent meal?

-She pays Quantum. Max Black is still unemployed.

-Of course. Remind me again why are you bothering with the secret identity thing?

-My face has been on every newspaper and magazine on the planet for three weeks, Vesta. How else am I going to order a cheeseburger in peace?

-I thought you didn't like…

-That's beside the point. However I *do* have enough money to pay for a decent dinner. How about Paris? We can be there in five minutes, you know.

-Oh, it's not the same now that they've built that horrible tower.

-We can go anywhere else…I can fly at the speed of light and you're quite fast yourself. You've been working day and night all month, you deserve a break.

-Oh don't worry, I don't need to sleep, so it's fine by me.

-So you're saying you're free this evening.

Vesta looks at Max with an innocently puzzled face. Then it hits her.

-Are you asking me out on a date?

-I'm trying to.

-Well, uhm, that's very sweet, I guess, but I don't date mortals.

Now it's Max's turn to look at her like she just landed from Mars. Vesta's face becomes so red that Max fears it's going to burst into flames again.

-Oh Gaea, I swear it's not a racist thing! It's just that I, I'm not really interested in, you know, mortals get old and want babies, or they die, or both, well actually they die whether they want babies or not, and and and it's not like I have something against dead people or anything…

-Man, you really suck at this, don't you?

-I've been single for hundreds of thousands of years, what d'you think?

A few moments of awkward silence pass, while Max keeps chewing his lunch.

-You don't look that old - he notes.

-Thanks. My family has some pretty amazing genes.

-Do you mind if I ask just how old you are? I know girls don't like the question but…well with being immortal and all…

-Actually I don't even know. I *think* I'm *at least* a million years old.

-Holy…wait a second. I flunked history at school, but even I know that Greeks weren't around at the time!

-My family was around long before the Greeks knew about us. It may sound like a long time to you, but I'm fairly young for a goddess. Dad was something like fifty million years old when I was born, grandma Gaea has been around as long as anyone can remember, as has most of Ra's family.

-Whoa. You mean *other* gods are real too!?

-Uhm, yeah, a few. Some of them were around before grandma Gaea discovered Earth.

-You haven't...by any chance, have you met *Him*?

Vesta sighs, whishing she'd kept her mouth shut. Why does EVERYONE living in the last two thousand years have the same question!?

-No, I haven't met Jesus. I lived on the other side of the planet at the time and didn't hear about him for like a hundred years anyway. As far as I know only what you'd call Greek, Egyptian and Sumerian gods are real.

-I was talking about Thor. You're telling me he's not real!?

-Afraid so – she answers, gently smiling. Apparently Max has different priorities than most mortals.

-It's not fair. Would've been cool to meet Thor. Not that there's anything wrong with Greek gods, mind you, but c'mon. Thor!

A few seconds of silence follow, while Max finishes his lunch and Vesta admires the city; she really can't get enough of the view. Then she asks:

-What do you think of Noriko, Max?

-She's cute, I guess, but way too young for me.

-Would you be serious for a moment!? I'm worried about her!

-Why? She's a genius millionaire. And if you didn't catch her saying it a billion times, she knows everything.

-I'm just not sure a young girl can carry such weight.

-She *did* save our backsides against that robot. I think she kinda proved she can take care of herself.

-I guess you're right.

More awkward silence.

-But just to be clear, she didn't save *my* backside. I could've taken the Talos.

-C'mon, Vesta, I was there too. We tried everything and we barely slowed it down.

-I could've...I dunno, I... I could've thrown it into the Sun!

-Then why didn't you?

Vesta opens her mouth to answer, but hesitates. Her face turns deep red.

-I didn't think of that – she mumbles, embarrassed.

-What?

-I said I didn't think of that.

The goddess and the hero look at each other. Then look around, as if to make absolutely sure nobody is listening to them.

-Let's keep that to ourselves – Max suggests.

THE MYRIDAN SAGA

Art by KodamaCreative

1-Recluse

All the 50 floors of Null Tower have been completely restructured in the past month. Before Noriko had bought it, the skyscraper was simply a residential building; now it's the center of the fastest growing enterprise in the country.

Bob Null reaches the top floor, where just like anyone else he needs to show his badge to unlock the blast proof door in front of the elevator.

"This is ridiculous; I need a badge to see my daughter. A badge!" he thinks, placing his hand on the scanner to show his fingerprints. A gentle female artificial voice answers:

-Welcome to the 50th floor of Null Tower, Robert Null. Please state the nature of your visit.

-Open the door, Nori, it's dad.

-No visits scheduled for the next unspecified hours and unspecified minutes. Please come back later.

-Noriko, open this door *now*. Don't make me shout.

-*One moment please. Mistress, request to allow unsolicited parental visit.*

Bob is about to lose his cool when his daughter's voice answers to the electronic voice.

-Permission granted, security override F3E57D35779-NULL. Come in, father.

The blast proof door opens by itself after a gentle ping. It's hard to see what's on the other side: there are no windows, and the eerie glow of computer screens is filling the air.

-What was that, Nori? – Bob asks, raising his voice in the dark. Noriko's voice is loud and clear, coming through speakerphones placed strategically.

-Hexadecimal password. Most commercially available computers would take about 16 billion years to crack it.

-I meant the thing that spoke back to me.

-Oh. That's I.R.I.S, as in Integrated Reconfigurable Intelligence System. I based her program on my understanding of the translation algorithm of the Talos.

-Cool. Listen, Nori, I know you must be doing important…stuff here, but we need to talk.

-Of course. Lights on.

Bright neon lights flood the room, which now Bob can see as far more chaotic than expected.

There's junk everywhere, for lack of a better word. Wires, computer parts, welding equipment, holographic projectors, dozens of empty pizza boxes, a basket full of dirty laundry.

Noriko is wearing her trademark leather jacket of an horrible shade of green and a black T-shirt with a white Ø sign. In addition, she's wearing futuristic metal gloves that she's using to work on holographic screens.

-Nori, when was the last time you left the room?

-86 hours ago. Before you complain, father, I eat regularly and this floor includes a shower.

-I see. How many shirts like that do you own again?

-365.

-Right; at least I don't have to worry about you maxing the credit card on a shopping spree.

-Did you wish to discuss a meaningful topic, father?

-I wanted to know how you're coping with all…all of this stuff. We don't talk anymore.

Noriko freezes for a second, calmly removing her gloves. Only now Bob can see that she's working on the Heart of the Universe.

-I'm doing great, father. The discoveries I make every day…Null Technology is going to change everything. And that's not counting what the others are doing! I.R.I.S, Vanguard status.

-*At once, mistress.*

Two new holographic screens appear in front of Noriko; one shows Vesta towing a lost cruise ship to a safe haven, the other shows Quantum rescuing people from a fire.

-By my calculations, the three of us have already saved 8.5 million lives.

-Does that include all the people you almost killed by dropping a chunk of the Moon on them?

-If you must be technical, yes. Why the sudden interest, father?

-I'm worried about you. You stay here day and night, building who knows what. I took calls from your friends for weeks and I don't think you talked to any of them for more than five seconds.

-They bore me.

-This isn't you, Nori. You don't meet your friends, you don't go out to dance or shop…you don't date, thankfully…I barely see you anymore.

-This *is* me now, father – she answers, raising her arms as to embrace the room full of technical wonders. Naturally, her silver eyes flash briefly. Bob is unimpressed.

-So this doesn't have anything to do with your mother.

Noriko didn't think she could still do a double take. An alien robot built by a god didn't faze her, but this is the strangest thing she's heard all month.

-How do *you* know that *I* know who my mother is?

-Maybe I'm not the smartest person on Earth, but I'm not dumb enough to forget that *you* are.

-Fair enough. But my interest in technology has *nothing* to do with my mother.

-*Terribly sorry to interrupt you, Mistress* – an artificial voice interrupts.

-We're not done – Bob warns.

-Of course we aren't. What is it, I.R.I.S?

-*A package from miss Leiko Tanaka of Scion Corporation is waiting for you in the atrium.*

Bob Null crosses his arms and smirks: it's not often he can corner his daughter like this.

-Okay, my mother *may* have something to do with it – she admits.

A few minutes later, Bob shows up again at the elevator. He's holding the package, giving a puzzled look at the address.

-It's from her, alright. This signature right here is her handwriting, but I don't know Japanese.

-"For her eyes only" – Noriko translates, reaching for the package…but she hesitates.

Bob notices her eyes aren't flashing: she's thinking, yes, but she's not accessing her power…she's just thinking, just like a normal teenage girl would. If things like these happened to normal teenagers, that is.

-Do you want me to open it? – he asks.

The eyes flash again. She's not trusting her human self to do this alone.

-It would be wiser if I saw it first – she says, taking the package in her own hands and opening it.

As soon as the slightest hint of oxygen can get inside, a green human arm thrusts out of the package punching Noriko in the face.

She takes a step back in pain, losing her grip. Before the package can hit the floor, the green substance inside has already grown at least a hundred pounds.

When Noriko understands what just happened, the package has delivered a fully grown woman with dark hair wearing green clothes.

-The Heart is ours – the Many states triumphantly, stepping forward to steal the Heart of the Universe.

-Over my dead body – Noriko threatens as she reaches for the Heart as well.

Both Noriko and the Many touch the Heart at the same time.

There is an extremely bright flash of light.

All of this has taken maybe five seconds from the moment when Noriko opened the package.

Bob Null didn't have any time to understand the situation. It takes a while for his eyes to recover from the sudden burst of light. When that happens, he doesn't like what he sees.

The Heart hasn't moved an inch, but the Many has disappeared. His daughter's clothes are lying on the floor: Noriko Null has vanished.

2-How I met her mother

Vesta's been busy last month, more than the last two thousand years combined. She's been flying from a crisis to another, helped by the fact that she can't get tired.

This is the first time she's had some time for herself. Legs crossed in the lotus position, floating a foot off the ground, looking at the ball of fire standing before her.

Someone knocks at the door.

-Hey Vesta, it's Max. You got a minute?

-Come in – she answers, somewhat surprised that Max has bothered to knock.

Max Black turns his body into x-rays, walks right through the door, and turns back into flesh and blood. This is the first time he's been into Vesta's apartment, so he looks around.

He's seen hotel rooms that felt more alive than this: every single piece of furniture looks brand new and never used. There's not a single personal object anywhere.

-Nice…nothing you've got here. Isn't that thing a fire hazard?

-I don't own anything, Max, but I need some kind of fireplace to meditate. It won't hurt anyone as long as I'm here.

-Wait, did Greeks meditate?

-I already told you I'm not Greek, I was just a Greek goddess for a while. I didn't learn meditation until…well I think it was a thousand years ago or something like that. Do you need anything?

-Actually, yeah. I wanted to talk about what happened on the Moon. That energy beam disintegrated me, right? Did you…well…

-Did I resurrect you? – Vesta asks, since Max is having trouble asking the direct question.

-Ah, yeah, I've been meaning to ask you that. I think I was kind of dead.

-Probably. I just pulled your molecules back together.

-You mean you don't know!?

-I'm just a goddess – Vesta shrugs.

Max is about to rebut, but he's interrupted by an artificial female voice:

-*Excuse me, miss Vesta. Your presence is required in the main laboratory.*

-I'll be right on it, thank you – Vesta answers, putting her feet back on the ground and making the fire disappear.

-What the heck was that!? – Max asks.

-Oh that's I.R.I.S. Noriko installed her yesterday.

-Really? She never tells me anything.

-*Your presence is required as well, mister Black. In case of sudden disappearance of the Mistress, I am programmed to gather the Vanguard immediately.*

-That makes sense. What's a vanguard? – Max asks.

A few minutes later, Vesta is floating above Noriko's clothes. They're just laying on the floor, above the wires and cables connected to the Heart of the Universe.

-It was definitely her. Nobody else would even think about wearing that ugly green jacket. Do you have any idea about how this could've happened, Bob?

-I'm not the brains in the family. She just touched the Heart and disappeared.

-Maybe she's still here. Maybe she's just invisible – Max suggests, slowly lifting the jacket off the floor. A black T-shirt with the Ø symbol and a bra fall off.

-I guess not. What if she's intangible?

-You're not helping, Max. Bob, we really want to find your daughter, by we have no idea where we should start.

-Yes we do – Max corrects her, transforming his body into light and reappearing a fraction of a second later on the other side of the room to pick up a package.

-You said the Many came out of this thing, right? So whoever sent it is probably responsible.

-It's from her mother – Bob says.

There's a few seconds of silence.

-I thought Noriko's mother was dead – Vesta finally says.

-Leiko left immediately after Nori's birth. Nori doesn't know about it: Leiko's family was powerful enough to erase all evidence; even the birth certificate shows a false identity. But that was before Nori became super-smart…she must've figured it out.

-And where is this Leiko now? – Max asks.

-*Miss Tanaka is currently hosting a fundraising party at Tokyo Imperial Hotel* – I.R.I.S answers.

-That's all I need – Max replies before disappearing in a flash of light.

Tokyo Imperial Hotel

When he turns human again, Max would be impressed if he ever bothered to watch international news. Only the biggest names of Japan's politics and finance are here, which means Max doesn't recognize anybody.

He also doesn't understand a single word anyone is saying, except the guys with sunglasses that are shouting orders and pointing guns. Bodyguards are the same anywhere.

-You sure know how to make an unnecessarily dramatic entrance – are the first words that anyone says in English. Max turns to look at whoever said it, and his jaw almost hits the floor.

The woman is holding a champagne glass and is standing next to the Prime Minister. She's wearing a black evening gown and she's the most beautiful woman he's ever seen.

-I am Leiko Tanaka. How can I help you, Quantum?

-We…we need to talk – he mumbles.

-Of course – she answers, then saying something in Japanese to the Prime Minister first and to the crowd later.

Nobody dares to say a word.

As Max follows Leiko, he finds it strange that nobody is following them. He's concentrating on her, however; not only on the fact that she's insanely hot, but that she doesn't have the slightest trace of an accent when she speaks English.

-Some party you have there. What's the occasion?

-The Prime Minister will be re-elected tomorrow. You don't know much about Japan, do you?

-This is my first time here. But I have a feeling I've already seen you somewhere.

-Probably last month when I met your President at the White House – she answers, using the same tone she'd use to give the time of the day.

-Yeah, I remember that! You're the hot Asian chick who…

Leiko turns to look him in the eye. She doesn't move a muscle on her face, but it's enough to send shivers down his spine.

-I mean, you're the one who donated tons of money to the refugees of that nuclear accident, right?

-Indeed I am. Luckily you weren't around at the time, or I wouldn't have been able to sabotage the power plant so easily.

-You…you did *what*!?

-I needed to discredit the Prime Minister and create a philanthropist image for myself.

The two have reached the destination: an hotel room on the floor just beneath the party. Leiko doesn't waste any time to complete her story, and Max is suddenly less interested in her body and more on watching his own back.

-The Prime Minister has a shot at re-election only because of my support. You probably don't realize it but you're quite big in Japan, Quantum. Just talking in public with a super-hero just boosted my favorability rating by at least twenty percent.

-So what's the plan? You want to be Prime Minister?

Leiko smiles. It's the scariest smile that Max has ever seen.

-Do you have any idea of how much power I'd have to give up to lead a country?

-And what's to stop *me* from telling all of this to the press?

-The Core.

-The whAAAAHH!!! –Max screams in pain, thanks to the energy blast that a floating metal sphere is using to confine him.

-*Intriguing specimen* – the sphere says with an unnaturally low voice.

-Scream all you want, Quantum. This room is completely soundproof; nobody will hear you.

-*He has been exposed to the energy of the Heart. Experimenting Drylon technology on lower life forms, what pitiful species. This abomination should be executed.*

-I want to talk to him, Core. But don't let him get away. Not just yet.

Max is crawling on the floor, feeling more pain that he'd thought possible. The Core is hitting him with some kind of energy that prevents him to turn into radio waves and escape.

Leiko sits down, crossing her legs. She looks like she couldn't care less if Max died right now.

Luckily the Core tones down his attack, and the pain becomes slightly bearable.

-How did you find me? – she asks.

95

-You sent a package to Noriko. You tried to kill her.

-My orders to the Many were simply to recover the Heart of the Universe. I take it she didn't succeed.

-Not a very original plan; the Many tried to kill us before and look how well *that* turned out.

-It turned out perfectly, actually. The Many wasn't under my command during your first encounter, but my operatives were able to recover samples from your fight. Fascinating organism, capable to recreate itself from a single cell. Extremely durable. Easily manipulated. And most importantly…it can operate the Heart of the Universe.

-Why is that thing so freakin' important!?

-*Ignorant savage. The Heart is the most powerful device on this pathetic planet. Only after I shared my knowledge with Leiko she could hope to rule the galaxy with it.*

-Core. Stop giving clues to the super-hero.

-I think I get it now, Leiko. You didn't care if Bob and Noriko had the Heart because you didn't know how to use it. But now you want it for yourself.

-*Leiko should've stolen the Heart right after reproduction and slaughtered her offspring. A pity her father and my former master prevented her from doing so.*

-That's enough, Core. Kill our guest, please.

The intensity of the energy increases again, and so does the agony. Max is shaking violently, his skin on fire and his brain full of jackhammers. Leiko is still sitting, calm and collected, watching him die painfully.

-The Core is a living database of a dead alien race more powerful than any god. The Heart was their greatest weapon; you don't even register on that scale. All these years Robert thought he was protecting our daughter, but he was only keeping an eye on the Heart for me. I offered Noriko a chance to continue her life in her blissful uselessness as long as she didn't interfere with my plans. I offer you the same chance now.

-Your…plan…sucks – is all Quantum is able to say through his teeth.

-Very well. I have uncovered enough Olympian technology to reverse engineer your powers from your dead body.

-Reverse…this – Quantum answers, gathering all the strength in his body to grab the Core and throw it out of the window like a baseball. Quantum stands proud in his energy form, ready for anything. Leiko stands up, fixing her long black hair.

-You should hurry. The Core can't fly very fast, but it will be back soon.

-Give me one good reason why I shouldn't tell everything to the press and throw you in jail.

-Nobody will believe you.

-Nice try, but I'm pretty big in Japan remember? Gimme another one.

-I know where your sister Kayla lives.

Quantum clenches his fists, looking into Leiko's cold eyes. And then he disappears in the blink of an eye, causing her to come very close to smiling.

3-A shot in the dark

A piece of the Moon is missing. While this is kind of a big deal, the public has not been informed of this because nobody knows where it went. This has made a lot of people really worried.

NASA took it very seriously, as did the people who fund it. This is the reason why, a little over a month after it happened, one of the satellites orbiting the Moon has been assigned to monitor this particular spot on a daily basis.

Vesta waits for the satellite to disappear over the horizon before landing on the Moon. She's wearing her usual outfit, consisting of an orange tube top and orange jeans.

Her bare feet touch the lunar soil, inside the giant crater which formed when Noriko accidentally teleported part of the Moon above New York City.

She takes a moment to enjoy the view: she's always loved the beautiful silence of the Moon.

"I really miss flying here just to get a tan, vacations were easier before they invented the telescope…there's just no privacy anymore. Oh well, back to work" – she thinks.

The crater is currently lighted by the Sun, which means the temperature is enough to boil water but not nearly enough to bother the goddess of the hearth.

Vesta looks very carefully at her shadow: something is growing on the ground, no longer sterilized by the heat of the Sun. Something green.

"Amazing…the Many is *still* alive. Noriko *vaporized* her before teleporting us back! She must've left behind…what, a couple of cells maybe? A couple of *molecules*!?"

Vesta's thoughts are interrupted when the green goo quickly forms a human hand, that tries to catch her ankle. Vesta steps back, disgusted, and the heat of the sun kills the hand leaving behind only the smallest amount of cells.

"Good Gaea, is there *anything* that can stop this thing from replicating!?" she wonders, waiting.

Without a shadow, the Many can't seem to be able to move again. Then Vesta understand what happened: the Many recreates its body each night, probably *more* than one body, and is killed again every time the Sun rises. There isn't a mountain or a crater or even just a

98

rock for *miles*, so the Many has died something like forty times already.

Taking it back to Earth is probably a bad idea, but there doesn't seem to be another way. Vesta gently grabs the green blob and holds it in her hand, setting it on fire.

"So far so good, it's not returning to human form yet. Let's hope this works" she thinks, flying back to Earth.

If Vesta cared about these things, she would wonder how she's able to create fire in a vacuum…but she's too busy wondering if a goddess can pray for a desperate plan.

Null Tower, New York City
The board of directors looks at Bob Null like he's from another planet. Not only he's the only one not wearing a tie here, he doesn't even know what the board *does*.

-I'm sorry, what was the question again? – he asks.

-"Where is your daughter?"

The man who repeated the question is Mark Stewart, the Chief Operating Officer of Null Technologies, looks like the polar opposite of Bob Null.

Bob is in his mid-thirties, has an head full of hair and not a care in the world. Mark is in his mid-fifties, no hair to speak of, only slightly balanced by a nicely kept goatee, and looks like he has the weight of the world on his shoulders.

-She's busy inventing, uhm, stuff. She'll be back soon.

-Really. Do you know how your daughter hired me, mr. Null?

-She offered you a ton of money?

-Well, yes. But she also told me that she founded Null Technologies not just for profit, but to change the world. And the things we're already building…holographic projectors, artificial intelligence, even the sound nullifiers…I believe we can. That's why I accepted.

-What's your point, mr. Stewart?

-My point is Noriko is supposed to brief me on any new projects, so don't try to sell me this bul###it about her being too busy inventing stuff. She's burned out, isn't she? She pulled out the last of her impossible inventions.

-Hey guys – Quantum says, appearing out of thin air.

He looks around, noticing the board of directors is looking at him. They're visibly scared.

99

-This is a private meeting, Quantum – Stewart greets him with the most glacial tone imaginable.
-Yeah, sure, whatever. You're the rich guy Null hired to manage the company, right?
-I am.
-I told her to keep an eye on you. You look like an 80s movie villain, y'know? Middle aged, bald, goatee, trying to steal the company.
-…
-Quantum is here to assist Noriko in one of her experiments, mister Stewart. In fact, we're just on our way to her lab – Bob explains.
-Of course. Please remember her to keep me updated – Stewart answers, watching Quantum vanish in the blink of an eye and Bob Null walk out of the room.
There's a full ten seconds of silence. He then addresses the board:
-I think we should discuss Leiko's proposition now.

On the top floor
The round-shaped rock called the Heart of the Universe is still sitting on the pedestal, hooked up to dozens of wires.
-Are you sure this is gonna work? – Bob asks.
Quantum and Vesta look at each other. Her right hand, which holds the last cells of the Many, is on fire. His left hand is now made of lightning.
-Nori said this thing works by thoughts, right? Enough electricity should jump-start it – Quantum answers, trying to sound like he knows what he's talking about.
-And the Many may be able to take Noriko back…somehow – Vesta adds, understanding how desperate the plan is when saying it out loud.
-Whatever; I just hope you're able to bring Nori back – Bob concludes, holding his daughter's leather jacket.
Vesta and Quantum look at him, puzzled either by his actions or by the jacket's horrible shade of green.
-What? She left her clothes behind. If we take her back naked, she's going to be upset.
The Heart starts glowing blue. It's very faint, but it's there.
-It's definitely doing something. I.R.I.S, is this good or bad?
-*Insufficient data for a meaningful answer* – is the computer's answer.

100

-I'm gonna go with "good" then. Ready? – Vesta asks.

-Ready – Quantum answers, touching the Heart of the Universe together with the goddess.

There's a blue flash of light, bright enough to fill the entire room.

When Bob Null open his eyes, Quantum and Vesta have vanished. Together with the horrible green jacket.

Tokyo, Tanaka Mansion

Leiko has fallen asleep on her extremely expensive chair, surrounded by laptops and holographic screens. She doesn't like to depend on her daughter's technology, but has to admit it's far more comfortable than laptops or tablets. She strives to look like a towering figure of power over her employees, but it does take a lot of work to be the head of Scion Corporation.

The sound of her cellphone ringing awakens her. It takes a while to recognize the sound: *nobody* calls Leiko Tanaka. *She* is the one giving the orders.

She looks at the phone, puzzled and half-asleep: she can't recognize the number.

-<Hello?> - she answers in Japanese.

-What did you do to our daughter?

That English voice is like an electric shock. She hasn't heard it in fifteen years.

-Robert!? How did *you* get this number!?

-Father of the smartest girl in the world. Remember? The girl you abandoned but promised you wouldn't harm!?

-I didn't do anything to *your* daughter, Robert.

Despite accentuating that "your", Leiko has regained her composure. Judging from his voice, however, Bob Null is simply furious.

-You want my grandfather's rock, don't you? The Heart of the Universe. It's what you've always cared about, isn't it? A f###ing rock!!!

-I sent the Many to recover it. I haven't heard anything back from her. You know why I'm telling you this, Robert? Because I didn't have anything to do with your daughter's disappearance.

-So you DO know she vanished!

-Of course I do. After the fight in New York your daughter is the most watched over teenager on the planet; you have two FBI agents infiltrated in your own building.

101

-Let me guess: one of them actually works for you.

-Don't be ridiculous. They both take orders from people who work for me. Since you've suddenly become smart enough to contact me, Robert, you might also be reasonable enough to understand my next offer.

-If the price is the Heart, you already know the answer's no.

-Do you seriously think I need your permission? I hold all the cards, as I always do. I'm simply giving you one last chance of losing gracefully.

-I'm not falling for that. I've already told you: I'm the one person you can't control.

Bob Null hangs up the phone, another thing that's never happened to Leiko Tanaka.

She doesn't care. She has everything under control. She always does.

-<Then I guess I'll have to make you even more irrelevant than you are> - she replies in Japanese.

4-Seeing double

Kari is bored. She's watching the sun disappear below the horizon. Waiting for something, for *anything*, to happen. You're not supposed to feel lonely on Myridia, *ever*, but she can't help it.

Like any Myridian she knows, she's been living by herself since she was fourteen. Like any Myridian, by age twenty Kari had seen absolutely everything her world has to offer.

Twice.

Unlike any other Myridian, this only made Kari bored out of her skull.

A sudden flash of blue light just below the water is about to change all that.

The last thing that Max Black remembers is touching the Heart of the Universe, then hitting a wall.

That's not what he did, but it's close enough. It could've been worse: if he'd materialized inside something solid, like a wall, he'd be dead by now.

Instead, when he opens his eyes, a beautiful white girl with purple hair and blue eyes is smiling warmly.

-Υοθ σcαρεδ με τηερε φορ α σεcονδ – she says.

-Unless I have a concussion, that's not English – he answers, trying to get his bearings.

-Τηατ σοθνδσ λικε γιββερισŋ. Υοθ σθρε υοθ'ρε οκαυ?

They're on a beach, who knows where; probably on the other side of the world, since it's close to dusk. He sure can't tell from the girl: not only he can't understand a word she's saying, he has no idea what language he's hearing.

The girl's appearance isn't of much help. The purple hair would've been weirder before he knew a girl with silver eyes.

-I'm Quantum. Y'know, the super-hero? Quantum – he repeats, more slowly.

-Jθστ μυ λθcκ. Φιρστ πεοπλε I μεετ, ανδ τηευ ταλκ νονσενσε.

-Yeah…whatever you just said isn't very helpful. Where's Vesta? – he asks, looking around.

Several feet away, the goddess is lying lifeless on the beach. There's another girl next to her, kneeling over her body attempting CPR.

Wearing the same pink dress and miniskirt of the girl with the purple hair.

-There she is. What's she doing? – Max wonders. When he tries to walk away, the girl with the purple eyes grabs his arm.

-Σταυ ηερε – she says. It sounds like an order.

-Girl, thanks for the help and all, but that's my friend over there - Max protests, struggling to free himself from her grip. She's stronger than she looks.

-I σαιδ σταυ ηερε – she adds. This time it sounds like a threat.

In the blink of an eye, Kari's body triplicates. Two identical Kari stand beside her, with the exact same pink dress and purple hair.

-What the – is the only thing that Max gets to say, before one of the Kari punches him in the face.

Another one kicks him in the shin. He falls to the ground, too disoriented to turn into energy.

The two duplicates disappear with a popping sound.

-Αρε ωε cλεαρ, ορ νοθ ωαντ με το kick your butt again? – she asks, suddenly making sense.

Vesta awakens with someone trying to resuscitate her. Kari is pushing her chest rhythmically to start her heart again. Only when the goddess awakens, she starts to breathe again.

-I hate teleporting – she complains, rising to her feet.

-Take it easy, you almost drowned – Kari advises.

-Come again?

-I pulled you out of the water, don't you remember?

-Not really, I was kind of dead at the time.

As soon as she's spoken, Vesta regrets her words: she just *knows* the girl will now look at her like she's from another planet.

-Yeah, I know, it's annoying when that happens.

-...

-I'm Kari Zel, by the way.

Max is massaging the back of his head. Kari is shorter than him, though not as much as Noriko, but she managed to take him down without the slightest effort.

-So, how come I can understand you all of a sudden? – he asks.

-That's probably me – Vesta answers, floating towards him a couple inches off the ground.

104

-Vesta, this is…uhm…what's your name?

-She's already met me. I'm Kari Zel.

-That's the name of the girl over there – Vesta answers, looking back. The girl who rescued her disappears with just a popping sound.

-I know, that's me too – Kari nods.

-What do you mean it's "probably you"? – Max asks.

-Gods can understand any language instantly. Sometimes, people around us can do the same.

-I should probably get used to answers that don't make any sense.

-Sorry to change the subject but did I just see that girl over there just…disappear!?

For once, Max shares Vesta's uneasiness with the current situation.

-There's definitely something funny going on here. She just made copies of herself a second ago.

-And? What's so strange about that? – Kari asks.

Vesta decides to change the subject entirely:

-We should probably just rest for a while. It looks like it's almost night.

-But it's not even dawn – Kari answers. She's definitely finding these people to be very strange.

-Then why's the Sun setting? – Max notes, pointing his finger towards the twilight.

-So? There's two more about to rise.

Max and Vesta look at each other, flabbergasted. Both swallow loudly, before Vesta asks:

-How many suns does this planet have?

-Six. I take it this is your first time on Myridia?

Later

Kari's house is just five minutes from the beach. It's nothing fancy, more like an apartment with a small garden outside the door. There's no other house in sight.

-So where are you guys from? – she asks.

-New York – Max answers.

-Earth – Vesta says at the same time.

-Never heard of it. Who's your god?

Again, the two visitors share a puzzled look.

105

-Your world. Which god owns it? – Kari clarifies, thinking there's something wrong with the translation if they can't understand such a simple question.

-You wanna answer that? – Max asks Vesta.

-It's…complicated – is Vesta's honest reply.

-Oh, disputed world. Gotcha. I thought you guys were acting strange…you're refugees, right?

-Sure, why not – Max shrugs.

-Don't worry, I'm not gonna report you or anything. For what it's worth, I think Myridia was better off before the gods came back.

They're now in the kitchen, where Kari takes the only chair. An exact duplicate appears right by her side, walking off to get something to drink.

-Sorry, I don't own another chair. I'm used to be by myself – Kari says.

-I can see that – Max notes, as the duplicate Kari serves him a glass of something vaguely resembling tea.

Vesta adjusts by crossing her legs and levitating, keeping the same distance from the floor like she would if she was on a chair. Interestingly, Kari doesn't seem to care that her guest can fly.

-Tell me about Earth. You're prime people, aren't you?

-I'm not…familiar with the term – Vesta admits.

-People from outside Myridia. You can't do this – Kari clarifies, creating another double and then making it disappear with a popping sound.

-That's…that's amazing. You mean anyone on…Myridia, right? Anyone on Myridia can create duplicates, just like that!?

-Of course. Hey, is it true that prime planets have cities with hundreds of people!? – Kari asks excitedly.

-Even more than that. Can anyone else do that? We know someone called the Many with a very similar power – Max asks.

-As far as I know, no. Never heard of someone called Many either.

-How about Null? Asian girl, late teens, silver eyes, never smiles?

-What's an Asian?

-This is getting nowhere – Max surrenders.

-Kari, you said that Myridia was better off before the gods came back. What do you mean with "came back"? – Vesta asks.

-Myridia didn't belong to any particular god for at least a thousand years; I think they just forgot about us. Three hundred years ago the

Oracles invaded and took over…they've been ruling the planet ever since.

-"The Oracles"? – Max repeats.

-They completely destroyed our industries and started the Harvest. Some say they turned Myridia into a paradise, but come on, they draft people for their stupid wars!

-"Harvest"? Kari…which god owns this planet? – Vest asks, biting her upper lip.

-Demeter. Does she own your planet too?

Vesta doesn't answer; she's noticeably paler and visibly shocked.

-What's up, Vesta? You know this Demeter?

-She's my sister. And we're in very, *very* deep trouble.

5-Who you are in the dark

The prisonerarrived days ago. They brought her here bruised, disarmed and naked.

She's a good fighter: only a teenage girl, but she managed to knock out the first guard twenty seconds after opening her eyes. If the guards weren't Myridians, she could've escaped right there.

But Myridians are tricky. They can create copies of themselves at will: if you want to knock out one, you better be prepared to do the same with an another thousand.

They tried to interrogate her, but the prisoner can't understand a single word. The guards are professionals: they don't resort to outright torture. They know how to break prisoners.

They provide her drinking water and nothing else. No food. No clothes. Not even a bed.

She just sits there, alone, on the cold floor of hard stone. Meditating. Thinking.

I am Null. I must remember that. I have to keep focused.

I can't remember what happened after the teleportation. I've been separated from the Many and imprisoned here…wherever "here" is.

I couldn't understand a word the guards said, meaning it wasn't any language known to mankind.

There is no way out. The walls are solid. There's a locket on the other side of the prison bars, but I can't pick it without any instrument.

They're either trying to break me or they don't care if I die. I'm cold. Hungry. Thirsty. Tired.

"Oh God I'm gonna die here alone and naked and scared!"

Shut up, Noriko. I'm trying to think here.

"Where's Dad? Where's everybody? What am I doing here!?"

You're not doing anything. I'm the one in charge.

"I was here first. I've been you until Athena messed things up"

Really. You're an angsty teenager with no original thought and no future. I am Null.

"You're the one afraid of her human personality. So afraid that you locked me in a corner of your brain and pushed away everyone we know. And now you're gonna die alone"

Shut up. I'm only hearing you because I'm tired and hungry and so far away from Earth that I can't connect to the worldmind.

"So basically we're going insane because you can't hear seven billion voices in your head anymore? That's a new one."

I'm not insane. Do you have any idea how hard it is to keep all the knowledge of the world inside your head!?

"Great, now I'm arguing with myself. You ever think Mom was right?"

Shut up. I am Null. I have no mother.

"She said I'm nothing. All that genius, and what have you done with it so far?"

Noriko is nothing. You are nothing. I am Null now. Null doesn't need anyone.

"Keep telling yourself that and eventually you'll believe it. Oh wait, that's exactly what you're doing now, aren't you? Come on big head, you're the smartest girl on Earth. You know what you need to do to get out of this mess"

Alright. We'll try things your way. But if we die, I'm never gonna listen to you again.

"What if it turns out I'm right? You're going to tell our friends that you're hearing voices?"

Don't push your luck.

I open my eyes, ready to take on the world. Then slam my head on the wall so hard I break my nose. This should work.

I regain consciousness with the unmistakable smell of disinfectant. There's something restraining my head, but I manage to look around enough to understand I'm in some kind of medical facility.

They have tied me up, but at least they've had the decency to give me an hospital gown.

"Did they have to dress me up while I was unconscious? Creeeepy..."

Why are you still here?

"It takes more than a broken nose to silence your fears."

That would be almost profound if it made any sense. I don't have time to argue with you right now, can't you see they're examining us? Look at that screen, it's showing all of my vital signs. That's probably the reason for the clothes...this "dress" is probably a sensor array.

"Yeah, I know, I'm you, remember? God, split personalities suck."
I'm going to ignore you right now. I can't believe I was ever you.
"I can't believe supersmart me is such a b###h!!!"
Shut up, you're making me waste too much brain power! Without a connection to the worldmind…
"You shut up! You pushed me away because you were afraid a human mind would go insane with that much information and responsibility!"
Well maybe it's better to be insane than to be you!
"Fine!"
Fine!
-You can stop pretending, I know you're not unconscious – a deep male voice intervenes.
"See? You took us right to the villain! He's gonna kill us now!!!"
Shut up, Noriko. I'm working on it.
"On getting us killed?"
…
"Shutting up now."

I manage to turn my head just enough to see him. A man in his early forties, utterly inconspicuous if not for the elaborate black robes. And the green, shining gem embedded in his throat.
-Fascinating piece of work. You have a self-sustaining brain: it's not drawing energy from the rest of your body. It seems to have its own independent power supply.
-You're speaking the same language of the guards, but I can understand you. Why? – I ask.
-No built-in universal translator, I see. Disappointing. I can't think of a major god making such a mistake. Maybe Dionysus, if he were sufficiently drunk…
-Stop ignoring me and release me at once! – I protest, testing the strength of my restrains.
As it always happens with any emotional reaction, my eyes glow. The screen signals a sudden increase in brain activity, then shuts down. I think I fried it.
-That…was unnecessary – he states calmly. The jewel in his throat glows.

All of a sudden, I'm free from my restrains. My first thought is to escape, but I'm not able to move a muscle: I float in the air, as he telekinetically draws me towards him.

-I am Drevel Viz, Oracle of Myridia and servant of Demeter. You will tell me your mission, how you managed to steal an highly classified biological weapon, and which god shall reclaim your corpse after I'm through with you.

Without lifting a finger, he throws me to the other side of the room. I swallow the pain and order my legs to stand up, but before I can do anything the Oracle telekinetically pins me against the wall.

The pressure on my chest is making it difficult to breathe. I know he could kill me right now, just by thinking about it, but I have one advantage over him. He's not Null. I AM.

-That all you got? – I manage to say.

The Oracle loses his cool. He doesn't raise his voice, but the increase in the pressure over my body is a telling sign.

-Only your head shows signs of genetic manipulation. I can remove organs and limbs from the rest of your body as I please. All I need from you is to know is which god created you.

-I'm not working for any god.

-I find that hard to believe. You can't have acted alone; no mortal could steal the Many on her own.

-Were you born this stupid, or is that jewel in your throat restricting the blood flow to the brain?

The Oracle raises an eyebrow, twisting my limbs so hard it feels like he's about to rip them out.

I can't give him the satisfaction to scream. I close my eyes and grin my teeth so hard it feels my skull will burst.

"Tell he what he wants! Tell him anything! Please!!!"

-Last chance to answer me without grievous harm, child. What manner of creature are you?

He steps closer. There's a permanent storm raging in my brain.

-I AM NULL – I shout, opening my eyes. They aren't silver anymore: they are white hot.

I am channeling all of the information stored in my head in a single, massive burst of electrical activity: another second and I risk melting my own eyes.

I was prepared to be temporarily blinded; the Oracle wasn't, and he releases me from his telekinetic control. The sudden shock leaves me an opening; I slip past him, jumping on his shoulders to grab his neck between my hands.

He could rip my head off with a thought. I reach for every drop of adrenaline in my body to strangle him as hard as humanly possible. He's doing his best to push me away.

I figured that if they bothered to install the jewel in the throat, blood flow to the head is important.It's not much of a deduction; more like a hunch. I'm betting my life on it.

I'm tired, hungry and dehydrated. But NULL. WILL. ENDURE.

The soldier standing guard just outside the lab opens the door. He's not supposed to interrupt the Oracle, so he didn't peek when he slammed me against the wall…but the fall of the Oracle made enough noise to arouse some suspicion.

He's wearing some kind of light armor and carries a spear. When he sees his boss lying lifeless on the floor, his first instinct is to create five exact duplicates of himself.

All of them look me in the eye. The girl half their weight who just took out their telekinetic master.

-I am Null. Does anyone else want to challenge me?

I'm bluffing. If I have to throw one punch I'll collapse from exhaustion. But from their body language alone I spot thirteen signs that they're terrified of me.

Five spears fall on the ground.

"Did…did we just win!?"

I did, while you were hiding in the dark. And that is why I am the dominant personality.

6-Alien ghost town

Vesta is flying above the city, carrying Kari in her arms. The Myridian girl is so full of joy she could explode any minute. To be up in the sky, literally free as a bird...

-This is amazing! And you can do this whenever you want!?

-Of course. I take this is your first flight; don't you have airplanes on this planet?

-We used to, but then the Oracles declared flying was an insult to Demeter.

-That is *so* like my sister.

-There it is! New Rhetra! – Kari exclaims, pointing her finger towards the city below them.

Vesta touches the ground a minute later. Max is waiting for them, sitting at the edge of the road.

-What took you so long?

-I couldn't break the sound barrier flying with her. So Kari, you think we can find our friend here?

The girl answers while fiddling with Noriko's green leather jacket. It's too small for her, so she's tying it around her waist.

-Old Man Vor lives here; if anyone can find her, it's him. Does this thing make me look fat? – she asks.

A duplicate appears in front of her, wearing the same exact pink dress with miniskirt but without the leather jacket, examining the original like she's in front of a mirror. While the two are pondering the possibilities of interplanetary fashion, a second duplicate appears.

-This is weird. I don't see any rickshaw – she says, completely uninterested in the jacket.

-What, Demeter thinks cars are an insult too?

-What's a car? - one of the duplicates asks, raising an eyebrow.

-Nevermind.

-This place used to be full of people pulling their own rickshaw – the original Kari clarifies.

-I checked the place before you arrived. This is some kind of ghost town – Max reveals.

-It can't be...this is a big city. There should be thousands of people living here.

-No really, I didn't see anybody. Granted, everything was kinda blurry at the speed of light, but...

-I'm sure it's nothing, Old Man Vor is probably asleep or something.

-Didn't you say thousands of people live here?

-Yes. Just Old Man Vor. Let's go find him.

Two new Kari appear out of thin air. They then split into four, then eight, then sixteen and so on, and in a few seconds there's a crowd of Karis marching in the streets.

-This place is *weird* – Max highlights.

Each Kari goes her separate way, creating more duplicates at every street corner. The only way to identify the original is the leather jacket tied around her waist.

-You're taking my being a goddess awfully well – Vesta notes.

-As long as you're not one of the evil ones it's no big deal, really. I know lots of boys who swear they've slept with Aphrodite.

-That is *so* like my niece.

-If you don't mind me asking, how does your power work? – Max asks.

Vesta is slightly relieved: she though he was going to ask how Kari's clothes duplicate as well.

-Everyone born on Myridia can do it. The Oracles say it's a miracle by Demeter; Old Man Vor says it's Drylon technology in the core of the planet.

-What's a Drylon? – Max asks.

-You ask the weirdest questions – Kari answers, shaking her head in disapproval.

-Humor us, please – Vesta insists.

-The Drylon ruled the universe before the gods. The gods are fighting over who gets their weapons. Look, there's Old Man Vor's home.

Kari runs towards the house, leaving Vesta and Black behind and confused.

-You never heard of this? – he asks.

-I've heard of the Drylon, but I never heard of anything predating the gods.

114

The city is old, but it looks positively ancient by Earth standards. It's like walking into a Western movie: an endless parade of two-story houses next to a dirty road.

-Can't believe we're on another planet. Where's the flying cars?– Max laments.

Just then, Kari crashes the window on the top floor. Vesta is ready to catch her, but waits when Kari creates a couple of duplicates beneath her.

Kari lands on her exact replicas, who disappear from existence with a loud pop.

A man smashes through the wall like it was nothing, landing like it was the most normal thing to do. As if it couldn't possibly look more like the Old West, he's wearing a duster and a hat...both worn out like they made it to hell and back.

-Tell Death if he wants the Old Man, he can come to get him himself.

-You mean Thanatos? He used to work for my brother! – Vesta says cheerfully.

-You don't say – the stranger answers. His face is covered by the hat's shadow, but it's clear from his voice that he's smiling.

A dozen swords of red energy appear in front of him. Unaffected by gravity, they shoot out in different directions...even though the stranger hasn't even touched them.

Vesta avoids the blades flying away. Two duplicates help Kari to jump high above them, but as soon as they're hit the vanish like soap bubbles.

Max doesn't need to move. Once he turns his body into light, the blades pass through him without cutting anything.

-Hm. That's new – the stranger comments, unfazed.

-All right, that's enough – Vesta intervenes, grappling him from behind. He struggles to get free, but there's no way he can overmuscle her godly strength.

-I agree – he answers.

Bright red swords materialize on his back, while Vesta is still holding him. The swords cut through flesh and bone, impaling her on the spot.

Max watches as her lifeless body fall to the ground, spilling blood everywhere. Just to be sure, the stranger creates yet another red sword, thrusting the blade directly into her skull.

115

Max knows he should be something, but this is the first time he's seen someone he knows murdered in such a brutal yet efficient way. It's just unreal.

Then the stranger turns towards him, taking off his hat to show what would pass for a common human face, if it weren't for the red skin.

-Your turn – he says.

Something snaps. Max delivers a massive energy blast; he doesn't know which kind of energy and frankly doesn't care right now.

The stranger effortlessly cuts the energy beam in two. The twin blasts miss Old Man Vor's house entirely, but end up turning half a dozen buildings into rubble.

Even so, the shockwave is enough to shake the house considerably. Old Man Vor loses his balance; if he were a few years younger, he could make a duplicate of himself appear to help him.

Instead, it's a couple of girls that catch him and help him get on his feet.

-Damn kids – he mumbles, pushing the girls away. The original is right in front of him, arms crossed and tapping her foot nervously.

-Well? Aren't you gonna say anything?

-Yes. That jacket's horrible.

-Your friend out there is killing *my* friends, and that's all you got to say!?

Vor looks at the girl, stroking his beard. Pink dress, blue eyes, purple hair. Pretty common on Myridia, but she *does* look familiar.

-I'm Kari! Kari Zel, remember? You saved me from the Harvest!

-Who's killing who? – Vor asks, already knowing the answer.

He walks towards the window, where he can see the red skinned stranger deflecting a barrage of lasers with a shield made of swords.

-Oh for the love of...TORN! STOP KILLING MY NEIGHBOURS!!! – the old man shouts.

-Fine – Torn whines, stabbing Max in the chest.

At the very last second, Max turns his torso into electricity; not only the sword hurts him anyway, but to his surprise he finds himself unable to change again.

-This makes far less sense than it should. Hey, come back here! What are you doing!?

Torn is back to Vesta's bloody corpse now, kneeling to grab the blade stuck in her head.

116

-Unkilling her.

He removes the blade; Vesta opens her eyes. She sits down, examining her current state: her formerly orange tube top is now red with blood, and there's a hole in her chest where the heart should be.

-Alien ghost towns suck – she says.

Watching the scene from the window, Kari is glad to see her friend is alive. Old Man Vor is unimpressed.

-Hm. Amateurs.

-You owe me some answers, Old Man! Who's that guy? Why is he red? Why did he try to kill us!?

-He's Torn. He does that.

-He shoots laser swords with his mind!!!

-So? We create duplicates at will and your friend over there turns into energy. It's a weird galaxy.

-Tell me about it. Is this place safe? Someone *must* have heard that blast.

-Don't worry, the guards of the nearest cities won't report anything. Being the former Minister of War of Myridia still carries some weight.

-Speaking of that, I have a favor to ask…

Just then, Torn's body smashes through the window. Kari's first thought is to create a duplicate to push the Old Man out of harm's way, but she doesn't need to.

Moving surprisingly fast for a man his age, the Old Man ducks the debris and catches a knife from his nightstand.

When Quantum turns back into flesh and blood, he finds the blade right between his eyes.

-Fight's over, son. Don't make me spill blood inside this house. I hate cleaning up the place.

-I could've handled him – Torn says, getting back on his feet. Despite flying through a wall, he's just fine.

-That's what they all say – the Old Man answers, turning suddenly to throw the knife at Kari.

One duplicate appears to push her away; another one grabs the weapon in mid-air. All of this happened in less than half a second.

-I see your training style hasn't changed much – the original Kari says.

-What just happened? – Quantum asks.

117

-Just a Myridian family reunion – the Old Man smiles.
-I'd hate to see your Thanksgiving…

Kari Zel by KodamaCreative

Torn by KodamaCreative

7-Get pants, save the world

Deka is one of the oldest cities on Myridia, and has been the capital of the planet for many centuries. Its population of five thousand might seem rather low, but since every Myridian can create at will up to ten thousand exact duplicates of him or herself, the actual population can rise to fifty million at any second.

Because of this, it's one of the very few cities on Myridia where buildings pre-dating the return of the gods are still standing. It resembles a modern Earth city, the only difference being the fact that a single Myridian can own an entire skyscraper.

The most striking feature of Deka is the statue of Demeter holding a sickle. It's over 600 feet tall, four times the height of the Staute of Liberty, and it was built over the ashes of the Myridian Parliament.

Nabric Ges has lived all his life in the shadow of Demeter's statue. He joined the Myridian Holy Guard right after reaching his Harvest year, and has been working as a guard for the Oracle Palace ever since. He's supposed to be on duty today, but nobody finds it strange that a dozen of his duplicates are moving crate after crate to his house.

This is Myridia, after all: people are supposed to be in many places at once.

Noriko Null is in the library, reading a book so fast it seems she's only flipping through it. She's sitting next to a pile of old books almost as tall as she is. She's still wearing the hospital gown.

When she notices Nabric opening the door, she doesn't slow down before commenting:

-This is amazing. Myridia already had a planetary government a thousand years ago. And did your people really go from iron age to industrial revolution in less than a century!?

-What's a century? And when did you learn to read Myridian?

-This morning, before breakfast. This is quite a collection of books, by the way. You don't strike me as the reading type.

-Yeah, you got me. It's my father's collection; all the books are more than three hundred years old, you know. Older than Demeter's return.

-I think I got this – Noriko declares, closing the book she's already finished – Thousands of years ago, the Greek gods established a

120

colony here by moving of humans from Earth. Considering your language, probably from Crete or Mycenae. Was it Demeter?

-I have no idea. My father thought it was Prometheus.

-Interesting. Still, you were able to build an impressive civilization…until Demeter claimed this world as her own private possession. That's as far as the books go; I take it they're illegal?

-I could be executed just for looking at them. The Oracles don't want us to know what life before Demeter was like. They say it can "inspire revolts".

Noriko walks towards Nabric; she's still weak from the days of dehydration and malnutrition, and he's a trained guard with twice her weight. Her silver eyes flash, making his soul shake in fear.

-Inspire me.

New Rhetra

Kari is trying to help Old Man Vor sit down on his chair, but he pushes away her duplicates.

-Did I say I needed help!? – he yells.

-This planet gets better and better – Max laments.

-Don't get me started on this planet – the Old Man whines.

Vesta floats towards him, feeling uncomfortable as she always is around old people. Old age is something completely alien to her, something that quickly steals the people she cares about.

-Sir, we could really use your help. We're strangers on this planet; Kari thinks you might be able to help us find our friend and to understand where we are. We will be eternally grateful for any information you can give us.

She gives a warm smile that even the Old Man can't ignore. At ninety-seven it really shouldn't have any effect on him, but Vesta's something else.

-You're a goddess, aren't you? I used to work for one.

Vesta "sits down" next to him, by crossing her legs and floating. The man with the red skin standing alone in a corner of the room looks at her suspiciously.

-She looks dangerous. I should kill her again.

-You have something of a one-track mind, don't you? – Max teases him.

The red-skinned man answers by creating an energy sword and pointing it at Max's throat.

-Torn! What did I tell you about killing my guests? – the Old Man shouts, then coughing several times. Torn makes the sword disappear, crossing his arms and looking away.

-You never let me kill *anyone*.

-You'll have to excuse Torn; he thinks everyone's an Oracle spy.

-Kari mentioned the Oracles. They're the ruling class, right? – Vesta asks.

-They are Demeter's representatives. You see, Demeter rules over a hundred worlds; despite her propaganda, she can't be in more than one place at a time. Maybe that's why she decided to conquer Myridia.

-I need to know what she did, sir. I haven't seen my sister for over two thousand years.

-There isn't much to say. You know Demeter's the goddess of the harvest, right?

-Yeah, she's always been into plants.

-She came here to harvest *us*.

Deka

Nabric Ges holds one of his father's books, as he recounts what has been passed from generation to generation. It's impossible to hide history from a civilization where everyone can whisper to ten thousand people at once.

-We had never met a goddess before; we didn't know what to expect. Demeter decimated our entire military force with her own power. Every industrial complex in the world was either sunk under the ocean or downright incinerated. In a single day, she sent us a thousand years back. Then she left the dirty work to the Oracles…her priests, each wielding a fraction of her power.

-The jewel on their throats – Noriko recalls.

-Godstones, yes. My father wasn't the only one trying to resist, to carry the memory of our old history. Each city has a dozen of libraries like this. The Oracles are brutal but patient: they know Demeter can wait. Another generation or two, and everyone will believe her lies.

-It can't be that hard to rebel. I stunned the Oracle with relative ease.

-Not a lot of people get the chance.

Noriko doesn't have anything to say. She's thinking how all of this is a little too convenient…the Heart of the Universe teleporting her

122

here, the Many and the Oracle defeated so easily, the guard conveniently ready to betray his masters…could there be Athena's hand behind this?

"Right, she almost starved to death and she calls it easy".

She had almost forgotten that annoying voice in her head. Her human mind is still too scared to come out: she has to keep moving to shut her up. She can do it: she is Null.

-I'll need anesthetic, a scalpel and copper wire. No, wait, you probably haven't developed how to extract it: just get me some bronze, a large glass bottle and a very hot fire and I'll think of something. Oh, and another thing.

Noriko jumps to her feet, looking at the hospital gown with disdain.

-Get me something decent to wear. I can't save the world without pants.

New Rhetra

-The Word of Demeter, the only legal book on Myridia, says that our purpose in life is to be bred for war – the Old Man explains.

-I don't like where this is going – Max warns.

-Myridian society follows precise rules. As soon as you hit puberty, you're kicked out of the house. You're expected to survive alone for a while; many build their own cities, like I did with New Rhetra. Then, if you're male and you're physically fit, you go to war. If you're female, you have as many children as you can.

-They have places called breeding camps. Women are chained and forced to…well… - Kari clarifies, hesitating before completing the sentence.

-What happens if you're not fit? Or if you can't have kids? – Vesta asks.

-The Oracles kill you – Kari answers.

There's a second of silence. The normally happy-go-lucky Kari is suddenly deadly serious.

-They call it the Harvest. Every season they inspect their crops. If you're weak, they kill you. If you're too old to duplicate, to fight or to conceive, they kill you. If you do anything they think Demeter won't like, they kill you.

-Still think I'm the one with the one-track mind? – Torn asks.

Vesta shakes her head: she can't believe her sister is responsible for something like this.

123

-I don't understand; what does she do with all these Myridian soldiers?

-What does anyone do with an army? Demeter isn't as powerful as the other gods, but thanks to Myridia she has an almost unlimited supply of soldiers.

-Demeter's at war? With whom? – Vesta asks.

-I lost track a long time ago. Gods help each other to fight one of their own, then break alliances when they feel like it. They've been fighting over the Drylon's arsenal for who knows how long.

-I knew I wouldn't like this – Max notes, approaching the old man.

Torn gives him a dirty look, but Max doesn't pay him attention. Noriko's mother and her weird floating metal ball mentioned the Drylon before; they must be close to something important.

-Old Man…we're looking for a friend. She may have used Drylon technology to come to Myridia.

-Then we're all dead – Torn says.

-Remind me again why you hang out with this creep? – Kari asks the old man, who answers:

-He saved my life once. I'm helping him survive the harvest. If your friend brought Drylon technology here, Demeter will tear this world apart to get her hands on it.

-Don't worry, she left it at home – Max answers.

-And she didn't take anything else with her? – Torn insists.

-She didn't take anything, not even her clothes – Vesta reassures him, before adding – Except…

-The Many! – Max and Vesta say at the same time.

Deka

Oracle Drevel Viz opens his eyes. He's in a dark room, laying on a table. His wrists and ankles are chained, and he doesn't have the strength to move.

His telekinetic powers, granted by the godstone embedded into his throat, should be enough to free him…except they don't seem to work.

Someone turns on the lights. Two duplicates of Nabric Ges are menacing him with spears, standard issue of the Myridian Guard.

Then there's the girl with the silver eyes. She's wearing clothes too big for her, mostly because they're supposed to be worn by a man.

There's something drawn with charcoal on the white shirt, a symbol that the Oracle doesn't recognize: Ø

-Unhand me and pray for Demeter's piety. Your death may be swift and merciful.

His voice isn't what it used to be. It's more like an angry whisper.

-You know a lot of fancy words, don't you? Good for you. Here's your word of the day.

Null is holding in her hand the godstone she removed from the Oracle's throat. Her silver eyes shine bright, and the jewel levitates.

-Tracheotomy.

She smiles. It's the most terrifying thing the Oracle has ever seen.

8- One of our oracles is missing

Women working in the Oracle Palace consider themselves fortunate. Unlike their mothers and sisters, they are not forced to give birth every ten months; unlike the males, they are not required to serve as guards or soldiers.

Women used to work only as maids in the Palace, but the recent increase of demand for warriors has led to a shortage of male administrators; this means that the Oracle Palace is the only place on Myridia where a woman can make a career. One day there might even be a female Oracle, as it's whispered already happens on many worlds.

The major problem is staying alive when Talas Khanos pays a visit.

The main gate opens without anyone touching it. A freakishly tall man inspects the scene: a dozen handmaidens, all duplicates of the same young girl, are covering the floor with rose petals.

Khanos walks forward, stepping over the petals humming a cheerful tune; nobody else dares to make the slightest sound.

-Nice crop, this year – he comments, telekinetically lifting one of the duplicates off the ground enough to look her in the eye. Despite being over seven feet tall, Khanos isn't very imposing: in the low gravity of his world, his muscles are somewhat underdeveloped. But there's something sinister in his purple eyes.

-What's your name, dear?

-Reilen Lal – she answers, shaking in fear.

-You're a fine specimen, Lal. Or is it Reilen? I can never remember how you people use your names. How old are you?

-I'm eighteen, Oracle Khanos.

-Wrong. You're only two minutes old – he answers, ripping her left arm out of the shoulder. She has less than half a second to scream, before her body disappears with a popping sound.

-Ah, I never get tired of that sound.

Reilen Lal isn't hurt like her duplicate, but that doesn't make watching Khanos dismember her any easier. The giant then looks at her, breaking one of her ribs with his mind.

As she kneels in pain, all of her duplicates do the same in an almost instantaneous reaction.

-Remarkable. I simply *must* ask Drevel to spare more specimen; your people make test subjects obsolete. Speaking of which, where is Oracle Drevel Viz?

Nabric Ges is lifted off the ground by an invisible hand. Khanos telekinetically squeezes his kidneys for maximum pain; since this is just a duplicate, he can't hit him or he will just pop out of existence.
-What do you mean you lost him!? – Khanos asks angrily.
-The Oracle...doesn't tell me...where he goes – Nabric answers through the pain.
Khanos looks the guard into the eye: he won't break easily. He quickly regains his composure.
-Have you ever heard of the Lampyrians?
The bricks of the wall disassemble themselves, opening a door where there isn't one. Khanos floats through it, carrying Nabric with him in the same fashion. As he talks, he passes through several rooms of the Palace; the walls close themselves behind him.
-Blue skinned all-female species from Aphrodite's Queendom. Most of the galaxy sees them as cheap prostitutes, but after vivisecting a few of them I reverse-engineered their reproductive system. You see, Lampyrian lifespan is fifty times shorter than a human's. That means they rarely live longer than a year, but they can also give birth five days after conception. I devised a way to push it to five *seconds* before I was old enough to grow a beard. Isn't biology a wonderful thing?-
Now they have reached the prison. Nabric is wondering why Khanos is here...he's already received his share of test subjects for the year.
-That's when I was approached by Demeter herself. She'd grown tired of Myridia...your people aren't particularly efficient. Yes, one of you can spawn ten thousand soldiers in the blink of an eye, but the duplicates are remarkably fragile...one good hit and you disappear. Not to mention it takes many years to grow a new soldier; replenishing Demeter's army takes time. That's why I created the Many.

The Many is kept in custody inside a glass cylinder full of water. Her body continuously spawns more copies to break out of it, but since there isn't enough space for them she has to reabsorb them. The cycle gives the container a pulsating appearance.

127

-Look at her. She can reproduce in half a second. She doesn't require food, water, air: she can extract energy from almost anything. She doesn't need clothing, housing, sex, human interaction. Infinitely superior to any mortal lifeform; drop one of her on a planet, and she will replace the entire population with other Many. The ultimate invasive species.-

Nabric doesn't really understand any of this. He's just a duplicate, created by the original Nabric as soon as he left the Palace with Null.

-I don't know…where the Oracle is…

-Drevel Viz called me to say he captured someone trying to smuggle the Many on this planet. A girl with strange eyes. I don't like people stealing from me, Nabric. Which is why, unless you tell me where your original body is hiding the girl, I will hold Myridia responsible for the theft. One hundred people will die each hour until I find her.

-You wouldn't do it – Nabric comments, calling his bluff – The Myridian people are personal property of Demeter. She values our lives.

-You are severely overstating your price. Where is the girl with silver eyes?

Noriko's makeshift laboratory is fairly impressive, given what she has to work with. She had to manufacture everything: from the magnifying glasses to see the finest details of her newest invention, to the electric welder, to the bicycles that Nabric's duplicates are using to power the welder.

-That looks like some fairly impressive technology – the original tries to compliment.

-Hardly. This is supposed to be the power regulator, but at best it's a steampunk microprocessor.-

She takes off the glasses and wipes the sweat off her forehead, showing off her latest creation.

It's a gun. The body is in brass, the holster is covered in leather, and the whole thing looks more like a glorified paint gun than a serious weapon. The weirdest part is the muzzle: it incorporates the godstone that she removed from the Oracle. The one that granted him telekinetic abilities.

-This little jewel resonates with brain activity, turning thoughts into pure kinetic energy. I theorize the Heart of the Universe works in a similar fashion; this technology might be an attempt to reverse

128

engineer it. Unfortunately, this means it only works if the user's nervous system has been specifically attuned to the godstone.

-I know you're talking Myridian now, but I have no idea what you just said – Nabric admits.

-The godstone needs to be physically connected to a human nervous system to work. Since I'm not keen to surgically connect alien technology to my own skull, I'm gonna trick it. Make it think it's attached to a brain. A brain with much more electrical activity, and therefore more power. Or, to make it short...

Noriko stands up, pulling back the gun's hammer. It makes a reassuring clicking sound.

-I call this the Genius Gun, Mark I. Now step back, please.

-Why?

-I need to charge it – Noriko answers, her eyes lighting up.

It's not the usual silver shine. Her eyes are now bleeding electricity and information.

People in Deka aren't used to new faces. Even though five thousand people live there, the same faces are everywhere: people send their own duplicates to run errands, use them to repair buildings or just to walk around. The result is that, no matter where you look, you end up meeting the same people over and over again.

Kari has created a dozen duplicates to help her new friends to stand out a little less, but it's easier said than done. Vesta's statuesque body can turn heads on any planet. Torn is covering his red skin as much as he can, but that only ends up making him stand out even more. But it's Max's own skin color that attracts the most attention; none of these people has ever seen an African-American.

-I think I just tripled this planet's black population – he comments.

-That would still leave it at zero – Torn says.

-It was a joke, Torn – Vesta clarifies.

-Unless the joke is that he can't count, I don't get it.

-How are we ever gonna find Nori in a place like this? – she adds.

-Most of these people are duplicates. They disappear if you hit them – Torn answers.

-And that helps us *how*? – Vesta asks.

-Your friend will be easier to find if we knock everybody else unconscious – he answers.

-You are NOT going to punch everyone in the city – Kari clarifies.

129

-Remind me again why we brought mister space samurai with us? – Max asks.

-He asked. I'm not gonna die again just to settle an argument – Vesta shrugs.

-You said your friend took the Many back to Myridia. We have a score to settle – Torn answers.

One of Kari's duplicates holds his arm, smiling cheerfully.

-I heard what you said to the Old Man! You said we need you. That's sweet!

Kari's duplicate disappears painlessly when Torn suddenly jabs her in the stomach with an energy dagger. The crowd doesn't even seem to notice.

-I am NOT "sweet". You amateurs wouldn't survive ten minutes in a fight with an Oracle. Unless we're subtle, they'll start another Harvest right away.

-"Subtle"? You wanted to punch the whole city five minutes ago! – Max protests.

-I *still* want to do that. What's your point?

-Guys, I think I found her – Kari says, standing on the shoulders of one of her duplicates and pointing at one of the skyscrapers.

She just saw a bright flash of light. After that, something inside the building explodes, blasting away the wall.

-Of course. If you want Noriko, just follow the explosions – Vesta comments.

9- First we take Myridia

City of Deka, planet Myridia

One of the advantages of a planet where anyone can make ten thousand copies of himself whenever he wants is that it's very easy to have a policeman on every street corner.

Officer Lar is patrolling the busy streets of Deka, when he sees the explosion on one of the top floors of the many skyscrapers.

As usual in case of emergency, most of the duplicates in the street disappear. Any duplicate can disappear at will, and most do once they have completed their purpose.

Officer Lar is a duplicate, of course: all policemen walking the streets are. He creates another couple of duplicates to check on the few civilians remaining in the area, and another one to enter the building. If the Oracles hadn't declared radio communications to be a blasphemous offence to Demeter, he could alert headquarters. But like most people on Myridia, he can rely only himself and his ten thousand duplicates.

The main door explodes, hitting the duplicate with enough force to make it disappear with a loud popping sound. Officer Lar would think it resembles a chewing gum bubble exploding, if the Oracles hadn't banned chewing gum decades earlier.

He holds his trusty spear, standard issue for any kind of law enforcement on Myridia, and creates enough duplicates to be ready for anything coming out of the building.

Silver eyes glow in the dark. Then a teenage girl steps into the light, holding a makeshift gun. Possession of unlicensed weapons is a capital crime on Myridia, meaning it would be perfectly legal for Officer Lar to stab her in the chest at this very moment.

But she's just a kid, not much older than his own daughter. He decides to go easy on her.

-Girl, you're in a lot of trouble, you know that? Put down the weapon and maybe I can convince the Oracles to make you choose a death that isn't painful.

He smiles, hoping to calm her down. Any crime is punishable by death on Myridia, so he's seen enough lost lives already. She cocks the gun.

-I am Null. I'm here to conquer this world and give it back to Myridians; if you wish join me, lower your weapon.

131

-Look kid, I don't know what kind of drugs you're on but…

She fires. There's no bullet coming out of the gun: just a fierce burst of wind, enough to lift seven duplicates off the ground and let them fall helplessly to the ground.

This would be enough to make normal duplicates disappear, but Lar has trained extensively to make sure his duplicates can withstand anything short of a lethal blow.

-That was a warning shot. This is when things gets serious – the girl boasts, rotating one of the dials of her gun. Her eyes shine for a fraction of a second.

Officer Lar grabs his spear, dusts himself off, and creates another twenty duplicates; all of them charge towards the girl, roaring their warring cry.

People on the street watch the girl shoot all of them with deadly accuracy; none of the officers are able to lay a finger on her. They're just common people who lived all their lives in a warped theocracy, sure to be killed on the spot if they ever dared to rebel.

The girl with the silver eyes lifts her weapon to the sky; hundreds of Deka citizens are looking at her, from the street and the skyscraper windows, and hear her shout:

-I am Null; swear allegiance to me and I shall give you back your world. Who is with me?

It the streets were busy before, all of a sudden they're positively jammed. Thousands upon thousands of people pop into existence without warning, wishing to see with as many eyes as possible what is going on.

-Man, and I thought New York was overcrowded – Max comments, pushed by strangers from every side.

-So much for reaching Noriko; we'll never get over there with all these people – Vesta notes.

-Indeed. Vesta, keep Purple Hair safe; Brown Skin, turn intangible – Torn orders.

-*What* did you just call me!? – Max asks, noticing that Torn's hands are emitting a red glow.

-Better do as he says – Vesta understands, catching the original Kari and flying above the crowd.

Torn inhales sharply, before shouting:

-CUT OF A THOUSAND DEATHS!

His hands release thousands upon thousands of red energy daggers, flying at incredible speed in every direction. The daggers carefully avoid any original Myridian, hitting instead all of their duplicates. For a bird's eye view, the streets have been made almost completely desert by a red wave of death originating from Torn.

Max Black whistles, impressed by the insane display of power and skill of his unlikely ally, and turns his body back from X-rays to human flesh.

-Street's empty now – Torn highlights.

It doesn't take much to fill them again, this time with thousands upon thousands of policemen charging towards the invaders, each carrying a metal spear.

There's a dozen originals in this district, each of them capable to create ten thousand duplicates, and they're facing three prime foreigners and a Myridian girl. This means it's 120.000 versus 10.003.

Vesta keeps a defensive position, allowing spears to break against her indestructible body and occasionally melting them with her fire.

Torn and Kari prefer hand to hand combat: the red skinned man with his energy swords and brutal efficiency, while the purple haired girl shows off her incredible agility and coordination.

The original Kari is no better than a normal human, but thanks to her duplicates it's like fighting hundreds of perfectly synchronized and choreographed martial artists.

Max Black is taking care of most of the battle, however. He cycles between one energy form to another, keeping down their numbers. The twelve originals can generate new duplicates instantaneously after one has been destroyed. But they're facing lightning, lasers, microwaves, fire, energy swords, daggers, blades, and even the girl refuses to be defeated.

Myridian security has only one strategy: attack with unrelenting determination and the enemy will eventually wear down and fall.

Whoever these people are, two hundred thousand spears aren't enough to make them break a sweat.

Two hundred thousand duplicates disappear, and twelve spears fall to the ground.

-We surrender – is all the policemen have to say.

133

-That was AWESOME!!! – Kari shouts, hugging Max and creating two more duplicates to do the same with Vesta and Torn.

-It's not over yet – Vesta warns her, pointing towards the immense crowd that is walking towards them. They're civilians, and they're led by a girl with silver eyes.

Despite its power, the Demeter regime is wildly unpopular. People have been waiting for decades for someone to rise against her and the Oracles, but the prospect of fighting telekinetic demigods has always prevented any sort of uprising.

Null has watched the fight from afar; Deka may be a large city, but two hundred thousand soldiers take a lot of space. And she saw the look on the Myridians when they finally saw in action people who have a chance of standing up to the Oracles.

"That was AWESOME!!! Did you see when Vesta kicked the ground so hard the whole street was shaking? And when Max shot laser with one hand and lightning with the other? And when the red dude hit five people right between the eyes with his daggers? At the same time!?"

"Yes, Noriko, I saw that. We are the same person, remember? You can see only what I can see."

"Y'know what that means, right? We're going home!!!"

"And of course I'm the one who's going to figure out how."

"Do you ALWAYS have to be all gloom and doom?"

"Shut up Nori. This isn't the time to argue with alternate personalities."

The purple haired girl is running towards her, untying a leather jacket from her waist. She may have risked her life, but the look on her face is unmistakable: this is the best day of her life.

She kneels before Null, like a knight paying his respects to the queen, offering the jacket as tribute.

-I believe this is yours, Lady Null.

The leather jacket is an horrible shade of green, but right now it's the most precious gift imaginable.

-Noriko! I'm so happy to see you! – Vesta greets her, hugging her with enough strength to make Noriko wish she was fighting the Oracle again.

-I knew you were still alive and kickin' – Max greets her, offering a high five.

134

-What took you guys so long? – is the very first thing Null says.
-Charming as always – Max comments, rolling his eyes and lowering his hand.
-These are Kari Zel and Torn; they're friends – Vesta intervenes, presenting the new allies.
-Close enough – Torn shrugs.
Then Max asks the question on everybody's mind:
-So, we liberated the city from these spear jerks; now what?
Null wears the jacket, immediately reaching for one of the inside pockets. She recovers the prototype N-Phone that was ready to hit the market before her disappearance, and connects it to the Genius Gun. She knew making the gun compatible with her previous inventions was a long shot, but it pays to be ready for anything.
-We take over the world – she says, firing a shot towards the sky.
The phone's holographic projector creates a large black Ø symbol in the sky, visible within several miles from Deka. The hologram resonates with the air molecules, creating a booming voice:
-<u>This city is now under the law of Null. Hurt my subjects and you will answer to me.</u>

Above the city, a man drops out of supersonic speed. Crossing his arms, he slowly descends to the ground like a disappointed parent ready to lecture his kids. He floats above the crowd, raising his voice to be heard; the jewel in his throat is glowing.
-This is an unauthorized assembly; you are all sentenced to death.
All of a sudden, the crowd's will to rebel against the system is fading; the cold eyes of this man wearing an elaborate black cloak are enough to make them shiver in fear.
-That's an Oracle – Kari whispers to Noriko.
-I figured as much. I am Null, ruler of Null City, and these are the Vanguard; I wish to discuss with your leaders the terms of your surrender.
-"Null City"? – the crowd wonders.
-"Vanguard"? We have a team name now? – Max wonders.
-"Surrender"? – the Oracle repeats, pronouncing the world like it's the most hilarious ever heard.
Without lifting a finger he telekinetically rips the road off the ground, together with Noriko and her allies.
-No one surrenders on Myridia. The will of Demeter is…
135

Null pulls the trigger, releasing the power of the Genius Gun: the Oracle is thrown against the nearest skyscraper, where if it wasn't for his telekinetic shield he would've been squashed like a bug against a windscreen.

The road falls with a roaring sound, almost as loud as the cheers of Myridians.

-Aww come on, I wanted to hear the villain's speech! – Max laments.

-You may get your chance – Vesta answers, pointing at the sky: one after another, new Oracles from all over Myridia are reaching the city.

10- The battle of Null City

Planet Myridia

For the last three hundred years, the Oracles have ruled Myridia with an iron fist. With the planet's infrastructure obliterated by Demeter, Myridians barely have any weapons.

While the Oracles lack the Myridian power to create duplicates at will, the jewel embedded in their throats grant them considerable telekinetic powers. It's hard to rebel against someone who can rip your head off just by thinking about it.

An Asian eighteen year old with silver eyes is now leading the latest uprising, which the Myridian police has been completely unable to sedate. With dozens of Oracles now reaching the city from all over the planet, she doesn't waste time taking charge.

-Vesta, Quantum, full frontal assault: they have telekinetic shields, but I've seen you power through a meteorite the size of a stadium. Torn, if any Oracle tries to land, disarm him or send him back to Vesta and Quantum. Remove the jewels and they're harmless; if you can't get close enough, lethal force is highly recommended.

-You want us to kill them!? – Vesta protests.

-We just declared a war against an entire planet. If you have time to worry about the safety of a superhuman militia that turned entire cities into concentration camps, be my guest. Kari, follow me.

Noriko leaves the trio, and the goddess of fire bites her lip nervously.

-This is wrong. I left Olympus because I hate stuff like this.

-Welcome back to the real world then. CLOAK OF DAGGERS! – Torn shouts, creating enough energy swords in front of himself to be used as a shield; he then run towards the Oracle who's just landed in the middle of the street, deflecting a telekinetic blast by cutting it in half.

-I have no idea how that's possible. You okay, Vesta? – Max asks, turning towards the goddess; as he does this, he turns his right hand into pure light to temporarily blind the Oracles.

-I'm not like my brothers and sisters, Max. I'm a pacifist. I don't know if I can do this.

-Listen, I don't like it either, but you heard Kari: these guys murder people for dressing the wrong way or for not having enough kids. We won't kill anybody unless we absolutely need to, but Myridians have suffered enough. We've got powers: it's time to be heroes.-

137

Torn is slammed into the ground by the Oracle; two more land beside him, ready to hit the red-skinned man with the walls they are now removing from the buildings.

-Less talking, more hitting! – Torn advises.

Moving faster than the eye can see, Vesta punches one of the Oracles hard enough to send him flying right through the building. Quantum takes care of the other one, melting the streetwalk with a focused microwave blast and making him lose his balance; Torn takes his chance and stabs the Oracle, carefully avoiding any vital organ but causing enough shock to render the Oracle unconscious.

-He'll live – is all Torn has to say; when the energy sword disappears, the blood it spilled drops to the ground. Vesta clenches her fists: she doesn't want to do this, but what have two thousand years of watching mortals die accomplished?

-Let's make this quick – she says, flying towards the Oracles.

Inside Nabric Ges' skyscraper, Kari Zel is watching the fight through the window. Oracles charging against Quantum's light form, only to be electrocuted when he converts his mass into electrons. Throwing weapon and objects against Vesta, only to see all of them incinerated. Torn jumping all over the place, using energy swords to scale buildings and shouting things like "stab of the back" when attacking from behind or "mind armor piercing" when cutting through the telekinetic shields, always removing the jewels in their throats with an energy scalpel.

Kari wonders if he knew he could remove them without killing the Oracles before trying. Every time he removes a jewel, he handles it to one of Kari's duplicates that run it back to the base.

Below the fight, the Myridians are revolting against the state police. Civilians outnumber policemen; when each and every one of them create ten thousand duplicates, the city is positively overcrowded with the largest riot this world has ever seen.

-I can't believe this; we're actually winning – Kari wonders out loud.

-Not yet, but I'm working on it – Noriko answers, without looking away from her newest invention.

It's hard to describe it, since it's built from salvaged components that the duplicates of Nabric, Kari and dozens of other voluntaries have recovered from all over the city, but the most striking part of it is the five feet wide reflector dish on top.

-That's, uhm, that's very...I have no idea what that is.

-Our winning card. The Vanguard is powerful enough to stall the Oracles, but they can't protect the whole planet. I want to conquer Myridia, not just Null City.

-Yeah, about that, when did Deka become Null City? Also, since when do you guys go as "the Vanguard"?

-In both cases, when I said so. I suppose I should thank you for helping them find me; I saw what you did during the fight. I know every single form of hand-to-hand combat developed on Earth, but I've never seen most of your moves. I'm not easily impressed, Kari Zel, but you are a valuable asset.

-Just Kari, Noriko. This is the most fun I've ever had. I mean, y'know, if you don't count all the people trying to kill me.

-Tell me about it. How many Oracles are down?

-Fifteen. And it looks like one of them is moving towards...

Kari doesn't end the sentence, interrupted by the Oracle that has just crashed through the wall. He grabs Noriko, wasting no time to exit smashing through the ceiling.

Talas Khanos is furious. He let this miserable planet alone for a few weeks, and now this child is ruining one of the most brilliant social experiments in galactic history.

She can barely hear him through the sound of the crumbling building, until both of them have finished smashing through all of the skyscraper's floors and are now floating in the air.

Khanos is holding her by the throat: even if they weren't flying, she wouldn't touch the ground since he's seven feet tall and she's barely above five.

-The girl with the silver eyes. What are you doing on Myridia?

-Sightseeing – she answers, firing the Genius Gun. Its kinetic blasts bounce off the mental shield of the freakishly tall Oracle; without it, she's completely at his mercy.

-You think this little riot changes anything? Myridia is the best flesh factory in the galaxy. Demeter will never allow it to rebel. She will burn this city to the ground and breed new humans; and she will expect me to keep it producing new soldiers with maximum efficiency. Myridian soldiers fight wars throughout the entire Olympian Galaxy, you stupid little girl; can you even understand the vision of such an endeavor?

139

-I can see what Demeter thinks of humans: animals to be bred and slaughtered at her will. Here's what I have to say about it.

Noriko fires the Genius Gun again, but not towards Khanos: she's aiming for the device, calculating its exact position. She's right, of course, and the kinetic blast provides the energy required to activate it.

-F##k Demeter.

The effect is immediate: an immense electromagnetic pulse spreads from the building, invisible to humans but not to Oracles.

They clench their throats, as the jewels shatter into thousands of pieces together with their power and pride. All over the world, dozens of Oracles find themselves plummeting to the ground or fall prey to the attacks of rebelling Myridians.

The last thing Talas Khanos can see before losing consciousness is the face of the girl with the silver eyes, while both fall to their deaths from the top of the skyscraper.

-Really shouldn't have let me enough time to study your technology – she says, pointing at the godstone integrated in the Genius Gun.

Torn catches them in mid air, using an energy sword as a grappling hook, slowing down their fall until they hit the ground. It's not exactly a perfect save, as Noriko almost passes out from the impact, but at least she's alive.

-Already over? I was warming up – Torn says.

Noriko catches her breath, checking if Khanos is still alive: he knows enough to prove useful. But that's not important right now: the sight of policemen surrendering to the rebels, Vesta and Quantum preventing falling Oracles to become blood stains on the concrete, the people dancing in the streets, everything is awe-inspiring. Even for Null.

"We did it! We saved the world!!!" her human side cheers.

"We completed a coup against an alien state police. This is far from over" Null answers.

"Spoilsport. Can't you at least enjoy the moment!?"

People are chanting her name, praising Null's might and genius. Enemies are praying for her mercy.

She reached Myridia naked, disarmed and helpless. In less than a week, she conquered the planet.

"I am, Noriko. Believe me, I am".

140

Her eyes shine, overseeing the endless possibilities of the galaxy's largest infantry at her disposal.

Her human side shivers.

Khloe VII, capital world of the Demeter Theocracy
Divine Palace

The planet is almost entirely covered in beautiful gardens, carefully tended by subjects from a hundred worlds of the Theocracy. The Gardeners must be sterilized virgins and they are executed after reaching thirty years of age; they are not allowed to see their families or their homeworld.

The Oracles carry out every other duty, constantly in contact with the many provinces of the realm. They report directly to the Lady-In-Waiting, the highest ranking mortal in the Theocracy who answers directly to the Holy Goddess Demeter.

Anesi Mithrades is the current Lady-In-Waiting, selected for the rank at birth and genetically modified to live much longer than a human. Although she looks slightly above fifty, Anesi is already 137.

On Earth she would be considered of Arabian descent; Demeter prefers her Lady-In-Waiting to be of darker skin than most of her subjects, to be able to recognize her at a glance.

She has changed her mind about this in the past, slaughtering entire breeding planets just because she happened to dislike their appearance.

Anesi enters the Divine Gynaeceum, where Demeter lives most of the time. Surrounded by all kinds of flowers, a bath tub the size of a swimming pool dominates the room.

Dozens of Lampyrians are attending the Goddess: stroking her hair, polishing her nails, massaging her feet, watering the flowers, humming tunes about Her glory.

Demeter can't recall if she created the Lampyrians or if she just came across this alien species. They look like human females, except for the blue skin; they can be clearly identified as slaves of Demeter because their bat-like wings have been surgically removed from their backs.

-Please excuse my interruption, Your Holiness. I have news from Icaria.

Demeter lazily invites the Lady-In-Waiting to go on with a casual wave of her hand.

-Hephaestus sterilized it with nuclear fire. Three billion dead and we have lost our stronghold in the sector.

-Don't we have more of those? Just have Myridia send a couple billion reserves.

-That's the other thing I have to tell you, Your Holiness. We have lost all contact with Myridia.

The goddess looks directly at Anesi, who swallows nervously. She lowers her head when Demeter stands up: the punishment for seeing her naked is disembowelment. The Lampyrians scatter, unable to follow their instinct to fly away like a scared flock. The green-haired goddess inhales sharply.

-Get me a towel and a spaceship – she declares.

11- It's good to be queen

Max Black enters the gym yawning. It's not easy to get some decent sleep on a planet with six suns.

It's *probably* still early in the morning, but Kari is already up. She's fighting her own duplicates, something that resembles kickboxing but is practiced with four opponents at a time.

-Hi Max; wanna join? – one of them asks while dodging a kick in the face.

-No thanks, I prefer to get my ass kicked after breakfast. Is, uhm, is any of you the original Kari?

-Nope, we're all duplicates – another one answers. It's slightly unnerving trying to have a conversation with one person while another identical twin answers, but he's getting used to it.

-How would you know?

-We just do. You can φινδ τηε οριγιναλ ατ νθλλ παλαςε.

-I didn't get the last part. Man, I hate this translation thing – Max whines; when Vesta is present he can understand Myridian language without problem, but lately she's been too busy helping with the reconstruction. Another duplicate appears, trying her best to communicate.

-Στθπιδ τρανσλατιον τηινγιε. Λετ'σ σεε...Kari has...hm... ηοω δο I σαυ παλαςε? Home? Kari has far home. Stand under? To speak me okay?

-I appreciate the effort but I have no idea what you want to say. I'll find her myself – Max answers, turning his body into light and disappearing.

It's been almost three weeks since the overthrow of the Oracle regime, and he hasn't picked up a word of the language. Kari has tried hard to learn English, though; her duplicates, at least, since he's never sure when he's talking with the original.

He turns human again on the roof of Null Palace, formerly the Oracle Palace. He knows from experience that trying to walk through the front door and try to talk with Noriko is a waste of time.

He's not alone on the roof: Torn is there, overlooking the city, duster blowing in the wind, leaning on an energy sword like a stylish cane.

-Hey red, have you seen Kari?

-No.

143

-Okay. Vesta?

-No.

-How come you can understand me even when she isn't around? You're not a god too, are you?

-No.

-Any chance you can say *anything else?*

-No.

-Sorry, I must be an idiot to expect a decent conversation from proud warrior guy.

No answer.

-Oh come on, I served you that one on a silver platter!

-You never served me anything. We don't eat together.

-It's just a turn of phrase. Oh I get it, that was a joke right? So you *do* have a sense of humor!

-How do you "turn" a phrase? – Torn asks, sincerely puzzled.

-Nevermind. Nice almost talking to you, Torn.

Sitting in the throne room, Noriko Null is bored. It's not *technically* a throne room because she's not *technically* the Queen, but it doesn't really make a difference. For all intents and purposes, she's now the supreme ruler of Myridia.

It was a natural step: the Oracles eradicated any form of democracy and imposed a complex hierarchy where everything must have a direct superior with absolute power. This is how things have worked for three hundred years, and even Null can't change that overnight.

Still, she's bored. She's typing the draft of the new Myridian Constitution on an holographic keyboard using her right hand, while resting her head on the left hand.

The physical reconstruction is the easiest part. With their power to create ten thousand copies of themselves, Myridians never lack a sizable workforce. They are also extremely fast learners: each duplicate can dedicate all his or her time learning something, and then be re-absorbed by the original transmitting all of the knowledge acquired. The concept of doing one thing at a time is completely alien to Myridian mentality, something even the Oracles were never able to break.

Still, it's a lot of work. Laws need to be written, infrastructure needs to be updated, breeding camps need to be converted to less horrifying enterprises.

Myridia lacks industries, free press, health care, transportation and pretty much anything invented after the 19th century. Agriculture is even more advanced than Earth's, but defense is severely oversized, especially now that Anti-Oracle Devices have been installed all over the planet. And of course many are still loyal to Demeter, even though by her estimation Noriko can count on the support of over 90% of the population.

She's been directing the reconstruction, helped by the fact that she only needs to sleep one hour per night. There isn't a single action involving more than a dozen Myridians that isn't under her supervision. She's bored out of her mind.

-Where do you want this? – Vesta asks, lifting with one hand the green container where the Many is imprisoned. Dozens of hands press against the glass, unable to break it from the inside.

-Throw it into the Sun. Any of the six will do.

-Are you sure? We could learn something from her. From it – Vesta clarifies; it's easy to forget that the Many isn't human.

-I don't have the instrumentation for a proper examination, nor the time to build it. Keeping the Many on the planet will only increase the chances of escape.

-If you say so. Any luck with Talas Khanos?

-He's not talking. Well, aside from proposing an alliance to rule the galaxy together. He's hiding something from me, I can feel it. Luckily I convinced the Provisional Council to commute the death penalty with life imprisonment for all Oracles; he'll talk, eventually.

-I like that. There's been enough death already.

-Vesta, we overthrew a planetary dictatorship with seventy-six casualties. I call that a miracle.

-The seventy-six sure don't – Vesta replies, flying out of the window carrying the container with her. There's no anger in her voice…she doesn't hold the deaths against Noriko…just sadness.

-Was that Vesta flying outside? – Max asks, suddenly appearing in the room.

-You just missed her. She's throwing something into the Sun – Noriko answers, no longer bothered by his habit of never knocking.

-Cool. Speaking of space stuff, I was wondering…when are we going back home?

-I'm working on it – Noriko answers, switching the holographic display from keyboard to a tri-dimensional model of the Myridian solar system.

-I knew you'd say that. It's like your catchphrase or something – Max chuckles.

-I don't have a "catchphrase".

-Sure you do. When was the last time you didn't say "I am Null" *at least* ten times a day?

-I don't say it *nearly* that often. Back to your question, this is the main star of Myridia; they just call it "Sun" in Myridian, but on Earth we know it as Castor.

-Wait a minute, are you telling me you actually *know where we are*!?

-Of course. I am N…Ehm. I've known for weeks; I just had to look at the sky. Although from Earth it looks like one star, it's actually six. It is the second brightest star cluster in the constellation Gemini, with both the star and the constellation named after the mythological Castor and Pollux twins. We are about 49.8 light years from Earth.

-So let me get this straight, the planet where people can create duplicates at will has a star that is actually six twin stars, named after a twin, in a constellation that *means* "twins". What are the odds?

-Significantly higher than the chances of an inhabitable planet orbiting six stars. Given the presence of Drylon technology, I assume Myridia was created artificially. Unfortunately for us, it also means that even you would need 49.8 years to reach Earth.

-Don't they have any spaceship?

-None to speak of, which is what worries me the most. Records show that Talas Khanos arrived with a spaceship shortly before the coup, which means it must have left the planet.

-So no free ride home. Bummer. But I bet little miss genius here can build a new one, right?

-Don't call me that. The Oracles don't have any records on how to build faster-than-light engines; I have some theories, but it would take me decades to build an Alcubierre warp drive. But that's not the worst part…not remotely.

The hologram changes form again: it zooms out to show the whole Milky Way Galaxy, entirely covered in colored patches. Each patch has a name on it: Demeter is right between Hephaestus and Artemis, but it goes on until it covers everything.

-They don't call it the Olympian Galaxy for nothing. There are twelve main regions, and Demeter's one of the smallest. Earth is right on the border with Hephaestus, and according to Oracle records they've been at war for a thousand years. And the only goddess we might count as an ally, Athena, is literally on the other side of the galaxy.

-Whoa. Kinda makes the whole "taking over the world" thing smaller.

-There are about seven thousand hostile planets in the galaxy. *Seven thousand*, Max.

There's something in Noriko's voice…something Max hasn't heard before. She looks like she's about to cry.

-You okay Nori?

-I…I don't know if we can do this, Max. What Demeter did to this planet…Earth would be crushed. And there are seven thousand more! I…I thought I knew everything, that I was prepared to face anything the world could throw at me…Athena was right. We are ridiculously unprepared for this.

Max places a hand on her shoulder. She can be *extremely* unpleasant at times, but he's come to consider her a little sister. A very bossy little sister, but still.

-It's alright Nori, the Vanguard is on your side. You even gave us a superhero team name, how cool is that? And the Myridians are free for the first time in their lives.

-I know, but keeping her in check has become harder. She hardly ever lets me out, and you haven't seen the things she's building in her mind…antimatter power plants, robot armies, death rays…she dreams of invisible spy satellites and low gravity castles on the Moon…

-Okay now you're creeping me out. Are you talking in third person again? Who is "she"?

-My other…

Before Noriko can say "personality", Vesta rushes back into the building; she's in such a hurry she bumps her head in the wall making a noticeable dent, but she's too upset to notice.

-Guys!!! Outside…it's a spaceship! They're invading us!!!

Max is too shocked to say anything; Noriko grabs his wrist to move his hand away from her shoulder. Her eyes shine brightly, quickly suppressing any tears and any glimpse to the girl inside.

147

-Not if Null has anything to say about it.

The spaceship floats right above Null Palace; it's big enough the cast a shadow on half the city.
-The sickle and the leaf. It's her – Vesta says, pointing at the large golden symbol painted on the bottom of the mothership.
-This is bad. Really, *really* bad…last time she was here, billions died – Kari adds; her happy-go-lucky attitude replaced with terror. Max approaches Noriko:
-Nori…about earlier…
-Not now. I'm thinking – she answers; her eyes are already shining like never before.
-Think faster. We're easy targets – Torn says.
-It doesn't matter where we are, if this is really Demeter, she's gonna…she's gonna… - Kari stutters, interrupted by a thunder loud enough to make the whole Palace shake.
Demeter is floating in front of the building. The resemblance with Vesta is uncanny: if it wasn't for the green hair and eyes, they would look exactly identical. She just stands there, surrounded by green energy that keeps her long skirted green dress from blowing in the wind.
The mothership is floating above her, casting a mile-wide shadow.
-Hi sis. You didn't really think you and your pets could take away my toys, now, did you?

Demeter
Art by KodamaCreative

12- The glorious war of sister rivalry
Planet Myridia

Under the shadow of her mothership, the *Twin Dragon*, Demeter is floating above the roof of Null Palace. Noriko, Quantum, Kari and Torn are staring at her, noticing how much she resembles Vesta: other than the green hair, the two sisters are identical.

She seems to have more pride than Vesta in showing off her perfect body, with a scandalously revealing cleavage in her green dress. As her hand is playing with a curl of her green hair, she's looking down at Vesta; not just because she's floating above her, but because Demeter exhudes a sense of pride and superiority.

-Well, well, little sister. Grown weary of that little planet of yours, I see.

-And you're still telling people how they should live their lives. How could you do this to a planet!?

-I know, right? Look at all these ugly buildings – Demeter answers, her eyes shining with green energy. It's been thousands of years since they've met, but Vesta can't forget that look.

-No no no please don't…

Null Palace is ripped in half by Demeter's mind, tons upon tons of steel and concrete straining under immense invisible pressure. She watches smiling, untouched by the large cloud of dust that is spreading though the city. Then she casually topples another building, like a child bored by his toy.

Over two hundred people are already dead. Despite the extremely low population density of Myridia, Demeter still needs to kill thousands more to clean her property.

Vesta flies through the thick cloud of pulverized concrete, yelling at her sister:

-What are you doing!?

-Pest control. You need to be careful with mortals or they'll spread everywhere.

-These are human beings! You can't just kill them whenever you want!

-Oh grow up Hestia. Your hobby was tiresome when were kids, now it's just pathetic.

150

As Demeter prepares to release another green blast, Vesta grabs her hand.

-**What are you doing!?** – Demeter asks, giving Vesta that terrifying look that only gods have.

-I won't let you kill mortals again.

Imagine beings so powerful to be unchallengeable. Immortal children who never lose an argument.

Try to stand up to those beings, those gods, and what do you get? Temper tantrums on a genocidal scale. A wave of Demeter's arm, and Vesta is pushed back at hundred miles per second.

Vesta smashes through three walls before she even realizes she's been hit. Her back hurts; not as much as it should after pulverizing concrete, but she isn't accustomed to pain.

There's a Myridian family in the building she's landed into. They must be refugees: fathers are not allowed to live with their wives and children after they're old enough to join the army.

They must know who she is…there's no Internet or television on Myridia, but word of mouth travels at the speed of light on a planet where everyone can create duplicates of himself. They don't say a word, but there's utter terror on their faces.

The last thing they'll ever see is Vesta's face when she says:

-I'm sorry.

There are over a hundred skyscrapers in Null City, remnants of the civilization Demeter harvested a hundred years ago. Now it's time to complete the job.

Six skyscrapers fly off the ground, surrounded by bright green energy, and are smashed together with maximum force. There are not enough words to describe the havoc of so many tons of glass and concrete exploding at the same time; the sound alone is enough to disintegrate eardrums.

Not counting duplicates, two thousand lives are abruptly ended in less than ten seconds.

Nobody sees the red-headed goddess wreathed in flames fly through the rubble at the speed of sound. Her unstoppable rage meets Demeter's telekinetic green shield.

-Why!? What did they do to you!? – Vesta shouts, her fists failing to do any damage to the shield.

-**They were born** – Demeter answers, her body now saturated with green energy.

151

The thunder created by her blast is loud enough to make the whole city shake. Vesta needs to gather all of her strength to resist its power; the wind alone will soon make more buildings collapse.

-**Is this the best you got? I know you've always been weak, but this is just pathetic.**

It's time for a change of strategy. Vesta grapples her sister and flies away, as fast as she can.

Maybe she hasn't used her divine powers for centuries, but flying is as natural to her as breathing.

Demeter is surprised by this kind of attack; their fights have rarely been so physical. The wind blows her green hair at twenty times the speed of sound. Within half a minute, by the time she understands what just happened, Null City is already a hundred miles north.

Even at this speed, Demeter's telekinetic abilities are more than enough to stop Vesta in her tracks.

Adding insult to injury, Demeter uses her momentum against her; luckily they're far away from any mortals, because no city could possibly survive the next assault.

First, Vesta hits a mountain with her face. Faster than sound, she can't hear her sister's feet pushing her head through the rock. Vesta can lift hundreds of tons without breaking a sweat, but it's not just her sister's weight pushing down. It's the full might of Demeter's mind.

-**And there you are, in the dirt, where you belong. Look at you, the Firstborn of Kronos, wasting her time with worthless mortals. Dad would be ashamed of you.**

Vesta's body is surrounded by flames hotter than the surface of the Sun, forcing Demeter to step back. Not out of pain or fear, since her shield is still intact, but out of surprise.

-I can't believe you're still obsessing over dad! He was an insane tyrant who ATE US!!!

-**He had a vision. A single god ruling the universe, worshipped by all those beneath him. That's the way it was always supposed to be...but you've poisoned the minds of your brothers and sisters. Made them weak. Attached to the mortals. I've worked hard to make things right.**

While listening to her sister's raving, Vesta realizes that the ground is shaking unnaturally. The clouds are moving closer and closer.

-**With this planet's Drylon technology I can rule the galaxy. Like dad. Nobody will take it from me. Least of all, you.**

The world starts spinning. Instinctively, Vesta floats…and her jaw opens wide, looking at the entire mountain rotate on itself to position itself above her. She looks down: there's just a hole below her.

"Did she just lift a mountain with her mind!?" she wonders, an instant before the mountain hits her.

Vesta never really tested the upper limits of her strength; she worked as a waitress until a few months ago. Now she knows she can't lift a dozen billion tons of solid rock.

Trapped beneath the mountain, she can't move a finger. She can't see anything. She can't breathe.

She doesn't need to, of course, but she's lived with mortals for so long that she still tries. She can feel the vibrations of the earthquake Demeter just caused, immensely more destructive than anything Earth has ever felt, and she prays she's taken the fight far enough from mortals.

She hasn't felt this powerless in a long, long time…

Rome, 753 BC

She wasn't there when it happened. The fire was burning in the temple, living proof of the devotion to the goddess Hestia. The goddess whose fire kept homes warm and families safe. The gentle goddess who never raised her hand against her brothers and sisters, who never shared their desire for power. The goddess who couldn't hurt a fly.

The goddess that the young girl worshipped, and whose pure white robes are now red with blood.

-She called your name, you know – Ares taunts her. She will never forget the glee in his voice.

-Praying for your help or some crap like that. She didn't put up a fight…it was quite boring, really. Maybe she was a little too young to be violated. How can you even tell with these mortals?

Hestia carries in her arms what used to be a twelve year old girl. Now she's a bloodied corpse.

-You know what's the most pathetic thing? You don't even know her name. And you know why? Because these fu###ng fleshy things

153

don't f###ing matter, that's why. So stop preaching Zeus and the rest of the fu###ng family to treat them with respect, will ya?

Hestia looks at her brother's son. Her eyes are burning with the heat of a billion stars, and her voice is on fire. Like her father's.

-Her name was Vesta.

Myridia, present day

The mountain melts under the infinite heat. A fiery mass of pure rage flies towards Demeter, grabbing her by the hair and flying towards the ground.

They fly so fast they are swimming through solid rock. The pressure rises as rapidly as the temperature, while the two sisters swim through the molten magma.

Tidal waves of lava will cause every volcano on the planet to erupt within minutes.

Demeter is struggling to break free: she didn't recall her sister to be *that* strong. Heat and pressure rise rapidly as the approach Myridia's core; this isn't a place for any living thing, even for gods.

Taking the battle here is hurting Vesta as much as Demeter, but she isn't thinking straight. She's thinking about the little girl that died 2500 years ago, the one she couldn't save, the one that gods and mortals forgot. The girl whose name will live until the end of time, thanks to her.

She was so naïve, she thinks now. She honestly thought rebelling against Olympus and forcing the gods to leave Earth forever was going to change things. Then she sees it.

There's something above the planet's core. A solid monolith, far larger than anything built by mortal hands. Just standing there, unaffected by the hell that is hurting the goddesses.

-You see that? That changes everything – Demeter says, freeing herself and throwing Vesta against the core itself.

Vesta knows there's a limit to her invulnerability. As her face is pressed against the core, as the flesh is melting in searing pain, she knows she has reached it.

-It's billions of years old. Older then Gaea, older than the oldest gods. It dwarfs even my power. And yet compared to what the Drylon have left us, it's insignificant. Just as you are insignificant now, sister dear.

154

If the descent into hell was quick and destructive, the return to the surface is faster and painful.

The two sisters emerge from the ocean floor. Demeter pushes the water out of the way; what isn't vaporized by the magma creates the largest tidal wave this world has ever seen.

Vesta regains consciousness on the beach. The sand becomes glass under the intense residual heat emanating from her charred skin. She looks like a third-degree burn victim; there's smoke coming out of her flesh. Strangely enough, she still has a full head of red hair and her clothes, though badly damaged and barely holding together, still have enough fabric left to protect her modesty.

Demeter lands on her back with the force of a sledgehammer. The green-haired goddess wipes the sweat off her forehead.

-**So. Ready to give up?** – she asks. Her short breath is the only indication that she just survived a battle with a goddess at the center of the planet.

Null City

Talas Khanos takes a deep breath, inhaling the heavy dust that is clouding the city. Everywhere, people are crying in pain and despair: the city is in ruins and death is everywhere. He takes it all in. It is the most beautiful thing he has ever seen outside of an autopsy.

-VEIL OF PIERCING!!! – somebody shouts. Red energy blades appear everywhere; the wind created by their rotation sweeps the city, clearing the air from the deadly dust.

They just ruined it. And Talas Khanos can see who did it: there's a man with red skin in front of him, next to a man with brown skin.

-Shouldn't that be "piercing the veil"? – Kari asks.

-Shouldn't you stop him, or am I supposed to do everything around here? – Torn answers.

The girl with purple hair pouts. One of her duplicates kicks Khanos in the shin, another one punches in the stomach, and a third one lands on his back. All at the same time. Finally, when he's forced on his knees, the original Kari kicks him in the face.

Khanos spits blood and a couple of teeth. He's starting to hate this planet.

-You don't understand; Demeter can't be defeated. She is a goddess.

155

Something cold touches his neck. It's a fully loaded Genius Gun, and Noriko is ready to fire it.

-I don't care who she is; she's never faced the Vanguard.

13- Our Lady of Kicking Ass

Max Black a.k.a. Quantum doesn't like bullies. He's met his fair share; they never seemed to understand how he could play football but also read comic books and know half of Star Wars by heart. Not until he kicked their asses to protect some poor geek who couldn't fight back.

And until now, he couldn't think of Noriko as a bully. But now he sees the five feet tall Asian teenager about to shoot the seven feet tall Talas Khanos in the head.

He moves at the speed of light to grab her wrist, trying to disarm her without hurting her.

-What do you think you're doing!?

Noriko Null stares at him with her silver eyes. He's known her for a couple of months now, and it's still creepy as hell. Almost as creepy as her deadpan voice.

-Max, my brain contains all the knowledge of mankind. I'm literally the smartest person who ever lived. I know *exactly* what I'm doing: I'm executing an enemy soldier.

-Well in case you haven't noticed, little miss genius, Demeter leveled half a city and *dropped a skyscraper on us.* It's 9/11 times a thousand here; *there's people who need our help.*

-Brown Skin is right. While Vesta keeps her busy, we have a shot at killing Demeter – Torn intervenes. For someone who dropped out of nowhere and tried to kill him, Max thinks that the red-skinned man is right.

-Killing a *goddess*? Isn't that kind of impossible? – Kari asks; a couple of her duplicates shrug.

Noriko is thinking it over. Everybody can see it when her silver eyes shine. She's glancing over the street filled with debris; now that Torn has dispersed the dense cloud of pulverized concrete, the ruins of Null City are in plain sight.

Countless deaths. The last remnants of a once proud civilization ripped to shreds. Children crying, people scared for their lives. Asking forgiveness to the goddess who would gladly slaughter them.

-Alright. Let's kick her ass – Noriko nods.

-As much as I'd enjoy watch you fail, this planet isn't safe anymore – Khanos intervenes, breaking something inside his mouth.

157

His body is suddenly surrounded by a green aura, then dissolves into a beam of light that shoots right into the sky. Everybody is shocked by his sudden disappearance, except Noriko who doesn't waste any time taking her N-phone from her leather jacket.

-Finally. I was afraid I'd have to tell him to do that – she comments, furiously typing something into her phone.

-Ah...what was "that", exactly? – Max asks, scratching his head.

-He had a transmitter inside one of his molars; remote-controlled teleport to the mothership, I suppose.

-Oh yeah, kinda forgot about that – Kari notes, looking up - It's hard to miss a spaceship floating over your head, unless someone *drops a skyscraper on you.*

-There. I can override the signal now. Kari, Torn, you're with me. Max, keep Demeter busy.

She activates the signal, and the three are surrounded by green energy. Noriko cocks the Genius Gun, celebrating the occasion with one of her rare smiles.

-Don't worry. I'll be back with a bigger gun.

Demeter's mothership

Despite being the capital ship of the Demeter Theocracy, the *Twin Dragon* has seen little to no combat in the last millennium.

The ship certainly looks intimidating, with its large wings and the two main cannons in the front, leaving the shadow of a two-headed dragon. But it's little more than Demeter's personal chariot.

It doesn't carry more than a token ceremonial platoon; there is only one guard in the teleporter's room. After all, who would commandeer the warship of a goddess?

The guard is still interrogating Talas Khanos, who beamed inside the ship without permission.

-I'm sorry, sir, but our orders are to keep guard and wait for Holy Demeter. We are not authorized to take you off-planet.

-*Unauthorized remote activation* – warns the teleporter's operator, frantically pressing buttons on his console.

-Clever girl – admits Khanos, stealing the guard's spear and using it to hit him in the face.

While he does this, the teleporter fills the room with green light and beams inside a male with red skin and two females, one with silver eyes and the other one with purple hair.

158

-Secure the control station – is Noriko's first order.

Talas Khanos presses a hidden button on the spear, releasing an energy blast. Torn deflects the blow in mid-air, while two of Kari's duplicates simultaneously disarm Khanos and knock out the guard.

Noriko fires the Genius Gun: the telekinetic blow hits the operator with enough force to throw him against the wall with enough force to take down a heavyweight boxer.

-Do I kill him? – Torn asks, pressing a red energy knife against Khanos' throat, where his godstone used to be.

-You have better things to do; Kari and I can handle the situation here – Noriko answers, nonchalantly disassembling the spear to recover its battery. She glances at the control panel: its flatscreen is showing a great deal of information, but it's not written in Myridian.

-Do you honestly think you can understand Olympian technology? – Khanos mocks her.

-Yes. But right now, I just need to know how to use it.

Using the tip of the spear as a screwdriver, she removes the flatscreen to expose the teleporter's internal wiring. Even she can't hack into a system without knowing its language: she'll have to manually connect the controls to her phone and jury-rig a new control design.

-Give me five minutes.

A mountain range several miles away

Finding them wasn't hard. Flying at the speed of light in his energy form, Quantum can be anywhere on Myridia in less than a second. As useful as it sounds, it also makes everything a very blurry picture. But the devastation left behind by the fight between Vesta and Demeter is so immense and widespread to be unmistakable, even at the speed of light.

Max doesn't want to think how many people would've been killed if the fight took place on Earth. Earthquakes, tsunamis and volcanic eruptions are devastating entire continents; even on this sparsely populated planet, there must already be tens of thousands of victims.

Vesta is on her knees; after surviving a trip to the center of the planet, she's not in the shape to fight anymore. Her skin is slowly growing back from her charred flesh, but Demeter is just fine.

-Just say it, sis. Just admit I am the rightful heir to the throne of Kronos and I'll let some of your pets live. What do you say?

159

-Go to Hades – Vesta answers.

-Our brother won't help you now, sister dear – Demeter says, preparing a devastating telekinetic blow. Before she can release it a blinding flash of light distracts her.

Without giving her time to think, the light then turns into ten thousand volts of electricity. The green-haired sister of Zeus isn't impressed; she withstands the attack with little effort.

Quantum turns back into human form, facing the goddess.

"Not even a scratch. This is gonna be harder than I thought" he admits.

-I don't know you. Are you a god?

-I'm a super-hero. And I'm not gonna quote movies.

-What?

As an answer, Quantum shoots a red laser in her face. To her utmost surprise, the telekinetic shield completely fails to protect her. He ramps up his attack, putting more and more energy into the laser until it's a solid stream of red death flowing towards her.

-How…how did you… - Vesta murmurs, struggling to get back on her feet.

-I can turn into energy, remember?

-No, how'd you get past her shield? I threw her at a planet and it didn't work!

-Her shield is green, but you can see inside it. It means that most visible light can get through it; it's just a matter of finding the right wavelength.

-That's…I fought her for thousands of years and I never thought of that.

-Then I guess Nori isn't the only genius in the team, right?

-ENOUGH!!! – Demeter shouts, generating a massive telekinetic wave. The ground shakes and collapses under the stress and the air itself catches fire from the sudden compression.

-To be honest, I got the idea from an old comic book – Max admits quietly.

-It's the thought that counts – Vesta consoles him.

Demeter is standing in front of them, infuriated. All the sweat and dirt of a long battle is finally beginning to show: her beautiful green dress is in tatters, yet despite facing a high powered laser that could melt titanium there's still enough fabric to protect her modesty.

160

-You are all beneath me! I am the Daughter of Kronos! I am a GODDESS!!! I AM...

There's a sharp whistle, the sound of a bomb dropping. Something lands on Demeter at a hundred miles per hour, sticking a red sword in her heart and a red dagger in her brain.

Demeter falls to the ground. Torn gets off her back, dusting himself off.

-You are too loud.

-Dude! Way to make an entrance! – Quantum greets him, showing him the palm of his hand.

Torn looks at him like he just landed from Mars.

-High five! – Quantum clarifies.

-Five what? – Torn asks back, looking around.

-Guys, I don't think we're done – Vesta notes.

-How'd you get here, anyway? I left you with Null and Kari. Shouldn't you, y'know, shout ridiculous names for your attacks back on the spaceship?

-I don't have to shout to attack. I only do it when I need to concentrate – Torn clarifies.

-Guys, Demeter's getting back up. I think we're screwed here.

-But you didn't call your attacks when you almost killed me and Vesta.

-Exactly.

-GUYS!!! – Vesta shouts, forcing her allies to look at Demeter.

The green goddess is floating before them, bursting with energy and hatred.

-Angry killer goddess. Right.

Demeter's mothership

Like the vast majority of the Theocracy's military, the crew of the *Twin Dragon* is Myridian. Since this mean that each of these soldiers can create at will up to ten thousand duplicates and Kari is just a girl in her mid-twenties, you'd think this is a pretty one-sided fight.

To their utmost surprise, however, they're having a hard time keeping her at bay. They multiply to block her passage and shoot on sight with their spears, but they never hit the original Kari.

When one duplicate disappears after being hit, another one is there to kick the soldier in the face, together with another one to redirect the fire towards another enemy.

161

They're trained to intimidate the opponent through sheer numbers, but Kari knows how to exploit it.

She forces the originals to create duplicates where she wants, preventing them to have a clear shot at her; the fact that spears can't be duplicated is another major point in her favor.

It's like a fast-paced chess game with thousands of players. With a lot of physical violence.

Her mind goes back to when she was just a kid on the run from the Oracles, rescued from her destiny by a former Minister of War.

"The average Myridian sees his duplicates as slaves" the Old Man taught her "They are just tools. You can be more than this, Kari. You aren't a girl with ten thousand slaves: you're a legion".

She stops to take a breath: all around her, the hallway is covered with unconscious soldiers.

She recovers a couple of spears and opens the door to the bridge: a dozen officers are taking aim.

-Last chance to surrender. You have an army, but I am Legion.

Nobody argues with the girl who just took down a Myridian platoon while wearing a pink miniskirt.

14- The day of the godless lightning

Kari Zel enters the engine room of the *Twin Dragon*, where Noriko has been busy since they took over Demeter's mothership.

The young Asian-American is busy building…*something*. Kari doesn't have the slightest clue about what she's looking at: it's a mess of wires, bronze transistors and godstones.

And it's connected to the main engine, the massive glowing sphere that is currently keeping the ship floating above the wasteland that was Null City.

-How's the rest of the Vanguard doing against Demeter? – Noriko asks, covering her silver eyes with a makeshift welding mask as she keeps working.

-They're keeping her busy. Do you really think we can defeat her? She's a freakin' goddess. I know Vesta is a goddess too, but still…

-She's not a goddess. None of them are – Noriko states.

-What do you mean?

-She has vast power over matter and energy, granted, but her actions don't supersede physical laws: she just works around them in ways that we haven't been able to explain yet. Her powers *might* be supernatural, but her actions are not.

-I don't think I follow.

-Max can transform into any kind of energy at will. Is he a god?

-He says he's a superhero, whatever that means; what's your point?

-Max was transformed into Quantum after interacting with an alien device called the Heart of the Universe. What if it's only the first stage of something more radical? What if somebody could control matter and energy with his or her mind? Wouldn't that make her a goddess?

-Like the Oracles do with the godstones. You're saying they're not magic stones, but some kind of godlike technology? Like the Drylon's?

-Godstones transform brain waves into kinetic energy; this ship's teleporter works by transforming matter into energy. I haven't had the chance to duplicate this technology, but I've learned to cripple it.

Noriko takes off her welder mask, then flips a switch. Her invention siphons energy from the main engine, slowly giving off the same eerie green glow.

-The Anti-Oracle Devices – Kari recalls. It's hard to forget something like that.

-Exactly. They cancel out the godstone's ability to sense brain waves by generating a counter-wave, much like my sound nullifier. I'm attempting to connect every A.O.D. installed on the planet to generate a massive wave that, if properly focused, *should* be able to overcome Demeter's mind and nullify her power.

Noriko wipes the sweat from her forehead, leaning over her masterpiece.

-I call it the God Eraser.

-Cool. And you think this thing's gonna kill my goddess?

-Call me a hypocrite, but I pray it does.

A crater several miles away

Demeter has rarely been this angry in the last million years. Not only her stupid sister and her pets are attacking her, they are *hurting her*. She hasn't felt pain for ages, and she doesn't like it.

Quantum returns to his human form, exhausted. Demeter just took a nuclear explosion in the face, *without* her telekinetic shield. He just put everything he's got in a blast that could level an entire city and all he did was piss her off.

-Impressive power. But I am a goddess, you worthless waste of flesh: unlike you, I never tire.

Her body is still glowing green, barely containing the power inside. Cuts and bruises are quickly healing, and even her dress is stitching itself back together.

Demeter watches as Vesta and Torn land beside their ally, the latter attempting another attach unleashing a storm of red energy swords. They all break like glass on her perfect skin.

-In retrospect, maybe attacking without a plan wasn't a great idea – Quantum admits.

-There was a plan – Torn answers.

-Oh really? What was it, fight until we're barely able to stand and die anyway?

-Distraction.

All four of them disappear in the rapid flash of the teleporter.

Null City

Demeter isn't used to disorientation. It takes her a few seconds to adjust her godly senses to her current situation: she's back into mortal-infected territory, where the flesh crops are watching her with religious terror.

These Myridians have never seen her before. They've heard about Demeter all their lives, how they should respect her every wish unless they wanted to be slaughtered. The first thing they do is fall on their knees and pray for her forgiveness.

-Now, that's more like it. Your kind has been trained well; I just might spare a few of you for the next harvest, if you bow down to me.

-Don't – Noriko orders, climbing the ruins of Null Palace to be seen by the people.

The Myridians look at her with a mixture of respect for the girl that crushed the former regime and fear of Demeter's wrath.

-This...*thing* you call a goddess is nothing more than a transcendental lifeform with the natural ability to control matter and energy at will.

-She's also bat##it insane – Quantum adds.

-I recognize you. You're one of my sister's pets. You want to appeal to my mercy?

-I am Noriko Null of Earth. I'm the most intelligent person in the galaxy. And I want you to surrender.

-Intelligence? HA! You does that measure up against GODHOOD!? – Demeters retorts, lifting her hand to deliver a telekinetic blast.

Noriko answers by pulling her gun and shooting first; the pure kinetic energy hits Demeter with the force of a freight train going five hundred miles an hour, and her body is thrown back by the impact.

-Pretty good, actually – Noriko boasts.

Noriko jumps off the rubble, walking towards the pile of dirt where Demeter has landed. The Myridians step aside, not wanting to be mixed up with the 90 pound teenager that just smacked around their goddess.

-This is a Mark II Genius Gun, Demeter. It fires focused kinetic energy with enough force to punch a hole into a five-inch thick steel plate. Which, from what I've seen, should hurt you less than a drop of rain. Now...how does this feel?

When Demeter tries to stand up, a shot to the knee forces her to fall into the dust again. She lets out a scream of pain and rage, but her voice has lost some of the power behind it.

-**What are you doing to me?** – she asks, watching her own hands. She can't make the dirt go away, and the blood coming out of her knee is spilling over the wreckage.

-The Mark II is linked directly to the God Eraser on your ship. I'm turning off your "godliness".

-**You can't...do** this...to me... – Demeter insists, gathering all of her strength just to stand up. In a way, Noriko admires her stubbornness: a human would've already lost consciousness for the loss of blood, but despite appearances Demeter is far from human.

-The hell I can't. You've killed millions of people, destroyed an entire civilization, elevated misery into worship of your petty ego. Somebody has to stop you.

-And you think you're the one to do it? *You* will pass judgment on a goddess?

-I won't – Noriko answers, throwing the Genius Gun away and opening her arms.

-<u>They</u> will.

Demeter doesn't understand, and looks around with a puzzled look on her face...until she looks up.

There's an immense dark cloud in the sky, gathering the total sum of all the knowledge of Myridia.

Static electricity fills the air. All over Myridia, every single mortal brain is downloading everything into the cloud. Demeter feels it, the same way she feels Noriko is somehow acting as relay for the three hundred million brains on the planet through the God Eraser's power.

She also feels what's in that cloud. Three hundred years of hatred for her.

Demeter has experienced fear before. Tired, dirty, bleeding, with no one to come to her rescue, she now knows what it means to be terrified.

-You can't do this to me! **My brot**hers and sisters…they will declare war **on y**ou!

Noriko is now at the center of this planet's mind. And for a moment she feels the same thing she felt the day that Athena granted her the knowledge of Earth.

The feeling that nothing is impossible. That <u>nothing</u> can stand against her.

-You still don't get it, you tiny little mind.

The cloud discharges all of its power with the most powerful lightning strike this world has ever seen. Three hundred years of death and destruction hit Demeter's mind; the God Eraser forces them to her very core, embedding every single image into her dark soul.

She sees the last memory of every man, woman and child she's killed. Her immortal mind, once capable of lifting mountains, is melting like snow. Feeling every moment of it.

Noriko is watching her, in front of the raging electrical storm. But in the last moments before Demeter's mind drifts into oblivion, she can see her not like a eighteen year old human girl.

She sees her negative image, silver eyes replaced with black, with black tendrils that link her brain to a magnificent web spanning thousands of years of knowledge.

-*I am Null. And I just declared war on the whole fu##ing galaxy.*

That dark voice echoing every word that's ever been spoken on Earth is the last thing Demeter will ever hear.

When the electrical storm passes, Noriko is standing on top of the motionless body of Demeter, the wind blowing her horribly green leather jacket.

Thanks to the link to the Myridian collective consciousness that just ended, no one alive today on this planet will ever be able to forget this moment.

That's when Noriko passes out.

Later

Noriko opens her eyes with a splitting headache. Her silver eyes shine when her superhuman mind races to assess the situation, escalating it to a migraine.

She's in a bed. She tries to sit down, but two duplicates of Kari prevent her to move.

-Don't even think about it. You need to rest.

-It'd be easier without all this noise. My head's already on fire, what's this music?

-There's people dancing in the streets. It's four days AL, but they're still celebrating.

-"AL"? – Noriko repeats, attempting again to sit down. She has to hold the sheets against her breasts; she's not wearing any clothes.

-This planet's habit to undress me while I'm unconscious is really annoying.

-"After Lighting"…that's what people call the day when you killed Demeter.

-So my plan worked. I wasn't sure I could do it…I never channeled another planet's collective knowledge before. I'd like to examine the body – Noriko adds, jumping out of bed…and immediately falling into the hands of the two duplicates, since her body is still too weak to walk.

-Easy there. You've been through a lot – says one Kari.

-Vesta already took her sister's body. She wouldn't say where – says the other one.

-Then I need to talk to her. There's so many things – Noriko adds, but Kari shuts her up by placing a finger on her lips.

-You've saved the world, boss; now you need to rest. The next impossible thing can wait tomorrow.

-Maybe you're right – Noriko answers, laying on the bed – It'll be a whole other week before we get back home.

15- How not to be a super-villain

Planet Myridia

Kari Zel is sitting on the beach. Two of the six suns are high in the sky, and a third one is near dawn; the wind keeps blowing her purple hair into her face.

Max Black, also known as Quantum, appears right next to her in a bright flash of light. She's not bothered for his sudden appearance; there's nothing unusual with it on Myridia.

-Penny for your thoughts – he says.

-What's a penny?

-Uhm, it's a small coin that, nevermind. I just wanted to know how you feel.

-I'm gonna miss this place, Max.

-Yeah, it's a nice beach.

-But I bet your planet's awesome too – Kari answers cheerfully, standing up and shaking the sand off her pink dress.

-You know you don't need to come to Earth with us, right? You could stay here.

Kari's smile fades. She recovers a backpack laying a couple of feet behind her; she moves it to make it clear that it's half empty.

-This is everything I own, Max. My family's been harvested years ago; I've been on the run since I was five years old. I'm tired of running…it's time to find something new.

-Fifty light-years away? Are you sure you're not running away again?

-Let me put it another way. If you had a chance to see a new world, would you throw it away?

Max smiles. This trip was worth it after all.

-If I ever do that, promise me you'll take me back to Myridia and never let me leave.

Twin Dragon, Demeter's former mothership
Orbiting Myridia at 1.200 miles altitude

Torn is leaning against the control station; his red skin and old duster stand out in the futuristic bridge. Noriko is laying with her back on the floor, working under the station like a mechanic in her workshop.

-Scissors – she orders, extending her hand from under the station.

-What?

169

-You create energy swords with your mind, don't you? I need a pair of scissors here.

-I don't know what that word means.

-Two blades joined by a swivel pin at the middle that allows them to be opened and closed.

-That doesn't sound like a useful weapon.

-I don't need a weapon, Torn, I just need something to cut a wire.

-I can cut the whole thing with my mind, you know.

-You can probably cut the ship in two, but I'm planning to use it. Scissors, *please*.

Torn sighs, and a pair of bright red energy scissors appears in Noriko's hand. He watches her work for a few seconds before she comes out of the station. He tries not to stare at her, but he can't help it: how could this frail child have killed a goddess?

-That was the last of the ship's tracking devices; now we can leave Myridia and no one will find out where we're headed. Are you sure you wanna come with us, Torn?

-Yes.

-You're not the talkative type, I see.

-No.

-What about Old Man Vor? I thought you had some kind of debt towards him.

-The Oracles are dead. He's part of the Provisional Government. We're even.

-You're not gonna tell me anything about who or what you really are, aren't you?

-No. You seem...strangely fine with the idea.

-I'll find out eventually; I am Null – she shrugs.

-I see.

-But we need to lay down some rules. You won't kill anyone on Earth without my consent, unless in self-defense after every other option has been tried. Understood?

-...

-It's not open for negotiation, Torn.

-Fine. I'll *try* not to kill people on your planet. Happy now?

-It's a start.

There's a flash of green light, signaling the arrival of Quantum and Kari by means of the ship's teleporter. Kari's two duplicates already

170

on the bridge rush to get her bag, while Quantum is busy enjoying the moment.

-Permission to come aboard, Captain – Quantum salutes, standing at attention and barely keeping a straight face.

-You're already on board – Torn informs him, confused.

-He's just quoting something. He does that – Null clarifies.

-Oh come on Nori, can't you crack a smile at least once? <u>We've got a freakin' spaceship!!!</u>

-What would I do without your ever so keen sense of observation – Null answers in the most deadpan way possible, recovering her N-Phone from the inside pocket of her horrible green leather jacket and activating the hologram generator.

The air fills with a tridimensional picture of the galaxy with a superimposed red dotted light.

-By studying the Oracles' records, I believe that Demeter's homeworld is about 40.000 light-years away from Myridia; since it took this ship 21 days to cover that distance, I estimate the *Twin Dragon* can fly at least 700.000 times faster than light.

-How long will it take us to reach your world? – Kari asks.

-Earth is 50 light-years away – Null answers, shutting off the hologram.

-So, how long? – Quantum asks.

-50 years divided by 700.000 – is what Null answers, even though she means "you should know this already".

Quantum and Torn look confused. Kari is counting on her fingers.

-38 minutes – Null clarifies, meaning "I can't believe I have to spell this stuff for you guys" – But since there are no records about Earth's stellar neighborhood in the ship's database, we should be as careful as possible. We'll keep a maximum speed of 70.000 times the speed of light.

-So, how long? – Quantum asks.

-You know what? I'm gonna go check on Vesta – Null answers, throwing her arms in the air.

Cargo bay 2

Gods don't have mourning rituals. They don't have centuries of traditions on how to pay their respects to their dead, because they don't believe that gods can die.

171

But Demeter is laying lifeless, arms crossed over her chest; her corpse looks more like a beautiful sculpture than a dead body. Vesta is sitting in front of the casket, tending to the live flame that floats before her sister's corpse.

Noriko approaches her carefully; from her breathing, she can tell Vesta's been crying silently.

-For what it's worth, she left me no choice. She would've killed millions of Myridians.

-I know, Nori. I don't blame you for this. It's so weird...we didn't get along. Gaea, she could be such a bi##h, but she was my sister.

-Maybe humanity's been rubbing off on you – Noriko tries to console her, placing her hand over the goddess' shoulder.

-She wasn't always like you saw her, you know. She was so happy, tending to her gardens; not a care in the world. Gaea, we were so young...

-What are you gonna do with her?

-You won't dissect her, Noriko.

-I didn't say...

-You were working your way around it. I'll throw her body into the Sun; maybe there she'll find the peace she lost a long time ago.

-Something tells me that's not open for discussion.

-I've never been a traditional goddess, but there are boundaries even I won't cross.

Null nods politely, taking a step towards the door.

-Nori. The weapon you used to kill Demeter...

-The God Eraser.

-You came up with it pretty fast, even by your standards. It wasn't designed to be used against me, right?

-Of course not – Noriko lies.

The *Twin Dragon* bridge

Max Black a.k.a Quantum is sitting on the golden throne that oversees the bridge; it's not just the color, it's a solid block of gold. Kari and her duplicates are manning every station, while Torn is brooding in a corner.

-Are you sure you know how to drive this thing? – Max asks.

-It'd be easier if I could read more of this stuff – Kari answers, punching some commands into one of the flatscreens to load information from the ship's systems.

172

-It's Ancient Olympian. Dead language – Torn explains.

Noriko Null enters the bridge from the only door that leads outside, adding:

-I've uploaded a translation program into the ship's computers; navigation and propulsion data can be accessed in English and Myridian now. I'll work on the rest as soon as I can.

-You translated the language of the gods? *In a day!?* – Kari asks.

-She does that – Quantum nods.

-Is there anything you can't do? – Kari insists, still amazed.

-Here it comes – Quantum mumbles, expecting another "I am Null, I can do everything".

Instead, Noriko looks each ally in the eye, one after another, and says:

-There is *one* thing I'm not very good at. Saying thank you.

-Well, what do you know, little miss genius *does* have a heart – Quantum comments.

For that, he gets a stern look from Noriko. Her silver eyes flash fiercely for a second.

-Max. That is <u>my</u> throne, if you don't mind.

The African-American hero moves away from the throne at the speed of light. Noriko takes her place, trying to sit down like a solemn queen.

She's too short for that, and when on the throne her feet don't touch the ground; she crosses her legs to seem a little less ridiculous.

-This is just the beginning. We sent a message to the gods: they can't treat mortals as personal property anymore. If we stay on Myridia now, we risk turning it into a bigger target.

-A word, Captain? – Max asks.

-*Please* stop calling me that – Noriko sighs.

-You were…quite passionate about the whole "taking over Myridia" thing. Not that I don't miss Earth too, but why are we *really* leaving so soon?

-I thought you of all people would've known, Max: I'm trying not to be a supervillain. Kari, are we ready to leave yet? – Null asks, quickly changing the subject.

-Engine is set for 70.000 lightspeed…I think – one Kari answers.

-Navigational control is on line. We can leave as soon as you give the word – another adds.

-Then set a course…for home – Max says dramatically, earning Noriko's patented death glare.

-Shutting up now – he promises.

Noriko adjusts her position on the golden throne, far too big for her. She glimpses at Max, whose body language is practically *screaming* "come on, say it". She decides to indulge him.

-Destination Earth, 70.000 lightspeed. Engage.

The *Twin Dragon* quickly accelerates beyond common physics, reaching over the stars.

16- A romantic slayer of gods

After Athena's gift, Noriko's brain doesn't need sleep anymore; since it's powered independently from the rest of her body, theoretically it can work forever.

Her body and her mind are another story, which is why she's fallen asleep on the golden throne of the *Twin Dragon*, the mothership stolen from Demeter.

She wakes up suddenly when something crashes into the ship so hard that Noriko falls from the throne. She's still half asleep when she hears Max:

-This can't be good.

-That felt like we hit something – one of Kari's duplicates says.

-In space!? – answers another.

-Report. <u>Now</u> – Noriko orders, getting back on her feet and fighting the urge to yawn.

Max disappears for a second, turning into x-rays and leaving the ship.

-There's nothing out there – he says when turning back into human flesh.

-Can we run a diagnostic? – Null asks.

-I can't understand what half of this thing is saying, what do you think? – Kari answers, pointing at the screen.

-We're in dark space – Torn intervenes.

-Care to elaborate? – Null insists.

-Ships can't fly here. Nothing moves faster than light in dark space.

-Nothing moves faster than light *anywhere* – Noriko states.

-Says the girl who hijacked a spaceship – Max objects.

-Alright, point taken. Kari, have Vesta translate what the ship is saying. Max, go back outside and explore the nearest light-minute, I want to make sure we're really alone out here. Torn, you're with me: I want to see if our "guest" has any clue about our situation.

Deck 7

Talas Khanos is sitting in his prison, waiting. He's so freakishly tall that he can look Noriko in the eye when she's standing up.

-I see you brought your butcher with you. Finally found the guts to kill me?

-Just wait – Torn teases him.

175

-Consider yourself lucky, Khanos; if I'd left you on Myridia you'd be in much, much worse conditions. I believe you know too much to be left out of my sight – Noriko explains.

-In other words, you need me.

-The first Oracle I met described the Many as a biological weapon; one that you created. Did Demeter deploy one of them on Earth?

-I don't know what you're talking about – Khanos answers, keeping his tone as neutral as possible.

-I met the Many a few *minutes* after my transformation. Someone must've transported it to New York; are there Olympian agents on Earth?

Talas Khanos laughs, exuding arrogance and condescension.

-It must be hard for you. Living your life in a miserable corner of the universe, believing yourself to be all-knowing, only to find out you're at the bottom of the galaxy's pecking order.

-What's that supposed to mean? – Noriko asks. Her silver eyes shine in anger.

-You're the genius; figure it out yourself.

The thin giant and the teenage girl look at each other, understanding that neither will admit that the other one knows a lot more than is willing to share.

-Let's go. This is a waste of time – she finally orders.

Bridge

Vesta is hunched over one of the control panels, trying to make sense of the situation. Ancient Olympian is her native language, so she can read perfectly the words the computer is writing. She just doesn't know what they actually mean.

-Give me some good news, people – Noriko asks, returning to the bridge.

-Life support is fine; we can stay here as long as we want. Well, at least I can; we've got a lot of rations but no way to grow new food, so...

-I don't plant to settle down here, Vesta. Is navigation working? I need to know where we are.

-We're five minutes from Neptune – Max answers, suddenly appearing next to Noriko.

-Isn't that one of Poseidon's old names? 'Cause I really, *really* don't want to run into Poseidon – Kari asks, shivering at the very thought.

176

-It's a planet in our solar system. Good job, Max.

-Just don't ask me to find Uranus next – he jokes, causing Noriko to roll her eyes.

-I don't get it – Torn comments.

-Lucky you. Five minutes at light speed, right? Given the current position of both planets in their orbits, that places us nearly four light-hours from Earth or 4.2 million kilometers.

Vest and Max look at Noriko with a puzzled expression. She corrects herself, used as she is now to think in metric like most of the world.

-2.6 million miles. Max can get there in four hours, but he can't bring any of us with him.

-I can get back too. I can fly in space, you know; I'll just get out there and push – Vesta boasts.

-Cool, what are we waiting for!? – Kari asks, excitedly.

-And when we get there? I don't think a ride like this is easy to park – Max highlights.

-I'm not planning on taking it to Earth. It's too dangerous to land there – Noriko objects.

-So you're going to…what, just abandon it here?

-I didn't say *here* – Noriko says, smirking.

Triton, Neptune's largest moon

With its surface covered by frozen nitrogen, this is the coldest place in the solar system at minus 400°F. The atmosphere is so thin here that the sound of the *Twin Dragon*'s landing is little more than a whisper.

Vesta steps out of the airlock wearing her signature orange tube top and pants; even she feels a chill when her bare feet touch the nitrogen ice.

She takes a deep breath, and flames start to erupt from the icy wasteland. A ring of fire surrounds the *Twin Dragon*, keeping it at a slightly cozier minus 100°F.

Noriko wipes the frozen moisture from the window with the sleeve of her horribly green leather jacket. She snaps a picture with her N-Phone.

-Look at it. It's so beautiful out there.

-It's ice – Torn comments.

-It's an alien world of ice volcanoes and geysers of sublimated nitrogen. It's right on our cosmic doorstep and we've only sent a probe in 1989. This…this is what we should be doing.

-Taking pictures. Of ice.

-What can I say? I'm a romantic – Noriko smiles, innocently. Torn looks at the seemingly unimposing girl and wonders aloud.

-Yes. A romantic slayer of gods.

Noriko ignores him, talking instead to the N-Phone and looking at the hatch.

-Last call, Kari.

-Just a sec! – the Myridian girl answers, hugging her duplicate. Or at least Noriko *thinks* so…they could *both* be duplicates for all she knows.

-Be careful out there – Kari warns.

-You too – the other one answers, closing the hatch and locking the only access to the escape pod.

-Everyone, remember where we parked – Noriko says. The last words she says on Triton.

Outside, on the surface of the frozen moon, red chains made of interlocked curved knives appear out of nothing, securing the escape pod. Vesta grabs the chains, carefully avoiding any sharp edge, and starts to float.

She gains altitude, ignoring the gravity that tries to keep her down, and quickly rises over Triton's feeble atmosphere. She takes a good look at Neptune, wondering if she'll ever see her brother Poseidon again. But her mind is on Earth now.

She once considered her exile on that planet as a badge of shame, but now she can't wait to see her home once again.

The escape pod isn't comfortable. There is limited space, which is why Max is traveling besides it in his radio wave form. Noriko is sharing the pod with two persons who have never seen Earth before. Then finally Torn, of all people, decides to break the ice.

-Khanos knows something.

-We're going back for him, right? I know he's behind bars and my duplicate's keeping an eye on him, but…I don't like the idea of her alone with that monster so far away from anyone else.

-I thought Myridians were never alone – Noriko recalls.

-It's what we tell ourselves – Kari answers, looking outside the window. She can feel the acceleration as Vesta kicks into high gear.

-If my estimation is correct, and of course it is, Vesta can reach a fifth of the speed of light in a vacuum. Even given time for a safe orbital re-entry, a Triton-Earth trip should take her less than twenty-four hours.

-You mean we can get her back in a couple of days?

-Unless he kills her – Torn clarifies.

-You must be *so* fun at parties – Kari retorts, sticking her tongue out.

-So you've *never* heard about Earth before? Demeter seemed to be barely aware of it.

-I've heard of planets without gods – Torn recalls – Once in a while the gods find worlds they'd forgotten. They don't do a very good job at tending to their domain.

-Now *that*'s an understatement – the Myridian girl underlines.

-No ship captain would explore a dark space system. The risk to be stranded is too high.

-What about a Talos? – Noriko asks.

-Hephaestus tin soldiers? They fly without ships. How do you know them?

-I defeated one on Earth a while ago.

Torn raises an eyebrow. Given the past weeks, Noriko knows it's the full range of his facial expressions.

-They're supposed to be undefeatable.

-I know, that's why I had to defeat it.

-I see. Since we're in dark space, if it sent a message to the other Talos it would take years for Hephaestus to receive it.

-It seems no god except Athena knows where Earth is – Kari says.

-Maybe she's the one who sent the Many to kill you – Torn suggests.

-Right after giving me all of mankind's knowledge? Sounds a little overcomplicated.

-Athena plays by her own rules – Torn replies enigmatically.

-Maybe. I can't shake the feeling someone's playing a completely different game than I first thought.

The awkward silence returns. None of the three people inside the escape pod have much to say for almost a minute.

-So, what're you gonna do when we get back to Earth? – Kari asks.

-A very long shower, a dozen cups of coffee and a change of clothes – Noriko answers, looking out of the window.

179

They're already way past Neptune, and all she can see are thousands of stars. Many of which, she now knows, are the personal property of genocidal gods.

-Then I need to talk to my mother – she adds.

OF GODS AND MOTHERS

Athena
Art by KodamaCreative

1- Fighting space gods doesn't pay the bills

Earth is finally visible from the *Twin Dragon*'s escape pod, looming large in the round window.

-Oh my gods, it's so beautiful – Kari says, almost crying at the view.

-I've seen worse – is all Torn is willing to concede.

-We need to decelerate. Max, can you hear me? – Noriko asks, talking to her N-Phone.

-*Loud and clear* – is the answer coming from the phone.

-How is he talking in space? – Kari wonders aloud.

-*By turning into radio waves. You know, we're going really fast out here. Vesta is doing her best to slow down, but we could really use some direction here.*

-Relax, it's an uncontrolled atmospheric re-entry. Just rocket science – Noriko replies.

-*If you're trying to reassure me, maybe you should switch to "piece of cake".*

-Same thing for me, really. Alright, here's what we gonna do.

There's a bright flash in Noriko's silver eyes, the same kind that always accompany the use of her superhuman mind. Only this time it's so bright it makes her eyes disappear in a pool of white fire, and she falls to her knees.

-Not now…need to…hold back…

Kari doesn't waste any time to help her, even though it hurts her mind to look at her eyes.

-What's wrong, Nori? Hold back what?

-H̲u̲m̲a̲n̲i̲t̲y̲ – Noriko says with a thousand voices.

-*Guys? We have a situation here!* – the N-Phone shouts.

Outside, Vesta is plunging into the atmosphere feet first, carrying the escape pod on her back; the friction is already surrounding it with flames. But it's not what worries her: she's the goddess of the hearth, and no flame will touch her friends if she doesn't want to.

But there's a storm brewing over the skies. A lightning storm that spans the entire planet…until all the electricity starts to rise and shoot a single, colossal bolt towards the prodigal sons of Earth.

-No. Freakin'. Way – are the words on Vesta's mouth.

Max turns his body into a pure electron flow, trying to somehow lead the lighting somewhere else. It's useless: the bolt carefully avoids both him and Vesta, moving as if it has a mind of its own, and hits the escape pod.

Inside it, the sparkles creep over the walls and leap straight towards Noriko. Torn quickly pushes Kari aside, but it's not necessary: the lightning strike isn't intended for her, and it's no lightning strike at all.

It's an update.

Noriko screams in pain as six weeks of information are fed directly into her brain; her body shakes uncontrollably, making the whole process similar to an epileptic seizure.

-What's going on!? – Kari screams.

-Looks like the same thing that killed Demeter – Torn answers, materializing a red energy sword in his hand and using it to cut the lightning.

Noriko's body goes limb.

Route 283
Ness County, Kansas

The escape pod is a bus-sized cylinder made mostly of titanium and aluminum; it should've disintegrated long before touching the ground. Instead, the drivers can see a red-haired goddess gently lay it down in the middle of a field.

-What the f##k happened!? – Max asks, materializing in front of the pod; he's so upset that he forgets to put on his Quantum mask. Torn cuts a hole in the pod's walls, and two Kari carry Noriko outside.

-The lightning attacked her. So I cut it – Torn answers.

-She's breathing, but something's not right – Kari says taking her pulse. A duplicate checks her eyes: the pupils are fully dilated. The eyes are more unpolished grey metal than silver.

-We need to take her back home – Max decides.

-A 1400 miles flight? In her conditions? – Vesta asks.

-I think she's coming to – Kari says happily. Noriko finally opens her eyes; their silver light is dim and intermittent, but it's back.

She gets back on her feet, leaning on Kari to avoid falling down, and she points her finger at Torn.

-Never…cut the signal…again.

-If you say so – Torn answers bluntly.

183

-You almost killed her, you idiot – Max says, giving him a soft punch to the shoulder. Torn doesn't flinch, which might explain why it's like punching a wall.

-Hardly. He simply disconnected me from the worldmind during my monthly update; I had to reboot my brain to fix the damage.

-Wait, you can *reboot your brain*!? – Max repeats, impressed.

-"Monthly"? You mean you have to be struck by lightning like that *every month*!? – Vesta asks; Noriko was in a lot of pain during the whole process. She can't imagine having to do it regularly.

-Why do you think I live on the top floor? Unfortunately, this means I have no knowledge on anything that happened on Earth during the last six weeks.

-Just great. So…now what? – Max asks.

-We head back to Null Tower. Normally I'd ask Vesta to fly me there, but with Torn and Kari…

-We need a vehicle. Gotcha – the Myridian girl nods, walking towards the road.

At every step, two duplicates appear by her side. When the first car approaches a few seconds later, twelve Kari have formed a human chain that prevent it from going any further.

The car comes to a screeching halt to avoid hitting any of them, and the driver starts to sound the horn and to shout:

-Hey, what's the holdup!? Stupid kids…

The driver walks out of the car, ready to deliver an ear-splitting rant to the purple-haired twins that are blocking the street. Instead he comes face to face with the most beautiful woman he's ever met.

-Excuse me, sir, but we need a ride to New York City. Would you mind taking us there? – Vesta asks with the most warm and kind voice the man has ever heard.

-No, I…I wouldn't mind at all, I guess – the man stutters.

Then something punches a fist-sized hole through the car's hood. The Genius Gun is still hot from the shot when Noriko aims it at the driver.

-Scram.

The driver doesn't need to hear the order twice, and starts running for his life. Vesta grabs the gun from Noriko's hand, like a mother scolding her child.

-What are you doing!?

184

-We just need the car. What if I told you he's a registered sex offender?

-How would you know? – Vesta asks, shocked.

-I am still Null – Noriko answers, sitting in the car. Torn follows riding shotgun; Kari makes her duplicates disappear and takes the back seat.

While Max turns into energy disappearing at the speed of light and Vesta lifts the car over her head, Torn asks softly:

-Was he really a criminal, or did you just need some space?

-I thought you were the quiet one – is Noriko's only comment on the matter.

She then just looks at the ground moving farther and farther away when Vesta starts flying, carrying the car on her shoulders in a 1400 miles trip back home.

New York City

It takes Max much, much less than the blink of an eye to be back: as usual, changing from flesh to energy and vice-versa takes most of the time. He flips the switch, but he can't turn on the lights: the apartment is still in the dark.

-Of course, it's been six weeks. Fighting space gods doesn't pay the bills.

It's easy to fix when Max's entire body changes into pure light. Now he can see that the room has been stripped down to little more than walls and floor.

There's no more shelves of comic books, no boxes of DVDs and comic books, no furniture with action figures sitting on top, and the comic books are also gone.

Not since fighting a killer goddess on an alien planet has Quantum been so mad.

Just outside the building, a man is holding a black plastic bag, mumbling to himself.

-What's the point of owning a building if you gotta take out the thrash?

A laser beam disintegrates his garbage. Terrified, the man's gaze follows the beam's trajectory…where a masked man is scowling at him.

-31B. What happened?

-I don't… hey you're Quantum! Can I get an autograph?

185

The man shields his eyes from the massive release of light, and finds himself with Quantum's hands holding his jacket.

-Apartment 31B. It's empty. Why?

-The black kid's room? He disappeared weeks ago. Dunno where he went.

-What about his stuff?

-Why do you care? Bunch of crap. Dunno why the suckers paid so much for it.

-"Suckers"?

-Chinese guys. Paid a couple grand to buy everything an' keep my mouth shut.

-Chinese. Why would the Chinese pay to get my...wait. You sure they weren't Japanese?

-Maybe. What am I, immigration? Look, I don't want any trouble, okay?

-You're not the one who needs to worry.

Quantum disappears in yet another flash of light, leaving his former landlord to wonder what in the world just happened, standing in front of the ashes of disintegrated garbage.

-I need more tenants like that.

Null Tower, Upper East Side

The sun is setting, and the giant Ø symbol on the top of the latest addition of the Big Apple's skyline is casting its shadow over the city.

Vesta carefully puts down the car right in front of the building; after sustained flight over half the country, the vehicle's definitely seen better days.

A duplicate of Kari appears in front of the car, opening the door.

-Nice ride – Noriko says, looking like she's seconds from throwing up.

-Sorry it took so long. I couldn't go supersonic without killing you – Vesta apologizes.

-We should do it again!!! –the original Kari says, jumping out of the car with the joy of an eight year old that's just been on her first roller coaster.

-Indeed – says Torn, with the enthusiasm of an eighty year old queued at the post office.

186

Suddenly Quantum appears in front of them, practically shouting at Noriko's face:

-You mother stole my comic books!!!

Noriko sights, rubbing her eyes. On top of her migraine, now *this*.

-Ma...*Quantum*. I'm gonna check whether the most powerful weapon in the galaxy is still where I left it. If everything's alright, *then* I'll worry about more trivial things. And after *that* I'll worry about your stuff.

Without saying another word, she reaches the front door...where two armed guards are waiting.

-I'm sorry, miss, but the Tower is in lockdown. No unauthorized guests.

-I am Null. This is my home. Let me in and...wait. I don't remember hiring you.

Suddenly, a hologram appears in front of the guards. It's another Noriko Null.

-*Unless you want things to go ugly, impostor, you will leave this place at once.*

-How dare you impersonate me!? I am Null!!!

-*Not anymore* – the hologram says with an evil smile.

-I'm never getting my comic books back – Quantum whines.

2- Home is where people don't try to kill you

It's eight PM and Jane Blake is watching TV with her parents. It's not how she thought to pass this Saturday evening, but the latest news left her no choice.

Vesta and Quantum have returned after disappearing for six weeks, and the news are having a blast speculating on their absence. But while she's captivated by the world's first super-heroes, Jane is more interested in the Asian-American they're working for: Noriko Null.

Noriko was her best friend before turning super-smart overnight; she hasn't heard from her for months. Like all of her classmates, Jane has been interview several times about Noriko...and like the others, she didn't know what to say.

-As you can see with this exclusive footage, teenage billionaire inventor Noriko Null has been seen leaving the scene after Vesta and Quantum flew away – the journalist says.

-Do you think they'll call you for comments, Jane? – her father asks.

-Probably. They always call when she does something weird.

-You should try to visit her. I always thought she was a nice kid – her mother adds.

-Even before she got stinkin' rich? – Jane mumbles, jumping at the chance to leave the room when someone knocks on the door.

-I'll get it.

Jane gasps when she looks through the peephole. When she opens the door, two silver eyes are staring at her.

-I need a place for the night – Noriko says.

An hour earlier, in front of Null Tower

Noriko is staring at a holographic reflection of herself, while two armed guards are keeping an eye on her. The silver eyes of both Norikos flash at the same time.

-I am Null. Let me in, <u>now</u> – the real Noriko orders.

-You have no power here, impostor. I can have security throw you out of sight – the hologram replies.

-We'll see. Security override F3E57D35779-NULL.

-Gentlemen, please keep this young girl out of my sight – the false Noriko says, before her image disappears leaving only empty air.

-Gotta admit, she <u>does</u> talk like you. Now what? – Quantum asks.

188

-That code gives me full control of the Tower, including the holographic generators. Which means whoever is generating my double has full control of the Tower's defenses.

After saying this Noriko puts a hand on her chin, pensive. It takes her a few seconds to formulate a strategy and simply add:

-We're leaving.

Now, Blake house

Noriko sits down on Jane's bed, studying the room. It's no different than any teenage girl's bedroom, and she's been here before on a couple of sleepovers.

But she was a different person the last time she was here; now a poster gives her every known fact about the singer, every book cover comes with every translation and commentary ever written, even just a piece of clothing relays volumes of selling graphics and history of fashion.

-I suppose I should thank you for resisting the urge to gossip about me to the press.

Jane doesn't comment, crossing her arms. It's one of the dozens of body language details that confirm to Noriko that she's upset.

-I suppose you also want me to apologize for shutting you out of my life.

-Give me one good reason for not throwing you out of the house – Jane answers.

-I think I know why I became what I am now.

Jane's taken aback by her friend's reply...she's not sure she's the same person. She certainly looks like Noriko...who else would ever wear that ugly green jacket...but nobody talks like that!

-Okay, I gotta ask: what the heck are you talking about!?

-Something made me the smartest person on the planet, Jane. Something larger than life, giving the janitor's daughter the power to reshape the world. Is it any wonder that my previous life was lost after witnessing the grandeur of humanity's knowledge?

-...

-I'm trying to apologize.

-You really suck at it – Jane says, hugging her best friend.

Noriko hugs back awkwardly; she doesn't feel sorry at all for embracing her newfound life, but she really did miss her friend.

189

-So, who's the lucky guy? – she asks amicably, with a sharp turn from her usual serious tone.

-What?

-I've known you since seventh grade. You only wear perfume when you're on a date.

-It's nothing serious. Besides, you don't know him.

-I am Null. I know <u>everybody</u> – Noriko answers. She makes an effort to lessen her eye's brightness; Jane isn't used to see them light up.

-What, you wanna talk about <u>my</u> life? With everything that's happened to you!?

Noriko's mind is bombarded with images of the past months...fighting the Many on the Moon, almost dying at the hands of the Talos, starving in a Myridian prison, killing a goddess...

-I could use a little girl talk. But if anyone asks, we're discussing the future of my empire.

A dark alley

Kari Zel is standing in front of the burning flame that floats in the air, but she's still shivering: it's way too cold to wear her Myridian sleeveless top and miniskirt.

-You should've told me it wasn't summer on <u>this</u> planet – she complains.

-I'm really sorry; I'm not used to take care of such things – Vesta apologizes; she's not dressed for the weather either, but it doesn't bother her in the slightest.

A streak of light illuminates the alley, when Max Black a.k.a. Quantum turns back into human form with a shiny golden necklace in his hands.

-I really have to ask – he says to Vesta – The first time we met you were working as a waitress. How in the world did you pay for this!?

-It was a gift from a Roman senator. Did you have any trouble finding it?

-I just had to turn into neutrinos and there it was, fifty feet under the Coliseum. Why didn't you sell it centuries ago?

-I don't have much use for money – she shrugs – But it should be enough to put a roof on your heads for the night.

-"Our" heads? You're not coming? – Kari asks, while an exact duplicate of herself is rubbing her arms to heat her a little more.

-I have to bury my sister. I'll be back in a couple of days – Vesta adds, starting to float away.

-I have no idea where we'll be in a couple of days! How are you gonna find us? – Max protests.

Vesta giggles. She can't remember the last time she enjoyed mortal company this much.

-I have a feeling you won't keep a low profile for long.

The goddess flies away, leaving Max alone with a purple-haired alien girl and her duplicates. He has no money, no home, no job, and the last order Noriko gave him was "Lay low; I'll contact you".

He also has fifty thousand dollars worth of gold in his right hand.

-Come on, Kari. Let's buy you some clothes, then I'll show you around New York.

-Where's Torn? – she asks.

Max looks around: there's no trace of a red-skinned alien swordsman. He slaps his forehead.

-Great idea, Noriko: put Quantum in charge of the team.

Another block

True to the stereotype, none of the New Yorkers that meet Torn stare at his red skin; in fact, few people seem to acknowledge his presence.

This isn't the first godless planet he's visited, but it's by far the most advanced. Most worlds forgotten by the gods are primitive and savage, but this is clearly a flourishing culture.

It's a little overwhelming to be exposed to an alien culture, even though the stoic Torn doesn't really show it. But when he sees something familiar, he's so overjoyed that the permanent scowl on his face almost disappears (almost: he's still Torn).

No matter where you are in the galaxy, there is always a bar.

The music is loud and the atmosphere is lively. Not his kind of bar, but a decent place to buy a drink.

He walks to the counter, where an attractive African-American girl is smiling at him.

-What can I get you, tall dark and painted?

-Sphinx nectar.

-I don't think I know that drink. How about a beer?

Before Torn can say anything, the girl is already filling a glass. He's clearly staring at her.

191

-How many species are there on this planet? – he asks.

-Excuse me?

-You're dark brown. I've seen light brown, dark pink, light pink, pale pink with strange eyes…

-I can't decide if you're weird or just plain crazy – she notes, puzzled by the customer.

He drinks the beer faster than anyone she's ever seen, and she's been to college. He then stares at the bottom of the glass, before placing it back on the counter.

-Tastes like warm hydra ichor.

The girl stares at him like he's from another planet. He is, but he can tell it's because she didn't understand what he just said.

-I didn't say stop – he clarifies.

-You *can* pay for this, right? – she asks while pouring another beer.

-Do you take Myridian Silver Obols?

-Sorry, just American dollars. This one's on the house, though – she says offering Torn the second glass: she doesn't want any trouble.

Torn stares at the counter, confused. Then looks at the girl, the counter, then the girl again.

-It is a tiny house indeed. Is there a beast I can slay in exchange of these "American dollars"?

-There's an ATM right outside – she answers, more and more confused.

-I'll be right back – Torn says, drinking the second glass. Then he walks towards the door; he stops there, pointing at the counter and saying:

-Put another drink on the tiny house.

Watching the weird man with red paint on his face, the girl shakes her head.

-Only in New York…

-BURDENING THE BEAST! – someone yells, followed by the sharp sound of something smashing through a wall. Someone is screaming.

Torn returns to the bar, lifting the ATM with one arm like a fisherman showing off his prey. Behind him, a trail of dollars flutter in the air. Both Torn and the banknotes are drenched in the red paint that makes the theft utterly meaningless…or if would, if Torn realized he had just pulled an ATM from the wall.

-Maid! I slew the beast. Is it worth enough dollars to wash away the taste of its foul blood with another beer?

The girl stares at Torn with her mouth open. She starts pouring another beer…for herself this time.

3- Alien underwear and silent killers

The Null Technologies Sound Nullifier™ is one of history's most unexpected inventions. It's not Noriko's most popular invention: that would be the holographic projector, the world's fastest-selling high tech device.

But people had been trying to build something capable of generating three-dimensional images for decades. Nobody really wanted something that could eliminate sound at will.

The most expensive model (hundreds of thousands of dollars) is the SN-140™, capable to nullify sounds up to 140 decibels…the sound of a jet engine. Most major airports have bought at least one since it hit the market.

Since most people can't afford the SN-140™, the most popular model is the SN-60™, barely able to nullify the sound of snoring. The most dangerous model is the SN-100™: priced at only a few thousand dollars, it can literally make it impossible to cry for help.

Noriko is sleeping on the couch of her best friend's house. Her adventure on Myridia has finally taken its toll, and the eighteen year old girl is finally getting some much-needed sleep.

Her mind may have superhuman stamina, but her body needs rest like any other human's. She doesn't hear the sound of people breaking the lock on the door; she can't, because the three people dressed in black are wearing an SN-100™.

They have machine guns and inspect the room carefully, approaching the couch with extreme caution. Noriko has kicked the blanket off the couch and is only wearing underwear stolen on another planet.

Her trademark horrible green leather jacket is on the coffee table. One of the three armed man takes it, checking the inside pockets: a screwdriver, a makeshift remote control for the *Twin Dragon*, her personal N-Phone and the Genius Gun. In sheer silence, he places everything in a separate plastic bag. The other man carefully examines the pants left on the floor, finding three godstones in the pockets. They are also taken away in little plastic bags.

The last man is keeping guard, watching over Noriko as she sleeps. He takes the pillow that has fallen on the ground. He waits for the signal from his two colleagues: when they're done, he places the pillow over Noriko's mouth and starts pressing.

On the other side of town

Leave it to New York City to have clothes stores open at 3 AM in the morning. The line to the dressing rooms is mercifully nonexistent at this hour, which is particularly handy since Kari and her duplicates need all of them.

The shop assistants could've sworn they saw only one purple haired girl coming inside instead of eight twins, though. Max Black is glad that she's not spending *his* money; the pawn shop paid a small fortune for Vesta's necklace.

-This is the best planet in the universe! – one of the Kari exclaims.

Eight identical pink dresses are thrown out of the dressing rooms. Max catches one of them, but it disappears in the blink of an eye when he touches it. All the other dresses do the same, with the exception of one that just lays on the ground. It must belong to the original Kari.

-I still can't believe you own *just one* set of clothes – Max says, picking up the dress: he's known Kari for several weeks now and he's *never* seen her wear anything else.

-Do you know how hard it is to buy duplicating clothes on Myridia when the Oracles have orders to shoot you on sight? – she answers.

-So if you duplicate when you're *not* wearing this…

-The duplicates are naked, yeah. So, what do you think? – Kari asks when the first duplicate shows herself wearing Earth clothes. One after the other, the other duplicates do the same, striking a pose.

-You look hot in anything – Max has to admit.

-I hope so, it's freezing outside! Can you pick these up?

All of the duplicates disappear with a popping sound; all of their clothes fall to the ground, leaving only the original Kari. She then creates other eight new duplicates, who don't waste any time to go back into the store for more shopping.

All of them are wearing only pink alien underwear.

"I think I'm in love" Max thinks.

Jane's living room

Noriko wakes up while someone's trying to kill her. She tries to break free, but he's too strong. When she starts kicking uncontrollably, the second man grabs her ankles and keep her down.

Nobody can hear her: with the SN-100™ active, even screaming at the top of her lungs wouldn't help. The world's smartest person, the girl who killed a goddess, defeated by a pillow.

She won't have it. She may be just a girl, but she's also Null. She will NOT die easily.

Her silver eyes shine so bright to be visible through the pillow; her brain is pulsating with the brain power of the entire hemisphere. It's enough to set off the Genius Gun.

The weapon fires on its own, responding to brainwaves of its mistress; the effect is the same of a grenade exploding. It reduces the coffee table to a pile of splinters, but it's also enough to distract her would-be killers. It still doesn't make a sound.

Noriko falls off the couch, breathing frantically. The three intruders are aiming their machine guns at her. She stands proudly, a skinny half-Asian girl against three well-built and armed men.

She dares them to make the first move.

Noriko wages her life on the hunch that the three men don't want to kill her messily. She leaps to the side, avoiding the first spray of bullets that miss her legs by an inch.

Using her lack of height as an advantage, she slides below the legs of the first enemy: his ally isn't as careful as he should be with his aim, injuring him. The man's scream of pain is nullified by the SN-100™: there are two left.

She jumps behind the couch while the second and third reload: contrary to what movies might lead you to believe, machine guns run out of bullets very quickly.

When they're ready, she has her hands on the Genius Gun once more. The telekinetic blast catapults the second enemy against the wall with the same force of a speeding car hitting a wall.

That leaves the third enemy. He's aiming at Noriko, the same way she's aiming the Genius Gun at him. They stare at each other for a few tense seconds, then Noriko lets the Genius Gun fall to the ground.

The third enemy doesn't get his eyes off her, gesturing to kick the gun in his direction. She doesn't get her eyes off him either, but she complies.

He reaches for the gun, very slowly, and takes it. Unarmed and facing two guns at point blank range, Noriko would have no change to get out of this alive if the third enemy could hear anything.

Because if he could, he would've dropped the Genius Gun the moment he heard it say:

-UNAUTHORIZED   USER.   DROP   THIS   WEAPON   IN
FIVE...FOUR...THREE...TWO...ONE...

Unfortunately for him, the Genius Gun warning goes unheard, and the third enemy receives an electric shock similar to a taser. He squeezes the trigger, covering the room with silent bullets, before losing consciousness.

Noriko takes a deep breath. She recovers the green jacket from the remains of the coffee table and wears it: much to her surprise, she's shaking. She takes the N-Phone, sitting down on the couch full of bullet holes.

-SOUND NULLIFIER DEACTIVATION ROUTINE COMPLETE – it says.

Then Noriko pushes three buttons on her N-Phone. She isn't shaking anymore.

-Hello, 911? Someone just tried to kill me. No, there's no rush.

A brief pause, while the operator talks. There are three unconscious men, two of which seriously injured, bullets everywhere. And the girl in alien underwear who just defeated them.

-Everything's under control.

Somewhere else in New York City

The elevator door opens; the original Kari is the first to exit, almost bouncing with excitement.

-This is so cool! I haven't been in one of these things in years!!!

Max follows her, carrying a dozen bags of clothes. Kari could've created new duplicates to carry them, but finding two rooms this late at night was already difficult without explaining another six twins.

-You had elevators on Myridia – he says.

-Only in the big old cities, and good luck keeping the lights on in the skyscrapers. But everything here's so clean, so brand new!

-I think you're the first person to call New York "clean and new" since the 1930s.

197

-Is that a long time? – Kari asks, without waiting for an answer when she reaches her room.

-Oh my gods, is that a bed <u>with sheets</u>!? – she exclaims, running inside.

-Again, you <u>had</u> sheets on Myridia, right?

-When we stayed at the Oracle Palace, yes, but I had to knit or steal sheets all my life. And no bugs! Your people live like kings! – she says, jumping on the bed like a little kid.

-Speaking of which my, uhm, my room is upstairs. Couldn't find two on the same floor.

-You've been great tonight, Max. We should have sex sometimes.

-Yeah, that'd be, what? – he asks, sure to have misheard.

-You don't have Oracles on this planet, so I guess you don't need permission to have sex, right?

-No, I mean yes, I mean…

-I know that look; I've said something really stupid again, haven't I? – she asks.

-We can have sex whenever you want – Max says, trying to make himself clear and make it sound as little desperate as possible given the circumstances.

-I'm looking forward to it – she answers to a warm smile, taking off her pants and throwing them on the bed. Still wondering if this is a dream, Max takes off his shirt.

-What are you doing!? – Kari protests.

-I thought you wanted to…

-I didn't mean on the first date!!! We have to find Noriko and Torn in the morning!

-This was a date? – he asks, puzzled.

Kari creates a duplicate, who pushes Max towards the door while the original undresses for the night.

-Get out; one of us has to get some sleep – the duplicate says, right before closing the door.

Max sighs, laying his forehead on the door.

-Aliens…go figure.

-Are we doing this or what? – Kari asks; she's behind him, or at least one of her duplicates is.

Max turns around; if he has something to say, he quickly forgets it when she sees the purple haired girl standing naked in the hallway.

-You mean…on the first date? – he struggles to say.

198

-What? Oh, I'm not the original, so it doesn't count – she says, walking towards the elevator without the slightest shame.

-This really is the greatest planet in the universe – Max thinks, hurrying to catch up with the duplicate.

Jane's living room

Noriko is tapping her foot nervously: Max isn't answering his cellphone. She should've asked him to charge it in the last six weeks, but in outer space it was a low priority.

Something else catches her attention: the bodies of the men who attacked her suddenly dissolve into blue goo.

"It was a nice try, mother" she thinks "But you shouldn't have signed it".

4- Person of the year

Max Black wakes up with the sound of someone bashing on the door of his hotel room. While he's still half asleep, Kari jumps out of bed and quickly recovers the clothes on the floor.

-Hurry! We're under attack! – she orders, throwing Max's pants on his face.

-Kari… - he starts to say, yawning.

-If I create enough duplicates, maybe we can get them to lose our tracks – she says frantically, running to watch the window like a caged animal.

-Kari, just calm down – Max says, pulling up his trousers and getting out of bed. Another bang on the door frightens the purple haired girl, who takes a step back into Max's arms.

-We're not on Myridia anymore, Kari. There are no more Oracles to hunt you down.

-Sorry. Hold habits die hard – she answers, trying to fix her morning hair to hide her nervousness.

-It's probably nothing; nobody knows we're here – Max adds just when there's another knock.

-Alright, alright, just wait a freakin' minute okay? Just wait over there, Kari.

-Why? The door's right here.

-'Cause you're naked.

-I don't get it – she says, genuinely puzzled. Max shrugs and opens the door.

On the other side there's a woman in a black suit, wearing sunglasses. He's never seen her before.

-Maximilian Black? Agent Ramirez, C.I.A. Please follow me – she says, showing her badge.

-Crap – Max says, instinctively transforming his body into light and moving almost instantly behind the woman's back. When he tries to catch her, however, his arms pass through the hologram.

-What the…

Max can't say anything else, because the real Agent Ramirez is down the hall and has just shot him with a tranquilizing dart.

-I said please – she quips, readying another dart. Kari runs out of the room: Ramirez's second shot doesn't miss her, but she was an easy target intentionally.

A Kari duplicate appears out of thin air right besides Ramirez, confiscating her weapon; a second one kicks her on the stomach, and a third one punches her on the nose.

Working together, the three naked duplicates incapacitate Ramirez in about five seconds straight.

-Don't move. I have you outnumbered – she threatens.

-I have backup – Ramirez manages to say, despite the pain of the broken nose. Just as she says it, two men in dark suits storm the hallway. They don't even get to aim their weapons: each of them is attacked by six Kari duplicates.

-That's all you got? I was chased by a whole planet for *years*. Nobody can lay a finger on me if I don't want them to.

-Good, you'll make my job easier. Someone is trying to kill your friends.

Police station

There's a man sleeping on the floor, seemingly oblivious to the men talking on the other side of the bars.

-Is that him? – asks the man in the black suit.

-The one with the red skin, yeah – the policeman answers.

-You said he pulled apart an ATM with his bare hands. How did you manage to catch him?

-He didn't resist. I'm not sure he understands he's in jail; he said he just wanted a place to sleep.

-Did you manage to get a name?

-Torn – says the red skinned man, without opening his eyes.

-Is that a name, a surname or a nickname?

-Yes. Go away now.

-Mister Torn, I'm Agent Warden, C.I.A. I'd like to ask you a few questions.

Torn doesn't say anything, just making a sound between a sigh and a grunt. He steps up, walking towards the bars still half asleep. Red energy swords appear out of thin air while he's yawning, slicing through the bars of his cell in less than half a second.

The policeman quickly draws his gun. Torn just glances at him, and a red dagger cuts the barrel in half before the man understands what's going on.

-This inn is too loud – Torn says, leaving behind him the cell and the policeman who's looking at what remains of his weapon.

201

-He…he just *looked* at it…

-Lucky you he's my problem now – says Agent Warden, hurrying to catch up to Torn while another man in a black suit deals with the legal minutiae with policeman.

-Mister Torn, wait!

-Just Torn.

-I was on my way to talk with miss Null. We can grab something for you on the way.

-How do you know I work for Null?

-That's classified.

Torn looks at Agent Warden with a puzzled look…or what passes for a puzzled look for Torn, whose eyebrows frown slightly more than usual.

-Well, actually it's a lucky guess, but I've been waiting to use that line for years – the agent admits.

Jane Blake is asleep on a chair, kept warm by a blanket left there by some thoughtful officer. She wakes up when a man with red skin sits down in the chair to her left, giving a very confused look to a donut.

-Why is there a hole in your food? – he asks.

-What? – Jane asks, still not fully awake.

-You shouldn't make holes in your food unless you need to kill it – Torn says, like it's some kind of ancient proverb.

-Don't tell me: you're one of Noriko's new friends.

-Close enough. You also know Lady Null?

-"Lady"?

-The man in black said you're one of her old friends.

-What man in black? – Jane asks, turning to catch a glimpse of the room where they've been interrogating Noriko for the last few hours.

-Oh crap. I really wish she'd keep me out of these things. She almost got killed last night, y'know.

Torn doesn't answer immediately, busy eating the donut with a surprisingly satisfied look on his face that almost gets close to a happy look.

-It would taste better without the hole.

-Someone tries to murder your friend and you worry about donuts!?

-Where I come from, someone's always trying to kill somebody else. Null can take care of herself.

-Yeah, I guess she can. I kinda miss the old Nori though.

202

-She wasn't always like she is now?

-Oh God no. She was always a little weird, something of a tomboy…I don't think you could get her in a skirt if her life depended on it…but she did, y'know, normal stuff.

-I see.

There's a full ten seconds without a word. Doesn't sound much, but try it in a police station.

-You have no idea what normal means, do you? – she finally asks.

-Does this conversation count as "normal"?

-Not even close.

-I see.

Inside the room, Agent Warden sits down in front of Noriko. She looks pretty ruffled up, having been rushed here in the middle of the night and questioned for hours.

-You have some interesting friends, I'll give you that – he says to break the ice.

-I don't know who you are. That shouldn't be possible – she answers, her silver eyes flashing briefly while she examines every face ever recorded on a database.

-Like people with red skin with mind swords or people who turn into energy, but what do I know. I'm Agent Warden, by the way, C.I.A.

-Since when does the C.I.A have jurisdiction over an assault on an American citizen on US soil?

-Since the head of an international corporation ordered an assault on an American citizen by means of biological weapons designed by aliens.

-…

-I had to practice the line in front of a mirror to say it with a straight face. To tell you the truth, Noriko…can I call you Noriko?

-No.

-I think you're either the best thing that ever happened to America or the most scary.

-The two are not mutually exclusive, Agent Warden.

-True, true. Take your Sound Nullifier: it made snoring a thing of the past. It also makes killing people without being caught a lot easier. I think the C.I.A. already buys them in bulk.

-I will track down who bought the Sound Nullifiers used by my would-be assassins – she boasts.

-No you won't. You're good, there's no denying that, but the people behind this are better.

-You have to excuse me, Agent Warden, but I've been off-planet for the past six weeks. If you want to discuss something, you need to fill the blanks for me.

-Fair enough. Who is Leiko Tanaka?

The irritation on Noriko's face shines through her stoic exterior. Warden is getting under her skin.

-Japanese businesswoman, age 33. CEO of Scion Corporation – she answers.

-Let me show you something – Warden adds, reaching for the inside pocket of his jacket. He pulls out a slightly wrinkled copy of a very famous magazine and puts it on the table.

The cover shows Leiko, arms crossed and oozing confidence, over the title in bright letters PERSON OF THE YEAR.

Noriko snatches the magazine, reading it so fast that it looks like she's just flipping through the pages. Then she angrily punches the table, and her eyes shine in anger.

-She STOLE IT!!! The Plasma Fusion Reactor is MY IDEA!!!

-You sold her the patent for an obscenely huge amount of money.

-That's a LIE! I was in space for the past six weeks! FIGHTING GODS!!!

-That'll hold in court – Warden jokes, unfazed by Noriko yelling in his face.

She looks aside at the mirror, thinking about who could be on the other side. They're probably recording the whole conversation. She calms down, rubbing the bridge of her nose in frustration.

-The men who tried to murder me are probably an imperfect copy of the Many. Bio-engineering based on an alien lifeform in six weeks; there can't be more than two people on the planet who can pull it off, including me.

-We've caught a few around the world…India, Pakistan, Korea. Even prevented a coup by the skin of our teeth. We can't *exactly* trace them back to Scion Corporation, but after your father told us about the Many…

-My father? Where is he now?

-In a safe location, don't worry about him. Anyway, he told us about the Many and the alien robot you fought in New York, the Talos. You'll never guess what powers it.

-A Plasma Fusion Reactor. It's where I got the idea – Noriko reveals.
-And Leiko Tanaka knows how to build another now. So we have a foreign businesswoman who, I remind you, is the daughter of an alleged big shot in the Japanese underworld, stealing the most important discovery since the atom bomb from an American citizen. Who she tries to murder with goons she can easily mass-produce in a lab. Oh, and to top it all off, they're probably made of recycled killer alien cells. Now, what does all of this tell you?
-She wants to take over the world.
-I wonder where she got *that* idea – Warden snarks.

5- Surrounded

Max Black a.k.a Quantum regains consciousness with a colossal headache. The first thing he sees is a duplicate of Kari tying up a woman in her underwear using the bedroom's curtains.

-What the…

-Oh thank the Gods you're fine – says yet another duplicate, created just to check if he's injured. The hotel room is already quite crowded: in addition to the woman and the Kari duplicates, there are three unconscious men on the bed, expertly tied up with sheets.

-I don't think I wanna know – Max says.

-They shot you with some kind of poison. This woman ισ τηειρ λεαδερ– Kari explains while completing the final knot, reverting to her native Myridian language.

-Crap, not this again. Where's the universal translator when you need it?

-Ωηατ? Cραπ, νοτ this again. Τρανσλατιον comeσ and goes. This ωομαν is their leader!

The woman mumbles something angrily, muted by the sock shoved in her mouth.

"By experience, I won't understand a thing Kari says until she's near Vesta again" Max thinks before removing the gag.

-I was trying to save you, morons!!! Untie me and give me back my clothes!!!

-Σηε ηαδ τηισ ωιτη ηερ – Kari says handing a plastic card to Max, who reads out loud:

-Agent Camilla Ramirez, C.I.A. How did you find me? And please don't say "we're the C.I.A.", I already take enough of that crap from Null.

-Are you kidding me? We've known your "secret identity" for months; you shouldn't carry your cell phone with you when you're Quantum. That's how we found out, and how we've traced you here. Now will you *please* untie me!?

-Not until you tell me the *real* reason you attacked me.

-I knocked on the door and asked you to follow me!!!

-Yeah yeah, listen I don't buy the whole "we're trying to help you" thing. I've seen way too many movies to fall for that.

-You're a moron. If we wanted to hurt you, we'd have…

Ramirez doesn't end her sentence, because a man in black military gear has just crashed through the door like it was made of cardboard. He doesn't make a sound, thanks to the SN-100™ in his pocket.

-Don't tell me: this is the guy I should be worried about – Max says, right when the man fires his machine gun at him. The bullets melt as soon as they leave the weapon.

-Microwave vision, dude. What else ya got? – Max taunts him.

The man doesn't have the time to answer, because two duplicates of Kari appear literally out of nowhere to violently slam him against the wall.

The man in black answers by creating a copy of himself in the blink of an eye, ready to fight.

-Another Many? No biggie, I have superpowers this time – says Max, definitely not impressed, shooting lasers from his hands with the intent of cutting his enemies in two.

It doesn't go as planned: the two men just stay there, taking it all in without flinching.

-This was probably a bad idea – Max understands, before the two men counterattack by firing energy blasts from their hands.

Back at the police station
Noriko and Torn are following Agent Warden to a black van.

-You have no idea of how many strings I had to pull to push the F.B.I off the case.

-Where are we going? – she asks.

-You ask too many questions.

-I'm accustomed to know all the answers by default.

-Well, welcome back to Earth then – Agent Warden says, opening the van's door for Noriko.

-Wait – Torn adds, placing his hand on her shoulder to stop her.

-What?

-That man is aiming at us – he says, looking at the nearby buildings. Noriko can't see anything thanks to the sun's glare, but she can hear the gunshot.

Torn shoves her aside, and she hits the floor with enough force to worry about a broken arm. Reacting faster than any human Torn creates a red energy sword into his left hand, and with a swift move he cuts the bullet in mid-air. Agent Warden hasn't even had the time to draw his gun.

207

-Go – is the only word that Torn spares.

The sniper fires again; while the other people around him scream and scatter, Torn effortlessly catches the second bullet with his bare right hand.

He examines the wasted ammo for an instant. Then he looks up: it's his turn to aim.

On the top of the nearest building, the sniper is aiming for Noriko again. A red chain of barbed wire appears out of nowhere, slicing his weapon into a thousand pieces.

Somewhere else in New York City

Quantum is gone and there's a large hole in the wall. There's no time to think: Kari's instinct and training take over. The men who attacked Quantum are larger than her, but there's only two of them. A dozen of her duplicates jump at the attackers, trying to overcome them by sheer numbers. But punches and kicks don't seem to bother the nameless enemies; they toss Kari aside as if she weights nothing. When the duplicates hit the wall, the impact is hard enough to make them disappear.

One of the men calmly walks out of the the hole in the wall. The second one attempts to do the same, but Kari creates a duplicate directly on his shoulder to bite his ear. But no matter how hard she bites, the man doesn't react. The ear comes off. Instead of blood, the man's head bleeds a blue gooey substance.

-Εωω – Kari says with a disgusted look on her face.

Then Ramirez shots him in the head. Kari doesn't ask how she was able to break free from the sheets while she wasn't looking or how did she find her gun so quickly. She's got a more pressing issue at hand: the man is still standing, with blue stuff pouring out of the bullet hole.

Agent Ramirez fires again and again, aiming for vital organs, but the man won't stop. He lifts his right hand; something blue comes off its pores, solidifying into an exact replica of Ramirez's gun.

When he shoots, Kari's body disappears.

Agent Ramirez looks with disbelief at the duplicate vanishing, when another Kari grabs her wrist.

-Λετ'σ γο – she says, dragging Ramirez away from the Blue.

There are other Kari in the room, and they start multiplying.

Outside the police station

Noriko tries to push aside Agent Warden, who is at the same time shielding her with her body and holding on to her to make sure she doesn't break free.

Torn still has his energy sword drawn, carefully keeping guard; it's not easy with the chaos that sniper fire can bring into the city.

-I lost him. You shouldn't have told me to not kill anybody – Torn says.

-Glad you take your promises seriously, but that thing probably isn't alive – she answers, recalling last night's fight.

-We should leave now; we don't know if there's any more of them – Agent Warden adds.

Just then, the sniper lands on the roof of the black van. The impact should've broken his legs, but instead his weight dents the vehicle's body.

This time Agent Warden has the gun in his hand, but there's no time to fire: the sniper is already aiming his own gun at Noriko.

A big red X cuts right through the man's body, splashing body parts covered in blue goo into every direction, as if a grenade had just gone off inside the man's guts.

-The #### are you doing!? – Noriko shuts.

-It's an attack called "slash of life". I didn't have time to call it – Torn apologizes.

-This blue thing is a copy of the Many! What do you think's gonna happen next!?

As predicted, the body parts of the Blue are already recreating full copies of the body. Which means that Torn just multiplied the assassin by four. Agent Warden and the rest of the C.I.A. operatives open fire, having as much success as Ramirez.

-I'm surrounded by idiots – Noriko says, climbing inside the van followed by Agent Warden.

Somewhere else in New York City

Max Black a.k.a. Quantum turned instinctively into energy when the Blue blasted him through the wall; it's the only thing that saved him from being disintegrated.

He turns back into human form in the middle of the street. A car brakes just in time to avoid hitting him; people in the street immediately start taking pictures with their cellphones. They hope to

209

catch a glimpse of Quantum's face, but even without his mask he's unrecognizable: his face is literally brighter than the Sun. Just because the C.I.A. knows his secret identity doesn't mean <u>everybody</u> should.

The Blue lands on the sidewalk; he's just fine despite falling from the fourth floor. Quantum's laser blasted through the black military gear, but he's still bleeding a thick blue substance.

-Okay, so you're not just uglier than the Many, you're weirder. Let's see how you like this – Quantum says before pointing his finger at the Blue, firing a lick laser at his head.

The Blue reacts by absorbing the energy and releasing it back with a blast coming out of his eyes. Quantum casually steps aside at the speed of light; all the Blue can do is dig a hole in the ground.

-Energy sponge? Look man, I've read enough comics to know how to beat someone like you.

Quantum fires again at the Blue, but this time pouring a lot more energy into his attack. The Blue absorbs it like he's supposed to; he can't release it, though, because Quantum isn't stopping. The Blue's body quickly inflates horribly until it can't take it anymore.

Overcharged, the Blue explodes into a million blue drops sprayed all over the street. Quantum crosses his arms to look more badass while the people cheer for him.

Then he hears a gunshot. He's back into the hotel in the blink of an eye.

The room is filled with Kari duplicates; Quantum has to turn into X-rays to get to the hall on the other side, where the original Kari and Agent Ramirez have rounded up the male C.I.A. agents. They're still out cold; Quantum makes a note to never get on Kari's bad side.

-What happened? Where's the Blue thing? – he asks.

-Στιλλ ταλκινγ αλιεν – Kari says.

-He's under the Kari dogpile. I think he's trying to shoot her...but your girlfriend's duplicates keep vanishing – Agent Ramirez explains.

-Yeah, they pop out if you hit them hard enough.

-What happened to the other guy?

-I hit him hard enough – Quantum answers with a satisfied smirk on his face.

Kari takes Quantum aside, pointing at the room and saying with a very worried tone:

210

-Τηισ τηινγ'σ λικε τηε μανυ! Ωε νεεδ βαςκθπ, τηερε μαυ βε τηοθσανδσ βυ νοω!

-What language is that? I don't understand a word - Ramirez says.

-Makes two of us. Kari, slow down, in English!

-Γοδσ ηελπ με. Do not…hit…by energy. They δθπλιςατε!!!

-Uh-oh. I know that word; they say it all the time on Myridia.

-What does it mean?

-"Duplicate" – Quantum answers, turning into radio waves to get back outside.

The good news is that the street isn't covered with blue goo anymore. The *bad* news is that there are now hundreds of Blue taking human form. The *worse* news is that the Blue is immune to energy attacks. The *worst* news is that they all want to kill Quantum.

-Some days, I miss Myridia.

6- Hostile takeover

Since she became the world's smartest teenager, Noriko has done some weird things.

Hiding in a black van while a C.I.A. agent is shooting the human-shaped biological weapons that are trying to kill her doesn't even make it to the top ten.

-What are you waiting for, take us out of here! – Agent Warden shouts at Noriko, who's behind the wheel.

-I can't reach the pedals – she admits, adjusting the seat to her five feet height.

The Blue lands on the roof, tearing it apart with his bare hands. Agent Warden fires a few shots, but the bullets are just absorbed by the Blue.

-How the hell did you kill three of those!? – he asks.

-They weren't bulletproof! They must be learning from each other!

Torn is right outside the van, slicing the Blue and wielding a red energy sword in each hand. Every time he cuts one of the Blue in half, two more take its place; he's already fighting eight.

He sees the Blue tearing the roof apart; from what he's seen, an unarmed Noriko doesn't stand a chance.

-Need some breathing room. SPIRAL INTO CONTROL!

Torn's body is suddenly surrounded by a whirlwind of red swords, which cuts the eight Blue into a million drops of blue goo. The Blue attacking the van notices.

He jumps off the vehicle and without saying a word walks menacingly towards Torn. The red-skinned fighter has four words to shout:

-NEEDLE OF THE EYE!

He throws the red energy javelin with enough force to impale the Blue's head to the van. Meanwhile, the blue goo is already forming a new army. Torn looks at the impaled enemy, still alive and struggling to free himself. But the Blue hasn't duplicated.

-Still one? Interesting.

Then he looks back at the blue substance shaping itself into dozen new copies of the Blue.

-Cut of a thousand deaths – Torn says, swinging his arm as if to thrust a weapon into the sky. A thousand red energy blades appear out of nowhere, suspended in mid-air like Damocles swords.

212

-Rain of terror – he adds, and all the deadly blades shoot downward to hit the Blue army.

Noriko steps out of the van to admire the many artificial humans impaled to the ground, still technically alive but unable to free themselves.

-I don't understand your urge to call your attacks, it doesn't work unless you shout them – she suggests. Torn gives her a confused look, pointing at the defeated enemy.

-They disagree.

Elsewhere in New York City

This is definitely Quantum's worst fight. Not the hardest…he's fought an indestructible robot, half a planet of telekinetic murderers and a goddess. It's not his worst defeat, because technically he hasn't lost. It's a stalemate…sort of.

He's fighting artificial humans called the Blue: they are immune to his energy attacks and they keep creating new copies of themselves. He can't harm them, they can't harm him.

He can't leave the fight, because right behind the hundreds of artificial humans there's a rapidly growing number of onlookers and journalists. As long as he's the target, they're safe.

So Quantum just stands in the middle of the enemy army, turning into an intangible and harmless mass of light. Yawning.

-You guys are really boring. At least the Many said something and was easy on the eyes…you're just nameless goons.

One of Kari's duplicates appears right in front of him, asking in broken English:

-What is you doing?

-I have no idea. Nothing works on these guys. Suggestions?

-ιμπρονισε – she answers in her native Myridian language. Two Blue try to grab her, but she makes herself disappear in the blink of an eye and they end up headbutting each other.

-What, do I have to make them fight each other? I can't just hit them, they just replicate whatever…

Then Quantum snaps his fingers. He knows how to win this.

-They just replicate whatever I hit them with – he repeats, transforming his own body a negative magnetic field. The Blue react in the only way they can think of: absorb.

213

Which means that when Quantum turns into a positive magnetic field, the Blue are immediately pushed towards him.

If Null were here, she'd explain that Quantum's understanding of what he's just done is scientifically impossible, but she wouldn't argue the following step: changing into pure thermal energy, Quantum vaporizes the Blue so quickly that they don't have time to adapt.

The result is that Quantum is once again standing triumphant in the now empty street. One of Kari's duplicates appears once again, jumping in excitement like a five year old.

-That was brilliant, wasn't it?

-Τηατ ωασ αωεσομε!!!

-And I can't brag about it because you don't understand a word I'm saying.

-Ωηατ?

-Yeah, I think this day sucks too.

The Sun

Vesta has been here many times before. Her uncle Helios used to take her here every few hundred years when she was younger.

Now she's here to bury her sister Demeter. She wonders if this is what she would've wanted…gods don't talk about their own funeral because they think they'll never get one.

They know they can die because it's happened before. But it's so rare that they can pretend it's impossible. And as far as Vesta knows, no god has ever been killed by a mortal.

She should probably ask Hades if there's a precedent. He knows everything about death.

Vesta is floating a few thousand miles above the Sun, holding Demeter's corpse in her arms. She can take the heat and the radiation, but resisting the star's gravitational pull takes all of her power.

-Goodbye, sister.

She lets go, no longer protecting the corpse from gravity. Demeter's lifeless body plummets into the star faster than the eye can see. Vesta doesn't know what will happen to her…it's possible her immortal body will survive the journey. But no one will ever disturb her.

She wipes the tears from her eyes, even though it shouldn't be possible for any kind of liquid to exist here, and she flies away.

An undisclosed location

From the outside this looks like any other generic storehouse, but it's just the entrance to a high security installation. Agent Warden has just led Noriko, Kari, Torn and Quantum to a well lit conference room which is barely furnished.

-So what's with the office building look? Where's the James Bond stuff? – Quantum asks, sitting down between Kari and Noriko.

-We're a little low on the budget. We should be able to talk in peace here, while our guys clean up the mess you left behind…again – is the agent's answer.

-ωιλλ σομεονε πλεασε τελλ με ωηατ'σ γοινγ ον? – Kari asks.

-ωορκινγ ον ιτ. Agent Warden, my N-Phone please – Noriko adds. It's not a question, it's clearly an order.

-I can't see why not. But I'm keeping your sci-fi gun for now – he answers, handing the phone back to the silver-eyed girl.

-Load N-Translator, English to Myridian. Κεεπ τηισ cλοσε το υοθ εαρ – she says to Kari, giving her the phone. The Myridian girl takes the device, commenting:

-Τηισ ωοθλδ βε εασιερ ιφ Vesta ωερε ηερε.

-*This would be easier if Vesta were here* - the phone translates.

-I agree, but apparently I can't trust Quantum to keep the team together for a single night.

-She flew away! What was I supposed to do!? – he whines.

-Follow – Torn answers.

-Says the guy who got himself arrested! – Quantum says.

-I was trying to get a drink – Torn explains.

-Do you guys need a minute? – the agent asks.

-Τηισ ισ φθcκινγ ριδιcθλοθσ. Ωηυ αρεν'τ ωε τακινγ τηε Τοωερ βαcκ?

-*This is expletive ridiculous. Why aren't we taking the Tower back?*

-Excellent question. Are the United States keeping me under arrest? – Noriko asks.

-The President is weighing his options – Warden answers.

-What would his options be if I asked the Vanguard to level this building to the ground?

Quantum and Kari are visibly worried by her question, but Agent Warden smiles.

-Nice bluff. You need us.

-I am Null. I've fought alien robots and gods. I don't need your help to take back what is mine.

-Then why didn't you do it as soon as you came back? Why hide? Look, you've been away for six weeks; a lot has changed and we can fill you in. In exchange, we want to know what the hell's been going on since you turned super-smart.

Noriko tries to keep her cool, but her shining eyes signal that she's exasperated by the situation. It's too dangerous to try taking the Tower back without knowing what happened to her father, to the Heart of the Universe, to her inventions…

-This is your fault. I'd be up to speed if you hadn't tried to save my life – she says to Torn.

-I'll ask permission before doing it again – he answers.

-Alright Agent Warden, you've got a deal. Tell me everything you know about Leiko Tanaka's plans and I will share my information on the Many, the Talos and the Heart of the Universe.

-Oh, I'm not the one you're supposed to talk to – Agent Warden replies, reaching for a remote control in his pocket.

The holographic projectors in the room are activated, creating a tridimensional image of a man wearing a very nice suit.

-It's a real pleasure to finally meet you, miss Null.

-Likewise, mister President.

Khloe VII, capital world of the Demeter Theocracy

The Divine Palace lies in ruins. A ten year old girl is walking through the gardens; the plants die with her every step, and a rotten decay spreads like a plague throughout the planet.

A decrepit old woman is patting the back of a Chimera, a monstrous fire-breathing lion with a snake for a tail, which is gleefully devouring one of the Oracles.

Anesi Mithrades, current Lady-In-Waiting and highest ranking mortal in the Theocracy, is kneeling before a beautiful woman with dark grey hair.

-Lady Hekate, I don't know where Holy Demeter is. She left for Myridia weeks ago.

216

-*Myridia. Didn't we own the place once?* – the grey haired woman asks, with a strange echo in her voice.

-*Who cares. When are we leaving? All this green sickens us* – says the old woman, with the same voice of the younger one.

-*Sending mortals to greet us. Instead of helping us in the war against Hephaestus, Demeter insults us* – says the child, holding a flower in her hand. It turns into dust in a second.

-*We agree. This world is beneath us* – the woman nods, lifting the Lady-In-Waiting by her neck. The looks her in the eye while Anesi ages thirty years every second, until all that's left of her are blackened bones.

-*Pack your things, girls. The Triple Goddess is going back home.*

7- Washington goes to Null

When Max Black got super-powers and became Quantum, he thought he'd be living the life of his comic book heroes…fighting evil, saving damsels in distress, that sort of thing.

Not sitting in a room with no windows, listening to the hologram of the President of the United States discuss energy policy with an eighteen year old genius girl.

-A Plasma Fusion Reactor can be assembled from scratch in about a year; converting an existing power plant can cut construction time in half if handled properly. I estimate that twenty reactors can cover the energy consumption of the whole country.

-As well as cut our dependency from foreign oil? – the President's hologram asks.

-You would also need to overhaul the infrastructure, but yes. Null Technologies would gladly oversee the project, but for the moment it seems I no longer speak for the company.

Quantum lifts a hand, interrupting the President before he can add anything else.

-I'm sorry, you kinda lost me there. Did you just invent clean energy!?

-Of course not. I did it eight weeks ago – Noriko answers, with a proud gleam in her silver eyes.

-During you absence, it seems that Leiko Tanaka of Scion Corporation stole the reactor blueprints – the President explains – We have already started talks with her, as have the governments of many other countries such as China, Russia and of course Japan. Except the Scion Corporation claims that it will take at least ten years to assemble a reactor.

-She's taking it slow. I don't think it's a good sign – Noriko says.

-It may be a good motive to kill you, miss Null. Officially, you sold the patent to the reactor to miss Tanaka, even though I understand she staged everything with the help of your holographic technology. It may be her way to kill the competition.

-Possibly. Where is the Heart of the Universe?

Despite the artificial quality of the President's image, Noriko can notice he's very tense when she asks the question.

-In a safe location. When you disappeared, your father feared for his life and turned himself into custody…together with Heart. We have the best scientists in the world working on it.

-You've also had the Talos for months. How many technologies have they been able to extract?

-They are having…technical difficulties with it.

-Of course. None of them is Null.

-Ωηατ αβοθτ τηε βλθε? – Kari asks.

-*What about the Blue?* – the N-Phone translated from Myridian.

-Good question. I understand using them as weapons, since there're less easily traceable than professional killers; for someone who isn't Null, at least. But why infiltrate them in several governments? – Noriko asks.

-And what is she doing with my comic books? – Quantum adds.

The room falls silent.

Triton, Neptune's largest moon

The *Twin Dragon*, Demeter's old mothership, is still on this ice world. Kari Zel, or more clearly one of her duplicates, is carrying a tray with a bottle of water and emergency rations.

On her way, she comes across a dozen other duplicates. Many more are working on the other decks: they're all extremely busy mapping every inch of the spaceship, down to every screw and bolt, as per Noriko's orders.

Finally, Kari reaches her destination: the prison. Talas Khanos is still in his cell, guarded by two Kari duplicates who pass the time playing cards.

-I told you to keep an eye on him – Kari says, creating another duplicate to which she handles the tray. The two Kari playing cards wearily acknowledge her presence.

-He's not going anywhere…we're in dark space and he doesn't have any powers without his godstone. Just look at him, he's fine.

The former Oracle is standing in his cell: at seven feet, he almost touches the roof. His eyes are closed and he's holding the palm of his hands upwards.

-What's he doing?

-Praying, I think. Check this out, sweetie: Full Hydra – Kari boasts, placing the seven cards on the table. Her duplicate slams her fist on the table, shouting:

-That's not fair, we agreed we wouldn't cheat this time!

-Oh yeah? Well I saw you deal from the bottom!

-Girls, not now, please – the third Kari intervenes, touching both players with her hands.

The duplicates disappear, transferring all of their memories to her.

-I really should stop cheating myself. Hey tall dark and insane, mind telling me what you've been doing in there for the past six hours?

Talas Khanos doesn't answer, but his sharp breath indicates how frustrating he finds the girl.

-Well? No speech on how you're gonna murder me for my sins against Demeter? Careful, we might take your godstone back if you don't gloat about how awesome you are, like all Oracles. Oh wait, we already did that!

-Do you want to know why I became an Oracle, child?

-Not really.

-The gods don't deserve to rule the galaxy. They are much more powerful than mortals, yes, but far more stupid and immature. Demeter thought turning me into an Oracle would make me a slave, but she made a mistake. The same one Null did…she gave me time.

-Time for what? Rot in prison? You better go back to praying…I have a feeling you'll need it.

-I wasn't praying, you worthless wench. I was concentrating.

Something opens the steel doors with enough force to crush them like cardboard. Kari gets ready for a fight, but her body is lifted and slammed against the wall by an unseen power.

Since this is a duplicate, the impact makes it disappear. Before she does, however, she instantly creates more duplicates; they are pushed aside just as easily.

What's keeping them at bay is a violet jewel floating in the air: a godstone. It quickly flies through the prison bars, embedding itself into the throat of Talas Khanos.

-Godstones transform brainwaves into telekinetic power. I've had one for years; you think I wouldn't find a way to activate it from remote?

Kari falls, no longer pinned against the wall. She gathers her strength, ready to summon an army to attack the prisoner. But her body disappears when Khanos telekinetically snaps her neck.

-That, my dear, is why I am Talas Khanos.

New York City

Agent Warden places the tray on the table, next to the pile of discarded circuits. He takes the large cup of coffee, while Torn grabs the can of beer.

-Isn't it a little early for that? – the agent asks.

-Would it have a different taste later in the day? – Torn asks, sincerely puzzled by the question.

-Well, no, but...

Torn doesn't simply open the can; he cuts off the top with an energy dagger, then drinks from it like from a normal glass.

-Where did you find this guy!?

-That's classified – Noriko answers, drinking the first espresso without taking her eyes from what she's building. She drinks the other four in a row, before Warden has the time to drink his own coffee.

-That can't possibly be good for your health, you know that right?

-Try six weeks on another planet without caffeine, then we'll talk about health. Torn, another godstone filament, please.

Still drinking his beer, Torn gestures towards the godstone on the table. It's already been cut in half, but the energy swords created by Torn's mind now slices it in tiny strings. Then he burps loudly.

Noriko takes her eyes off the device in front of her, to look the red skinned man into the eyes.

-I don't know about your planet, but on Earth that's just disgusting.

-We don't have beer on my planet – Torn answers. If she didn't know Torn, Noriko would've thought he was sarcastic.

-And what planet would that be? – Warden asks.

-That's classified too – Noriko answers, before Torn can say anything.

-Cute. You really expect the CIA to keep an eye closed when you bring two aliens on Earth?

-No, I expect you to try and fail to gain intelligence from me – she clarifies, using pliers to carefully place the godstone filament inside the ring-shaped device she's been building for the past hour.

-If this is about the NSA trying to infiltrate your servers...

-Agent Warden, when I became the smartest person on the planet I had a limitless number of options to make money. Do you know why I decided to use my talent on a quiz show to gain my first million dollars?

221

-I figured it's got something to do with your massive ego.

Noriko's silver eyes flash intensely; while she doesn't show other signs of anger, Warden knows he's touched a nerve.

-It was the best way to amass a large sum of money without owing anything to anyone. Now that Scion Corporation has the Plasma Fusion Reactor, after I regain control of Null Technologies I will own most of my fortune to them. But it will be the last time. Nobody steals from Null; not Scion, not Tanaka, not even the United States government.

-Is that a threat?

-A promise. We are allies now; but try to cross me, and Null will destroy you.

The ring-shaped device is now complete. Assembled with parts cannibalized from the room's holographic projector, the N-phone, the Mark II Genius Gun and the godstone.

When Noriko wears it on her left wrist like a bracelet, it lights up to show the circuitry of godstone filaments. And it talks.

-N-Watch activated. Psychic broadband connection established.

-Done. This will give my brain remote access to the Tower's systems.

Outside the door, Quantum and Kari are taking a pause from the endless debate.

-So, still thinkin' my planet is awesome? – he asks.

-Ι ηατε τηισ τρανσλατιον τηινγ – she answers with a weary tone.

-I hate this translation thing – the N-Phone says with a monotone artificial voice.

-I take it this is a bad time to discuss last night, isn't it? I mean, with the CIA and the killing blue guy and all...

-Υοθ ηαδ σεξ ωιτη μυ δθπλικατε. Ωηατ'σ τηερε το δισcθσσ?

-You had sex with my duplicate. What's there to discuss?

Of course, Noriko chooses this exact moment to come out of the room. She glances at Kari, then at Quantum while raising an eyebrow disapprovingly.

-What? – he asks defensively.

-Nothing; this doesn't even make it to the top one million things on my mind at the moment.

-Any chance that list includes the theft of my comic books?

-Don't push it. We'll discuss it after we've taken back the Tower.

-Not that I mind some action, but why exactly do you need us? Can't you just use your newest thingamajig to waltz right through the front door?

-I think I need a translator too – Torn says, puzzled by Quantum's words.

-Joιν τηε cλθβ – Kari adds.

-*Join the club.*

-The N-Watch has a limited range; I need the Vanguard to get me past the Nullbots.

-"Nullbots"? You mean the Tower has *actual robots!?* – Quantum asks.

-Killer robots – Noriko clarifies.

8- Prototype

Null Tower is one of the newest additions to the New York City skyline, with the large Ø symbol on top and its windows of mirror glass.

As the home of the world's richest and smartest billionaire teenager who invented clean energy a few weeks ago, it's also under constant watch by pretty much every important person on the planet.

There are two armed guards in front of the entrance. Their job is mostly to intimidate any unsolicited visitor: Null Tower has been in lockdown for weeks.

Four people walk out of a black van and step towards the Tower. There's an African-American man with a fancy mask, a twenty-something girl with purple hair, a man with red skin, and a teenage Asian who looks just like the Tower's owner.

-No visitors – one of the guards warns.

-Whatever – the Asian girl says with a deadpan tone, keeping on walking.

One of the guards reaches for his gun. The man with red skin blinks, and red energy swords cut through the weapon reducing it to shiny confetti.

Before the guard can say anything, three exact duplicates of the girl with purple hair are already kicking him into submission from three different directions.

The second guard looks at the man with the mask and drops his gun.

Inside the Tower, the lobby is flooded with red lights and the sound of an alarm. The Asian girl keeps walking towards the elevator; it doesn't take long before the hall is filled with another dozen guards, armed and ready to shoot.

The girl with the purple hair cracks her knuckles, but her Asian leader raises a hand as if to say "let me handle this".

-A word of advice. Between them, the people you're facing can summon an army of ten thousand fighters, cut through matter with a thought, shoot laser beams at the speed of light and unleash destruction faster and more devastatingly than you can imagine. We are the Vanguard. We killed a goddess once. You do not want to pick up a fight with us.

The guards stare back at Noriko, and for a few seconds you could hear a pin drop.

Then their image falters, like a bad TV signal, revealing what's beneath the hologram: robots.

Their proportions are clearly human, but their metallic bodies are covered by a shiny black coating and they have no face.

-Cool – is Quantum's first reaction.

-Listen to me very carefully: these things cannot leave the Tower – Noriko orders: her voice went straight from arrogant to extremely worried.

-Understood. CUT OF A THOUSAND DEATHS! – Torn shouts, releasing a flood of red energy dagger. They cut multiple times through head, chest, arms and legs of each and every robot, disappearing before they reach the walls.

The Nullbots don't move. They keep their balance, with internal wiring showing through the multiple holes. Then all of their wounds start to heal: the black metal simply regenerates, and the forearms split down the middle to reveal machine guns.

-Great. You built these things!? – Quantum asks Noriko.

-Just the prototypes – she apologizes.

Triton, Neptune's largest moon

Even for a goddess, reaching the edge of the solar system takes time. Vesta started her trip right after burying her sister Demeter into the Sun…she should've gone for Noriko, but she needs more time to cope with her loss before meeting her again.

Catching up with Kari's duplicates on the *Twin Dragon* will do her good. She likes the Myridian girl like a little sister. Well, like what a mortal would call "like a little sister": Vesta's little sisters are Demeter and Hera. The first is a dead genocidal tyrant and the second…she decides not to dwell on the thought. She floats above the alien ship for a few seconds.

Then something assaults her mind, shutting it down with the force of a jackhammer.

Inside the ship Talos Khanos waits another ten minutes before disconnecting the God Eraser, just to be sure.

Back on Earth, Null Tower

The custom-made machine guns can't even dent Torn's shield made of intertwined daggers; if it wasn't for that, Noriko and Kari would be dead.

225

-So let me get this straight. Leiko had killer robots all along, yet she sent those crappy Blue things to get you? – Quantum asks. He turns his body into light, so that the bullets fired by the Nullbots pass right through him.

-Each Nullbot costs about 90 million dollars; they're not as effective to mass produce as a biological weapon – she explains.

-Why do I find it creepy that you've thought about this before? – Quantum wonders aloud.

Kari isn't following the discussion: the N-Phone is having trouble translating the conversation with all the noise from the machine guns. She gets the gist of it: the others don't know what to do.

She creates her first duplicate just outside the shield. She's no match for a Nullbot, but math is on her side…the robots kill anything on their sight, and she's making sure their targets are *always* busy. It's impossible to end your fight when the girl you're trying to murder can create ten thousand duplicates in the blink of an eye.

-Gotta hand it to her, nobody dies like Kari. Now what? – Quantum asks.

-The main server is on the tenth floor. I need to be there to reprogram the Tower – Noriko explains.

-I'm on it – Quantum says. Before Noriko has the time to say "wait", he's already disappeared.

The first thing Quantum tries is X-Rays. They're fast and they go through almost anything; he just needs to be careful to avoid using it to pass through people. But the walls of the tenth floor have lead panels built inside, so he needs something else.

He tries radio waves, but there's some kind of interference that makes it almost painful. He tries to think of something else, but he knows the only thing left to try are neutrinos.

Elementary particles that pass through anything, neutrinos are always tricky to turn into. But this time it actually hurts: when Quantum transforms his mass into neutrinos, it's like being hit by a million of tiny needles all over his body.

When he returns to the ground floor, Noriko and Torn are running towards the elevator doors.

-I can't get through! What the hell is on the tenth floor!? – Quantum asks.

-A Plasma Fusion Reactor - she answers, pushed aside by Torn to avoid a blast from the Nullbots.

-You put a nuclear reactor in your own house!?

-It's not nuclear, and I'm a little busy right now – she adds, calling the elevator.

When the doors don't open, Torn glances at them. A giant red X appears over them as he slices through metal with his mind; just a moment later, the door crumbles.

-Go. We've got your back – Torn says, exuding confidence as usual.

Noriko nods, grabs Quantum by his sleeve and runs towards the elevator. They leave behind Torn and at least fifty Kari, facing a squadron of fully armed Nullbots.

-You know, I'm kind of tired of dying now – she says, creating more duplicates as human shields.

-They're not very bright. We just need to stall them – Torn answers.

-You understand what I'm saying!?

-Only when you say things that make sense. DEFENCE OF THE LINE!!! – he shouts, creating a lasso made of intertwined razors to slow down the Nullbots.

-And he thinks I'm the one who's not making any sense – Kari shrugs.

Tenth floor

A laser beam cuts a hole in the elevator door. Noriko Null crawls through it, careful not to touch the white-hot edges. Quantum is waiting for her on the other side.

-Honestly, who makes elevator doors with an inch of lead inside!? – he whines.

-The whole building is shielded from radiation. Just in case – she explains.

-The question still stands, but I'm a little worried. Is the Tower gonna send killer robots here too?

-It tried. I already hacked the internal security system; only external hard drives like the Nullbots are unaffected, but we should have a few minutes before the whole system reboots.

-Hold on a second, when did you hack in? You haven't touched anything!

-Didn't need to. My mind is faster than any computer on the planet; the N-Watch interacts directly with it, so I no longer need to type anything. Here we are: the main server.

The room is very close to what Quantum expected. The supercomputer towers cover pretty much the entire floor; everything is clean, sterile and very, very quiet. Unnervingly quiet.

-Is something wrong? – he asks.

-This is too easy. I expected the system to try a plasma discharge from the reactor.

-Which means…

-It could've vaporized us. I had countermeasures but…it didn't even try. I need to check it out.

Worried that Noriko sounds disappointed by the fact that somebody *didn't* try to kill her, Quantum follows her to an isolated room.

There are thousands of cables leading to a single elevated platform, which houses a tiny round object. It's the size of his fist and made of glass, containing a ball of ionized energy that constantly shoots tiny strings of electricity towards the glass.

-It's…it's a plasma lamp!?

-A Plasma Fusion Reactor. Well, the prototype, actually.

-All this mess because of that tiny thing!?

-That "tiny thing" can generate enough energy to power half the city. And apparently it generates enough antineutrinos to hurt you.

-No need to add salt to the wounds. Just looking at it makes me dizzy. Now, are you going to shut it off or what? In case you forgot, your robots are trying to kill Kari and Torn!

-Right. Hard reset, authorization code 5CF4343C8B82D40-NULL.

-*Code accepted. Encryption keys randomized. System reboot in five second*s – an electronic female voice answers, and the server powers down. Together with the reactor and the lights.

Exactly five seconds later, the lights come back with a cheerful female voice.

-*Integrated Reconfigurable Intelligence System active. How may I help you mistress?*

-I.R.I.S, I'm downloading a new operating system into your secondary drive. Transfer all active commands to the new drive and run a system-wide diagnostic. Load the chronology of all operations inside the N-Watch and…

-A-hem – Quantum coughs to get her attention.

-Oh, yes. Shut down the Nullbots, please.

-Is it just me, or was all of this waaaay too easy? – Quantum asks.

-I agree. None of this makes sense. What is Leiko's plan!?

Scion Corporation headquarters
Tokyo, Japan

Leiko Tanaka is sitting in an empty room, her legs crossed. Other than her and the chair, there is absolutely nothing else here. But when the holographic generator is activated, another person appears. It's only the silhouette of a man; there is no other detail visible.

-*Any progress?* – the hologram asks, with a heavily distorted voice.

-The Nexus is back on Earth. She is…unlikely to recover the Heart soon.

-*What is the global readiness level?*

-Unchanged. It will take years before society adapts to the reactor technology. I have agents in most of the major governments, but progress is slow. If a god finds us now, Earth won't last a day: a direct intervention might be your only choice.

-*I will ask my superiors* – is all the holographic shadow has to say, before disappearing.

Leiko smiles. If her gambit pays off, in a few weeks she will own the whole planet.

9- The talk

Washington D.C.

The limousine halts outside the hotel. Kari has been staring outside the window the whole trip, fascinated by the most mundane things. Everything is alien and wonderful to her.

Torn has fallen asleep a couple of times.

-Stay here – Noriko orders, stepping outside the car.

When she does, Kari is already by her side, pointing at the Capitol clearly visible at the end of the road.

-Is that where your king lives? – she asks.

-First off, he's not a king, he's a President – Noriko answers – Second, we're meeting him at the White House later today. Third, didn't I tell you to stay in the car?

-But I am in the car – Kari says, confused.

The original Kari waves from the car. Noriko shrugs, knowing there's no reasoning with the Myridian girl. Despite being seven years younger, Noriko acts like her big sister most of the time.

She doesn't say anything, covering her silver eyes with a pair of sunglasses. She can't help but think that there's some credit to Quantum's idea to have a secret identity: when you're one of the most recognizable faces on the planet, it's hard to go unnoticed.

The leather jacket of a horrible shade of green is still dead giveaway this is the real Null, though.

The Secret Service has orders to screen all visitors; luckily, Noriko and Kari have papers personally signed by the President.

-You and your father are pretty close, aren't you? – Kari asks.

Noriko hesitates before answering, leading the purple-haired girl to apologize.

-Sorry, I don't mean to pry. Is this thing on?

She taps the tiny purple earring with her finger. It's a miniaturized version of the N-Phone translator…it receives words in English and immediately translates them into Kari's natural Myridian. Working through bone conduction, only Kari can hear the translation.

When she talks in Myridian, the other earring translates her words into English; the Sound Nullifier in her belt makes sure people hear only the earring's voice.

It's a little jarring for people when they notice that her words don't match the movement of her lips.

-You're not a duplicate, you're the original one – Noriko realizes.

-Well your father doesn't talk Myridian and I can't duplicate your inventions. I'm studying English right now, back in New York.

-You mean your duplicates are.

-You're not answering the question. You don't get along with your father?

-We were close before... - Noriko answers, pointing at her head.

-Before Athena?

-Yeah. He raised me alone, you know? He pretty much gave up his life for me.

-Is that unusual on Earth? – Kari asks. On Myridia, you're lucky to have *one* parent caring for you long enough before they're recruited as soldiers or breeders of soldiers.

-He went through hell with Social Services to keep custody and won. He had all the reasons in the world to abandon me, but he didn't. My mother is one of the richest persons in the world and he never asked her for money. He never even told me who she was.

Noriko is about to knock on the door, but Kari stops her. She's not very tall, but she towers over the teenage girl.

-You're mad at your father for not telling you about Leiko, aren't you? He was protecting you.

-He shouldn't have made the decision for me – she answers, her silver eyes briefly shining.

-He probably had his reasons. Your father sounds like a very wise man.

-Hold that thought - Noriko says, knocking.

A few seconds later, the door opens. Revealing a naked blonde woman covering herself with a white towel.

-Your father is *definitely* not what I was expecting – Kari says.

-Oh my GOD you're HER, aren't you!? – the blonde shouts, trying to take Noriko's hand.

The teenage genius takes a step back at the speed of sound.

-I'm, like, your BIGGEST fan! I saw you on the news with that robot thing and, GOD, I just HAVE to get your autograph!!!

The woman runs back inside, leaving Noriko to scratch her head.

-So...that happened.

-Nori!!!

231

Someone else comes out of the room. A man who reaches Noriko so fast that neither her or Kari have the time to do anything. He puts his arms around her and holds her so tight that has trouble breathing for a second.

-Hello…father – she manages to say.

Bob Null is hugging his daughter for the first time in six weeks; his voice is broken, like he's holding back the tears. She doesn't hug him back: she just stands there, uncomfortable.

-I was so worried! Are you alright? Did they hurt you in space? They didn't probe you or anything like that, right?

-Your dad looks…*very* wise, Noriko – Kari says, taking a good look at Bob.

-I am fine, father. Can we <u>please</u> continue this conversation with both us wearing pants?

-Oh, sorry – Bob answers, recovering the towel from the floor to cover himself. Once he's adjusted it around his waist, he places his arm around Kari's shoulders.

-You didn't introduce me to your friend. Nice hair. Purple eyebrows too, never seen that!

Noriko's death stare would be frightening even without the shining silver eyes.

-What? – Bob asks, well used to his daughter's disapproval of all of his partners.

-Well at least you're not seeing Deena anymore – she concedes.

-Nice to see you too – answers a new female voice from the room.

There's a brunette in her underwear standing near the door, holding back the blonde woman which now has a pen and a magazine in her hands.

-Deena. Still sleeping with my father, I see.

-Noriko. Still wearing that ugly jacket.

-I should've stayed in the car – Kari understands.

A few minutes later, Noriko and Bob are alone. Deena didn't have much to say, while the blonde was a little too excited to have Noriko's autograph…even though it was dedicated to "GO AWAY". Kari wanted to stay, but preferred to let Noriko some time alone with her family.

Bob has finally put on some clothes, failing miserably to hide under the bed the undergarments left behind by his latest conquests.

-The President told me you were treated fine, but I don't think this is what he meant.

-You met the President too? Nice guy. I think he paid for the room. I suppose you want to know what happened when you disappeared, right?

-Someone reprogrammed the Tower's computer to impersonate me and give control of Null Technologies to Leiko, so you took the Heart of the Universe and gave it to the US government.

-Uhm...yeah, pretty much. You're not mad 'cause I gave away that alien thing?

-It was a good move, father. With the Vanguard gone, you were not in a position to protect it. It won't be easy to take it back...even for me, unfortunately.

-You plan to steal it back? From the government!? – Bob asks, then he quickly covers his mouth and looks around suspiciously.

-I'm working on it. Don't worry, I disabled the microphones the second I walked in – Noriko explains, showing the N-Watch at her wrist.

-So now what? – Bob asks.

-I'm in Washington to meet the President and testify before Congress about...well about a lot of things, starting from the Talos attack in New York. Then we'll go home.

-That's great, kiddo! Just give me a minute to pack my things and...

-Father...I have to tell you something.

There's something strange in her voice. A trembling emotion, a sliver of frightened humanity.

-Oh my God you're pregnant – Bob reacts, sitting down on the bed.

-What!?

-It was Quantum, wasn't it? I knew I shouldn't have let you two sleep under the same roof. If mister super-hero thinks he can...

Noriko waves her hands to get his attention back, frantically explaining:

-Father, please, you're <u>completely</u> off track!!!

-Then who? You've hardly ever left the Tower after...you're not pregnant, aren't you?

-<u>Definitely not</u>.

-Whew. Dodged a bullet there. So the girl with purple hair...

-Kari Zel.

233

-I get it. Look, Nori, there's no need to be embarrassed. I don't care if you like girls.

-What? No! What are you talking about!? – Noriko asks, blushing.

-It's not that much of a surprise, I mean, you haven't worn a dress since you were like five, you've always been <u>very</u> close to Jane, and that guy you used to date, whatshisname, I could tell you weren't all that much into him...

-Kari and I are not in a relationship <u>andIreallywishtodropthissubject</u>...

-It's not Vesta, right? 'Cause that would just be wrong.

-This snowballed fast – Noriko says, slapping her forehead. She takes a deep breath to find the strength; of all the ways she predicted how the conversation would pan out, this wasn't on the list.

-Dad, I killed someone.

Bob Null hasn't heard his daughter call him "dad" in months. He walks towards her, with a small warm smile on his face, and places a hand on her shoulder. She's holding back the tears.

-It's okay, Nori. You don't need to be strong all the time in front of me. What happened?

-We were on Kari's planet, Myridia. There was this woman, Demeter. Their goddess. She was a tyrant and...and I killed her, dad. She was too powerful and too insane; Myridia deserved better.

-You think you made the wrong choice?

-No. Demeter deserved to die – Noriko answers, sniffing.

Nobody is ready to hear these words from a crying teenage girl. Bob simply hugs her and strokes her hair, offering a shoulder to cry on.

-What's <u>really</u> wrong, Nori? You know you can tell me.

-I want to do it again – she explains, sobbing. She's really crying now, hugging back.

A cold chill goes through Bob's spine. She's not just hugging; she's clinging to him like her life depended on it, and her voice becomes more passionate and angry.

-People were afraid of me. They called me a goddess. They wanted to worship me and...and I loved it so much, dad. I can't stop thinking about it. It's eating me inside. *I want to take over the world.*

The unnatural voice startles both father and daughter, who break off the hug. Bob is doing his best not to look afraid, but he's failing miserably. Noriko's mask of detachment has melted completely:

she's crying, and her eyes are completely black for a second. Two empty holes.

They turn back to white and silver. She's still trembling, terrified.

-What's happening to me?

Bob clenches his fists. Nobody does something like this to his daughter and gets away with it. He recovers a suitcase from under the bed and frantically puts some clothes inside it.

-Call the President and cancel. The White House, the Senate, everything. You can do it, right?

-Of course – Noriko sniffs, wiping off the tears – I am Null. But why?

The following words are some of the most difficult Bob has ever pronounced.

-We're going to see your mother.

10- Flight

Null Tower, New York City

Max Black a.k.a. Quantum opens the door to his room, leaving the suitcase on the floor. Kari Zel is behind him, wearing her pink Myridian clothes and carrying a couple of bags full of comic books.

-You don't have to do this, really. I don't have a lot of stuff to move – Max says.

-No problem at all! Right now I'm only taking five English and three history classes, flying to Japan with Noriko, sparring with Torn in the gym, watching TV, cleaning up the place, keeping guard of our spaceship on Neptune and sleeping. I've got time to help you.

-...

-What?

-Nothing, I'm just trying to understand if you're the original Kari or one of her duplicates.

-The original is sleeping. I'm kind of lazy.

-Only you can call doing a thousand things at the same time "lazy".

-If it makes you feel better, I don't understand how Earth people can get anything done without duplicates. Speaking of which, haven't you talked to your family yet?

-I don't know what to say to them – Max answers honestly, shrugging.

-"Hey guys, I'm back on Earth, I'm fine, bye"? – she suggests.

-My folks don't even know I'm Quantum…we don't talk much. My sister knows, but she doesn't really approve of my superhero career.

-You know, when siblings fight on Myridia it's generally for stuff like who's going to live and who's going to sacrifice himself to the Oracles. But I guess your Earth problems are important too.

-I don't mean to sound insensitive, but are you going to play the "Myridia sucks more than Earth" card *every time* we disagree on something?

-Yep. Is it working? – Kari asks, smiling innocently.

Quantum groans, recognizing the girl *does* have a point, and disappears in a flash of light.

Triton, Neptune's largest moon

The only thing Vesta can remember is the cold. As the goddess of the household fire, she's not used to it…in fact, she barely recognizes the feeling.

Despite the absence of a decent atmosphere, flames immediately surround her body to heat her. A human would've crumbled to a dust cloud of ice crystals in minutes; she just shivers.

She doesn't know how much time has passed; she never carries a watch. But it's been enough for the *Twin Dragon* to take off.

She tries to stand up, but her legs won't support her. She falls down again, gathering all of her strength just to remain conscious.

"Is this what Demeter felt before dying?" she wonders before fainting.

First class, international flight

Kari Zel is bored out of her skull. She knows she's just a duplicate, sent to accompany Noriko in her journey to Japan, but that makes the experience even more irritating.

She's not used to fourteen hours of sitting down in a closed space without any other duplicate. Noriko is passing the time working on who knows what invention on her N-Phone, oblivious to anything else. Her father Bob however notices Kari's exhaustion; his seat is on the other side of the corridor, so he leans over to talk to Kari.

-Enjoying the flight? – he asks.

-I've flown before with Vesta, but compared to that this is sooo boring. How do Earth people stand traveling like this?

-Don't ask me, this is the first time in my life I can afford a flight. So you're really from outer space?

-No, I lived on a planet too. You're…surprisingly cool with it.

-Hey, the last thing coming from space was a homicidal robot trying to conquer New York, and before that there was this crazy green woman who almost destroyed the city with a piece of the Moon. A cute girl with purple hair trying to help my daughter really isn't the worst that could happen.

Bob gives her a big smile, and it's hard not to be at least a little charmed by his simplicity.

-She doesn't like it, you know.

-Who doesn't like what?

-Noriko. When you flirt with other women. You never noticed?

Bob glances over to his daughter, certain to receive a lecture, but she's too busy on her work.

He leans over towards Kari a little more, asking in a much softer tone:

-What happened to her on your planet?

-She killed a goddess.

-Yeah yeah, I know *that*, but before it?

-I don't know. What happened to her on Earth? I understand she wasn't always like this.

-She was stuck by lighting and turned super-smart.

-Yeah I know but...does she know anyone beside the Vanguard? This Jane she met...

-She was her best friend. Before the lightning, at least. I don't think she's met any of her other friends lately. Although it seems she's making a habit of making friends on other planets.

-And she keeps us at a distance, too. I can see she's trying but...what was she like before the lightning?

-Why the sudden interest? – Bob asks. Kari seems harmless enough, but he really doesn't like people asking too many questions about his daughter.

-I worry about her: she saved my people. She's my goddess now.

-Well if you don't mind, your goddess has to go to the bathroom – Noriko intervenes, standing up.

Kari and Bob react as if they've just been caught doing something wrong by their parents.

-Nori, you weren't...

-Listening to anything important? Unlikely – she cuts them off.

Her father and her friend watch her as she walks away; she's clearly upset. Bob notices that she's left her N-Phone behind and reaches for it.

-You really shouldn't. Your daughter's an adult now – Kari chides him.

-She's also very good at getting into trouble – he answers, looking at the N-Phone screen.

It takes him a while to understand what it is. Kari watches it too, but she's not very good at reading English.

-What is it? Another weapon?

-It's...it's stock. She's just buying stocks. By the truckload.

-Oh that's nice. What is a stock, anyway?

238

-To be perfectly honest, I don't know – Bob answers.

The Twin Dragon, Demeter's former mothership
Kari Zel is used to watch herself die. She's witnessed the death of countless duplicates.

When Talas Khanos used his telekinetic powers to break free, she expected to experience it firsthand. But instead she wakes up tied to one of the chairs on the bridge.

She turns around, seeing the former Oracle sitting on the golden throne at the center of the room.

-Good morning, sweetie.

Kari's first instinct is to create a duplicate to untie her. But when she does, the metal collar on her neck releases an extremely painful electrical shock. She falls down but doesn't hit the floor: Khanos is lifting her with his mind.

-It's called the Agony Ring. Try to use your Myridian powers again and it will fry your brain.

-You won't kill me…you need me to pilot the ship – she manages to say through her teeth.

-Do I? I may not be Myridian, but I can do more than one thing at a time as well – he answers, gesturing towards one of the control stations. The flatscreen quickly responds to his mental commands, despite being several feet away.

-Then what do you need me for? I'm not your slave.

-That's a good question. You're just a duplicate, so vivisection is out of the question: you'll pop out of existence the second I touch you with a scalpel.

Something bumps against the *Twin Dragon*; it's enough to shake it despite the inertial dampeners.

-Well what do you know. The birds sure are hungry today if they attack a mothership.

-"The birds"? – Kari asks.

-Harpies. Have you ever seen them eat a person? – Khanos asks, with the excitement of a kid.

Kari shakes her head nervously.

-Too bad I can't let you duplicate. I just <u>love</u> Myridians watching themselves being eaten alive.

First class, international flight
239

Noriko is in the bathroom, looking at her own reflection. She's visibly tired: tiny red veins are starting to become visible around her silver eyes.

"You should get some sleep. You look like thirty-five or something" the reflection thinks.

"Can't I get some privacy here?" Noriko thinks back.

"Hey, is that the way to treat your other personality? Geez, you're really a stuck-up"

"I will not have an argument with a figment of my imagination"

"Say, when you're done talking with mom, what do you say we meet the old gang?"

"First, Leiko is not my mother. Second, what old gang?"

"You know. Jane, Liz, Asha and Stacy. You think Jeff is still mad at me for dumping him?"

"Is that everything that matters with you? Friends and boys?"

"So what? We're rich now. We're popular. Isn't this what we always wanted?"

"I wanted to be more than the janitor's daughter"

"Well you're the smartest person in the world now. What are you going to do with it?"

-Is this a bad time?

Suddenly hearing a voice that isn't coming from inside her head, Noriko jumps back and bumps into Quantum.

-I'm in the bathroom, what do you think!?!? – she says punching him in the arm.

-Sorry! I bounced off your N-Watch as radio waves and didn't watch where I was going. Good luck you weren't, y'know…

-Get. Out – she says, her eyes shining with her death stare.

-I can't; I don't have a ticket, remember? And if people see us get out of the same bathroom…

-What are you doing here!?

-Oh, right. I can't find my sister.

-She's not here, nice seeing you, goodbye.

-Come on Nori, this is serious! She quit her job and nobody's seen her in the past six weeks!

-Sounds familiar – she acknowledges.

-Both the CIA *and* your mother know I'm Quantum. What if one of them kidnapped her while we were gone? You know, to blackmail me.

240

-It's a possibility. We'll land in Tokyo in seven hours; wait for me at the airport.

-Right. Enjoy, uhm, enjoy your flight – Quantum answers before beaming out as a stream of light.

"As if I don't have enough things on my mind already" she thinks, pulling down her pants to sit on the toilet.

-I forgot, Kari wants to know when... - Quantum asks, stopping mid-sentence when he notices the girl's embarrassing situation. Her eyes are blindingly shining with rage.

-I...should probably...

-**<u>Get. Out</u>** – she repeats with an almost demonic voice.

Quantum could swear he disappeared faster than light this time.

11-Old stories

Scion Corporation Headquarters

Tokyo, Japan

Noriko Null looks up to the top of the building. Brand new, old-fashioned and imposing: Scion couldn't ask for a more accurate image.

-It's much bigger than our skyscraper – Kari says with her typical enthusiasm.

-It's not *that* big – Noriko tries to minimize.

-Leiko always did like to show off – her father Bob chimes in.

Kari and Bob take a step forward, but turn back when they notice Noriko is still looking up. Her hands are clenched in fists, and she's visibly shaken.

-You don't have to do this – Bob tries to reassure her.

-Yes I do. It's just…I haven't seen her since the lightning strike. Since I was…normal.

-If it makes you feel better, I haven't seen her since the day you were born – Bob says.

-It doesn't – Noriko answers coldly, entering the building like she owns the place. Kari doesn't waste time to ask Bob:

-I know you said Leiko left you when Noriko was little but…on the day she was born!?

-You need to know only one thing about Leiko Tanaka, Kari. She doesn't have a heart.

Bob follows his daughter, leaving Kari to look around. First New York, now Tokyo…she thought Earth was a paradise, left untouched by the evil gods that slaughtered her people.

-What kind of a planet is this? – she wonders out loud.

The Twin Dragon, Demeter's former mothership

Over the years, Kari Zel wondered how her first travel in outer space would be like. It was just a child's dream: only males could become soldiers and leave Myridia. And they never came back.

But she could hope that space was a simpler place, where gods left people in peace.

-Take this. You'll need it – Talas Khanos says, handing her an Oracle lance. The mere sight of it brings back painful memories of people being killed to appease Demeter.

-What do you need *me* for!? Can't you use your freaky mind powers to stop them or, I don't know, the ship's defenses!?
-Think, you pathetic carrier of genetic material, think. Harpies are strong enough to survive in the vacuum of space, but they can't fly faster than light. And we're *years* away from the nearest system.
-You mean somebody brought these things out here!?
-Would you *please* just go ahead and die?
The first harpy rips the hull apart. The air is quickly sucked out of the spaceship with enough force to lift a person off his feet. Talas Khanos uses his telekinesis to avoid this fate, but Kari is in much more trouble. She plants the lance firmly into the floor and holds on to it, fighting against the decompression. Khanos watches her for a few seconds, chuckling as she gasps for air, before sealing off the wall.
-Couldn't you do it earlier? – Kari asks, exhausted.
-I prefer specimen that are hard to kill off.
Kari doesn't have time to recover: the creature is spreading her bat-like wings. It's far more alien than Kari imagined…the bird legs, the talons that could crack her skull, the thick reptilian blue skin, wings where the arms should be…and that horrible, horrible head.
Curved horns. Four bulbous eyes. And half a face filled with white, sharp fangs.
-I was talking about the Harpy, of course. But if you survive, you'll do fine as well.

Scion Corporation Headquarters
Leiko Tanaka enters her office, followed by her assistant carrying a holographic tablet. Noriko, Bob and Kari are sitting on the three chairs in front of her desk.
-<What do you want?> – she asks in Japanese, without even looking at them.
The resemblance to Noriko is striking. Mother and daughter seem to have done everything possible to look different from one another…traditional versus rebellious, long versus short hair, expensive office suit versus cheap leather jacket, skirt and high heels versus jeans and combat boots…but the similarity still shows.
-<They can't understand you> – Noriko answers, pointing at Bob and Kari.

243

Leiko sends off her assistant with a hand gesture and asks again, this time in English:

-What do you want? – Leiko asks again, this time in English.

-We haven't seen each other for eighteen years. And you tried to kill our daughter. Don't you have anything else to say!?

Leiko doesn't say a word. She just stares at Bob blankly, waiting for an answer.

-I wanna know what you think you're doing. Stealing my technology, installing reactors all over the world, infiltrating the Blue in foreign governments and, yes, trying to murder me in my sleep – Noriko says. Her silver eyes flash briefly when she raises her voice.

It's the only moment when Leiko shows any reaction; it's the first time she sees this. But she doesn't look surprised…just awestruck, even if it's just for a second.

-Have you read the Odyssey? – Leiko asks.

-Of course – Noriko and Kari answer simultaneously.

The Myridian girl gets astonished looks both from Noriko and Bob.

-What? It's popular on Myridia. Of course Demeter didn't want us to read about a guy flying around the Galaxy when every other god wants to kill him, but we read it anyway.

-There is no interstellar travel in the Odyssey, Kari.

-I…don't think we've read the same version, Nori.

-The Odyssey…the original one, not the bastardized version we read on Earth…talks about the attempt to organize a human resistance against divine dictatorship after the end of the Second Trojan War – Leiko explains.

-Wait wait wait, time out – Bob interrupts her – How did we jump from attempted murder to the freakin' Odyssey!?

-Don't interrupt – Leiko and Noriko answer at the same time; neither of them seems to be proud to use the same words of the other one. Then Leiko continues:

-Before dying of old age, Ulysses managed to recover several Drylon artifacts and hide them on a planet forgotten by the rest of the galaxy, hoping that someday the mortals of that world would rise against the tyranny of Olympus.

-The Legend of Lethe, yeah, everyone knows about that. Wait, you mean to tell me that Lethe actually exists and we're standing on it!? – Kari asks, dumbstruck by the notion.

244

-So you recovered the original version of the Odyssey and learned about the Heart of the Universe. It doesn't explain much – Noriko complains.

-I'm not trying to explain anything. I'm just stalling you – Leiko answers calmly, looking at her watch. She presses a hidden button under her desk, and the whole room is filled with a diffuse light.

Quantum appears suddenly, collapsing on the floor. Bob does the same. Kari creates a couple of duplicates to lift herself, but they also fall under the immense pain they are feeling.

Noriko is the only one capable to remain conscious for a while. She can feel the circuitry of the N-Watch and the N-Phone being fried, and crawls to the desk to lift herself up.

-Took you long enough. I almost thought you weren't going to make it – Leiko says, opening a small box on the desk.

A ball of metal, not much larger than a baseball, rises up and talks with an inhumanly deep voice.

-*If you were sufficiently evolved to use primitive technology to generate an anti-neutrino field that also stimulates pain receptors, you wouldn't need me* – the Core answers.

Noriko manages to stand up, but it takes all of her strength. And just looking at the Core makes her silver eyes burn.

-Just knock her out. If she keeps this up, we risk damaging the Nexus.

These are the last words Noriko hears before passing out.

The Twin Dragon, Demeter's former mothership

The Harpy tries to bite Kari in the neck, which given how massive its jaw is would probably decapitate her. Kari is quick enough to avoid her; then she unstuck the lance from the floor and uses it to fence off the alien creature.

-Having fun!? – she asks Talas Khanos, who is just a few feet away.

-Not really. Needs more disemboweling – he answers sincerely.

In an open environment, Kari would be dead by now. The Harpy would take flight and strike with its powerful talons; she's already seen that the creature's legs are strong enough to rip the hull to shreds. But there's not enough space to fly here, and the Harpy doesn't have arms: it can only bite, and the lance keeps it at a distance.

-It's really something to see one of them in the wild, isn't it? One of the few truly alien species of the galaxy. They're almost extinct; we're close to Artemis space, so this one probably escaped the reserve with her family.

-"Her"? You mean this thing's female? – Kari asks, poking the Harpy in one of the eyes; the creature lets out a chilling scream, like knives on a chalkboard.

-Of course, all harpies are female. Since she came inside alone, the others are probably her children.

-Great; I can deal with mommy here, but what are we gonna do with the rest!?

-What indeed – asks another female voice.

A woman comes through the wall like a ghost. She has blue skin, no nose and large bat wings coming out of her back, and her blue hair barely cover the trimmed horned crest on her forehead.

Other than that, she could easily be mistaken for a stunningly beautiful woman. The harpy roars again, waving her wings; she looks really pissed.

The blue woman spreads her own wings, hissing. The harpy groans something and steps back, crouching and wrapping herself with her wings.

-What the Hades just happened!? – Kari asks.

-I told her not to eat you. I am Elytra Elater, captain of the *Distant Horizon*. Who is your god?

-Null.

Kari's answer doesn't seem to satisfy the blue woman, who draws her gun and points at her.

-Can we trust her?

-She's just a Myridian and I gave her an Agony Ring. She's harmless – Talas Khanos answers.

-Wait, you two know each other!?

-Oh yes, Elytra and I go way back. Her family's been providing me new specimen for over 60 generations…which for a Lampyrian like her means about thirty years.

-You're a Lampyrian? But I thought…

-That my people were only cheap prostitutes? I heard the same thing about Myridians. Khanos, what is going on? I've heard all kinds of rumors coming from Demeter space.

-The fall of the gods is arriving, Elytra. Soon we will rule the galaxy. Well, not you *personally*, since you've got only a few months to live but...

-Why do you <u>always</u> bring up my lifespan? – she asks, putting the gun away.

It's Kari's only chance: she jumps at the blue woman with the intent of knocking her out and stealing her gun. Instead, she just goes through her intangible body.

Her first thought is that she's just a hologram, but the punch in her stomach is definitely real.

-Unless you want me to punch you in the brain next time, don't do it again – she threatens.

Sensing the anger of her mistress, the Harpy roars.

"I'm starting to think Myridia wasn't so bad after all" Kari thinks.

12- Flashback, part 1

Nineteen years ago

Bob Null's life changed one Friday afternoon, coming home from high school. Someone was waiting for him. It was a Japanese schoolgirl, complete with uniform, holding a suitcase in her hands. The petite and demure Asian wasn't really his type, but he had to admit she was beautiful. She was standing in front of his rundown apartment building: the two really didn't seem to belong to the same world.

-Excuse me, are you Robert Null? – she asked.

-Uhm, yeah. Call me Bob – he answered, hoping she wouldn't notice how much he was staring at her. She bowed respectfully.

-Tanaka Leiko, it is a pleasure to meet you. Is your grandfather Professor Heinrich Null?

-Maybe. Why? – he asked back. When your grandfather is a Nazi you tend to talk about him as little as possible.

-May we speak in private?

Nazi grandfather or not, Bob was a fifteen year old boy in front of a cute girl in a school uniform. Of course he immediately invited her to his apartment.

Once inside, Leiko took off her shoes and looked around, confused. Like Bob, she realized this really wasn't her world.

-Sorry about the mess. We moved in three weeks ago and with Dad doing overtime at the factory…

-Does anyone else live here?

-No, my mother passed away and I'm an only child. What about you? – Bob asked to get a chance to change the subject to something else.

-My brothers died of overdose and my mother is in a mental institution – the girl answered. There wasn't the slightest emotion in her voice: she could've given him the weather.

Bob didn't know how to follow that, and just watched her retrieve a picture from her suitcase.

-Have you ever seen this object? – she asked. The picture showed an old black and white picture of Professor Heinrich Null holding a baseball-shaped rock in his hands.

-Sure, come here – he said, taking her by the hand and leading her to his father's bedroom.

248

He will never forget how cold her hands were that day.

The object was on his father's nightstand. He hadn't bothered to unpack most of his clothes yet, but the rock had been in its rightful place since the day they moved.

Leiko was overwhelmed and seemed on the verge of crying; even her composure had limits.

-Are you alright? You look a little pale – Bob asked.

-The Heart of the Universe. Mom was right: it was on Earth all along.

-Look, it's just a rock. Grandpa said it was the most important thing ever or something, but he was kind of crazy.

-What do you want for it? – Leiko asked.

-How about a date? – Bob asked with a big, warm smile. Leiko turned around to look him in the eye: he was positively towering above her, but she was clearly the one in control.

-Are you proposing a romantic encounter or sexual intercourse?

-What!? No, nothing like that! I was just, look, you're taking this the wrong way. How about we just go for a walk?

Leiko's stare was unsettling. She hardly ever blinked and her voice never changed tone.

-That will do – she agreed.

They talked for what felt like ages. Leiko let it slip that she was fifteen and that she was some kind of prodigy already in college, but that was the extent of what she wanted to reveal. At first she let Bob do most of the talking, intervening only when necessary to avoid turning it into a monologue.

But over the hours she started to talk about her family. How her father had always been cold towards her, more interested in her brothers and in his own career; he was a very important businessman with very, very shady connections. She didn't talk about her mother.

Eventually, the two found themselves sitting on the beach of Coney Island, looking at the sea.

Saying nothing, just happy with each other's company.

-It is late. Your father will worry – she broke the ice with her cold voice.

-He's used to it. I come here often. What about you? Do you have a place to stay?

-Yes. I should go back to it – Leiko answered, wiping the sand off her skirt. Then she looked up at the sky, with a sad look. It was the first time Bob saw any emotion on her face.

-There are no stars – she said.

-Yeah, that's too bad. Too many street lights or something. It's funny when you think about it: we've managed to pollute everything, even the sky.

-None of this matters. We could be nothing and the universe wouldn't notice.

-What's wrong, Leiko? What aren't you telling me? – Bob asked. The girl looked like she'd been carrying the weight of the world on her shoulders her whole life. He'd been trying to get inside her head the whole day, and this was the first time she didn't bother shielding herself.

-I know what is out there. Gods and monsters and scary things. If they come back, nothing will matter. Not the stars, not humanity, not you, not me. The universe doesn't care about us.

-Will you cut out that gloom and doom bull##it?

Leiko was surprised by Bob's reaction; he grabbed her shoulders and tried to shake her off her shell-shocked detachment.

-You got hurt by something, badly, I can tell that. But don't go around saying crap like that; people matter. You matter.

-The universe disagrees.

-F##k the universe! Why don't you go beyond the impossible and prove it wrong?

Bob expected to receive a slap in the face. Instead Leiko threw herself in his arms and kissed him.

It was a long, passionate kiss by a girl who hadn't left any emotion break free of the absolute control she had over herself.

Noriko Null was conceived on the same night.

Today
Scion Corporation Headquarters, Tokyo

-You know, father, you don't have to tell me everything – Noriko laments, blushing.

-I think it's romantic – Kari says, sniffing.

They are all in the same meeting room, handcuffed to their chairs. Quantum is also there, under the constant surveillance of the Core that floats above him.

250

Unaffected by his daughter's embarrassment, Bob Null continues:

-Leiko rented one of the apartments and assembled some kind of lab in the basement. We told everyone she was an exchange student; I didn't know she was pregnant. Then, two months later, she just vanished.

-I thought she left you *after* Nori was born – Kari notes, confused.

-No, I mean she literally vanished. One day I came back from school and found that stupid rock inside one of her devices. Her clothes were on the floor, underwear and all.

-Just like when I was teleported to Myridia. But *how*? Nothing I tried has worked – Noriko wonders.

The doors open. Leiko Tanaka enters the room, followed by two people with surgical masks and another three dressed with military gear.

-Have you tried being pregnant? – she asks.

-<u>What?</u> – is the collective question.

-The Heart is programmed to answer only to beings with two distinct genetic codes. There's only one known alien species with this kind of biological structure – she explains.

-The Drylon – Noriko understands.

-Olympians can't use it because they don't have real DNA. The Many can fool the scanning process thanks to its unstable genetic code; probably a side effect of the shapeshifting. But a pregnant female human is registered as a single individual with two distinct DNAs.

Noriko's silver eyes fill up with electricity. It still hurts, but she's too mad to care.

-So that's the only reason I was born? **To be a password!?**

-Essentially, yes – Leiko acknowledges, gesturing one of the men with surgical masks to come closer. He's holding a syringe.

-Why'd you contact me? I didn't know you were my mother. There was no need to offer me money to keep it a secret and prevent me from traveling to Japan.

-I had to test you. I needed the final proof that you were the failure of a human being that I thought you were. You had no talent, no ambition, no goal; in a few years you'd be working in a fast food. You could've accepted my bribe and used it to become someone, or to blackmail me. But instead you chose to run away like a spoiled child.

251

-You do have a strange idea of child support – Quantum quips.

-How can you talk to our daughter like that!? – Bob protests, struggling to break free of the handcuffs.

-Robert. You think you're so special just because you can procreate? A dog can do it. Don't suppose to be better than me just because my life revolves around something greater than fulfilling what animals are programmed to do.

-I am not a failure. I am Null – Noriko says; her eyes are blindingly bright now. All of her muscles are tense, pulling the handcuffs away from the chair, but there are hardly any muscles to speak off on her eighteen year old body.

-And what does that mean? You are the smartest person on the planet. You have all the knowledge in the world. And what are you doing with it? Building toys and an ivory tower where you can hide because the world is too scary? I had access to your scrapbook for six weeks and I changed the world without even trying!!!

The man with the syringe is coming closer. Quantum is trying to turn into any kind of energy, but the Core's power is preventing him from doing anything. They walked right into Leiko's trap...she was waiting for them the whole time.

Then he notices the room is getting darker. They're right in front of a very large window; he can see there are black clouds gathering above the city, moving unnaturally fast.

One of the armed men is holding Noriko steady while the doctor is about to inject something in her arm. She just needs a little more time.

-You stole my comic books – Quantum intervenes.

If Leiko is surprised by the sudden change of subject, she doesn't show it.

-I was studying you. Learning how you think. But you're just a loser wasting the gift to change the world on a juvenile power fantasy. Much like my daughter.

-Maybe. But if I was a character in a comic book and the bad guy was making a big speech when I was prisoner, you know what I'd say right now?

-Enlighten us.

-"Shazam".

The lightning smashes through the window, headed straight for Noriko. Leiko's men are pushed back, and the syringe falls to the floor.

If this were a normal lightning strike, it would already be over. But this is an update for Noriko's brain: it will take several seconds to complete.

Fueled by the indescribable adrenaline surge that accompanies the update, Noriko breaks free of the handcuffs. Still engulfed in electricity, she punches Leiko right on the nose.

-WHO'S A FAILURE NOW!? – she screams through the pain.

For the first time in her life, Leiko can't hide the fact that she's afraid.

13- Flashback, part 2

When the lightning smashes through the window to reach Noriko, the Core's anti-duplication field falters. The interference lasts only a moment, but Kari can create duplicates in the blink of an eye.

A new Kari pops into existence right in front of the Core; she grabs the baseball-sized alien device and runs to the window, throwing herself off the building.

As shocking as watching a duplicate throw away its life so carelessly can be, Quantum knows there are more important things to do. With the Core away, he's free to use his powers.

The armed guards are disarmed with a simple blast of concentrated microwaves, which melts their weapons from the inside. A right hook takes care of one of the doctors, because you can't feel like a super-hero if you don't punch somebody in the face every once in a while.

In under a minute, all of Leiko's men have been taken down. The proud owner of Scion Corporation is on the floor, with a hand on her broken nose trying to stop the bleeding.

-Security will be here in a minute and your alien friend can't stop the Core from coming back. You are not going to… - she threatens, stopping when she notices Noriko's stance.

She's zoned out, staring at her blankly with silver eyes filled with electricity. Staring her own hand soiled with blood, Leiko watches the electrical current still flowing from her own head.

-What are you seeing? – she asks.

Twenty-eight years ago

Leiko wasn't allowed in her mother's room. There were no pictures of her in the house and her father never talked about her; Leiko had to discover who she was by reading her books.

Wakahisa Noriko had been a respected professor of archeology and comparative mythology, so most of what she wrote went right above Leiko's head. She was smart enough to read them despite being only five years old, but even child prodigies have limits.

One night she sneaked into her room. She was laying on her bed, hooked up to a machine that recorded her vital signs; people said she had a stroke shortly after Leiko's birth, but there was nothing wrong with her body. She kept talking.

-The stars are rebelling hide the hearts make room for the dark galaxy build more gods seal the edge of the universe build more gods the stars are rebelling...

-Mommy?

-*What are you doing here?* – something asked, with a scary deep voice.

Leiko screamed: there was a metal ball floating above her mother's head. In the dark, with the moon's light coming through the blinds, it looked downright demonic.

-What are you doing to my mommy!?

-*This primitive storage device cannot sustain a Drylon operating system. I am attempting to correct that flaw, but the biological hardware has sustained heavy damage.*

-What's a Drylon?

-*Would you like to know?*

Eighteen years and six months ago

Leiko found herself naked inside some sort of storage room. There were boxes everywhere; she was in front of a ten feet tall statue of a man in a toga. The head and arms had been cut off.

There was some kind of alarm. The room was filled with armed angry men shouting orders in a foreign language that she couldn't understand, pointing weapons at her.

They ran all kinds of tests on her for several days. She was treated fairly, giving her time to study her captors. She identified all races she knew among them, and a few skin colors she'd never seen before. They spoke softly and never looked each other in the eye.

After they'd exhausted every possible kind of physical test feasible on a human, they started to ask questions. Every person they sent spoke perfect Japanese.

They wanted to know about Earth. Which god did they worship? When was the last time they saw one? What did they know about the nearby stars? What were the other planets in its solar system like? How advanced were their weapons? How many warships did they have?

Leiko answered every question. It was enough to break any teenager, let alone someone who by now knew she was pregnant. Leiko never complained, not even once.

After weeks of captivity, they took her to a poorly lit room where she waited alone for four hours.

Finally her contact arrived. He was freakishly tall, at least eight feet, and his skin was extremely dark. Judging by how other people reacted to his presence, he was in charge of the place.

A woman with long blue hair followed him with, taking notes on a digital device. Leiko could've mistaken her for Native American.

-State your name, planet and god – he said in perfect Japanese, sitting down. Even so, he was taller than Leiko would've been standing up.

-I am Tanaka Leiko of planet Earth, and I have no god.

-We have no record of a planet with such a name – the Native American with blue hair explained – However judging by the description of its solar system we believe it is a new name for Lethe.

-The planet forgotten by the gods. What do you know about a man called Ulysses? – the tall man asked.

-That he took the Core to Earth two thousand years ago. My grandfather discovered it in China during the war and claimed it as his own personal property.

-How do you know about the Core? – the tall man pressed her. Leiko didn't lose her composure.

-I have read the Odyssey. The real one.

The tall man and the woman with blue hair looked at each other. They seemed very worried.

-Has anyone else read it on Earth? – he asked.

-Only my mother. She discovered the original text; that's how she found out about the Core and met my father. It has shared its secrets with me. And it wants to help you.

-You know who we are, then – the tall man realized.

-The Mortal Liberation Front – Leiko answered.

Eighteen years ago

Leiko was sitting on a medical bed floating a few inches off the ground. The doctor placed the ultrasound sensor on her belly; she was in her eight month of pregnancy.

The tall man walked into the room, carrying a very heavy metal suitcase. He glanced at the monitor that was showing the heart rates of mother and child.

-Aren't you *at least* a little nervous? You're making my men look like amateurs – he said.

-We have another month before birth. Enough time to take all precautions.

-I hope you are right. We had to sacrifice three worlds to get this.

The tall man opened the suitcase. It contained a small device, no bigger than a fingernail, shaped like the symbol for infinity.

-The Nexus. Are you sure it will activate properly once on your world? – he asked.

-There are more than five billion people on Earth; it should be enough. You don't have another choice: if any god finds out about a Nexus activation they will burn its planet to the ground.

-Very well. Proceed – the tall man ordered.

On Earth, such a procedure would've been fatal. However Leiko didn't even feel any discomfort when the needle went through her belly and straight into the child's brain, installing the Nexus.

But then Leiko's eyes turned silver, and all the medical monitors went crazy.

There was a bright flash of blue light. When it ceased Leiko had disappeared, leaving her clothes on the medical bed.

Today
Scion Corporation Headquarters, Tokyo
A slap in the face makes Noriko come back to the present. While she gets her bearings, Kari snaps her fingers in front of her.

-Hey, are you there? You're not going into shock again, are you?

Just then, security rammed through the door. They were pointing their weapons and shouting orders in Japanese. Leiko composed herself, still holding her bloody nose.

-Settle down. Just a minor disagreement; miss Null was just about to leave.

-The hell I am. You put some kind of alien device inside my head!!!

-This is private property, miss Null, and you are no longer welcome here.

-Your shareholders probably disagree. Have you watched the news, lately?

Null Tower, New York City

257

Vesta knocks on the window, stroking her right arm to warm it up. She can <u>still</u> feel the cold from Triton…even space didn't feel so cold.

Kari's original body, still wearing her pajama, opens the window to let her in.

-Vesta, what took you so long? – she asks yawning, while creating a duplicate to hug the goddess.

-Someone stole the *Twin Dragon*.

-Really? That's too bad. Are you hungry?

Kari calmly walks towards the living room, followed by Vesta who is floating a few inches off the ground.

-Aren't you worried about your duplicates?

-Nah, I can take care of myself.

-Hey girls, we're on the news! – another Kari shouts.

In the living room, six different copies of Kari gather in front of the television. Torn is also there, almost invisible among the collective excitement of the duplicates.

The TV is showing four people walking out of a building, escorted by the police: Noriko, Bob and two Kari. Then it shows amateur footage of a lightning bolt striking the Scion Corporation skyscraper, then images of a hole in the sidewalk with the same size of a baseball.

-*More news from Japan where the headquarters of Scion Corporation were the scene of several unexplained phenomena: a lightning bolt striking the upper floors despite the clear sky today in Tokyo, and reports of a woman falling off the side of the building but disappearing before hitting the ground. We have reports of teenage billionaire Noriko Null being present in the room struck by lightning; she was seen leaving the building accompanied by her father Robert and two unidentified women. There are also unconfirmed sightings of American super-hero Quantum in the building.*

-You guys better watch the…oh hi Vesta – Quantum says after appearing in the room.

At this point, nobody is really surprised to see him show up all of a sudden without warning.

-What happened over there? – Vesta asks.

-It's…kind of a long story.

-Did you find your sister? – the original Kari asks.

258

-No, she wasn't there. Wait, here it comes!

-But the big story today is the near meltdown of the Japanese stock exchange, with Scion Corporation stock falling dramatically over the course of the day after what experts describe as "the most aggressive hostile takeover in history"; reportedly, Null Technologies has acquired over 80% of Scion Corporation stock for less than 2 dollars per share. The Japanese finance minister has said, quote, "If she does this again we can kiss the financial system goodbye", but later added that his comments were taken out of context.

-Don't you get it? Leiko just lost everything she had. We won!

-Did she lose control of the Blue, the Core, the Fusion Reactor or of any technology she stole from Noriko? Or of the alien technology she clearly already has? – Kari asks.

-Well, no, not really. We lost her and the Core when we left the building. Now that I think about it, she probably wants to kill us even more now. But I got my comic books back!

-Nice job – is Torn's final statement on the matter.

14- Consequences

The Twin Dragon, Demeter's former mothership

Kari Zel can feel the ship has landed, but she has no idea where. Talas Khanos hasn't told her anything, and she doesn't know if she can trust Elytra, the Lampyrian who hijacked the vessel.

All she knows is that she ceased to be useful to her captors days ago, which knowing Khanos means he's just waiting for the best moment to kill her.

The door opens. The man approaching the cell wears an uniform, but it's very different from Elytra's…not just because of the gender and the absence of holes on the back for the bat wings.

It's an orange form-fitting armor, seemingly made of metal but as thick and flexible as silk.

-Hands on your head and no sudden moves – he orders; he's holding a pair of handcuffs.

Kari obliges, assessing the situation: the only weapon he carries is a knife.

-Where are you taking me? – she asks when he opens the cell's door.

He's too slow to avoid Kari's sleight of hand: with one swift motion she handcuffs him to the prison bars, then steals his knife before he can do anything about it.

-Amateur. Never escort a prisoner alone – she comments. Years of avoiding Oracles finally pay off.

-I'm never alone – the man answers. An exact duplicate of him appears behind Kari.

She headbutts him so hard that the duplicate disappears; just in time, because a second later she's faced with another three duplicates.

She's fought plenty of Myridians before, of course, but with the Agony Ring on her neck she doesn't have the luxury to create her own duplicates this time.

"It's gonna be fun" she thinks before ten male duplicates jump on her.

Bangkok, Thailand

There is a large silent explosion in the middle of the street, leaving a gaping hole in the ground.

Quantum retakes human form, gasping for breath: this is getting harder every time.

He watches the rain of blue goo which not long ago was a true army of soldiers marching towards the City Hall.

He touches his right ear with a finger, as if to touch an invisible headplug, and asks:

-Quantum to Null, are you getting this? Hello?

-*You don't have to say anything, Max. The Neural Headset translates your brainwaves into radio waves* –a familiar female voice in his head answers.

-Yeah yeah, I still think it's creepy. I've dealt with the Blue here, can I go home now?

-*Not just yet. Follow the signal to Vesta and Torn's location, they need your help.*

-The invulnerable goddess and the proud warrior guy asked for help!?

-*I didn't say they _asked_.*

Riyadh, Saudi Arabia

Vesta's fist is on fire when she punches the Blue, but it doesn't matter: at this point, the Blue are completely fireproof. Luckily, they are vulnerable to being punched into the stratosphere.

-This is starting to be really, _really_ annoying – she complains when twelve new Blue charge her.

-Why? CUT OF A THOUSAND DEATHS! – Torn shouts, releasing a stream of red energy daggers that obliterates the Blue.

-Are you kidding me? This the fifth Blue attack this week!

-I know. This planet is growing on me – the man with the red skin notes, coming dangerously close to smiling. Quantum appears right by his side.

-Hey guys. I see you've got everything under control – he notes, interrupted by Noriko's voice.

-*They don't. Vesta, the Blue have set fire to an oil field 400 kil…250 miles south of your position.*

-Oh Gaea, _another one_!? – the goddess complains before taking flight.

-*Max, I think the Blue are adapting to Torn's power. Gather as much as you can and sterilize the remains with high-energy gamma rays. Torn, the authorities will try to get their hands on them, try to dissuade them.*

-Can I fight them?

261

-*Not this time, Torn. I've got enough international accidents on my hands as it is.*

-Look at this mess – Quantum says looking at the city: it looks like a warzone – Your mother must be really pissed off that you stole her company.

Null Tower, New York City

Noriko Null takes a step back from the holographic display and sighs: Quantum is right, the Blue have intensified their attacks after she acquired Scion Corporation.

She still doesn't understand why; what good is all of this chaos to Leiko? Does it have anything to do with what she saw during their brief telepathic contact?

-*Mistress, the President is calling on line three. Shall I put him on speaker?* – asks the Tower's artificial intelligence.

Noriko looks at the hologram of the planet: it's full of red points, indicating where the Blue have attacked. She also hasn't had the time yet to deal with the acquisition of Scion Corporation or the mess left behind at Null Technologies during her disappearance.

-I already have eighty-five callers on hold, I.R.I.S. Tell him I'll call him back.

-*Mistress, you have requested to be reminded not to hang up on him again. The last time-*

-I'll call. Him. Back – Noriko punctuates. Her silver eyes shine in anger and frustration.

-*Very well, mistress.*

Noriko closes her eyes. It's going to be a rough day.

"So we're not going to acknowledge what we've seen in mom's mind?" a voice in her head asks.

"Don't call her mom. She just gave birth to me to gain access to the Heart of the Universe"

"Yeah, whatever, but what about that Nexus thing she put inside us?"

"It doesn't show up in any kind of test I can think of. Even the Oracle on Myridia that examined me didn't seem to find it. Although it <u>does</u> explain why Athena chose me: she didn't give me any power, she just unlocked it"

"And here I thought we were just that awesome"

"You're just an alternate personality. I'm the awesome one. I am…"

262

"If you say "I am Null" I'm gonna give you the worst headache ever. So Athena activating the Nexus is what made you super-smart, I get that. But why did mom put it there in the first place?"

"We'll deal with that later. I'm kind of busy now"

"I want to know what else you saw during the psychic link; I know you're hiding something"

"I don't know what you're talking about"

"I'm you, remember? Well, the part of you that isn't a total b##ch, anyway"

"You won't go away until I show you, isn't it?"

"Yep"

"Remember: you asked for it"

Eighteen years ago

Leiko might be the coldest person in the world, but her father was absolute zero. Daichi Tanaka didn't show the slightest emotion beating her fifteen year old daughter, nine months pregnant.

-I told you not to get involved in my business – he said, kicking Leiko in the face.

-You've been exposed to the Core too much; you're not thinking rationally – she said, defiantly.

Her reward was her own father almost breaking her right hand by stepping on it. She kept talking through the pain.

-Drylon technology...causes...emotional detachment...delusions of grandeur...adult brains...can't adapt...that's why mom went crazy...why you can't see...the bigger picture...

Daichi rolled Leiko's body over, moving his foot over her belly. She felt the baby kicking.

-This bastard child. Will he be able to adapt to what you put inside him?

-Her. It will take years...the Nexus needs time to mature...and she must be away from the Core.

-Will we be able to extract the Nexus after it's active?

-Not without killing the host.

Daichi seemed to think it over for a while, while Leiko moaned in pain. Finally, he snapped his fingers to order one of his men to open the door.

They let a Japanese girl in. She didn't look like Leiko at all, but she was fifteen and pregnant.

263

-This is Haruka Yukimura. Records will show that she is the mother of the bastard child of the American. None of you will see the baby after the birth. Understood?

-Yes father – Leiko said. But Noriko can also hear what she thought: "You will die before the Nexus is active. I will make sure of it".

Noriko opens her eyes again. The flashback is gone; this is the extent of what she saw.

"Oh my God, that was...Haruka Yukimura. Isn't that..."

"The name shown on my birth certificate, yes. Left the United States after my birth. Died a month before I met Leiko the first time...a car accident, officially. Daichi died a year ago"

"Did Leiko kill them both?"

"I'd be very surprised if she didn't. And after what I've seen, I can't say I'm overly sad about it"

"I understand why you didn't show me that memory. We come from a family of horrible people"

"A family with connections to the Mortal Liberation Front. I don't know if Leiko is working for them or just using them, but it's not a good sign"

"Still, it's nice to have at least some *answers about our past, isn't it?"*

"I suppose"

Noriko approaches the holographic display again, struggling to maintain a professional detachment.

"Noriko...about the whole "Drylon technology makes you insane" thing..."

"I don't wanna talk about it"

The Twin Dragon, Demeter's former mothership

Kari adjusts the orange uniform stolen from the guard, admiring how it adheres perfectly on her body. A big step forward from her pink dress.

-Not bad. Wish it came in another color.

-He should be out cold for a few minutes – her duplicate says, adjusting the Agony Ring on the guard just to be sure he doesn't create more copies of himself.

-Let's hope this thing doesn't have some sort of locator or this will be a very short escape – the first Kari says, activating the helmet that grows from the uniform to completely cover her head.

264

The other duplicate is handcuffed and escorted out of the ship. It's a very easy trip…there seems to be nobody else on the *Twin Dragon*.

Everything changes when she steps out of the ship via the cargo bay. There are two other guards, a man and a woman, with the same uniform Kari is wearing. Only they don't have the helmet on.

Both the Kari wearing the uniform and the pretend prisoner act casual, but the woman stops them.

-Hold on. Where do you think you're going?

-I'm escorting the prisoner. Captains' orders – Kari answers. Luckily, the helmet distorts her voice.

-Varesh Yel was supposed to do it. Where is he?

-I don't know, ma'am. You should check with his direct superior.

-*I* am his direct superior. Who are you? Why are you wearing the helmet indoors?

-Look, I'm just following the captain's orders.

-So am I. Varesh, this is Zvareya, do you copy?

-*Varesh, this is Zvareya, do you copy?* – the radio on Kari's belt repeats. The two guards immediately draw their weapons, and both Karis sigh at the same time.

There are very few people alive who can defeat Kari Zel in hand to hand combat, and these two certainly aren't among them. Before they can sound the alarm, they're knocked out by a punch in the throat, a kick in the groin and an elbow blow at the base of the skull. All at the same time.

-It won't be long before they start looking for me – the Kari in uniform says, discarding the radio and stealing the guns.

-They're gonna have their hands full – the prisoner Kari says, before creating a hundred duplicates.

15- Oldest one in the book

New York City isn't the easiest city to find a decent house, especially if you're unemployed, but when you know Null it's not really a problem.

-This is awesome, isn't it? – Max Black exclaims, with hands on his hips as he proudly examines his new apartment. It's nothing to write home about, really, but to him it's a castle.

-I still don't get why you can't live at the Tower like everyone else – Vesta complains, effortlessly carrying three boxes of comic books balanced on one hand.

-That place gives me the creeps, with all those Nullbots. Thirty robots and less than ten people in a skyscraper that has a nuclear reactor...not the best place to live.

-It's not nuclear. And Torn likes it.

-Yeah but c'mon, he's Torn. The dude makes the Grim Reaper sound like the life of the party.

-Hades isn't so bad once you know him.

Max looks at her like she's from outer space, which isn't far from the truth. Then he takes something from his pocket: a pair of glasses.

-You should get ready, my friends will be here soon. Put these on.

-What for? – Vesta asks, taking the glasses.

-I have a secret identity, remember? If they see me with Vesta, they'll know I'm Quantum.

-You've got to be kidding me.

-Oldest one in the book. Besides, I don't think they're gonna look at your face.

-You know I'm older than...wait, what did you say?

-Nothing!

-He said they'll be looking at your breasts. Hi Max! – Kari introduces herself, followed by two duplicates who are moving the couch.

-Kari – Vesta greets her, crossing her arms over her low-cut tube top.

-Hey, if you got them, flaunt them – Kari taunts her, lifting her own breasts.

-You've been watching TV again? – Vesta changes the subject.

-No, I've got a dozen duplicates doing that for me. By the way Max, I met your friends downstairs, they'll be here any moment now.

-They saw you use your powers!?

266

-Just relax, I told them we're twins – one of the duplicates reveals.

-This is so stupid – Vesta complains, wearing the glasses. Her hair quickly turns from bright red to dark brown, shortening from shoulder length to a bob cut.

-Since when can you do that!? – Max asks.

-I don't know, since the Crusades I think. Are you sure this is a good idea? There are so many crises in the world we could...

-Later. We can't do Vanguard business 24/7 or we'll go insane. We need to have fun sometimes.

-Besides, with Leiko and the Blue gone, it's not like there's any big threat now – Kari shrugs.

Outer space

An army of five thousand Kari duplicates is swarming the docking bay, keeping the guards too busy to notice the woman in the orange uniform fleeing the scene.

"Oldest one in the book" this Kari thinks; by the time they've dealt with the other duplicates she'll be long gone.

She takes one of the elevators out of the docking bay. It runs through the outside of the installation, so Kari can finally understand the situation...which isn't good, to say the least.

It's a space station built on an asteroid. She can see the *Twin Dragon*, Demeter's former mothership, but it's far from the only ship docked here.

Hundreds, if not thousands, of smaller ships are ready for departure. They come in all size and shapes, but they all have one thing in common: a golden bow painted on the hull.

"Artemis Hunters. Since when do space pirates have a fleet this size!?" she wonders, when the elevator doors open.

Elytra Elater, captain of the *Distant Horizon*, is on the other side. Pointing a gun at her.

-Kari Zel of Myridia, I presume?

Before she can finish the question, a dozen Kari duplicates are already attacking her.

Earth, Max Black's apartment

Vesta is drinking a beer, watching Max having fun with his friends and the three Kari duplicates.

267

He told them he has a job at Null Technologies and that Vesta and Kari are co-workers...which isn't far from the truth and isn't so unusual: Noriko is hiring so many people these days. She may be a genius but Plasma Reactors, Sound Nullifiers and N-Phones don't build themselves.

A fourth Kari duplicate appears next to the fridge to get a few beers, asking:

-Mind telling me why you're here by yourself?

-This was a bad idea. Sooner or later they'll find out I'm a goddess.

-And what's so bad about that?

-You don't understand...it's happened so many times. They fall on their knees asking me to make them immortal, or to heal the sick, or to return their loved ones from the dead. I can't do any of these things, I'm just the goddess of the household fire. And once they discover it they try to drown me, or burn me at the stake, or worse.

-Look, they're just watching a game. Nobody's gonna ask you to raise the dead.

-I appreciate the thought, Kari, but I'm not one of them. I look human, but I'm not.

-So what? You're the only goddess I know that acts human, and that's what counts. We've both been running away for too long, Vesta. It's not what you're running away from, but why.

-Hey there's a fourth one!? – one of Max's friends exclaims.

-Kari has many "twins" – Max says, giving a disapproving look at the original Kari.

-Yes. Large families are quite common on Myridia – she says smiling.

-Myridia? Never heard of it.

-You wouldn't know it. It's not on Earth.

-America – Vesta whispers.

-I mean it's not in America. It's in, uhm...

-Russia – Vesta suggests.

-Yes. Myridia, big town in Russia. Very big. Like, five hundred people big.

The room fills with laughter; thinking she just made a joke, Max's friends go back to watch the game. Kari resists the urge to clarify that five hundred is a lot of people for a Myridian city, since it means five million duplicates. Instead she says to the goddess:

-Thanks for the assist. Where did you tell them you're from?

268

-Greece. They seemed to buy it.

-Why can't I come from Greece too?

-Because "Kari Zel" doesn't sound very Greek. By the way, if anyone asks, my name's Olympia.

The goddess and the Russian twin with purple hair drink their beer, watching humans.

-What are the rules to this "football"?

-I have no idea – Vesta admits.

Outer space

It should be an easy fight: as a Lampyrian, Elytra isn't as strong as a human being. However she's able to become intangible to avoid all of Kari's hits, although the Myridian doesn't know how: as far as she knows Lampyrians don't have powers.

Elytra becomes solid again to fire her gun at one of the duplicates, who disintegrates on impact. Kari takes advantage of this to attack, but stops when Elytra phases her arm inside Kari's chest.

-Make a move and I'll squeeze your heart – she threatens. By the tone in her voice, she means it.

-What's going on here? Where are we?

-I ask the questions. Are you alone?

-Myridians are never alone.

-Don't give me that propaganda bull###t. Are you working with Talas Khanos?

-Why should I? He's a monster.

-I know. But I need him. My people need him.

-Why?

Elytra looks at Kari in the eye. She's trying to understand if she can trust her.

-I'm five months old. I won't live longer than twelve months; neither will my daughters. Khanos is a master geneticist; he says he can extend our lifespan to match humans.

-And he needs the *Twin Dragon* for that? Can't you see he's just using you?

-We're going to take over Myridia – Elytra reveals.

The mere mention of her home planet is enough to make Kari's heart jump. Her world has already seen so much death; she can't bear the thought of an invasion.

269

-You're Artemis Hunters. Space pirates. Myridia doesn't have any resources to steal.

-Except a Drylon artifact that gives everyone born there the power to duplicate at will. I have hundreds of thousands of pirates under my command; in a few years, they will be billions.

-And how's that gonna help the Lampyrians?

-Khanos needs to experiment on the Harpies.

-The Harpies? Why would anyone want those man-eating beasts to...

-They're our mothers. Zeus fu##ed so many of them that Lampyrians evolved as a separate species. But Harpies are practically extinct; Artemis is the only one who doesn't want them dead, and she keeps them just for the hunt. If we take them to Myridia...

-In a generation all Harpies will have the power to duplicate – Kari understands.

-Yes. Talas Khanos will have enough Harpies for his experiments and my daughters will have a chance to live more than a year. And the Hunters will be a force to be reckoned with.

-Why are you telling me this?

-Because Khanos told me what happened on Myridia. You helped Null kill Demeter.

-I didn't do it to hand over Myridia to a bunch of pirates and monsters!

-No, you did it because you wanted to save your own people. I want the same for mine.

-Threatening me won't do you any good, you know that. I'm just a duplicate: if you hurt me I will simply disappear. And you will gain nothing from me.

-I know. That's why I'm doing this – Elytra says, taking her intangible hand out of Kari's body.

Kari checks if there's any sign of damage, but she's completely unharmed. And Elytra is holstering her gun.

-Why are you telling me all this?

-Because I need your new goddess. I can't trust Khanos; if he betrays me, I need Null to finish the cure. If she's half of what I think she is, she can do it.

-And you think Null will help you out of the goodness of her heart?

-No. I think she will help me because if she doesn't, I will make sure that the Harpies eat each and every Myridian on that planet.

270

The two women study each other for what seems to be an eternity. The fight could start again at any moment. Finally, Kari asks:

-How do I get out of this place?

-I will give you one of my ships. No tracking devices: you can check if you want.

-I will. If this is some kind of double cross...

-If I wanted you dead, do you honestly think you'd be able to walk away from here alive?

Kari doesn't answer. She knows that look: Elytra is a killer. She's not bluffing.

-If you hurt my people, you won't get away from me. Intangible or not.

She's not bluffing either.

16- Unfinished business

Fairbanks, Alaska

The ship enters the atmosphere at the wrong angle, surrounded by a cloud of flames. Thanks to a last minute correction it doesn't crash into the ground, but drags on the snow for several miles before finally coming to a halt.

Nothing happens for over an hour. Then the area surrounding the crash is quickly isolated by the United States Army, which is under orders to keep it under control and to await further instructions.

The ship is only slightly bigger than a bus, and the wings have been completely ruined by the crash.

As the soldiers approach the ship, something flies above them at supersonic speed. Realizing it missed the target, it turns back. Then it lands with so quickly and displaces so much snow that it looks like something just exploded.

When the snow has settled, the soldiers can't believe their eyes. It's a woman with long red hair, wearing just an orange tube top and tight jeans. Barefoot in the snow.

-Uhm, hello. Was anybody injured? – Vesta asks.

-Step away from the vehicle, ma'am – someone shouts. Like his fellow soldiers, he's holding a weapon and seems ready to use it.

-Look, I don't want to cause trouble, but I'm taking the ship – she says, walking towards the vehicle. The first soldier shoots, and the others follow.

The bullets ricochet on her body; they're as harmless as raindrops for her, but they could damage the ship even more.

She raises a wall of fire around the ship. This distraction gives her enough time to reach the ship, raise it over her head, and fly away from the army's orders and imprecations.

Null Tower, New York

Max Black walks through the door as radio waves, then turning back into human flesh.

Kari Zel is laying on the bed, unconscious and full of bruises. It's not a normal bed: strange devices scan her body from head to toe, then project a tridimensional hologram of her internal organs.

Noriko Null is studying the hologram with a serious expression on her face. Another Kari Zel is by her side, dressed in civilian clothes, together with Vesta and Torn.

-I got here as soon as I could. Is she gonna be alright?

-I'm working on it – Noriko answers.

-I recognized the symbol on the ship. Artemis Hunters. Lousy drivers – Torn explains.

-What ship? Where is it?

-I had Vesta park it where nobody's gonna find it – Noriko reveals.

-The Moon – the goddess clarifies.

-Are you done yet? – Kari asks impatiently – I wanna know what happened.

-She suffered multiple internal injuries. She's not gonna wake up anytime soon – Noriko answers.

-So? I can just absorb her back.

From the looks of the others, the Myridian girl understands they are unfamiliar with the concept.

-What? I can absorb duplicates if I touch them. I gain all of their knowledge.

-Is it safe? She is in critical condition – Noriko stresses.

-What happens to the body of a duplicate has no effect on the original. Watch.

Kari touches the shoulder of the other Kari. The one on the bed simply disappears with a loud popping sound, leaving the sheets to fall on the bed.

The original Kari falters; only Vesta's help prevents her from falling down.

-I'm okay, I'm okay. Just a little dizzy. Gods, she really went through a lot these past weeks...

-What did you learn? – Noriko asks.

-You may want to sit down for this one...

A five-star hotel in Tokyo, Japan

Since she lost control of Scion Corporation, Leiko Tanaka has been out of public view. There's no need to make a spectacle of herself fighting it: this wasn't part of her plan, but it's working.

She closes the door to her room and recovers a small object from her purse, the size of smartphone.

Her scientists assembled it from the circuitry the Olympian vase she recovered; it is the same device that brought the Talos to Earth months ago.

She checks herself in the mirror before activating it. There are still bandages over her broken nose; all in all, a small price to pay for the cause.

Once the device is active, it creates the holographic shadow of a man. It's impossible to see anything other than a dark silhouette.

-*You missed your last scheduled report* – it says.

-There's a new development. The Nexus has discovered my plans and defeated the Blue. She will soon have complete control over the deployment of reactor technology.

-*Have you been compromised?*

-She managed to establish a psychic link for a few seconds. I believe she suspects that I work for the Mortal Liberation Front.

-*Your orders were to update the global readiness level in case of an Olympian invasion. Instead you managed to hand the planet over to the Nexus. My superiors will be...disappointed.*

-There is a way to turn the situation to our advantage.

-*How? We can't trust a Nexus with an entire planet. It's too dangerous.*

-Then conquer the planet and give it to me as your lieutenant. The gods don't know anything about Earth so you don't risk to be discovered, and you can isolate the Nexus to work for you.

-*First you wanted us to attack the planet because its technology wasn't progressing fast enough, now you want the same because the Nexus is working too fast? My superiors will find this fixation with planetary conquest troubling.*

-I gave up my own daughter to the Nexus. <u>Never question my loyalty to the cause!!!</u>

Leiko's sudden burst of emotion seems to affect the shadow. He takes time before responding.

-*We don't have the resources for a full-scale invasion. But I will inform my superiors about your proposal. In the meantime, make no contact with the Nexus and await further instructions.*

The shadow disappears, leaving Leiko alone once again. If she were anyone else, she would smile.

"Sentimental idiot" she thinks, putting the device back into her purse together with the Core.

274

Null Tower, New York

All five members of the Vanguard sit at the round table: Null, Quantum, Vesta, Kari and Torn.

At the wave of Null's hand, the lights dim and the table projects the holographic image of the Milky Way Galaxy.

-This is so cool. It's like being in a Justice League meeting or something – Quantum whispers to Kari, who nods pretending to know what he's talking about.

-This is the map of the Olympian Galaxy I recovered on Myridia – Noriko explains. Two red dots appear over the map: one labeled "Earth" and the other "Myridia".

-43 light-years towards the galactic centre there is a border between five kingdoms, each ruled by an Olympian god: Zeus, Hermes, Artemis, Demeter and Hephaestus. Earth lies on the edge between the Hephaestus Collective and the Demeter Theocracy. Myridia is deeper into Demeter territory, 50 light-years away from us. Even if the Hunters manage to conquer it, they will have to defend it against the power of five Olympian gods.

-That's why they need the God Eraser. Can Myridia hold its own against the Hunters? – Vesta asks.

-No – Torn answers.

-Excuse me? Myridia has the best infantry of the galaxy! – Kari protests.

-They're good. The Hunters are better.

-You've run into them before? – Noriko asks. It's always a chore to get information out of Torn.

-Not personally, but anyone capable to make it big in Artemis space is dangerous. It's a rough territory, crowded with the kind of space monsters she likes to fight. She's not really interested into running the place but hates being told what to do, so there are no real governments. The Hunters are just one of the many factions fighting for control; they don't follow any rule, except for the only law existing in their sector.

-Which is? – Quantum asks.

-"Don't f##k with Artemis".

-And what about Elytra's story on the Lampyrians? Can she be trusted? – Vesta asks.

275

-She's a Hunter and she works with Talas Khanos. It could be a trap – Torn advises.

-Wait. We're not seriously considering sitting this one out, aren't we? – Kari asks, understandably worried about her people. The others don't seem very excited, with one exception:

-Yeah, I mean c'mon, space pirates guys! – Quantum says.

-This is happening because we killed Demeter and let Khanos take control of the God Eraser. It's our responsibility to do something about this! – Kari insists.

-I didn't say no – Noriko clarifies. She strokes her chin; judging by her shining eyes, she's not taking the situation lightly.

-I can't spare the whole Vanguard on this; we have unfinished business on Earth.

-I'll stay – Quantum volunteers, to the surprise of all present. Even Null.

-I know, I know, I'm gonna miss the space pirates. But I still haven't found my sister and if Leiko tries any more monkey business with the Blue I'm the most qualified to deal with it. Besides, who else is gonna stay? Little miss genius here is the only one who can fix the spaceship and disable the God Eraser, Torn is the only one who knows anything about the people you're gonna fight, Kari knows the planet better than anyone else, and if you're gonna fight spaceships you need Vesta to kick some pirate butt.

-This is...surprisingly mature for you – Noriko compliments.

-Hey, I'm like ten years older than you!

-Nice to see you're finally starting to act like it.

-You really suck at being nice to people – Quantum pouts.

Project Silver, classified location

The President of the United States is walking through the brand new facility, accompanied by the Secret Service and a balding man wearing a lab coat.

-Are you sure this can work, professor?

-As sure as we can be, Mister President. We believe the Heart keeps memory of whoever has gained access to it; our tests show that it was suitable to interact with the biological samples we recovered from Robert Null. This should work with anyone sharing enough DNA with the previous user.

-But obviously we can't fully trust the father of Noriko Null. She has shown complete disregard of international law and refuses to testify before Congress about her actions.

-Do you think she's a threat, sir?

-She is Null. I've learned not to trust that girl.

-I understand, Mister President. As soon as you give the order, we're ready to begin.

On the other side of the bulletproof glass there's one of the most advanced laboratories in the world. Everyone inside is wearing hazmat suits; everyone except the African American woman strapped to the apparatus that has been connected to the Heart of the Universe.

-This is strictly voluntary, miss Black. Just give the word and we will abort the procedure – says the President through the lab's microphone.

-I want to do this, sir – she reassures him.

-Very well then. Operation Ascension is go – the President orders.

The electrical charge passes through Kayla Black's body, and all of her muscles contract as she tries to remain conscious.

She lied: this isn't what she wanted. But who can give up the chance to be a goddess?

277

17- Hekate rising

Null City, Planet Myridia

The planet's reconstruction has been astounding: anywhere else, the city would still be in ruins after the Vanguard's battle with Demeter. But no other place can count on a population with the power to create ten thousand duplicates of all of its citizens.

There is much to do, of course: it will be years before Myridia is completely healed, but for the first time in three hundred years its people can hope to remain free.

All of that changes when Demeter's mothership, the *Twin Dragon*, suddenly appears over Null City. The Artemis Hunters find little to no resistance: the Myridians can duplicate and have plenty of personal weapons, but nothing to withstand a full-scale invasion.

Elytra Elater flies above the battleground surrounding Null Palace. It's nice to finally be able to stretch her Lampyrian wings; as captain of the *New Horizon* and leader of the Hunters, she doesn't get to do that very often.

Of course someone tries to shoot her down, but every shot passes through her as she goes intangible. When she lands on top of the Palace, someone approaches her.

-Call off your men. We surrender – the man says, raising his hands over his head.

-Are you the ruler of this planet?

-Velazer Tes, Prime Minister of the Provisional Government – he identifies himself.

-Elytra Elater. I claim this world for Lady Artemis, Goddess of the Hunt.

-We know how to treat gods here – the Prime Minister says, pointing at the giant statue of Demeter in front of the Palace: the head has been cut off. Null's symbol, Ø, has been carved over her breasts.

-I like your style. New Horizon, this is the Captain, blow up the big statue please.

A beam of light pierces the sky, carving through the statue's chest like a knife and vaporizing the entire torso. When the rest of the statue collapses, the entire city shakes.

The edge of Myridia's solar system

Since Myridia orbits six stars, navigating through the multiple solar winds and magnetic currents is extremely tricky. Kari is doing her best to keep the ship steady, but it is far from a comfortable journey.

-Are you sure you've done this before? – Vesta asks, firmly holding to her seat.

-I did reach the Earth with this thing, didn't I? – Kari answers, not very convincingly.

-When the engine worked – Torn notes.

-*Sorry if I didn't have the time to build a brand new fully functional spacecraft* – Noriko answers through the Neural Headset installed in her head. The ship is so small that the others can hear her kicking the inertial dampener in the engine room.

-Whoa. I just picked up something on the scanner. Something big – Kari notes.

-*The Hunters?*

-Worse. It's the Covenant of Witches – Torn says with a serious tone. Well, slightly more serious than his usually serious tone.

-*Say again!?*

-Hekate's fleet – Vesta translates.

Tens of thousands of Witches surpass the Vanguard's salvaged ship. It's an immense cloud, composed only of women flying under their own power; they move like a swarm of locusts.

-Why the f##k are there witches in freakin' space!? – Noriko asks once she's reached the others.

-They're like Oracles but work for Hekate – Torn explains.

-There was no Hekate on the galaxy map. What's she doing out here? Any ideas?

-Nothing good, that's for sure – Vesta muses, looking a billion miles away.

-I need more than that and you know it – Noriko scolds her.

-She sided with Zeus when he overthrew my father Kronos, who was the brother of her grandparents. She's much, much older than me. We haven't met since...Gaea, it must've been a hundred thousand years ago. Nobody in the family really liked her except Demeter; Hekate was the only one besides her to oppose the marriage between her daughter Persephone and Hades.

-Makes sense. There's a Hekate sector in Demeter space – Torn remembers.

-What do you know about her? – Noriko asks him.

279

-Never meet Hekate unless you want to die.

Myridia

Hekate watches over the planet as her Witches descend into the atmosphere. The three bodies of the Triple Goddess...the child, the maiden and the crone...are the same aspects of the same being.

The Child is ten years old, with short grey hair and a black tunic.

The Maiden is thirty years old, with long grey hair and a black dress with generous cleavage.

The Crone is eighty years old, with her whole shriveled body completely covered by black robes.

This is not her original form, of course. Hekate is over a hundred million years old.

-This planet smells wrong – the Crone says.

-We don't sense any goddess here. Only mortals – the Maiden nods.

-We thought we convinced Demeter to get rid of them. Honestly, these young gods never learn – the Child concludes.

Among the thousands of Witches and Hunter vessels plunging into the atmosphere, one stands out.

-We see a goddess there. One of the children of Kronos – the Maiden announces.

-Go after her, sisters. We will handle things here – the Child orders.

The *New Horizon* looms above the planet. The capital ship of the Artemis Hunters, it's got enough firepower to destroy a small moon. On the bridge, the main viewscreen shows the Child glowing with purple energy, targeted by every weapon the ship has.

-All weapons to maximum! This is the only shot we have! – the ship's second-in-command orders.

The Child smiles.

Her purple energy swarms inside the ship, hunting down each and every person inside. Their blood evaporates instantly, leaving behind only desiccated corpses. The males are the lucky ones, since they're left there to mercifully die. The females are reborn as dead emaciated bodies animated by Hekate's power. They are her latest Witches.

280

Finally, the ship explodes with the power of a thousand nuclear weapons. Even in the coldness of space, the Child's laughter is chilling.

The outskirts of Null City

Noriko wipes the dust off her leather jacket of a horrible shade of green. Kari does the same with the dust stuck on Noriko's hair; she's now wearing the duplicating skintight armor she stole.

-You know, just once I'd like to have a safe landing – Noriko notes.

Vesta is putting out the fire around the wreckage of their ship, looking worried at the sky filled with Witches and spaceships fighting each other.

-Poor planet. I don't think we'll be able to save everyone this time.

Kari places a hand on her shoulder to console her, while Noriko adjusts her N-Watch.

-You forget you're with me. Activating Anti-Oracle Defense Grid...now.

An invisible energy sweeps the planet. Designed to nullify the telekinetic abilities of Demeter's minions, the Anti-Oracle Devices interfere with the Oracle's ability to use their powers.

Demeter's Oracles simply revert back to humans. But the Witches are corpses reanimated by Hakete's power: without it, they can't even prevent their own flesh from falling apart.

Once the Grid is activated, dead bodies start to fall all over Myridia.

-It's raining Witches! – Kari exclaims with a mix of excitement and disgust.

-There's more coming – Torn adds, pointing at something approaching their location at high speed.

-You're on – Noriko says to Vesta.

The Maiden and the Crone land. Even at a distance, their purple energy is sickening.

-*What are you doing here, Hestia? This planet is ours* – the Maiden says.

-The name's Vesta now. And this planet doesn't want to have a goddess anymore.

-*We don't care about the planet. We only want the Drylon device inside it* – the Crone explains.

-So that you can try to duplicate yourself again? – Noriko asks.

281

Her friends look at her; it's clear they don't know what she's talking about.

-Think about it: one goddess, multiple bodies. Except we know Drylon technology doesn't work on gods. You tried to use it, but something went wrong and you're stuck like this. Am I getting close?

-*Don't address the Triple Goddess unless spoken to, mortal* – the Maiden says, pointing her finger at Noriko. She's ready to incinerate her, but Vesta grabs her hand.

-I don't want to fight you, Hekate. Go back to whatever dark corner of the galaxy you're from.

-*You presume to give orders to the Triple Goddess? Daughter of the Titans of Necromancy and Destruction?* - the two Hekate asks simultaneously, their bodies engulfed in the fiery purple energy.

Vesta's body catches fire; the ground beneath her is vitrified thanks to the extreme heat.

-I am the Firstborn of Kronos, Lord of the Titans, the Devourer of Gods. My title outranks yours.

Even Noriko takes a step back. She knows Vesta is bluffing, but it's still a scary sight. Vesta wasn't able to overpower Demeter, but Hekate is hesitating; she hasn't met Vesta for so long, it's possible she really has become as powerful as her father.

None of this matters, however, since the *Twin Dragon* chooses this moment to fire the God Eraser.

For Vesta, it's like having a billion needles stuck under her skin while someone pours acid into her brain. The God Eraser creates interference within a god's mind, making it impossible for them to use their powers. As Demeter proved, intense exposure can even kill them.

Hekate screams. The Maiden and the Crone phase in and out, their image flickering like a bad TV signal. Not only they're not used to pain...something common among the gods...but they share the same mind, meaning the damage is greatly amplified.

Noriko, Kari and Torn are completely unaffected. All they hear is a deep humming sound.

-Hang in there, Vesta, we got this – Noriko reassures her. The N-Watch creates a tridimensional hologram of the *Twin Dragon*, showing the blueprints and highlighting the location of the engine.

-Are you sure you can do this? You only get one shot – she says to Torn.

-I know – he answers, creating a bow and an arrow of red energy.

Noriko can't help but wonder how he's able to do this. He can't be a god because he's not affected by the God Eraser. Presumably he's not a demigod for the same reason. Can his powers come from Drylon technology? He's earned his privacy, but she can't help but wonder.

He fires the arrow, which flies right through the ship's hull and walls. Something inside the *Twin Dragon* explodes, and the ship starts to rapidly lose altitude.

No longer under the influence of the God Eraser, Vesta wants to fly under the ship to prevent it from crushing the city. Before she can do it, however, something unexpected happens.

Someone else catches the ship. Someone with large, white angel wings.

-Nike!? What's <u>she</u> doing here!? – Vesta wonders, catching her breath.

The Crone and the Maiden are returning to full power as well. And it's clear from the madness in their eyes that they have all the intention to kill Vesta.

-*You will pay for this insolence, spawn of Kronos!* – the Maiden threatens her.

Before they can do anything, lightning strikes the ground between them. When it's over there is someone else in front of them: a woman in full Ancient Greek armor, wielding a shield and a spear.

-Ladies. Let's keep things civilized, okay? – she asks.

-Athena!!! – Noriko recognizes her.

-Hi kid. You look thin; have you been eating enough?

The Crone jumps at Athena, filled with rage and deadly purple energy, ready to kill.

-*THE TRIPLE GODDESS WILL NOT*-

Athena stabs the Crone in the heart, and one of the aspects of Hekate falls to the ground with a spear in her chest.

-The Triple Goddess will shut up – Athena says.

283

18- Who wants to rule Myridia

Vesta and Athena share a sincere hug, while Hekate watches with disdain. They all look the same age, despite coming from three wildly different generations of gods.

-I've missed you, Aunt Vesta. I meant to visit you, but you know how it is.

-You know I can't stay mad at my favorite niece. Athena, these are... – Vesta tries to introduce her allies, but Athena interrupts her.

-Kari Zel of Myridia, yes I know. And your other friend here is called Torn.

-How did you...

-Goddess of wisdom, remember?

-You mean you've been spying on us – Noriko says. The others are shocked to hear the harsh tone on her voice, since she's talking to one of the most powerful gods in the galaxy.

-I'm sorry, but isn't anyone gonna acknowledge the corpse and the big-ass invasion!? - Kari adds, pointing at the lifeless body of the Crone Hekate lying on the ground.

-*You will pay for this, Athena* – the other body of Hekate, the Maiden, threatens.

Athena recovers her spear from the Crone's heart, pointing it instead at the Maiden's throat; it's still dripping divine blood.

-I'm also the goddess of war, in case you've forgotten. If you want to challenge me, you will discover that it's not a honorary title.

-*As a matter of fact, we will. Since Demeter is dead, we claim her dominion by right of conquest.*

-You didn't conquer anything. Right now you're not holding a very strong hand, Hekate.

-*If we make our move to conquer Myridia and you stop us, her domain will be yours. Are you prepared to defend it against the forces of Hephaestus, Hermes and Persephone?*

-Dammit, Hekate – Athena says, removing her weapon from the enemy's throat.

-You're not seriously considering leaving Myridia to her, right? – Vesta asks.

-I have to. I can't commit too many ships to this sector without weakening my border with Apollo.

284

-Then who will rule Myridia? – Kari asks.

-Whoever wins the war for the planet and is able to hold it against the other gods.

-Hold on a second – Noriko intervenes – I may not be an expert on divine law, but shouldn't something called "right of conquest" apply only to territories that were actually conquered?

-Nori? Where are you going with this? – Vesta asks, but Noriko continues.

-I killed Demeter. By your logic, shouldn't Myridia be mine by right of conquest?

-*Don't be ridiculous. Mortals can't invoke right of conquest!*

-Actually...there is no specific law against it. Nobody thought this would happen – Athena notes.

-*This is madness. It goes against everything divine rule stands for.*

-Really? And who decides what is and what isn't divine rule?

Athena, Vesta and Hekate look at each other, then Athena answers Noriko's question:

-Themis, Goddess of Divine Law. We need to go to trial.

Earth, New York City

Max Black and a duplicate of Kari are walking the stairs to his apartment; he's carrying two sport bags, she has four tennis rackets.

-I'm sorry, but what was I supposed to do? I didn't bring enough clean clothes! – she complains.

-Next time just tell me and we'll play one on one instead of couples, okay? Don't make your duplicates disappear in the showers!

-But I like playing against myself. Hey, what do you say next time we play ten versus ten?

-How are you gonna explain nineteen twins playing tennis!?

When they reach the door to the apartment, there's a woman waiting for them. Caucasian, about Kari's age, wearing glasses.

-Can I help you, miss? – he asks. Kari jumps in front of him, looking at her uncomfortably close.

-You're not from the CIA, are you? – Kari asks.

-Don't mind Kari, she's Russian.

-You're Max Black, right? Kayla's brother? – she asks with a British accent.

-Yes, it's me. You're a friend of Kayla's?

-Not exactly, I'm...this is going to sound awkward. My name is Erika. I'm Kayla's girlfriend.

The Aegis, in orbit above Myridia

Kari and Torn have decided to stay on the planet to meet Old Man Vor and Vesta volunteered to keep an eye on Elytra, but Noriko couldn't resist the offer to visit Athena's mothership.

Compared to Demeter's ship, the Aegis is visibly more modern: the endless corridors are filled with displays at every corner, with blinking lights everywhere.

"Max would've loved this. This feels like an episode of Star Trek" Noriko thinks.

Everyone crossing them salutes Athena by placing the right fist over the heart; it looks like a military salute of some kind. The atmosphere is very cordial: they don't look intimidated by Athena.

Noriko has to admit that she is intimidating. Still wearing the armor, the goddess looks even taller than six foot five, especially next to Noriko's five feet.

Nike is also dressed in armor, with the breastplate leaving her back completely exposed to make room for her rather large angel wings. Both armors seem rather impractical, leaving a lot of flesh exposed (Noriko notices that Athena doesn't have a navel); if they're as powerful as Vesta and Demeter, the armor is probably for show. In fact, judging by Hekate's reaction and recalling the extent of her dominion, Noriko suspects that Athena is far more powerful than them.

-The Hunters have retreated to the southern continent, ma'am. They have made an official claim for Myridia in the name of Artemis – Nike informs Athena.

-It figures that my step-sister would get involved somehow. What about Hekate?

-The Child and the Maiden have retired into Hermes and Persephone space respectively; they will likely look for their assistance. The Crone corpse is under our custody.

-And what about Talas Khanos? – Noriko asks.

-He has requested asylum to the Hunters.

-That would be all, Nike; please transmit your report to the Senate and inform them that I will be pleased to answer their questions tomorrow.

286

-Yes ma'am – Nike says; she bows respectfully and walks away.

-"The Senate"? – Noriko repeats.

-My approach to divine rule is somewhat...different from the rest of my family – Athena admits, opening the door to her quarters. As she does, the armor disappears to be replaced with civilian clothes. It's really strange to see Athena wearing a feminine dress that wouldn't look out of place on a manager, even though it has the same colors of her armor...bronze and gold...and her symbol over the left breast: a lightning bolt on a cog. It's the same symbol of her golden earrings.

-You see, the Athenian Federation includes over eight hundred worlds, spanning almost ten percent of the Olympian Galaxy. Every world is free to leave if they want to and I don't force them to worship me, although many do.

-So you're a democratic goddess? Sounds a little too good to be true. What's in it for you?

As they talk, Noriko can't help by admire Athena's private quarters: they are on a spaceship, but she couldn't tell it from here. It looks like the Hall of Mirrors from the Palace of Versailles.

-I am genuinely loved by my subjects. Nobody else in my family can say the same.

-And you get to rub it on their faces.

-Great minds think alike.

They have now reached the table, where a lavish meal is awaiting them.

-I wasn't joking earlier: you need to put on some weight. You're too skinny for a warrior.

-Athena, I want to talk about the Nexus.

-And you can't do it over lunch?

-I know what you're trying to do. You're playing up your role as the mother figure I never had growing up. It's not going to work.

-Seriously? I grew up without a mother too, but I would've liked to have one – Athena answers, taking her seat.

Reluctantly, joins her...and while she doesn't want to admit it, shares the best lunch she ever had.

-You knew all along that my mother placed the Nexus inside my head and decided to activate it.

-Yes. I have to admit, when I intercepted Leiko's first message to the Mortal Liberation Front I wasn't overly fond of Earth. I was ready to kill you myself if it meant destroying the Nexus.

-Why is it so important?

-Drylon technology is always important. But the Nexus...I believe it's what the Drylon used to become smart enough to create technology so advanced we can't understand it even now, five billion years after they disappeared. I even tried to use one on myself, as you can see by my silver eyes, but it didn't work. I've used other Nexus on a number of mortals over the years but...power corrupts, you know. Slowly, inevitably, mortals go insane. But before they do, they create amazing things...things that can hurt the gods. You've done it yourself. Eventually, Zeus decreed that every Nexus should be destroyed.

-So there are no other Nexus? I'm the only one?

-As far as I know, yes. I thought they'd all been destroyed, but Ulysses managed to hid one. What a fascinating mortal, that one. A real shame he couldn't live forever.

-I understand why you wouldn't want Leiko have something like that. But why risk angering Zeus to activate the Nexus inside me?

-Oh, Zeus won't lift a finger against his most loyal and beloved daughter. As for the "why"...I have to admit I saw a little bit of myself in you. No mother, a womanizing father without a clue, little interest for feminine things...you're still a virgin, right?

Noriko almost chokes on her food on the question, quickly turning red for the embarrassment.

-It's okay if you're not anymore. I really don't care about these things.

-Are you the only Olympian who knows where Earth is? – Noriko quickly changes the subject.

-There is at least another one. I don't know who, but I didn't send the Many to your planet. Someone else must have intercepted Leiko's messages, stolen the Many from Demeter and sent them after you. I do have some theories, but no proof.

-I saw the galaxy map. Earth is in the worst possible place. Can't you defend it?

-I have responsibilities to the Federation. That's why I made you the Nexus: I'd hate to see Earth gone now. If mankind manages to survive, I'd like it to join the Federation someday.

-Wow. This really does feel like Star Trek after all.

They talk for what feel like hours. Despite her best efforts, Noriko can't help but feel a bond between them. And she has no doubts that Athena knows it too.

She retires to the guest room for the night; of course, it's far bigger and fancier than she'd imagined.

The other gods will arrive tomorrow. Since there's no chance to get anything done without Athena watching over her shoulder, she decides to indulge in her new stepmother's generosity.

She can't remember the last time she's had a relaxing bath. There's always something to build, someone to fight, the fate of the world on her shoulders. This is the first chance to unwind she's had in a long time; she just soaks in a tub the size of a pool, allowing her brain to rest.

Then someone touches her tight, and Noriko lets out a high-pitched scream.

-I have to say, Athena's choice in protégés is admirable.

Noriko tries to slap the boy's face before even seeing him, but ends up missing: he has teleported from her right to her left at the speed of thought.

-Now now, is this the way to greet a god?

-WHAT THE F##K ARE YOU DOING HERE!?!? – she screams, trying to cover herself.

The boy teleports on the side of the pool and bows. He looks in his very early twenties, has curly hair and is completely naked. Noriko does her best to be as discreet as possible when she looks.

-Hermes, god of travelers, traders, thieves, trespassers, tricksters and many other things, at your service.

19- The stalking god

The Aegis, Athena's mothership

Noriko has already met several goddesses, but Hermes is the first male god she's encountered.

And of course it has to happen when they are both naked. Hermes seems to be unconcerned by it, but he has the decency to lend Noriko a towel when she makes it <u>very</u> clear that she's not.

-This Athena's ship. How did you get in? – she asks, covering herself.

-Oh please. I come and go anywhere I want in the universe; even the goddess of wisdom can't keep up with me.

-So you're the one who stole the Many from Demeter and send it to kill me.

-Who, me? Your sense of humor rivals your beauty.

-Drop the charm offensive, it doesn't work on me. Now would you **please** put on some clothes!?

-If you insist, sunshine – Hermes answers, disappearing for a fraction of a second. When he's back he's wearing a toga, and so is Noriko. She is not pleased with his initiative.

-Don't. Do that. Again.

-Since apparently you hate fun, let's talk business. Are you really going to claim Myridia?

-If it prevents Hekate or the Artemis Hunters from destroying it, yes. I did kill Demeter after all.

-Yes, well, I can't complain about that; Aunt Demeter was a heartless bi##h. But I've had my eyes on her domain for a looooong time, so I'm going to claim the planet too.

-Of course you are – Noriko comments, massaging her temples. There's a migraine coming up.

-I understand your concern: Hekate is a psycho and Artemis an anarchist. But you and I, sunshine, we could come to some sort of agreement. And nobody else needs to know about it.

-Why would I make a secret deal with a creep who stalks me when I'm taking a bath?

-You mean other than the whole "handsome god who rules a tenth of the galaxy and could kill everyone I know in their sleep if he wanted to" thing?

290

Hermes moves again, too fast for the naked eye. Now he's behind Noriko, touching her shoulders.

-Because if you hand me Myridia nobody will be killed. You have my word.

-And how much is the word of the god of liars and thieves worth? – she asks, pushing him away.

Or at least she tries. Hermes has the body of a slim twenty-something but weighs like a brick house.

-Think it over, sunshine. I did enjoy our time together; try not to get yourself killed.

Hermes vanishes a final time, leaving Noriko conflicted, embarrassed and tired.

"Great. There goes my chance to get some sleep" she thinks.

"I don't know, I'm definitely dreaming. Did you see his..." the other voice in her head thinks.

"Shut up. Stupid sexy god" she complains, headed straight for the bed.

Earth, New York City

Erika Rhys is sitting on the couch; Max Black hands her a glass of water, before sitting down next to her. Kari stands beside him.

-Thanks for letting me in. I wanted to call before dropping by, but you're not on the phonebook – she says with a British accent.

-It's okay, any friend of Kayla is welcome. Although I understand you're more than friends.

-Yes, we've been together for a couple of months. I wasn't sure you knew...

-That my sister's a lesbian? She doesn't exactly keep it a secret.

-Wait, you're from Earth but your sister's from Lesbo? How does that work? – Kari asks him.

Erika looks at her confused, then looks back at Max.

-Don't mind Kari. She's Russian – he answers. It's become his default excuse for all of Kari's quirk behaviors; Erika doesn't seem to buy it completely, but doesn't insist.

-About eight weeks ago she left her job as a security guard; said she received a better offer.

"After we left for Myridia" he thinks, but actually says:

-Did she say anything about her new job?

-Only that it wasn't in Chicago, were we both used to live. She said I probably wouldn't hear from her for a long time and that if I ran into trouble I should call you.

-That's odd. Didn't you say she never called your parents? – Kari asks to Max.

-Yes, but it doesn't surprise me. Mom and dad...let's just say they're not exactly progressive.

-That explains why they yelled at me when I called them. I don't like this, Max...it's not like Kayla to abandon her loved ones without a good reason.

-I know. I've been looking for her, but she's dropped off the face of the Earth!

-There was something else. She said if you weren't able to help me I should contact Noriko Null, you know, the teenage billionaire?

Max and Kari look at each other, then back at Erika.

-Why are you looking at me like that? – she asks.

Null Palace, Myridia

Two duplicates of Kari kiss Old Man Vor on each cheek; even the grumpy old man can't hide the fact that he's happy to see her again.

-You've definitely moved up, Old Man! Look at this place! – a third Kari exclaims. She's been to the Palace before, but it was immediately after the revolution. Now that everything's been restored, she can't help but marvel at the luxury.

-I miss my old house. It's drafty here – he complains. He's still Old Man Vor after all.

Torn isn't sharing Kari's enthusiasm. He's looking outside the window, where he can see fifty thousand Myridian guards gathered around the Palace.

-I'm surprised they made you Minister of War again. You worked for Demeter – he says.

-Ah, it's just ceremonial crap. They know that if anyone invades we're screwed without you guys.

-How's the Provisional Government holding up? – Kari asks.

-Pretty well, all things considered. There's a few people who miss Demeter, but they mostly keep their mouths shut. We still haven't figured out how to contact all the soldiers Demeter stationed outside Myridia, so for the most part we're concentrating on rebuilding.

-The Artemis Hunters. What can you tell us about them? – Torn asks, straight to the point.

-Ruthless bastards. Artemis keeps changing her mind whether pillaging and raping are illegal or not in her sector, so those who leave her domain are the scum of the galaxy...they're no better than those junkheads from Dionysus space or the Mortal Liberation Front.

Torn and Kari exchange looks. The Old Man notices, and after a fit of cough warns them:

-Don't ever get involved with those guys. Believe me, you have no idea what they're willing to do to achieve their goals.

-Elytra seems to be equally ruthless – Kari says, recalling the last time they met.

-I don't know about her, but her family's been ruling the Hunters since I was a kid. Don't make her good looks fool you, the Ghost Maker she inherited makes her damn near invincible.

-"Ghost Maker"? – Kari repeats.

-She can turn intangible at will. Drylon technology.

-Isn't using Drylon technology punishable by death? – Torn asks.

-Artemis makes an exception for the Elater family. I don't know if that's because Lampyrians don't live long enough for that technology to drive them nuts, or if Artemis enjoys their company a little too much...if you know what I mean, eh eh.

-Which means Artemis will never allow Elytra to find a cure for their short lifespan – Kari says.

-I don't think Talas Khanos cares about what Artemis allows. If I were you I'd keep an eye on that one...that guy's not right in the head.

On the other side of the planet

Thousands of ships are stationed in the vast swamp that covers most of this continent. Their weapons are targeting Vesta, who is floating above them with her arms crossed and a stern look on her face. She's here to prevent them from getting any ideas. The Myridian Army would have little to no defense against an aerial attack, but the Hunters know better than to attack the flaming goddess whose fire is not extinguished by the heavy rain.

Elytra Elater returns to the base camp, saluted by her troops. She shakes her blue bat wings to dry them off, being careful not to touch any of the parts salvaged from the *Twin Dragon*.

293

-Have you had any success fixing it? – she asks to Talas Khanos.

-It's late. You should get some sleep – he answer while telekinetically lifting another piece of equipment, attempting to connect it to the other fragments of the God Eraser he's holding up.

-I'll sleep when I'm dead. Can you fix it or not?

-In time, maybe. We won't be able to use it during the trial, unfortunately.

-Damn. We better get rid of it before Artemis arrives tomorrow.

-Already? I thought her hunting grounds were near the galactic core.

-Hermes is here – Elytra answers.

-Ah, of course. The god who makes travel distances meaningless. Although I question how Athena was able to get here *before* him, seeing how her dear Federation is so far away.

-She asked for a lift – someone answers.

Elytra quickly draws her gun and fires, but Hermes catches the shot mid-travel. Despite the fact that it's a laser gun.

-Good reflexes. I like a woman who fires first and asks questions later. But you know what I like better? Winning a war without firing a single shot.

-You're the one who brought the girl with silver eyes to Myridia – Khanos guesses.

-I'm afraid I can't take credit for that. But when Athena said she needed a quick trip to Earth I couldn't help but peek at what she was doing over there, and the rest is history. Can you believe that her ship is so slow that it would've taken her a whole month to reach Earth?

-What do you want? – Elytra asks, still aiming her gun at Hermes.

-Demeter wouldn't let me marry his daughter Persephone. So I'm going to steal everything she had and spit on her grave...wherever *that* is.

-Why are you telling us this?

-Because, my dear blue angel, I like the idea of Lampyrians with a longer lifespan. Humans have become quite boring lately...no offense.

-None taken – Khanos answers.

-You know Asclepius? God of medicine, son of my dearest step-brother Apollo? If I ask him to create a cure for your people, I'm sure he would gladly do so out of the goodness of his heart. And not, of course, because a certain someone could accidentally let it slip that he's been trying to poison his own father for the past two thousand years.

-You're lying – Elytra says.

-Pff. As if the god of tricksters needs to lie to achieve his goals. The very thought, seriously...

-What do you want us to do? – Talas Khanos asks. He's not overly fond of gods, but knows that having one as an ally is always a major asset.

-Renounce the claim to Myridia. It's a pretty good offer, considering the alternative is not seeing your grandchildren grow and, what else? Oh yes, watching the Hunters slaughtered by Hephaestus.

The mention of the name fills both Elytra and Khanos with dread.

-He's...he's coming here too? – she asks nervously.

-Demeter wasn't more than a nuisance to Hephaestus; he'll wait to see who gets her stuff before sending his army. I wonder if the Hunters can last more than a day against a legion of Talos robots.

-I...I will talk Artemis into leaving Myridia to you – Elytra says, reluctantly.

-You do that, my sweet blue angel – Hermes says, kissing her delicately where her nose would be if she had one. Then he turns to Talas Khanos.

-And you. I've seen your work with the Many...you've got some talent. And yet, you betrayed your own goddess to seize power at the first opportunity.

Hermes teleports in front of Khanos...or walks so fast that it's impossible to see the steps, it's hard to tell with him. For a moment, Khanos fears for his life...he knows just how powerful Hermes is.

But Hermes just extends his hand, waiting for Khanos to shake it.

-Would you like to become one of my Oracles?

295

20- The Sword of Justice

Space station Sword of Justice, above planet Myridia

Vesta is waiting in front of the large marble door, waiting impatiently; she could never stand for all the pomp and circumstance of her fellow gods.

-Why is this taking so long? – Noriko asks, tapping her foot.

-Themis doesn't usually give an audience to mortals. Give her time, Athena will convince her.

-I still don't like it. And why are you dressed like that?

Vesta looks at herself: instead of her normal Earth clothes, she's wearing an orange *himation* that covers all of her body except the right arm and shoulder.

-It's a formal occasion. Aunt Themis is the Goddess of Divine Law. I don't want to disrespect her.

-Speaking of disrespect, Hermes made me an offer tonight.

-I don't think I want to know – Vesta says with embarrassment.

-Not that kind of...nevermind. He wants me to drop the claim to Myridia in his favor; he promised in return to treat its people fairly. Do you think he can be trusted?

-I honestly don't know. You can never tell with Hermes.

The door opens, revealing a fully armored Athena; she's even carrying her spear and shield.

-We're ready. Hold on, young lady, where do you think you're going dressed like that!? – she complains, pointing the spear towards Noriko. She's wearing her usual attire: combat boots, jeans, black T-shirt with white Ø symbol, leather jacket of a horrible shade of green.

-Told you so – Vesta smirks.

-You need to change into something decent. An armor? No, you don't have the figure to fill up a nice breastplate. Maybe something from Earth?

Athena touches Noriko's shoulder with her spear, and the girl's clothes change instantaneously. She's now wearing a black pantsuit over a green shirt. The white Ø symbol is a medal on her chest.

-It's a good look for you Nori. You look just like... – Vesta starts to say.

-Your next words better not be "like your mother" – Noriko interrupts her angrily.

-...like someone ready to meet the Goddess of Divine Law – Vesta concludes hastily.

-That's better. But did you <u>have</u> to give me high heels, Athena? I hate these things.

-Let us hope that remains the worst of your worries. Shall we go, ladies?

Now that she has all the knowledge of mankind and she's met several gods, it takes a lot to leave Noriko speechless. However when she looks at Themis, sitting at her desk, her jaw drops.

Themis doesn't have eyes; there's only smooth skin where they're supposed to be. She wears a golden crown over her white hair. And she's twenty stories high.

-All bow before Themis, daughter of Ouranos, King of the Heavens, and Gaea, Queen Mother of the Titans – is the shout of a woman who looks just like her but only as tall as a human being.

Both Athena and Vesta bow respectfully. Noriko does the same, whispering to Athena:

-I thought we were going to see Themis alone.

-That's her daughter Dike, the goddess of mortal justice. She's just here as a formality.

Themis then talks; due to her size, her voice resonates in the immense room they're in.

-The Court acknowledges Hestia, daughter of Kronos, Lord of the Titans, and Rhea, Queen of the Titans. Athena, daughter of Zeus, Ruler of Olympus, you may address the Court.

-Your Honor, we hereby confirm the death of Demeter, daughter of Kronos and Rhea, and formally request her domains to be assigned with right of conquest – Athena says.

-The Court accepts the testimony and formally declares Demeter as deceased. Which one of you, Athena and Hestia, claims the right of conquest?

-I do – Noriko answers. Themis chides her raising her voice:

-THE MORTAL WILL ADDRESS THE COURT ONLY WHEN SPOKEN TO.

-We both formally forfeit our right of conquest and recognize this mortal as legitimate heir to Demeter – Vesta quickly adds, to prevent Dike from punishing Noriko for her insolence.

The immense room falls silence. There's no guarantee Themis will accept: this has never been attempted in recorded divine history, which goes back several million years.

-What is your name and parentage, mortal? – she finally asks.

-Noriko Null. Daughter of Bob.

-You have the right to invoke any god you desire as your representative before this court.

-I choose no god. I killed Demeter and I will defend my claim.

-Very well. The Court accepts to deliberate on the claim of Noriko Null, daughter of Bob, over the domain of Demeter, including all of her vassals, stars, planets, ships, worshippers and any other kind of personal property. The Court dismisses Dike, daughter of Zeus and Themis.

The goddess without eyes bows before her mother, walking away from her desk. She heads out of the room; she doesn't acknowledge Noriko. She does a curtsy for Athena, then turns towards Vesta and spits on the floor. Vesta doesn't seem to be particularly surprised by it.

-What was that about!? – Noriko asks.

-I didn't exactly leave Olympus on the best of terms – Vesta answers timidly.

Null Tower, New York City

When Erika Rhys walks through the front door, she looks around in amazement. The holographic Ø that looms over the entrance, the sight of people discussing without emitting a single sound thanks to the Sound Nullifiers, the Nullbots guarding the elevators...it's even better than she'd imagined.

-Oh my God. When you said you worked for Null, I didn't think...I mean there's plenty of offices and power plants popping out everywhere, but my God, we're in the actual Null Tower!

-So I take it you like the place? – Max Black asks.

-Her God apparently does, whoever he is – Kari Zel comments, finding the enthusiasm of the British woman a little over the top.

-Are you kidding me? This is where the future is! Can you believe it's been, what, six months since Null made her first million dollars with that awful TV show?

One of the Nullbots steps in front of Erika, blocking her access to the elevator.

-*Authorized personnel only* – it says with its deep mechanic voice. Like all the other models, the Nullbot resembles a human male covered head to toe by a black sheet of metal. Given the grave voice, the fact that it doesn't have a face, and the only note of color being the white Ø symbol on the chest, it's pretty imposing.

-Gee, I'm sorry. She's with me – Max says, jumping in before Erika can have a heart attack.

-*Let me see your badge. Please* – the Nullbot reacts. The pause before the last word make the scene seem particularly creepy. After Max shows him his badge, the Nullbot takes a step to the side.

-You may proceed. Have a nice day.

Max, Kari and Erika finally make it inside the elevator. When the doors close, the latter can finally allow herself to breathe again.

-That was a robot! An actual, working robot! Can you believe what could be done with these things if we can mass produce them? They could do anything from construction work to housecleaning!

Max looks at Kari with an expression on his face meaning "can you believe this woman?"

-Before your head explodes, need I remind you we're here to find clues about my sister?

-Right, right, sorry. I just can't wrap my head around the fact that Kayla's brother works in the most important place in the world. What do you do here, exactly? – Erika asks.

-I, uhm, I'm a... – Max hesitates, elbowing Kari to get some kind of suggestion.

-Don't look at me. I'm Russian – Kari shrugs.

Space station Sword of Justice

Just outside of the hall, the claimants are waiting for the next session. Athena and Vesta don't seem to mind the wait, but Noriko is constantly fidgeting with her uncomfortable shoes.

-Seriously, how long is this gonna take?

-We have to wait for all the claimants to arrive. Not everybody is as fast as Hermes – Athena explains; there's a touch of disdain for her step-brother in her voice.

-So what do you think? Should I consider his offer?

-It's up to you, Noriko. I can' take any official position on the matter.

-Why? We are both sponsoring Noriko's claim – Vesta asks Athena, who elaborates:

-I share a border with the Hermes sector. If I'm seen pushing for him to inhering Demeter's sector, it could be considered as an attempt to create an alliance between us. Something that Ares and Apollo would not like at all; it would destabilize the entire galaxy.

-So you're saying I shouldn't give him Myridia and the other worlds?

-I can't tell you that either. You must understand, what happens here can potentially affect thousands of planets; I am dealing with political intrigues and balances of power the likes of which you can't even begin to comprehend.

-You'd be surprised by what I can comprehend – Noriko answers with a veiled threat, punctuated by her shining eyes.

Then a very heavy door opens slowly, and a familiar voice announces:

-All bow before Her Royal Highness Persephone, Queen of the Underworld, daughter of...

-ENOUGH WITH THE FU##ING RESUME, HEKATE.

The girl approaching has nothing regal about her. Green hair, black lipstick, she wears a black jacket full of rips and holes, with rolled up sleeves to leave room to spiked metal bracelets. It's left open to show off the iron bra and panties, not to mention the green dragon tattoo. Chains binding her tights and high heeled metal boots complete her outfit.

She doesn't look much older than Noriko; more than a Greek goddess, she looks like a weird combination of punk, metal and goth fashion nightmares.

-WELL LOOK WHO'S HERE. THE OLYMPUS UNF##KABLE HERSELF.

-Persephone. Unpleasant as always – Athena greets her.

-AND HESTIA. I THOUGHT DADDY SENT YOU TO PLANET GOATF##KERS TO FINALLY TASTE SOME C##K.

-It's Vesta now. And I see you haven't matured one bit in two thousand years. What are you doing here? Don't tell me you actually want to rule Demeter's worlds.

-F##K NO, WHO CARES ABOUT THESE S##THEADS. I'M HERE BECAUSE THE OLD C##T FINALLY KICKED THE BUCKET AND I WANT TO CELEBRATE. IS THIS THE LITTLE B##CH WHO F##KED HER BRAINS OUT?– she asks, looking at Noriko.

-If you mean if I'm the one who built the God Eraser that killed your mother, yes I am.

-GOOD JOB, LITTLE B##CH.

-It's Null.

-WHATEVER. NEXT TIME I'M ON PLANET GOATF##KERS, DRINKS ARE ON ME. LET'S GO, TRIPLE C##TS – she calls to the two forms of Hekate present, the Child and the Maiden. Despite exchanging some threatening looks, the three goddesses leave for the Themis hall without saying anything.

-Well...that was unexpected – Noriko comments, still unsure of what just happened.

-Don't let her childish behavior and vulgarities fool you. Persephone is far more cunning and ruthless than her own mother – Athena explains.

-I don't understand why she's here; isn't she supposed to be with Hades? – Vesta asks.

-Demeter offered her 10% of the galaxy to drive her away from Hades; that's why her current estate is so limited compared to other gods of her caliber. Instead of divorcing Hades, Persephone expelled every living being from her domain and rules it part time, dividing her time between the Necropolis and the Underworld. If she inherits the rest of Demeter's estate, she will do the same with it...or will leave everything to Hekate.

-So let me get this straight. Persephone would exile everyone, Artemis would give the place to pirates, Hekate would kill everybody...and if I inherit everything, I will have to deal with all of them!? I hate to admit it, but an alliance with Hermes is starting to make sense.

21- Outbursts

Null Tower, New York City

While Null Technologies employs thousands of people, very few of them work at the Tower itself. One of the upper floors houses all the Tower's living quarters: Vesta, Kari and Torn live here, as do Noriko and her father Bob. Max Black a.k.a. Quantum is knocking at Bob's door.

-This is probably a bad idea – Kari whispers to him.

Max doesn't have the time to answer before Quantum opens the door, greeting them.

-Yes, what can I...oh hi Max. It's been a while.

Kari does a double take: she's used to seeing multiple people with the same face, but she didn't expect to see Max shaking Quantum's hand. But despite not knowing they're the same person, Erika seems to be far more shocked.

-I can't believe it. You...you are...

-Quantum, the Man of Energy, at your service – he answers, taking a bow.

-Q, this Erika, my sister's girlfriend.

-You know Quantum? HOW!? – Erika asks.

-Yes, how exactly? – Kari repeats, crossing her arms.

-Max and I go way back. In fact, I was the one to suggest Noriko to hire him. Now, I suppose this isn't exactly a social visit? – Quantum asks.

-I'm afraid not. My sister's missing and we were hoping to use the Tower's computer to find her.

-Sure, why not. You can use the I.R.I.S terminal, two doors to the right. I'm afraid I can't stay here to help you; you know, places to be, people to save, that kind of stuff.

-Of course. It was a honor to meet you, sir – Erika manages to say, stuttering.

-We better get started. See ya later, Q, I owe you one – Max adds, taking Erika's hand to drive her away from Quantum.

Kari watches them leave, then turns towards Quantum. She tries to touch him, but her hand goes right through him

-A hologram. I.R.I.S, is that you? – she asks. Quantum answers with a metallic female voice:

-Forgive the ruse, Kari Zel, but Mistress Noriko programmed me to save Quantum's secret identity.

-Then why do I think that she's not gonna be very happy when she finds out that we brought a stranger into the Tower?

-She also instructed me to avoid answering rhetorical questions.

-She <u>does</u> think of everything, doesn't she?

-She also instructed me to avoid answering rhetorical questions.

-Just my luck...

Space station Sword of Justice

The hearing has been going on for hours. Not a long time for gods, but as much as she tries to hide it, Noriko is exhausted. She has fallen asleep, resting her head on Vesta's shoulder.

The red-haired goddess instinctively warms the air around them a little bit.

-You care about her – Athena says. There's no emotional attachment to the sentence: the goddess of wisdom is simply stating a fact.

-She's my friend. I hope you're not pushing her too much into this.

-I'm not pushing her to do anything.

-Athena, please. You can fool Zeus, but I know you. <u>Everything</u> you do is part of a plan.

-True enough. For what it's worth, aunt Vesta, I never intended to leave you stranded on Earth for such a long time.

-You should try it, Athena. Live between mortals, experience time as they do. Take it slow.

-I'd go crazy within the hour.

The two goddesses chuckle, taking care not to wake up Noriko. The awkward silence that follows lasts a few seconds, before Vesta takes the courage to ask:

-How's the family, Athena? I was thinking...

-You're still not welcome on Olympus – Athena cuts her short.

-After all this time?

-Said like a mortal. But don't worry: sooner or later, they will understand. They have to.

-Demeter didn't.

-And what happened to her?

-It wasn't my fault, Athena. I'm not the one who gave Noriko her power.

-But you did allow her people to grow too fast. No wonder their Nexus killed the first hostile divinity she encountered.

-I was sentenced to exile. I wasn't supposed to rule or influence mortals.

-Since when do you follow your family's orders, Vesta?

The family reunion is cut short when someone opens the doors with the force and subtlety of a battering ram. Still frightened by the noise, a dozen of ten year old girls leave rose petals on the floor and chant together:

-All hail Artemis, daughter of Zeus, Ruler of Olympus, and Leto, The Concealed.

The sound wakes up Noriko, who jumps on her feet to meet the latest would-be ruler of Myridia.

Artemis looks like a fitness model. All of the goddesses Noriko has met have perfect bodies (as well as Hermes, no matter how much she tries to forget him), but Artemis' clothes seem designed to emphasize her well-defined muscles. Aside from the dark blue low-cut shorts and shirt that leaves her abs exposed, she's only wearing metal bands on her wrists and ankles.

Her white hair is very short with a boyish cut; there is a deep, nasty scar over and under her right eye, which hasn't healed completely.

The children step aside to let her pass, bowing respectfully. Artemis ignores Athena and Vesta, going straight to Noriko who does her best not to look intimidated: she's almost two feet taller and looks like she could break her in half without a sweat. To answer her stare, Noriko's silver eyes shine menacingly. Artemis doesn't seem to care.

-Elytra says you're the mortal girl who killed Demeter and wants to rule her worlds.

-I am Null. Do you have a problem with-

Noriko doesn't have the time to finish before Artemis grabs her by the jacket's collar, lifting her effortlessly with one hand, and kisses her.

Athena sighs, rolling her eyes. Vesta is too embarrassed to do anything for the first five seconds; but then she sees that Noriko is clearly panicking when her efforts to break free are in vain.

-Artemis, stop it! That's enough! – she shouts, trying to separate her friend and her niece.

She's not strong enough to move Artemis by more than an inch, but finally she ends the kiss.

-Hm. Still don't understand what all the fuss is about.

Noriko coughs heavily as if she almost drowned, which isn't far from the truth. Vesta immediately tires to help her, noticing that her eyes are now more shining than ever.

Noriko jumps towards Artemis; Vesta has to hold her to stop her. She's never seen her like this.

-How dare you!? I am Null! Slayer of gods! I will have your head for this!!!

-I can see why you like this one, Athena. I think I'll keep an eye on her – Artemis adds, leaving to join the hall of Themis.

Athena doesn't react. Noriko is still mad with rage; Vesta is still holding her to prevent her from running straight into the hall. She's acting like a caged animal: it's only a matter of time before she hurts herself. And her eyes are now painful to look at, even for a goddess.

-Athena, a little help here!? – Vesta asks.

-I warned you about this – Athena explains, touching Noriko's forehead with a finger.

Noriko calms down immediately. She leans on Vesta, too dizzy to stand on her own. As she catches her breath, with her heart still pounding, she recalls:

-"The darkest part of humanity crawling inside your head". You said it when you gave me the power. It's happening, isn't it?

-The Nexus gives you access to mankind's knowledge. Experience and intelligence, yes, but also unbridled ambition and aggression. When you lose control over it, this is what happens.

-I felt it before...when I killed Demeter, when I faced Leiko...but nothing like this. It's getting worse. Why didn't you do anything!?

-I can't. Nobody using the Nexus has ever been able to fully control it.

-No, I'm talking about Artemis. Vesta tried to help me, but you just stood there and watched!!!

-Artemis is very persistent; taking you away from her would've made you even more desirable in her eyes. Her lust is satiated for now. It was a calculated move; there's no need for emotional outbursts.

-The hell there isn't – Noriko says, pushing Vesta aside and walking off, away from the hall.

305

Vesta crosses her arms, giving her niece a stern look.

-I hope you're happy. First she learns that her mother is a monster; now you watch her being molested and you don't even care!?

-You're a million years old, aunt Vesta. It's time you grow up.

-Yes. Maybe it is – she answers, leaving the goddess of wisdom to follow her friend.

In an empty corridor, Noriko is sitting with her eyes closed and her forehead on her knees.

"I'm not going crazy. I'm not" she thinks.

"Can we go home now? This place is scary" another voice replies from within.

"Let me out again. I want to kill that b##ch"

"Oh great, another one! It's getting crowded in here!"

"Shut up! Both of you! I'm trying to think!!!"

"Build another God Eraser. We can kill all of them in a single shot and rule the galaxy!"

"Who cares about the galaxy, give them what they want and let's go home!

-Noriko? Is everything okay?

She looks up: Vesta is offering her a handkerchief. She didn't even notice she was crying.

"Hug her and cry on her shoulder!"

"Cut out our her heart and weaponize it!"

-I could use your help – Noriko answers, taking the handkerchief. Vesta sits down besides her.

-I'm sorry about what happened. I should've warned you about Artemis. And Athena. And...well I'm afraid everyone in my family is nuts. I shouldn't let you get mixed up with them.

-I'm just tired to be a pawn is someone else's game. Leiko wants to use me to rule the world, the Mortal Liberation Front wants the Nexus as a weapon, the gods want to use me to mess with each other...and the worst part is I've been helping all of them without even knowing it. I can't even trust myself because there's a piece of alien technology in my brain that will eventually turn me insane.

-I trust you – Vesta says.

-Why? You're a goddess. You could rule Earth if you wanted. Why are you still following me?

306

-Because beneath the rude and bossy exterior you're a good person. Maybe Leiko and Athena gave you your power for the wrong reason, but so what? It can still be used to do some good.

-Pretty hard to do when the Nexus keeps pushing the worst part of humanity inside my head.

-I'm sure you'll eventually find a way to use it to your advantage. It's what humans do.

Noriko's eyes flash intensely. She stands up, snapping her fingers.

-That's it! Why didn't I think of that!?

-What? What did I say?

-Come on; I have to talk with Hermes before it's too late!

-About what? You're going to accept his proposal?

-I need his help to win Earth and Myridia back. But I have to make him think he's winning.

-You want to trick Hermes? He's the GOD of tricksters!!!

Noriko smiles. It's the smile of someone who has just figured out how to beat impossible odds.

-Do you have any idea of many millions of lawyers there are on Earth? They are all here – she says, tapping a finger on her head.

22- Alliances

Space station Sword of Justice

Unlike his fellow gods, Hermes doesn't have a mothership; in fact, he never travels by ship. Noriko is just outside his residence inside the Sword of Justice, accompanied by Torn and Kari Zel.

-I don't like it. This place gives me the creeps – Kari says.

-Believe me, you're not the only one who finds Hermes...uncomfortable. But there's no way we're going to be alone in the same room again – Noriko answers.

-"Again"? – Torn asks, raising an eyebrow.

-Don't ask.

The door opens on its own. The three enter the god's room, which is illuminated by dozens of candles whose flame trembles as they walk by. Hermes is slouching on some kind of throne; much to the visitors' dismay, Talas Khanos is standing next to him.

-What's he doing here!? – Kari protests.

-He's my new Oracle. To what do I owe the pleasure of your presence, Lady Null?

-I have...reconsidered your proposal.

-Teenagers. You just can't trust their hormones – Khanos comments, solely to provoke a reaction.

-Not. That – Noriko answers through her teeth.

-Oh, this I've got to hear. Leave us alone, Khanos.

-As you wish, my Lord – he bows, disappearing in a flash of green light. Kari gives a worried look to Torn: it's the same effect of the teleportation device from Demeter's ship.

-Yes. Hermes Oracles can teleport on their own – Torn answers the unsaid question.

-So, let's get to the point, shall we? Why are you really here, sunshine? – Hermes asks.

-I'm willing to renounce my claim to Demeter's planets in your favor. You're a sleaze, but so far you're the least insane of the claimants. And you don't really need Myridia.

-Interesting assumption. Did Athena brief you about my domain?

-No need. Everybody else wants Myridia because the Drylon monolith inside it can grant them an instant army. You don't need that: you've got the Many that you stole from Demeter. The fact that you're now employing Talas Khanos, the creator of the Many, confirms it. The only reason you're doing this is because you don't want anybody else to have Myridia.

-Clever girl. This could be the start of a truly wonderful alliance between us.

-It doesn't mean I trust you. You sent the Many to kill me immediately after Athena chose me. If I deliver Myridia to you, I want something in return.

-Of course. You could rule Myridia in my place, if you're willing to become my Oracle.

-No. Myridia will choose its own rulers and you won't force them to worship you.

-You're in no position to make demands, sunshine.

-Myridia hasn't fully recovered from what Demeter did; if you want to rule a strong planet, you need to give them time to heal. What's a thousand years for a god?

-A very busy god. I can't wait that long. I can give them a hundred years of freedom.

-Three hundred. It's how long Demeter's rule lasted.

-I'm not Demeter. Two hundred and fifty years.

-Let's make a deal. A hundred years of freedom for Myridia...and you won't reveal the position of Earth to anyone. Even indirectly.

-You do realize, sunshine, that Earth is in Demeter space. If I get Myridia, I get Earth as well.

-I know. But what if some other god defeats you? If they don't know the location of Earth, it will take time before they attack it. They haven't found it in more than two thousand years.

-Hm. Good point. Very well, I accept your proposal.

-And you will declare it in front of Themis, of course. Your word alone isn't worth enough.

-You hurt my feelings, sunshine.

Artemis Chariot

The ship has a unique design: it's built around a large sphere that hosts the most diverse habitat Vesta has ever seen. It hosts all kinds of animals, even extinct or alien ones, in a perfect reproduction of a forest. Artemis sits on her throne of animal bones, petting a deer.

-It's nice to see you again, aunt Vesta. I did miss your company all these years.

309

-You look...you look the same as ever, Artemis. Except that, uhm...
Artemis instinctively touches the deep scar on her eye when she answers:
-You missed all the fun.
-We have <u>wildly</u> different concepts of "fun", Artemis. But we do have something in common.
-Are you sure you don't want to talk to Athena about this? She's the asexual one, not me. Although I still haven't figured out if she's sterile like you.
-I see that rudeness still runs in the family. I was talking about leaving mortals alone instead of forcing them to worship us and treat them like slaves. The mortals of your sector are free, right?
-As long as they acknowledge my superiority to other gods, yes. Why do you ask?
-You know I <u>technically</u> own Earth, right? According to divine law, that is.
-What's your point?
-Renounce the claim to Myridia and I will formally surrender Earth to your rule.
Artemis' stare gets more intense. The two goddesses haven't always seen eye to eye, and do say that their family has some history with double crossing would be an understatement.
-What's in it for you? – Artemis asks suspiciously.
-I care about Earth; someone has to defend it and right now I'm not up to the task. Leave it alone for some time...say, a hundred years. By that time Earth will have grown strong enough to give you a significant edge against the other gods.
-I can't protect Earth against every god in the galaxy.
-You won't need to. Only Athena and Hermes know where it is, but won't attack.
-I can see why Athena wouldn't, but what about Hermes?
-He can't attack without revealing its position. If he does, he'll automatically lose Myridia and open his sector to an assault from Persephone, Hekate, Hephaestus and you.
-It looks like your precious Noriko has figured out everything, Vesta. Why do you really need me?
-Hephaestus. One of his Talos has already attacked Earth but hasn't reported back; it's only a matter of time before he finds it and retaliates. We need you to defend the Earth against his army of

310

indestructible robots...and I know you can't possibly resist a challenge like that.

-Hmmm. I can't deny that. And I do despise that deformed blacksmith and his metallic army. Very well, I accept your offer...with one adjustment. How old is Null?

-Eighteen years, but I don't see what's it got to do with...

-She won't be attractive a hundred years from now, won't she?

-I...I suppose not, it's close to how old humans can get.

-What about fifteen years? She'll be a fully grown woman by then.

-Where are you going with this, Artemis?

-I will defend Earth against all gods for the next fifteen years without them even knowing. Then they will acknowledge me as their ruler and worship me...and Noriko Null will be my queen.

-What!? That's ridiculous, she'll never accept that!!!

-Either I take her in fifteen years or the Earth is doomed – Artemis sentences.

-Why are you doing this? You own hundreds of planets. Can't you choose somebody else?

-My step-brother fancies her. It's reason enough for me.

-I'll ask Noriko. She won't be pleased to know you're risking the fate of her world and possibly of half the galaxy just because you suddenly want to get in her pants.

-We are gods. Mortals need to please us, not the other way around.

"Why did I miss my family again?" Vesta wonders.

Null Tower, New York City

The I.R.I.S terminal is rather different from any other computer: it doesn't have any kind of physical interface, just a holographic keyboard and a paper-thin screen.

-You think this will find Kayla? – Erika Rhys asks.

-This baby can cross-reference any database on the face of the planet – Max Black boasts.

-What does that mean? – Kari Zel asks.

-I have no idea. But it sounds cool, doesn't it? There, I think it found something – Max says, pointing at the screen. All the information available about his sister's movements are highlighted, but the most recent one is several weeks old: a flight from Chicago to Colorado Springs.

-Dead end? – Erika asks.

-I.R.I.S, do you have anything else that might help? – Kari asks directly to the computer.

-*I would suggest analysing all personal details about the people on the same plane.*

-Wait a second, what kind of computer makes suggestions? – Erika intervenes.

-Ours – Max shrugs – I.R.I.S, do it.

-*Done. Five passengers were Air Force military officers. Should I break into the Pentagon servers to learn more about them?*

Max, Kari and Erika exchange very, very worried looks.

-Wouldn't that be kind of very illegal? – Max finally questions.

-*Yes. But I am programmed to request permission before breaking the law.*

-That's both reassuring and creepy at the same time – Erika highlights.

-Yeah, welcome to Null's world. Go ahead I.R.I.S but <u>please</u> make sure nobody finds out.

-*Information recovered. Displaying details.*

-That was fast. Does this mean anything to you? – Kari asks Max, who's studying the screen.

-This is bad. I.R.I.S, if I'm reading this right, all of those people work at NORAD?

-*They were indeed assigned to the North American Aerospace Defense Command, but they have been re-assigned to Project Silver four weeks ago.*

-What's "Project Silver"? – Max asks.

-*Unknown. There are no details in the Pentagon servers. All information relevant to Project Silver is classified as "Cosmic Top Secret".*

-I guess it's not a nice thing – Kari whispers to Max.

-It's from the Pentagon. They don't do "nice" – he whispers back.

Project Silver, classified location

The two-star general is sitting at his desk, reading the latest report. When the red phone on his desk starts ringing, he stands up to adjust his uniform before pressing a button.

The hologram of the President of the United States appears, acknowledging the general's salute.

-At ease, General Anderson – the hologram says.

-Always a pleasure, sir. I wasn't expecting you to be back so soon.

-I wish we had these holographic projectors during the campaign; we're saving a lot of gas lately.

-I would suggest we use the projectors for most visits, sir. As you know, the secrecy of Project Silver is vital and, to be honest, Air Force One isn't exactly discreet. We already took a considerable security risk with your last visit.

-I know, but I couldn't ask miss Black to volunteer without meeting her. Has she recovered?

-Almost completely. The doctors tell me her body has fully absorbed the energy from the Heart of the Universe; we're running any possible kind of medical exam to be absolutely sure it's not harming her, but so far she's as healthy as humanly possible. We made it, sir.

-That's a relief, general. What about her psychological profile? Can we be sure we can trust her? She is Quantum's sister, after all.

-Things would've been easier if miss Black was a soldier instead of a security guard, sir, but I think she has the right stuff.

-Let's hope so. Because if she turns out to be half as powerful as her brother, miss Black is the most powerful weapon at our disposal.

23- New order

Space station Sword of Justice

The twenty-story tall Themis walks into the hall, taking her place on the throne. Noticing that Athena, Vesta and Hermes rise up when she arrives, Noriko does the same.

She is wearing once again her formal attire: it's not her style, but the occasion warrants it. As Themis takes her time before talking, Noriko glances at the other goddesses present.

Persephone has her feet on the desk, unwilling to show any kind of respect to anyone: she even gives the middle finger to Noriko when she notices her. Artemis is at least more composed, but doesn't bother to hide her utter and complete boredom.

All the three bodies of Hekate are present: the Child and the Maiden are sitting next to the Crone's corpse, whose head is mercifully covered by her dark hood.

-The Court formally abolishes the Demeter Theocracy and recognizes Noriko, daughter of Bob, as her conqueror. However, since there is no legal basis for a mortal ruling a planet without the consent of a god, this Court will now divide the former realm of Demeter to the following gods. Persephone shall rule the following: Athosia, Lantea, Orvan and Syba.

-GREAT, I WIN A COUPLE BILLION GOATF###ERS. I HOPE THE C##KSUCKER THAT GETS THE REST OF THE OLD C##T'S STUFF HAS ROOM FOR THEM, 'CAUSE THOSE A##HOLES AIN'T STAYING AT MY FU##ING PLACE.

Themis doesn't react to Persephone's vulgarities and continues:

-The Court also assigns the following planets to Hermes: Dagan, Revana, Satedia and Myridia. While the Court cannot assign a planet to Noriko, we hereby declare that the rule of Hermes shall follow her requests: Myridia shall be governed by its own mortal population for the next one hundred years, during which there shall be no forced attempt to influence their worship. Hermes and all of his vassals, oracles and subjects shall also refrain from revealing the position of Earth to any other gods, either by direct or indirect action. In the event that such rules are not followed, ownership of both Myridia and Earth shall be turned over to Persephone.

-SWEET MOVE, LITTLE B##CH!

-*WHAT!? Myridia is mine by right of conquest!!!* — the Child form of Hekate shouts, causing the Crone's corpse to lean over the Maiden.

-Only gods can invoke right of conquest. The Court will consider Hekate as merely two thirds of a goddess until such time when all of her bodies are resurrected.

-*We shall see about that* — the Child hisses.

-The Court also assigns ownership of Akadia and Earth to Artemis. The latter shall be governed by its own mortal population for the next fifteen years.

-I object. How am I supposed to respect the borders of Artemis space if I can't disclose its location? — Hermes intervenes. Noriko expected him to be mad, but he's strangely subdued.

-Nice try. You know where it is, just don't go there and you'll be fine — Athena answers.

-WHAT ABOUT THE REST OF MOM'S S##T? YOU JUST ASSIGNED TEN FU##ING PLANETS, WHERE'S THE OTHERS?

-The Court has assigned all planets for which there has been a specific claim. According to divine law, in the absence of a conquering god, all unclaimed planets shall be assigned to any god which had submitted a formal declaration of war against the deceased. While the deceased was at war with Ares, no formal declaration of war has ever been submitted. It is therefore decided by this Court that, with the exception of the planets already assigned, all of Demeter's domain shall be inherited by the only other god at war with her: Hephaestus, son of Zeus and Hera of Olympus.

-This is bad — Athena comments coldly.

Her fellow gods don't react with the same demure, but start shouting louder and louder:

-*This is unacceptable! We will appeal to Zeus himself!!!*

-There's no way I'll let that bastard keep all that space without a fight! — Artemis echoes.

-I'LL CUT THAT #####'S #### AND #### UP HIS #### WITH MY OWN ##### INSIDE HIS #####!!!

-Interesting — Hermes ponders, raising an eyebrow.

-SILENCE!!! — Themis says, pounding her giant fist on the desk. The thunderous sound is followed by absolute silence. Even Persephone keeps her mouth shut.

-Any god that does not obey divine law shall taste the wrath of mighty Zeus. Anyone willing to challenge him may proceed. The court is adjourned.

One by one, the gods leave the hall after looking at Noriko. Their stares range from homicidal to challenging, and none of them leaves a good taste in her mouth.

-What just happened? – Vesta asks to Athena.

-Hephaestus just received ninety worlds and twenty billion new subjects. Thanks to his robot armies he doesn't need them: they will all be dead before the end of the year – Athena answers coldly.

-So I just killed twenty billion to save seven billion – Noriko realizes.

-No. Hephaestus just won a war without doing anything; he now owns the largest territory in the Galaxy, which gives him a significant advantage over both Dionysus and Artemis. It won't be long before he declares war on both of them. If we wins, which is extremely likely, I estimate that at least another fifty billion people will die – Athena explains coldly.

-She couldn't possibly have known – Vesta excuses her.

-On Earth you know everything, Noriko. But out here, you are dealing with forces beyond anything you can control – Athena concludes, before leaving the hall.

-For now – Noriko whispers.

Project Silver, classified location

When General Anderson enters the room, the two female soldiers keeping guard salute him.

-At ease. How are you feeling, Black?

A stream of white-hot plasma flows out of the African-American woman, incinerating a block of granite. The power still runs through her veins when she's done.

-I'm feeling great, General. I've already learned how to shoot a dozen different types of energy.

-And no side effects? – he asks, not only to Kayla but also to the scientists in the room.

-I still want to run some tests, but it's very unlikely at this point – one of them answers, leaving his colleagues to analyze the ashes before continuing the explanation.

-Why can she only generate energy but not turn into it like her brother?

-You said Quantum was disintegrated by the Heart. It's possible his own body shares the same power of the Heart, which we know can alter matter and energy. Since we couldn't disintegrate miss Black...regrettably...and we only irradiated her blood, it's possible there simply isn't enough power inside her to do more than transforming just a few cells into small amounts of energy.

-"Regrettably" isn't the word I would've used – Kayla highlights.

-Or "small amounts" – the General adds, looking at the vaporized stone.

Myridia

The southern continent is mostly uninhabited, and for good reason: it's a never-ending swamp where plants grow uncontrollably, feeding off the light of the planet's six suns.

The Artemis Hunters have stationed here since the invasion, and they couldn't hate it more. They are space pirates that thrive off the chance to rape and pillage entire planets, but they've seen little to no action since their landing.

Elytra Elater knows this forced inactivity is hurting her leadership. The Ghost Maker she carries makes her literally untouchable, so she has little fear of assassination attempts, but mutiny is a real possibility at this point. She needs something to make the Hunters remember why they follow her.

Luckily, a scoutship from Athena's fleet just landed three people inside her camp.

Kari Zel is one of them: she's going to put up a fight. She doesn't recognize the man with red skin wearing a worn-off duster; she's never seen a human with that skin color, for that matter.

But the third one is Noriko Null. The girl with silver eyes. Much shorter than she'd expected.

Noriko has never seen a Lampyrian before. Elytra resembles a slim woman with blue skin, large bat-like wings and no nose; not very physically imposing, even with fully spread wings.

-Null, The God Slayer. Nice of you to drop by – she says.

-"God Slayer"? – Noriko repeats, glancing at Kari.

317

-It's what they call you on Myridia now. You've got something of a following – Kari understates.

-I want you off Myridia and, from what Kari tells me, you need my help curing your people.

-Yes, I...

Elytra can't complete the sentence: she vanishes before she can say a single other word. For once Noriko is caught off-guard, until she hears someone behind her saying:

-I appreciate the effort, sunshine, but I do my own housecleaning these days.

-Hermes. Why are you still here? – she asks, barely containing her distaste for the god.

-What's not to like about Myridia? Good food, beautiful women, a Drylon artifact of limitless potential. And a very cute precious little thing that just managed to piss off half a dozen of the most powerful beings in the Galaxy. I look forward to meeting you again, sunshine.

Hermes moves forward, kissing Noriko on the cheek. She vanishes in the blink of an eye.

Null Tower, New York City

In front of the elevator door, Erika Rhys shakes Max's hand, offering to do the same for Kari but receiving only a nod and a cold stare.

-Thank you so much for helping me find Kayla – Erika says, apparently missing the purple haired girl's hostility.

-I'm sorry we couldn't find more; all we know is she's involved with Project Silver, whatever that is, and maybe NORAD – Max answers.

-Still, now at least I have an idea where to look. I'll let you know if I find anything – she concludes.

Max watches the British girl with glasses leave the building; when she's out of sight, Kari adds:

-I don't like her.

-Why? She seems nice.

-Isn't it a little too convenient? Your sister just happens to find a girlfriend while you're off-planet, then only when you're back *and* Noriko is missing she just drops by to get help?

-Now you're just being paranoid, Kari.

-Your sister's been kidnapped by your own people, how come *you're* not paranoid?

318

-I didn't say I'm not worried about Kayla. Believe me, I am. But losing our head isn't gonna help.

-You're saying you won't let me send a duplicate to follow her and keep an eye on her?

-I'm an optimist, Kari, not an idiot...

Just then, there is a bright flash of light in front of Max and Kari. They get ready for anything...and are a little disappointed when they see it's just Vesta, Torn and Noriko.

-I HATE that god – the latter fumes.

The Aegis, Athena's mothership

As the ship exceeds the speed of light, the handmaiden fills two glasses with ambrosia. Both Athena and Hermes take a drink.

-I have to admit, Athena, I didn't think it would work. I mean, a mortal killing Demeter! But now she's gone and nobody can trace the killer back to us.

-Not if everybody believes it was the Heart of the Universe that brought Noriko to Myridia instead of you. However we may need to take it from her; she's smart enough to figure it out.

-I can't argue with that. The fact that she managed to trick me into keeping Myridia free for the next century is intriguing...professional jealousy, if you will. Very, very intriguing indeed.

-Just try to keep your pants up, Hermes, galactic stability depends on our success.

-Sister dear, somehow I doubt that the citizens of your Federation, or sweet Noriko for that matter, would approve the idea of inciting a massive war between your enemies.

-Mortal feelings are irrelevant, Hermes. Peace is the ultimate goal of all my actions.

-And to think they consider you a war goddess. How many will die to bring peace to the Galaxy?

Athena looks outside the window; her cold, silver eyes shine over the reflection of the stars.

-As many as it takes.

Hermes
Art by KodamaCreative

24- The world will be enough

The dawn is breaking over New York City. Despite one of the nicknames of this metropolis, most of its residents are still asleep.

But not its most famous one. The one who lived her whole life thinking she was just ordinary, until the weight of the whole world was put on her shoulders.

She raises her hand, calling the sky to give her everything this planet has, and the sky obliges. A lightning strike hits the roof of Null Tower, downloading everything that's been added to humanity's collective knowledge since her last update... and somewhat unsurprisingly, it's both a lot of information and a little more than a drop in the ocean.

-What does it feel like? – Max Black asks her, having materialized a couple feet behind her.

She's not surprised; at this point it's almost a given that getting super-powers is a disaster for anyone's social skills.

-What are you doing up so early? – she asks back.

-I never get tired of this view – Max answers sincerely, looking at the sun's rays navigating through the city's skyline. Noriko just nods, enjoying the moment for a few seconds.

-On the right days, it feels like this – she finally answers.

-Like what?

-Like everything's where it's supposed to be. I wish everyone could see it, Max... there's nothing like feeling the world's mind. It can be messy and complicated and really, really ugly if you look at it up close. But if you step back, and watch it from afar, there's an undeniable beauty and sense of purpose to it. The world's mind is a beautiful sunset.

-Wow.

-Sort of puts thing into perspective, doesn't it?

-What? No, I was just thinking that's the girliest thing you've ever said – Max jokes, receiving a playful punch on the arm.

-Don't play dumb with me, Max!

-I'm not! You always pretend you're so above-it-all, it's just funny to see that you're still human.

-Perhaps I am. But I'm still Null, y'know.

-What are you guys doing up so early? – a third voice joins the conversation, as Vesta flies from one of the lower floors and lands on the rooftop.

-That seems to be a common concern lately. What are *you* doing here? – Noriko asks her.

-I don't sleep, and I saw the lighning. Is everything okay?

-Yes. The world is still unaware of most of the danger that lies above its atmosphere – Noriko answers, to which Max reacts by rolling his eyes.

-Forget what I said, no human talks like that!

-Is everything okay? – yet another voice asks, this time belonging to Kari: she's kicked open the door that leads to the roof. Torn is behind her, silent as usual.

-Are we going to have to do this *every time* I do an update!? – Noriko complains.

-Should we? We're just worried about you, that's all – Vesta tells her.

Noriko hesitates before answering. They've known her long enough to pick up the clue: she wants to tell them something important that she's not comfortable sharing.

-Since you're all here, I should probably do something I should've done properly a long time ago.

-You're welcome – Torn interrupts her, before she has a change to say anything.

-Aw come on! – Max complains.

-The *one* time she wants to be nice with us and you interrupt her!? – Kari asks.

-I am nice to you guys! – Noriko objects.

-Occasionally – Vesta comments.

-You too, Vesta?

-Sorry, girl – the goddess shrugs.

It's just a small moment, but the members of the Vanguard share an awkward and yet genuine laughter between themselves. Noriko herself giggles discreetely, and Torn even raises an eyebrow.

-Is it just me, or does this feel like one of those cheesy last scenes of a TV episode? – Max asks.

-It's just you – both Vesta and Kari answer at the same time.

Noriko retakes control of the discussion:

-There are rough times ahead of us, guys. The Galaxy is heating up: sooner or later, what we have started will reach Earth... and I have a feeling my mother's far from defeated.

-Whatever it is, we'll face it together – Vesta says, with her words carrying a lot of weight.

Noriko looks at her team... the goddess who regained her faith in humanity, the slacker who rose up to the occasion and became a hero, the refugee who helped her save her whole planet, and Torn.

-You're awfully quiet – she tells him.

-I am.

-What? You don't think we're going to make it? – Kari asks him.

-This is only one planet. We face an entire galaxy of evil gods. Based of what I've seen, the world will be enough – he declares.

-And if it doesn't... – Noriko adds, pausing.

Her silver eyes shine with the light of seven billion minds, focused throught the determination of a single girl who really doesn't know how to give up.

-...we'll just have to teach the Galaxy how to behave.

CONTINUES IN BOOK 2:
NEUTRON STAR TEA PARTY

Made in the USA
Coppell, TX
16 October 2020